I Remember You

Heartbroken Tess Tennant is leaving London and moving back to her picture-perfect home town to take up a teaching job. It's time for a fresh start, one with warm stone cottages, friendly locals in oak-beamed pubs and of course Adam, her childhood best friend, who never left Langford.

But something isn't right in the town: Adam is preoccupied with a new girlfriend and the past – which Tess thought she'd put behind her – is looming large again.

So by the time she has to take her class on a trip to Rome, Tess is feeling reckless. She is swept off her feet by a mysterious stranger, and falls in love. But her magical Roman Holiday is about to turn into a nightmare . . .

Back in Langford, as autumn creeps towards Christmas, Adam is gone and everything has changed. Tess has to decide, once and for all, where she belongs and who she belongs with.

Rich, witty and moving, *I Remember You* is for anyone who likes to dream about a new life – and for anyone who still remembers their first love.

Harriet Evans is the author of three previous novels, *Going Home*, *A Hopeless Romantic* and *The Love of Her Life*, all of which were bestsellers. She lives in London and now writes full time, having given up her job this year to do so.

She would love to hear from you: please contact her at www.harriet-evans.com

Also by Harriet Evans

Going Home
A Hopeless Romantic
The Love of Her Life

HARRIET EVANS

I Remember You

HarperCollins*Publishers*

HarperCollins*Publishers*
77–85 Fulham Palace Road,
Hammersmith, London W6 8JB

www.harpercollins.co.uk

Published by HarperCollins*Publishers* 2009

1

A catalogue record for this book is available from the British Library

ISBN: 978 0 00 724384 6

Set in Meridien by Palimpsest Book Production Limited,
Grangemouth, Stirlingshire

Printed and bound in Great Britain by
Clays Ltd, St Ives plc

Mixed Sources
Product group from well-managed
forests and other controlled sources
www.fsc.org   Cert no. SW-COC-1806
© 1996 Forest Stewardship Council

FSC is a non-profit international organisation established
to promote the responsible management of the world's forests.
Products carrying the FSC label are independently certified
to assure consumers that they come from forests that are managed
to meet the social, economic and ecological needs
of present and future generations.

Find out more about HarperCollins and the environment at
www.harpercollins.co.uk/green

For the Don, my wonderful dad Phil,
with all my love

When my life is through,
And the angels ask me to recall
The thrill of it all,
Then I will tell them I remember you.

'I Remember You', *lyrics by Johnny Mercer*

PROLOGUE

Spring had arrived in Langford early that year. A sprinkling of bluebells carpeted the lanes, and daffodils nodded proudly in the breeze which rolled in from the hills behind the small town. As Tess Tennant raced up the hill from the bus stop, she caught sight of her mother and her mother's friend Philippa, outside the Tennants' house. They were laughing in the bright sunshine.

'Hello, Tess darling!' Emily Tennant called out to her daughter, who ground to a halt, panting. 'I was just telling Philippa your news.'

'You haven't told Adam yet, have you?' Tess said, between breaths. She unhooked herself from her school bag, trying to look nonchalant and grown-up; she was almost eighteen now, after all. By the time Cleopatra was eighteen, she was ruling Egypt with her brother. By the time she was twenty-two, she'd got rid of her brother, seduced Caesar and had his baby. Of course, she was dead at thirty-nine, and had wrecked Egypt with civil war, so perhaps she wasn't someone one should slavishly emulate – but she'd been to Rome, got to shag Mark Antony in the process and wear some awesome gold jewellery as well as being super-empowered and all that, so it wasn't *all* bad.

'No, of course not,' said Philippa, brushing her wild dark hair away from her face as she smiled at Tess. 'But well done, sweetheart. That's wonderful. He's going to be so pleased for you.'

'He's got a scholarship to Cambridge,' Tess said, brushing her hands through her hair. 'He won't remember who we are in a few months' time, he'll be too important. He'll be going to posh college dinners with E.V. Rieu and Oliver Taplin, people like that.'

'E.V. Rieu died in 1972,' said a voice behind her. 'I'd be extremely surprised if he rocked up to dinner.' Tess turned around to see Adam, her best and oldest friend, standing in front of her with an expectant look on his face.

'I got in,' she said, beaming. 'I'm going. I'm going to UCL. If I get three Bs.'

'Oh, my God,' Adam said, a wide grin breaking out over his face. He threw his arms round her. 'That's completely, completely brilliant. You are totally bloody brilliant.'

'Come in and have some tea,' Tess's mother called out to them, as Philippa smiled at them, hugging each other tightly.

'No, thanks, maybe later though,' said Tess. Adam released her, draping his arm round her shoulder and squeezing her tight. 'Hurrah,' she whispered happily. 'The meadows?'

'Yep,' he said, nodding.

'Oh,' said Philippa, pleased. 'Bye, you two! Have a nice time! Get me some garlic on the way back, Adam. Have a – oh, yes. Bye!'

As they walked down the lane together, Adam rolled his eyes at Tess. They both knew their mothers were watching them.

'For someone who despises the conventions of marriage, your mum is surprisingly bourgeois,' Tess said (she was doing Politics A level).

'It's weird, isn't it,' said Adam, chewing on a piece of grass. 'So mysterious and bohemian, and yet she wants her teenage son to go off with the girl next door.'

* * *

No one knew where Philippa Smith had come from. She had arrived in town nineteen years ago like Mary Poppins, on a wild, windy day in early spring. She was moving into the cottage opposite the Tennants: Frank was a GP and he and Emily had one child, Stephanie, who was nearly two. Philippa was nearly eight months' pregnant, Emily barely showing.

She had been teaching in Dublin, she told them, and the father of the baby was Irish, a fellow lecturer at the college where she worked. She spoke of him without rancour, but she wasn't going to see him again. Beyond that, Philippa said nothing more about herself. She had no apparent family or friends; she barely scraped a living marking A- and O-level exams and writing textbooks on early English history. Parts of Langford were scandalized; but Emily, who had a young child and had moved with Frank from London to live in this small, strange town, adored her immediately. Philippa accepted her neighbours' friendship – their invitations to join them for pot luck, their casual enquiries checking that she was all right – up to a point, and then she would retreat back to her draughty cottage and her books. For someone with virtually nothing – no family, no other friends, no back-story – she was strangely imperious.

Philippa had her baby son, Adam, six weeks after she moved to Langford; Tessa (to use her full name) was born a couple of months after that, and it was always accepted that the two babies would grow up in each other's pockets. The sight, however, of the blond, tall Adam, and his determined blue-eyed sidekick with black hair that bobbed round her head like a halo, trotting hand in hand towards the shop around the corner, was irresistible. It was impossible not to smile, put one's head on one side, and say, 'Aah . . . aren't they adorable?' And when they were thirteen, and Adam was still tall and a darker blond, now a weekly boarder at a good school thanks to a combination of scholarship and sponsorship, and Tess was still small and stocky and determined, but both of them were shyer, it was rather affecting to see them putting their childhood closeness behind them, behaving slightly awkwardly around each other. People had stopped wondering where Philippa came from, and instead smiled fondly when her sweet-natured, shy son appeared anywhere with Frank and Emily's daughter.

'I think someone's got a little crush on someone . . .' a well-meaning person would hiss, delightedly, as Tess ambled casually over to Adam, shyly, at a drinks party to say hi.

'You can tell he's awfully fond of her,' someone else would say. 'Look at them!'

Tess and Adam had long accepted there was nothing they could do about it. It wasn't their parents. It was the whole bloody town: Mrs Sayers the primary school secretary, Mrs Tey the solicitor's wife, the lady at the newsagent's – even Mick, who ran Langford's best pub, the Feathers, had been heard to say, 'They make a sweet little pair, don't they?'

It was one of the reasons Tess was desperate to get out.

The water meadows were flooded in winter, but as spring arrived and the water receded they began to dry out so that, even in the full heat of summer, the grass was always lush and green, the butterflies colourful and plentiful, the honey bees always busy. On this sunny April day they could sit on the tree by the river, swinging their legs over the bubbling water, drink the beer Adam kept in the knothole and smoke illicit cigarettes, the butts of which they were always careful to collect and remove when they left. Not just to save their own hides, but because they were country children and, along with other things like never leaving a gate open, they would sooner eat a cigarette butt than leave it lying in a field. Especially the water meadows. They'd been used in a Merchant Ivory film and the Prince of Wales had visited them last year. Everyone in Langford was proud of them.

Adam took a drag of his cigarette. 'So, you're really moving to London, then,' he said.

'Yep,' Tess said, swinging her legs happily. 'Can't believe it. You'll have to come and visit me.'

'I'll visit you, but I'm not so crazy on London,' he said.

She nudged him. 'Don't be silly. You don't even know it!'

'I know it well enough to know I don't like it.'

Tess stared at him, trying not to look impatient. Adam was not especially open to new things, and it annoyed her, though she hoped university would change that. She wanted to take on the world, to run full tilt at life. He was content to sit and watch the world go by outside his window while he worked.

'I'm serious,' he said. 'Cambridge I can cope with – although it's pretty flat, at least there's countryside nearby. London –' He shrugged his shoulders. 'Too noisy. Too crazy. Too many people! No green spaces, nothing. I think you'll miss it.'

Tess turned and stared at him. 'Have you lost your freaking mind?' she said, half-seriously. 'I'm eighteen, bruv! So are you! Just because we're studying Latin and Greek doesn't mean we have to turn into old men with bushy moustaches and elbow patches who talk about the good old days.'

'Well, you especially,' said Adam. 'I'd love to see you with a big bushy moustache, T.' He nudged her, but she glowered at him and he relented. 'OK, I'll come and visit you.'

'You'd better,' she said firmly. 'We are going to parrrrtay. When Cleopatra first met Caesar, she said—'

'Oh, shut up about Cleopatra,' said Adam, who was highly bored of Tess's Cleopatra obsession. 'Her parents were brother and sister, no wonder she was crazy.'

'Adam!' Tess said, in outrage.

Adam rolled his eyes. 'OK, OK.' He patted her on the back. 'You really can't wait to get out of here, can you?'

She looked at him, and shuffled along the wide branch, suddenly a little uncomfortable. 'It's not that. I just want to do something different, get away, you know? I feel like all these things are just round the corner waiting for me, and

I'm sick of the same old faces, same stupid tourists gawping over the same boring things.'

'Yeah,' Adam said slowly. 'I know. Still . . . I'm going to miss it.' He looked around, at the meadows that stretched before them, the shocking green of the trees in bud, the blue sky, the fields folding out away to the horizon. 'It's a nice life here, that's all.'

'Of course it's a nice life for you,' Tess told him. 'You're Adam Smith. The richest woman in town paid for your education. You're tall. You're super-intelligent. You've got a cool bike. And all the girls at my school have a massive thing for you and you could basically snog anyone you wanted. You're a superstar.'

'Tess!' Adam laughed, embarrassment written over his face. He blushed. 'That's rubbish.'

'It's not,' she said. 'Why would you want to leave? You've got the perfect life.' She stood up; a piece of bark was digging into her. 'Me, I *want* to leave. I want to live in London. I don't want to turn into an old lady before my time.'

'You'll come back, though,' Adam said, still sitting on the branch. 'Won't you?'

Tess felt sad suddenly, and she didn't know why. She turned to face him, and stood between his legs. She pinched his cheek lightly. 'Don't bet on it. I can't see myself living here.'

'I know what you mean, but *omnia mutantur*. All things change,' said Adam.

'Yeah, they do,' said Tess. 'But we change with them, that's the rest of the quote.' They were silent for a moment; both of them took another swig of beer. 'Still,' she said. 'We've got ages till we have to go. We've got the whole of the summer. And then –' She lifted her beer and clinked it against his. 'The rest of our lives.'

They were right, of course. Things do change, but neither of them could have foreseen in what way. Because already, part of Tess and Adam's future had been written, set in stone long before they were born.

PART ONE

I'll tell you of a tiny
Republic that makes a show well worth your admiration –
Great-hearted leaders, a whole nation whose work
is planned,
Their morals, groups, defences – I'll tell you in due order.
Virgil, *Georgics*, Book IV (trans C. Day Lewis)

Langford College

Classical Civilization Tutor Required
For A levels, Term-long courses and Seminars
Immediate start preferred

Langford College is one of the most important and well-regarded adult educational facilities in the country. This private training college for further education is set in a Grade I listed Victorian manor, former seat of the Mortmain family, in twenty acres of beautiful grounds near to the historic market town of Langford.

Due to unforeseen circumstances, the position of Tutor in Classical Civilization now becomes vacant. We are urgently seeking a replacement, to arrive in February to prepare for the Summer term. The applicant must be educated to MA level or beyond in Latin and Greek. Three years' teaching or lecturing experience essential. The applicant must be prepared to guide his or her students on a field trip, one per annum.

Applications are now invited by post, including CVs with *two* references, to Miss Andrea Marsh, c/o Langford College, Langford, —shire. No email queries, please.

'Per Artem Lumen'

CHAPTER ONE

The old woman sat at her window, her usual position, and watched, waiting. It was noon in Langford, and if there was to be any activity on the high street (described as 'one of the most beautiful streets in England' by DK Eyewitness, 'picture-postcard perfect' in the Rough Guide, and 'chintzy' in the Lonely Planet), it would be at this time.

There might be a couple of ladies walking to lunch at the tea shop. Or some weekenders emerging from Knick-Knacks, one of the many gift shops that sold Medici Society notelets, Cath Kidston cushions and 'vintage' mirrors. Or perhaps a group of American tourists, rarer at this time of year, distressingly loud, having visited the house where Jane Austen spent several months staying with an old friend. (The house, formerly known as 12 St Catherine's Street, was now the Jane Austen Centre, a museum which contained a glove of the great author's, a letter from her describing Langford as *neither incommodious nor invidious, yet I cannot like it*, and a first edition of *Emma*, inscribed, *'To Lord Mortmain, in respect of his great knowledge, this little offering.'* But since the author was anonymous until she died, it was generally agreed it wasn't her, anyway.)

Perhaps she might spot a bus trip taking people to Langford Regis, the famous Roman villa nearby (home to some of the best mosaics of Roman Britain, and a new heritage trail promising a fun day out for all the family.) Perhaps even a film crew – they were increasingly common in Langford these days. But whatever it was, Leonora Mortmain would have seen it before, in some form or another. For, as she was fond of telling her housekeeper Jean, she had seen most things in the town. And nothing surprised her any more.

She watched them walk past with a weary disdain; the tourists, lured from London or Bath for the day, even on this cold January morning, clutching their guide books, reading aloud to each other. And there was her old adversary, Mick Hopkins, the publican at the Feathers. He was putting a sign out on the road – what did it say? Leonora couldn't make out the bright chalk lettering, and her glasses were on the other side of the room, in the bureau. Something annoying, no doubt; some quiz night that would mean everyone became disgracefully inebriated and staggered out onto the street, calling names and making noise, waking her all too easily from a restless sleep. Leonora Mortmain sighed, and her long fingers briefly clutched her skirt. Sometimes she wondered, quite literally, what the world was coming to. The town she had known all her life was changing. And she didn't like it.

There was a picture in the town hall (renamed the Civic Centre in the eighties, now mercifully re-renamed). Leonora had a copy, too. It showed the Langford Parish Council on Easter Day 1904, outside St Mary's Church, behind the high street. Men in morning suits, top hats and gloves, walking sticks, their sepia faces serious and respectable, their wives demurely on their arms, expressionless and slim in pintucked, ruffled Edwardian dresses. Everything correct, respectful. The church noticeboard in the background was freshly painted. Even the urchin playing in the street in the foreground, unseen by the subjects of the photograph – even *he* was clean and *presentable*! The previous day, Leonora had watched in amazement and horror as a mother – she presumed she was the mother – pushed her child along the high street in a buggy with one hand. The woman was fat, red-faced and sweating, holding a cigarette with the hand that steered the buggy and eating a pasty of some description in the other. She was dressed in pink jogging bottoms; the child was filthy. And she was shouting at it as she went. 'Shut the **** up, Tiffany!' she'd screamed as the child screamed back. And then later that same day, as evening came, a troupe of girls, no more than teenagers, walking along towards the bus stop, wearing jeans and trainers, and tops that displayed more than enough of their cleavages, smoking and drinking out of cans. One of them – no more than fourteen, Leonora estimated – stopped and kissed, in a most unseemly way, a youth of the same age, whose hands had roved over her body like – like oil in a pan. And under her clothes! Leonora had watched it all from the window.

Extraordinary! Incredible! That the town had come to this, and Leonora increasingly had no remedy for it. *O tempora, o mores*, her father had been wont to say (although he disapproved of Cicero in many ways). Well, what Sir Charles Mortmain would have made of his beloved town now, she shuddered to think. She simply could not imagine. Leonora Mortmain shifted uneasily in her seat, and her hand restlessly stroked the bell that lay near her at all times.

Her father was a man who cast a long shadow: a passionate classicist, author of *Roman Society* (Heinemann, 1933) which expounded the virtues of Imperial Rome – its organization, its rules, its ruthlessness – omitting many of its more interesting vices – vomitoriums, poisonings, slave boys. Young Leonora (many doubted such a beast had ever existed but it had) had lived in fear of him, desperate for his approval. He had died in 1952. She wondered, often, what he would have made of things now.

The fact that his own daughter had been forced, because of death duties, to sell Langford Hall, the Victorian Gothic manor house at the edge of the town, was something that still, nearly forty years on, gave her pause. Langford Hall was now Langford College, a private institution that at least taught respectable things, like History of Art, French classes, the Classics, of course, and so on. But no matter how respectable it was, she knew Father wouldn't have liked it.

Leonora Mortmain took a deep breath. Thinking about her father brought back painful memories. She had been feeling older lately, and these days she kept thinking about the past. More and more. She had a final plan underfoot – one that she knew was right, but which sometimes made even her quail at the thought of what she was doing . . .

Something caught her eye, and Leonora sat back in her chair. A tall, darkish blond boy – well, she supposed he was a man now. He appeared outside the pub and started chatting to Mick Hopkins. He clapped the older man on the back as they laughed about something, his wide, easy smile infectious.

Leonora knew them both. Mick Hopkins had been at the Feathers for more than thirty years now. They said he was a good landlord – Leonora had never been inside the pub, though she had lived opposite it for forty years. She supposed he was an inoffensive man in his way, compared to some of the people she was forced to watch on a regular basis, but she didn't care for him. He was responsible for so much of the bad behaviour she saw outside her window, and whenever she complained he brushed her aside, politely, but she could tell he was laughing at her . . . She hated that, hated it.

Her eyes fell, almost greedily, on the man he was with. It was Adam Smith, Philippa Smith's son. Leonora watched him carefully, knowing she was spying, but just for once letting her curiosity get the better of her.

When he was eleven, Adam had won the top prize at Langford Primary, for outstanding achievement. Leonora had offered to pay his school fees. It was the right thing to do. He was an extremely intelligent boy, he had been offered a part scholarship, as a weekly boarder, to — School, and his mother couldn't afford for him to take it up. Leonora had stepped in, enjoying the slightly surprised murmurs of approval that greeted the announcement that she was paying for his education. She would do it every year, she said, fund the brightest pupil from the school through to their graduation, as a memorial to her father.

But to Leonora's immense displeasure, Adam had gone to the bad. His mother had died, suddenly, when he was almost eighteen, dropped dead in the street of a brain aneurysm. A terrible thing and a shock to everyone, but Adam had gone to pieces. He had failed, soon after his mother's death, to get the results he needed for Cambridge, and he had gone on failing ever since. He didn't seem to care about that fine mind of his after that; he would rather loll about on the street chatting and laughing like a common idiot, not like the gentleman he should be. She had had such high hopes for him, had seen it as her chance to create something out of nothing, and it had failed ... Leonora Mortmain blinked, realizing she was staring rather too intently out of the window at the young man.

She rang the bell with fury, shaking her head querulously. Too tiresome to think about all that now.

'Mrs Mortmain?' Jean Forbes bustled into the room. 'Are you all right, Mrs Mortmain?' The 'Mrs' was a courtesy – no one quite knew why or where it had started, but no one dared call her 'Miss' now. Much less 'Ms', though some would have loved to have tried.

'I am well,' said Leonora, collecting herself once more. She looked out of the window, searching for composure. Her eye fell upon a girl in jeans and a light blue top, ambling slowly along the street towards where Adam Smith stood with Mick from the Feathers. 'Tell me, who is that?'

The inhabitants of Langford believed Jean Forbes put up with a great deal. Leonora Mortmain didn't pay well, and she was an extremely difficult woman, who almost went out of her way to be unpleasant. Poor Jean, people said. That awful, dried-up old crone – imagine having to live with her! Did you hear, she tripped Ron Thaxton up with her walking stick, because he was in her way? She told Jan Allingham that she believed charity should be in the home and nowhere else, when she came round collecting for Cancer Research. The list went on and on.

For her part, Jean knew they said it – on certain days, she couldn't blame them for saying it. But luckily for Leonora, Jean's nature was good and kind and, most importantly, patient. 'You rang very loudly. I thought you were—' she began.

'What?' snapped Leonora. 'I asked you who that –' She jabbed the window with a long finger, painted magenta and crowned with a thick gold and garnet ring. '– was.'

Jean looked now as if she were about to say something, but she thought better of it, and leaned out of the window. The girl and Adam had recognized each other, and were embracing, laughing heartily as they did so. He patted her on the back, lifting her up so her feet were off the ground as Mick went inside, leaving them chattering happily together. Jean screwed up her eyes.

'Oh, my goodness,' she said, after a moment. 'Isn't that Frank and Emily's daughter?'

'And *whom* might they be?' asked Leonora Mortmain.

'Tess,' Jean said. 'I'm sure that's Tess Tennant. Ah! Bless her! Sweet girl. The doctor's daughter. Dr Tennant? He came when you had that problem with your foot. You used to like her, remember, she went off to become a Classics teacher. She and Adam were such friends. Looks like she hasn't seen him for a while.' She clapped her hands together. 'Of course! Didn't Carolyn Tey tell me that she's joining Langford College in a couple of weeks? She's the new Classical Civilization tutor there.'

'Is this true?'

Jean blinked. 'Well, yes, of course it's true. Do you remember, Derek what's-his-name had to leave before Christmas, he got shingles? They've been desperate for someone ever since.' She looked at her employer, realizing she was gabbling, and sighed. 'Carolyn's signed up for a course, Mrs Mortmain! They're going on a trip to Rome in May!' Jean sighed. 'Ooh. I'd love to go to Rome.'

Rome. Rome, in May. In the plans that Leonora had had when she was young, Rome had figured large. And it would mean she could go back to the house, legitimately go back once more, as a student, not as a young girl living there. Just once more, before she died. Leonora pretended to ignore Jean, leaning back towards the window, watching Tess who was explaining something to Adam. He stood listening intently to her, hugging himself, his hands tucked under his armpits. Tess ran her hands through her black hair, and it stuck up a little at the back. Rome. *Rome*.

'Hm,' said Leonora. 'Well, I don't remember her.' She wrinkled her brow, as if searching for a memory.

'You do remember, Mrs Mortmain,' Jean said. 'She used to play with Adam – Adam Smith all the time. Best of friends when they was little. It's nice to see her again,' she said ruminatively. 'Nice to have a young face move back to the town, isn't it?'

'Ye-es,' said Leonora slowly, not really listening. Her gaze had slid from the girl to the poster she was now reading, stuck crudely onto the old blackened wood of the archway. 'Jean – ah, what does that poster say?' she asked.

'"Stop the Out-of-Town Superstores,"' Jean read slowly. '"Shame on the Mortmains! Save Langford!" Oh,' she said, realizing what she'd just said. 'Oh, Mrs Mortmain, I'm sure it doesn't mean . . .'

15

Leonora stood up; leaning heavily on the windowsill as she did so. She was shaking. She peered forward, the better to see the poster:

STOP THE OUT-OF-TOWN SUPERSTORES
SHAME ON THE MORTMAINS!
SAVE LANGFORD!
SAVE THE WATER MEADOWS!!!!
If YOU want to stop Leonora Mortmain from ruining OUR town with these plans for 2 megamarkets, a homeware store and 4 other retail outlets, to be built on the historic Langford water meadows, which will make HER RICH and KILL THE TOWN AND OUR BEAUTIFUL WATER MEADOWS, come to the Feathers, March 15th, for a town meeting. Call Andrea Marsh, Ronald Thaxton or Jon Suggs for more information! **Get involved!**

'Oh, dear,' said Jean, as her employer sank back into the silk chair, breathing fast. 'I didn't want you to see it—'

'Don't be stupid,' Leonora snapped. Her mind was racing, almost as fast as her heart. 'It was bound to happen, sooner or later. And the sooner they realize it's our land, to do with it what we wish, the better. The plans are already approved in principle.' She looked around her lovely sitting room, and then out onto the street again, at the poster, as Tess and Adam walked away, still talking. Adam looked across, towards the house. Leonora shrank against the curtains. She did not want him to see her.

'So,' she said. 'It's started, then.' She paused. 'Well, everyone needs to understand. It's for the best.'

Jean Forbes said nothing as Leonora Mortmain turned to the window again, and continued to stare out onto the street.

CHAPTER TWO

'So when did the train get in?'

'An hour or so ago. I dumped my stuff at the pub and you're the first person I saw.'

'You're staying there?'

Tess said grimly, 'I need to find somewhere to rent, fast. It's expensive, the Feathers – what's happened?'

'I can't believe you're back,' Adam said, smiling at his oldest friend as they walked down the High Street. He made to put his arm round her.

'Ow!'

'Oh sorry,' he said, rubbing her shoulder where he had jabbed it.

'It's fine.' Tess picked up her speed; she was small and he was tall and she remembered, then, that they didn't walk well together: always out of step. There was an awkward pause.

'It's really you! Man.' Adam shook his head, looking at her. 'It's been a long time, Tess. I can't think of the last time I saw you.'

She looked up at him. 'I know.' Her eyes searched his face. 'Your hair got darker,' she said, eventually.

He tugged at it. 'Oh. Probably not.'

'You used to be so blond,' she said. 'Especially in summer.'

'Not for years,' he said. 'That was when I was a boy.'

'Remember your mum used to call you the Milky Bar Kid, and you'd get so cross?' She smiled, but a look of pain shot across Adam's face at the mention of Philippa's name, and she regretted it. Was he still not able, after all this time, to talk about his mother?

'I'd forgotten,' he said, though she knew he was lying, he remembered everything. 'You just haven't seen me for a while, that's all. You are a heartless girl.'

Tess shook her head firmly, glad to move the conversation on. 'You never come to London, that's the problem.'

'Hey.' He grimaced. 'You never came home, *that's* the problem.'

'Rubbish,' Tess said. She avoided looking at him, trying not to sound defensive, keeping her voice light. 'Anyway, Mum and Dad don't live here any more, so why should I?'

'Typical,' said Adam. 'A brother. I've been like a brother to you all these years, and you just don't care.'

'A brother?' Tess laughed, rolling her eyes, she couldn't help it. 'Right.'

Adam seemed not to hear her. He looked at his watch. 'So – how's Stephanie?'

'She's great. She and Mike just moved to Cheltenham – but you knew that.'

'Sure,' said Adam, stopping to let a tiny old lady clutching a green string bag pass on the crowded street. 'She sent me a Christmas card. Morning, Miss Store! How are you?'

'Good morning, Adam dear,' came a bright voice back. 'I'm very well, thank you. I have some lovely rhubarb, if you'd like some. Didn't you say you were coming round later?'

'Yes, please, that would be great.' Adam smiled, and they walked on. Tess chuckled.

'What's so funny?' Adam said. 'She's a very nice lady.'

'OK, OK!' Tess said. 'Where are we going later?'

'I'll explain in a bit,' Adam said. 'I hope you're pleased.'

Tess pulled her ponytail out and rubbed her scalp, letting her hair fall about her shoulders. She looked around her again, frowning. 'Well, I'm back.'

She had to remind herself how, back in Balham before Christmas, dumped, unemployed and miserable, the job at Langford College had seemed, quite literally, like a miracle. Not only was it a job, which in these times was a rarity itself, especially since she was a Classics teacher and not someone providing a necessarily indispensable teaching service, but it was also a way out, a new start, a way to leave behind the misery she'd felt and start over again. But now she was here . . . It was eighteen months since she'd been back; even longer, she realized now, since she'd really taken stock of Langford, of what were to be her new surroundings. Like someone walking through their new house and wondering if they've made a terrible mistake, she now saw the town again, as if through fresh – and rather dismayed – eyes.

Take, for example, the high street. It was like walking through Toy Town. The shops looked smaller; the church of St Mary's at the end was tiny. Even the side gate, the entrance to one of the medieval lanes that skirted around the edge of town, seemed minute to her, as if a child could climb over it. Compared to London, to her old street in Balham, which was three times as long as the high street, it was hilarious. She'd forgotten, when she first went to London, how huge every-thing seemed, even though she knew it already. How it took her a term of wandering around Bloomsbury to get used to it, the size of the squares, the vast classical columns of the university buildings, the height of the houses, even the size of the theatres. She was taken to the ballet by a boyfriend from university, and Covent Garden seemed as huge a football pitch.

And the shops! Everything here was either an antique shop or a gift shop or a tea shop, or else a crappy homestores place that only seemed to sell frozen Findus pancakes and ready-made Yorkshire puddings. She peered into the window of a shop called Jen's Deli, noting with some relief that there was at least *one* shop that sold parmesan and prosciutto. She may have lived in Balham, but even Balham had a shop that sold Poilane bread.

'Penny for them,' said Adam's voice, behind her.

'What?' said Tess, momentarily disconcerted. She glanced up, and saw his reflection in the window, watching her. She brushed her hair out of her face. *I was just thinking how glad I am that at least there's a half-decent shop here that sells fresh parmesan*. She was ghastly. 'Oh, well. Nothing!' she said brightly. 'So – tell me. How's it going? How is – everything?'

For a while now, Tess hadn't known the best way to ask what Adam was up to, but she knew it drove him mad, the pussyfooting. After Philippa died, people pussyfooted all the time, half-asking him what he'd do. 'You're – not going to Cambridge? Ah! What will you do here instead? A job at the pub? Sounds like a good one, Adam, keep you behind the bar instead of in front of it, eh! Ha! Ha!'

'Ah, so you're working in the museum now too? Well, no one better than Jane Austen! If that's what you're going to . . . So, how long do you think you'll be – oh, you don't know, well, of course, that's absolutely right – isn't it! Quite right.'

To Tess's father Frank, who had asked Adam straight out a couple of months after his mother died, why he wasn't going to Cambridge, why he wasn't even going to defer for a year and then go, Adam simply replied, 'Things have changed, I'm afraid. I'm not going.'

'I think Philippa would have wanted you to go,' Tess's father had said. Tess had watched, terrified, her fingers in her mouth.

Adam had said, evenly, 'I know she'd have understood why I'm not going. There are reasons why. She would understand, trust me. Thanks, though.'

'What for?' Dr Tennant had said, bewildered.

'For asking directly in the first place,' and Adam had said

it so politely that Tess had looked at him, almost in despair, and then at her mother whose hand flew to her chest, as if clutching her heart in some sort of pain. He was heart-breaking, this young man, completely alone in the world, prepared to throw away his best chance at life. But what could they do? They couldn't bind him and bundle him in the back of a van, then drive east and dump him outside the gates of his college. And there was no one else they could talk to, either. All Adam – or Frank or Emily – knew about Adam's father, the Irish professor, was that he'd moved to America many years ago, and there were no details for him; Adam wasn't even sure of his surname.

He was only just eighteen, and he was alone in the world. There wasn't really anything the Tennants could do now, except watch out for him, help him as much as they could. Watch, as everyone's favourite boy passed his twenties living in the small cottage where he had grown up with Philippa, never clearing out her possessions, and alternating jobs between the bar of the Feathers and the Jane Austen Centre, where he worked behind the front desk two and a half days a week. He never talked about his mother, or what might have been. Never.

Looking at Adam now, Tess knew she wasn't going to get an answer out of him.

He said, 'Things are the same as they've always been.'

'Still working at the Feathers? I didn't know the barman when I went in to drop my stuff.'

'Yep,' said Adam. 'Suggs is doing a couple of nights a week there, actually.'

Suggs was Adam's best friend and his housemate in the cottage.

'How's the Jane Austen Centre?'

'Oh, you know,' Adam said. 'Pretty full-on. Tiring.'

'Really?'

'Yes, you know. We'll have to rearrange Her Glove soon, and some people are talking about moving the furniture in the Writing Room. Phew.' He saw her expression. 'I'm joking, you idiot.' He pushed her gently. 'It's dead, deader than a dodo. Especially this time of year. We get tourists, but it's ten a day at best. Even I can cope with tearing off ten ticket stubs.'

Tess was embarrassed, and tried to cover her embarrassment. 'Right. I see. Well, it sounds like you're keeping yourself busy!' He gave her a strange look. 'Er, let's take a look in here, shall we?' she said, almost wildly, and pushed the door of the deli open before Adam could stop her.

'No – er – Tess –' he called after her as she went inside, but she ignored him.

'Hi,' said a friendly-looking person behind the counter, wiping her hands on a tea towel. 'Can I get you anything?'

She was beaming in a welcoming way which made Tess, less than two hours off the train from London, instantly suspicious of her. 'Just looking, thanks,' Tess replied repressively and turned to the shelves.

'They've got some good stuff in here,' Adam said, in a low voice. He swivelled round, so they were both facing the shelves. 'Nice pasta, and the vegetables are fresh. They get them from George Farm, it's a good arrangement.'

'I love cooking,' Tess said. She sighed with pleasure.

'How long are you staying at the pub for?' Adam asked her.

'Till I find somewhere,' Tess said.

'You should have stayed with me,' Adam said. 'It's ridiculous, you paying to stay there.'

'I didn't—' Tess began, then she stopped. 'That's so sweet of you.' She patted his arm, touched and grateful for the presence of him, and shook her head.

'That's OK,' Adam said, still in a low voice.

'Why are you speaking so softly?' Tess said. She turned back to the counter. 'Perhaps I should get some—'

'Adam?' said the friendly girl eagerly, her pale face lighting up. 'I thought it was you. Hi – hi there!'

'Hi, Liz,' said Adam neutrally. 'How've you been.'

He said this not as a question, more from a need to say something. Tess watched this exchange with dawning understanding.

Liz wiped her hands on her tea towel again, beaming with pleasure. 'It's good to see you! I wondered where you'd been.'

'Ah – ah.' Adam took a step back, and Tess smiled wryly, looking at her feet. Just like the old days; nothing had changed. She knew what was going to happen next.

And it did. 'This is Tess,' Adam said, putting his arm around Tess and squeezing her shoulders. He kissed the top of her head. 'Tess, this is Liz. She's from London too.'

'Actually, I'm from Nantwich,' Liz said. 'But I live here now. Moved down here last year.' She held out her hand bravely, smiling a little too enthusiastically. 'It's great to meet you, Tess!'

'Yes,' said Tess, shaking her hand. 'You too.' She cleared her throat. 'I've just moved back and it is great to catch up with people like Adam,' she said woodenly. 'Because he is my oldest friend. And is like a brother to me.'

'Right! Right!' Liz tried and failed to hide her pleasure at this news, and stared at Tess with something like adoration. Adam, meanwhile, glared at his oldest friend with something like loathing.

'So –' Tess went on, evilly, getting into her stride. 'It's great to meet you. Are you two –'

'That wasn't fair,' Adam said a couple of minutes later, as he bundled Tess out of the shop, having guilt-bought far too many overpriced deli items and leaving Liz smiling pleasantly behind them.

'It wasn't fair of you to do that to me, the old routine again,' Tess said firmly. 'Or to that nice girl. *I* remember you and your ways, Adam. But poor Liz doesn't know about you.'

'What about me?' Adam said tetchily.

'That the main reason you work at the Feathers is to pick up women,' Tess told him. 'And that you should be in the tourist guide as a well-known landmark.'

'I only slept with her a couple of times,' Adam said, ignoring this.

Tess hit him on the arm. '"I only slept with her a couple of times,"' she mimicked, crossly. 'God, men. You think that means it doesn't mean anything! Oh, you are so useless. She's mad about you! She's been waiting for you to call her!'

'Well . . .' Adam said. 'I bet that's not true. I mean, I like her, but—'

'Oh, I know, you can't be bothered to actually talk to her, after you've shagged her,' said Tess, and it came out sounding angrier than she meant.

'Don't split your infinitives,' Adam said, brightly. 'Call yourself a Classicist?'

'It's not funny,' Tess said. They walked down the road towards the pub and after a pause she burst out, 'God, sometimes I really hate men.'

Adam glanced at her swiftly, and was silent for a moment, then said, 'So, er – have you heard from Will?' He patted her arm. 'Don't hit me again. I'm serious. I'm sorry about you two, I thought it was all going well.'

'I thought so too,' said Tess. 'I was wrong, obviously.'

'Do you know why . . .' Adam began, and trailed off.

'Yeah. He's seeing someone else.' Tess said. Adam nodded. 'Someone called Ticky.'

'I don't know what that means.'

Tess gazed up at the thick white January sky. 'No, I don't either. Except I hate her.'

'You see, just like a girl,' Adam said. 'You should hate him, he's the one who did you wrong.'

'You sound like Mae West,' Tess said, trying not to sound miserable.

'I mean it. I never thought he was . . .' he trailed off again. Tess nodded, and shoved her hand through the air in a 'I know, I know' gesture. Adam had met Will a couple of times and she had come to accept – so she told herself – that there were some people with whom Will was not destined to get on. Adam was one of them. He was too ready to laugh, too ready to take the piss out of Tess; they knew each other too well, perhaps, for Will ever to be the third side of the triangle.

Will had not been a laugh-a-minute. Indeed, that was one of the things that Tess had originally liked about him. Here she was, this poverty-stricken teacher, frittering her twenties away in South London pubs, wearing too-short skirts and drinking Pernod and Black, her only claim to cultural superiority being that she taught Classics (though bribing bored fourteen-year-olds with a bloodthirsty description of the Emperor Nero's brutal murder of his mother Agrippina as a back route to telling them about the fall of the Roman Empire did not necessarily indicate the highest levels of academic achievement, she knew). Their friend Henry, whom Tess knew from university and Will from school, had introduced them at a birthday party. It was a hot summer's day and Tess was wearing a shirt dress which emphasized her curvy form; her eyes were sparkling, her thick dark hair shining, and she had a tan, having just returned from two weeks in Greece with Fiona, another friend from university.

Will had been impressed with this clever, pretty girl and – height being a sensitive issue with him, since he stood less than five foot six inches high in his shoes – what he particularly loved was the way her tanned face looked up to his, her blue-grey eyes smiling at him, as she described her holiday. He had barely listened as she talked, and so he never heard that they were staying in an all-inclusive resort, and to his question, 'Did you go to Mycenae?' never heard the answer,

25

'Well, we went to a karaoke bar called Mycenae Mike.' He merely smiled as she chattered, wondering how easy the promising shirt dress which revealed just enough of her breasts would be to remove.

Three dates did it; by then Tess, who had been rather unsure about him at the beginning, since he was so unlike her in so many ways, had fallen for his adept flattery, and by Christmas she was head over heels in love with him. For the first year all was wonderful; Will liked the fact that she was a little different from his usual (tall, thin, blonde, posh) girlfriends, and Tess for her part liked the fact that he was a little different from her usual (young, puppy-dog-eager) boyfriends. Their differences were a badge of honour in her eyes: they weren't each other's usual type, she told herself, and anyone who'd care to listen, including Adam. That's what made it work so well – to start with.

'I've asked myself if I knew when it went wrong,' Tess said. They were walking towards the edge of town, down to the ancient walls. It was mid-afternoon but the sky was getting darker, almost as if night-time was approaching.

'And what conclusions have you reached?' said Adam.

She looked sideways up at him, pushing her hair out of her face, as they walked along the windy street. Here, at the edge of town, the breeze was often strongest, whistling through the lanes like a dervish. Tess wished she could tell him the truth. But he, of all people, was not someone she wanted to talk to about it. She gave a little wince, as if she were speaking an unfamiliar language, trying to frame the words correctly.

'He –' She shrugged her shoulders. 'He just went off me, I think. I wasn't right for him.'

'Well, it's also that he wasn't right for you,' said Adam, but Tess wasn't really ready to hear that, she still remembered the Will who stood up when she came back into the room, who was always on time, who sent her flowers to work on a regular basis, who bossed her around, in an amused, rather despairing way, which made her feel like a naughty schoolgirl, instead of the matronly teacher she feared becoming.

'He wasn't,' she said, slowly. 'But . . . I thought he was.'

'Did you have the Dealbreaker, though?' Adam said.

'The what?'

'Come on!' Adam smiled at her. 'You remember the Deal-breaker.'

'My God, do you still use that?'

The Dealbreaker was Adam's cut-off point, the moment when you knew, he said, by some tiny action, that this woman was never going to be for you – though he insisted Tess apply it to men, too. It was his excuse to be picky, she always thought. It had seen off Cathy (gobbled her food), Laura (pigeon-toed), Alison (never heard of Pol Pot) and Belinda (allegedly, hairy chest). Tess shook her head, wondering at him. Twelve years since she left for university, nine years since she moved permanently to London, and Adam was still working in the same place using the same terminology, pulling with the same frequency. But who was she to judge any more? She'd moved back here, after all, and she no longer had any idea who she was. He at least seemed to know.

'Sure I do,' he said. 'It's good, I'm telling you. There's always a Dealbreaker. The fatal flaw. In any relationship, until they're the One.'

'There's always a fatal flaw if you always look for one, Ad,' Tess said pointedly. 'So, what was the dealbreaker with Liz?'

'I'm not telling you,' said Adam. 'Though it's pretty bad.'

She stared at him, curiously. 'Oh, go on.'

'No,' said Adam, and she knew he meant it. 'What was the Dealbreaker with Will? Come on, there must have been one.'

'There wasn't . . .' She shook her head.

'Bollocks, Tess,' Adam said. 'Are you seriously telling me there wasn't? I know there was.'

She said, slowly, 'God, there really was.'

'So?'

Tess laughed up at him, her eyes sparkling. 'Not telling you either.' He smiled. 'Not because you won't, honest. Just 'cause – it's –' She shook her head again. 'Too embarrassing. Get me drunk and I'll tell you.'

'That's a promise,' Adam said. 'So,' he said, changing the subject. 'What do you need to do first?'

'Find a place to live,' Tess said. 'No idea where to begin. I'll probably have to get a flatmate, too.'

'When do you start?'

'Four weeks' time. But my lease came to an end, and I just wanted to leave London,' Tess said, walking fast to keep up with him. 'Beside, they wanted me here early to prepare for the summer term.'

'When did the job end?'

'Last week,' said Tess. 'They're folding my classes into Mr Collins's – he's the head of Classics.'

'Two people teaching Latin and Ancient Greek at a secondary school in South London, eh,' said Adam. 'Wow.'

'Wow exactly, and that's why I'm the one who got made redundant,' Tess said, in a small voice.

'Sorry,' Adam said, putting his arm round her again. 'You're back now. You've got loads of time to settle in, too.'

'Exactly. I thought I'd use my redundancy to come down early and scout the place out for a bit, before I start at the college.' She shook her head. 'Funny, isn't it. So posh. Going from Fair View comp to this.'

They had reached the end of town; they were standing in the last lane that overlooked the medieval city walls. It was still strangely dark for the middle of the afternoon. Tess peered over, down to the valley, the hills opposite, the gathering clouds above them. 'Hey,' she said quietly. 'The water meadows.'

'Yeah,' said Adam. 'Did you know, they're –' he started, but then stopped abruptly and held out his hand. 'It's raining.'

'What were you going to say?'

'Doesn't matter.' He patted her arm. 'T – it's great to have you home again.'

'I need somewhere to live,' she said, uneasily. 'Then I'll start to feel like I'm home.'

'Fine,' said Adam, clapping his hands. 'Let's go and see Miss Store.'

'Who? Oh, the old lady with the bag – why are we going to see her?'

'Because,' said Adam, looking pleased with himself, 'Miss Store's neighbour has just moved out, and there is a cottage for rent by the church, which I am pretty sure you will love.'

She stared at him. 'Adam, that's – wow!'

'I told you,' he said. 'I know everything in this stupid small town. I'm like a fixer.' She laughed. 'And I want my oldest friend to be happy now she's back. Shall we go?'

'Is it called something like Ye Olde Cottage?'

'It's called Easter Cottage,' Adam said, smiling. 'And it's on Lord's Lane.'

'Of course it is,' said Tess. 'You are wonderful.'

'Let's go,' he said, and they turned away from the water meadows.

'Aw,' Tess said. She stopped and hugged him, her voice muffled against his jacket. 'Oh, Ad. I missed you, man. I'm sorry. I'm sorry it's been so long.'

'S'OK,' he said, squeezing her tight. 'I missed you too, T. But you're back now. Back where you belong. And it's brilliant.'

CHAPTER THREE

Several weeks later, Tess sat on the sofa in the sitting room of Easter Cottage kicking her shoes against the worn flowered silk of the sofa. Her feet beat a steady, echoing rhythm against the fabric in the silence of the room as she gazed out of the window, lost in thought. It was late afternoon. From the direction of the high street, sounds of small-town life drifted up to her – each one, it seemed, redolent of the world she was now in, each one serving to emphasize once again the world she had left behind. The sound of friends meeting in the lane. The ring of the shop bell in the Langford gift shop. A dog barking. Evening was fast approaching, another evening alone in this still-strange new cottage. She was living in a *cottage*, for God's sake. She shivered. Tess was uneasy. Unhappy, even.

She remembered, as she had done several times, the conversation she'd had with her mother the night before she'd moved back to Langford.

'I'm sure you'll enjoy being back there,' Emily Tennant had told her daughter. 'Just mind you don't turn into an old lady.'

'An old lady?' Tess had said, amused. Three years ago, the week after Stephanie's wedding, her father Frank had sold his GP practice and her parents had retired to the coast. Tess had thought they were mad, moving away from home. Still did, especially now she was on the eve of going back there. 'I still don't understand why you moved. I mean, the new house is great, but – Langford's Langford! It's beautiful.'

'Of course it is,' her mother said soothingly. 'But we wanted a bungalow. Somewhere easy to manage. We wanted to have some fresh air, be by the sea. Take the dogs for walks in peace, and put in double glazing and a satellite dish if we want it.' She sighed. 'I was just sick of feeling like a tourist in my own home. Langford's full of second-home owners and day trippers and tea shops. Sit at the table where Jane Austen sat, and all of that. Trust me, I know,' she had added, mysteriously. 'It's wonderful, Tess dear, but – don't get sucked into all that heritagey stuff. You're still young.'

'Oh, Mum, calm down!' Tess had told her, slightly indignant. Was it not she who had danced on a bar in Vauxhall the previous week, and done three tequila shots in a row before snogging the barman? 'I'm thirty. I'm in the prime of my life. I'm not an old lady.'

That afternoon, in the sweet little shop next to the Tourist Centre at the far end of the high street, Tess had bought a tea towel with a map of Langford on it. It was really nice, and she needed some more tea towels; Easter Cottage was lovely but it had virtually nothing in it. But it had cost her six pounds, and she was starting to see her mother's point. She was pretty broke, and she was lucky to have got this job.

Summer term at the College would be beginning soon; Easter was early that year. It seemed impossible that three months ago she'd been living with Meena in Balham, in the depths of despair, dumped by Will and sacked by work (well, rather smoothly told her job was being 'folded into' her boss's). Added to which, the week before Christmas, a boy who looked about ten had mugged her and taken her purse, just outside Stockwell tube. That had been the final straw.

Well over a month had passed now since she'd found Easter Cottage and she was still without a flatmate. Tess was starting to realize how foolhardy she'd been. People didn't turn up somewhere like Langford looking for a place to rent. They were either retired, or young married couples, or weekend-home owners. Not like Tess, that's for sure.

There was Adam. But Adam still lived in the cottage he'd grown up in. He couldn't afford to rent somewhere else. There was Suggs, Adam's best mate, but Suggs smelt of stew, and only had one pair of socks, and besides, he lived with Adam. She didn't really know anyone else. Perhaps she would, soon. Apart from anything else, it was such a lovely cottage. She could be so happy here, she knew it.

Tess sighed, and looked around the sitting room and the tiny galley kitchen. She had tried to make it a cheering sight. Her mugs, gaily hanging on their little white hooks; the old fireplace, which she'd filled with a jug of daffodils; and the framed poster of the equestrian statue of Marcus Aurelius in Rome hung above the sofa, which was festooned with bright, pretty cushions. It was a cold spring, and she was enjoying the cool nights, enjoying nesting in her small, sweet new home. Usually, she liked it when night came and she could draw the curtains and settle down on the sofa.

But tonight, the fog of gloom that she'd been trying to shake off all day seemed to settle firmly over her head. Tess shook herself. It was the countdown to starting her new job; she just had to tell herself that after Fair View Community College it'd be a walk in the park, teaching middle-aged people about Augustus and gladiators and the Senate. So why was she so nervous? There was an alarm bell sounding somewhere, a note of disquiet, and so she did what she always did in these situations, which was to enumerate her worries out loud to something, an inanimate object. In her flat in Balham, this had been the photo of Kanye West on the kitchen wall (Meena was obsessed with him and knew all the words to 'Gold Digger').

Now she looked around for something similar. But Mrs

Dawlish, Miss Store's old friend from whom Tess had rented Easter Cottage, was clearly not a fan of *Late Registration*. Marcus Aurelius was not suitable – the horse would get in the way. There was an old map of —shire on the wall, printed on olde-worlde textured parchment-style paper, and next to it a print of Jane Austen, the well-known watercolour by her sister Cassandra. It was a pretty shocking print, JA's colouring resembling that of someone afflicted by a rough bout of seasickness *and* jaundice combined, but it was considerably better than nothing. Tess nodded.

'Right,' she said aloud. 'Let's go through it, one by one. OK?'

There was a silence. She felt stupid, her voice echoing loudly in the small room. 'OK,' she made Jane Austen say, though she didn't really think it was the kind of thing Jane Austen would actually say, and she made a mental note to look up the word 'OK' to see whether there was any record of its usage in early nineteenth-century Hampshire.

'I'm worried about my new job,' she said in a small voice, crossing her legs underneath her on the sofa. When she said it out loud, it sounded – what? Silly? Or even more terrifying than she'd thought?

'And why is that?' she heard Jane Austen say.

'Erm . . .' Tess screwed up her eyes and stared at the picture, to try and see that small, pursed mouth moving. 'Well . . . I'm worried that, even though it's supposed to be less of a challenge than my old job, the people are going to be more difficult.'

'What do you mean?' Jane Austen asked, sounding a bit like Julie Andrews in *Mary Poppins*, Tess realized.

'Well, I've got more to lose,' Tess admitted. 'I grew up here.'

'True,' Jane Austen said, 'but I'd have thought teaching Classical Civilization in a failing comprehensive in South London and getting some teenagers who don't care about anything to even remotely be interested in the Roman Empire is worth much more than impressing Mrs Flibberty-Jibbit of Langford, wouldn't you?'

Tess paused. Then she said, 'Good point, there, Jane. Do you mind me calling you Jane?'

'I do, rather. I prefer Miss Austen. Next?'

'Well, I'm worried about money.'

'Aren't we all, dearie,' said Jane Austen. Tess realized she was now making her sound like someone from a *Carry On* film. 'Proceed, my dear Tess,' she amended.

'I need a flatmate, otherwise I'm screwed,' she said. 'I'm really stupid.'

'Yes, that is rather naive of you, committing to this house without a companion to share the rent,' said Jane Austen. 'Did you place an advertisement outside the inn?'

'Yes,' said Tess.

'Well, why don't you go down the pub tonight and ask Mick if anyone's interested?' That wasn't quite right. 'Mayhap you should repair to the inn and enquire as to the results of yon advertisement placement.'

'I was in there yesterday . . . and the day before,' Tess said sadly. 'He's going to think I'm stalking him.'

'Ask Adam to meet you there, then,' said Jane Austen, rather impatiently.

Tess sighed. 'I texted him. He said he's busy tonight.' She cupped her chin in her hands and said gloomily, 'He wouldn't tell me what he was doing, either. I think he's bored of me. Already. He's my only blimming friend here and he's trying to ditch me.'

She breathed out heavily, making a sound like a car engine winding down.

'Well,' said Jane Austen reasonably, 'it sounds to me as if you are in need of some new acquaintance. After all, you left London for a fresh start. Think of what Will would think if he saw you, sitting all miserably by yourself here, moping around?'

That was it.

34

'You're bloody right,' Tess said aloud, as she stood up. 'Honestly, Tessa Tennant. What's wrong with you? Get a grip! You're out of London, you're back here in this lovely town. No more tube strikes, no more congestion charge.' She took a deep breath. 'No more waiting ten sodding minutes to be served at the pub, no more strange men staring at you on horrible bendy buses, no more skinny teenagers staring at you in TopShop, and definitely no more horrible boyfriends going off with girls with stupid names!' She thumped her fist on the wall; it echoed, disconcertingly. 'You're back! It's good! You've got a bloody good job and you're lucky!'

Somewhere in the eaves of the old building, a bird trilled, an early evening call. 'There you go,' Tess told herself firmly. She stared at the picture again, and it stared impassively back. 'Now, go to the pub, get a drink, and cheer up.' She shut the window and dumped her now-cold cup of tea on the kitchen draining board.

'Thanks, Jane!' she yelled, as she headed towards the door. 'I'm off to the pub! See you later!'

She collected herself. 'I'm going mad,' she said softly, shaking her head at the print, which hung by the front door. 'Sorry.'

CHAPTER FOUR

The Feathers had been in Langford for four hundred years. In its day, it had been one of the great coaching inns, the resting place for the beau monde on their way down towards the great estates of the South-West. Charles I had hidden in a cellar there for a couple of weeks, and Beau Brummell had stayed the night before visiting the Roman Villa and signed the visitors' book. *'Passing comfortable,'* he had written. *'A charming little town, Langford. I pay you my compliments. Brummell.'* Langford, which had always thought of itself as a deeply correct place, and regarded with suspicion the new claims of towns like Bath (vulgar nouveau Regency), Stratford-upon-Avon (American tourists everywhere) and Rye (smugglers' money!) had collectively swooned at this, back in the day. In fact, nearly two hundred years later, it still continued to swoon; the visitors' book was in the great hallway that led through to the dining room; in a glass case, open at the page on which Mr Brummell had flirted with the town. The Feathers was, geographically and symbolically, at Langford's very heart for this reason.

The dining room had huge wooden settles, carving it up into different sections, so that coachman and nobleman could eat in the same room, but not be troubled by the other. A huge, leaded oriel window, giving out onto the high street, let in the light, and at the back there was another window, with a perfect view of the countryside as the town sloped down the hill, stopping before the valley, with the Vale of Langford opening up before them.

Tess, coming into the dining room on that March evening, armed only with a copy of *Persepolis*, which she was re-reading, and the paper, was struck once again with the sensation that hit her: the clear, seductive light, the musty, clean smell, the quiet reassuring sounds of a working pub on a slow Wednesday spring night. The bar, a long L-shaped affair, was low and welcoming. Tess pulled up a stool, waiting for Mick to appear, her eyes scanning the blackboard for the day's specials: she was suddenly very hungry.

And then, from the corner of the bar behind her, someone spoke.

'Scuse me,' said a husky, female voice. 'Can I take this stool?'

Wheeling round, Tess looked up suspiciously to find a girl about her own age looking at her. Of course. It was That Girl. That Girl, as she had wittily christened her in her own mind, was staying at the Feathers, and was the sort of person, based solely on outward appearances, that Tess had always secretly yearned to be. Sophisticated, mysterious, effortlessly glamorous; Tess had seen a Mulberry handbag swinging from her arm as they'd passed in the street a couple of days ago. Tess had been pinning up her advert, wrestling with a rusty pin and a hard wooden board; That Girl had sashayed past, smiling pleasantly at her. That Girl's long, glossy hair was – well, toffee-coloured, that was the only word for it. Her clothes just sort of hung off her, like they were meant to. She definitely wasn't a local, That Girl.

'Er,' said Tess, pushing the stool next to her away from her, swiftly, feeling like a spotty teenage boy. 'Here, of course . . . Yes.'

That Girl pushed her hair away from her eyes, behind her shoulders. 'Sorry,' she said. 'I'm Francesca.' She smiled, briefly, and held out her hand. 'I saw you yesterday, didn't I? Are you staying here as well?'

'Um, no,' said Tess, sitting upright. She wasn't dwarfishly short, but she was self-conscious about her height, and girls like Francesca made her feel peasant-like, a pear-shaped lard-arse. She smiled and tried to flick her hair out behind her back too, but her thick dark locks were too short and unwieldy. They swung back in her face like bouncing wire wool, so instead Tess shook her head, nonchalantly, trying to pass this off as a normal cool hair-move, and said, 'I live here, actually. Just moved back from London.' She felt this was necessary, she didn't know why. 'How about you? Are you on holiday?'

Francesca stroked a corner of the small blackboard with her long creamy fingers; the chalk smeared into swirls. 'Not exactly,' she said. 'I'm just staying here for a while. I'm from London too.' She looked down, and was silent.

'Oh,' said Tess, not sure what to say next. 'Well.' She cast a glance around the almost empty pub. 'It's a great town, anyway.'

'Yes,' said Francesca, more eagerly. 'I love it here. Everyone seems really nice. So you – you're from here, then?'

'Sort of,' Tess told her. 'I grew up here. But I've been in London for the last ten years. I've just moved back to Langford. I got a new job.'

The words on her lips still sounded so strange, foreign. She would have to get used to them. She didn't know what else to add to this but her companion said,

'Wow. So you've been back a few weeks, right?' Tess nodded. 'That must be great.' Tess nodded again, slowly. Francesca pushed the blackboard away, and cupped her chin in her hands. 'But it must be weird too, I bet. Coming back here – are you on your own?'

She said it in a friendly tone, in the spirit of polite enquiry; at least, Tess chose to take it that way.

'I'm not on my own – I mean, er, I *am* on my own, yep,' Tess said nonchalantly. She pushed the ball of her palm firmly over her forehead. 'I had a bit of a crap time, last few months.' She hesistated, debating as to how much detail was necessary. 'And I was unemployed, too. So – I saw this job advertised and I applied and I got it – that's how I decided to move back. Plus, you know, it was time to leave London,' she said, getting into her stride. 'I wanted to live in a proper community again. Escape from the town, shop in local shops, walk everywhere . . . just be with people who I – you know.'

Francesca was nodding politely. 'Wow,' she said. 'That's so cool of you. Let's hope they don't build that out-of-town shopping centre, then!'

'Oh. Well, exactly,' said Tess. 'I know. So – why are you here?' she blurted, curiously.

'Oh, I'm just meeting someone for a drink,' Francesca said. 'Just someone I met.' She shook her head. 'Sorry, you didn't mean that, did you.'

Tess smiled. 'I don't want to be nosy.'

'God, no,' said Francesca. 'The weird thing is, it's the same reasons as you.' She gave a little smile. 'I'm here to escape from London too. Except I was never here in my life before, and I have no idea *why* I'm here.' Her eyes met Tess's; Tess saw something in them, something vulnerable, and she suddenly liked her, this stranger. 'I'm a lawyer. Well, I trained as a lawyer, but most recently I'm a banker.' She made a slicing motion across her throat. 'An unemployed banker. Doesn't get much more tragic than that.'

'I'm sorry.'

'Don't be. I was heading for a burnout anyway,' said Francesca. 'Seriously, if I hadn't been given the heave-ho I'd have done something stupid. It's the best thing to happen to me in years. That's the weird bit.'

'Why? What happened?' Tess said.

'Can't remember, really,' Francesca said frankly. 'Last few months are a bit of a blur. I was working twenty-hour days. For about two months. Then I went to a wedding, someone at work, and after a drink apparently told one of the partners to fuck themselves. Then I tried to kiss another one. Then . . . well, the first round of redundancies was before Christmas, and I knew I'd be the first to go, so they didn't have to pay me a bonus.' She said it as though reciting a lesson. 'I got a few months' redundancy pay. My flatmate's just moved in with his girlfriend, so I rented out my flat and . . . I'm here.'

Tess could only gape as the barman appeared. 'Hi, Mick!' said Francesca. 'Get me a gin and tonic, would you?' She waggled a finger at Tess and looked at her watch. 'My drink date isn't here yet. What do you want?' She stopped. 'I'm so sorry. I don't even know your name.'

'It's Tess,' Tess said, and they shook hands again, smiling at the formality of it.

'God,' came a voice from the door behind them. 'Francesca, can you ever— Oh. Tess?' The deep voice stopped. 'Is that you?'

Tess whirled round. 'Adam? I thought you were—'

There, striding towards them, was her oldest friend, a look of bemusement across his face. His thick light brown hair was standing up in tufts, as it did when he was in a hurry, or confused, and his eyes were questioning. He smiled as he reached them, and she nodded, behind Francesca, smiling back at him. Of course . . . of course.

'This is a nice surprise!' he said, squeezing her arm, just a little too hard.

'Yes, isn't it,' she answered, taking his hand in hers and scratching his palm with her middle fingernail. He jumped in surprise.

'I thought I—'

'You said you were busy tonight,' Tess said, unnecessarily loudly. 'How lovely to see you. I just came in to check up with Mick about my ad.'

'Ah, of course,' said Adam. 'Well, lovely to see you, Tess.' Francesca was looking at them, confusion spreading over her lovely face. 'Yes, I am busy tonight, as you can see.'

'Yes,' said Tess, trying to think of some appropriate come-back, but she had missed her chance for Adam leaned forward, towards That Girl again.

'I really am sorry for being late,' he said, smiling at her. Francesca looked up at him, her cheeks flushed, hair falling in her face, her composure momentarily disturbed.

'Oh, that's fine,' she said, shyly.

'I had to lock up at the museum, and then I found a little chick barely alive in the lane . . .'

'Country Boy,' said Francesca. She turned to Tess. 'I called him Country Boy the first day I was here. He's so funny.' Her eyes met his again.

'I'm not,' said Adam. He was smiling at her. 'I'm a sophisti-cated international man of mystery, that's me. Call me Adam Bond instead.' Francesca gave a gurgle of laughter. 'So you've met my oldest friend, then?'

'Wow, really?' said Francesca, turning to Tess with pleasure in her eyes. 'Isn't that weird!'

'Hilariously weird,' said Tess, ignoring Adam's glares. 'We grew up together. In fact—'

'Let's get a drink,' Adam said hurriedly.

'I've got one, but – great idea,' Francesca said, turning to the bar. 'Tess, what did you say you wanted?'

Tess felt as welcome as a red sock in a white wash, nor did she wish to stay and watch Adam perform his moves on yet another unsuspecting victim – although in this case she was fairly certain she wouldn't be called upon to pretend to be Adam's girlfriend, as with Liz from the deli.

She said, warily, 'Oh, I really can't—'

'Yes,' Adam said, too quickly. 'It's really sad, but unfortunately Tess can't stay.'

Tess looked at him, and she thought of walking back down the lane to the cottage again, opening the door, seeing Jane Austen's somewhat disapproving face on the wall. 'Oh, go on then,' she told Francesca. 'Just one, then. I'll have a gin and tonic too, that'd be lovely. Thanks.'

'Brilliant!' Francesca said happily, moving off towards the centre of the bar.

Tess narrowed her eyes and glowered at Adam. She said, under her breath, 'I can't believe you! I don't *want* to be in this situation, you know!'

'OK, OK. Don't kill me.' Adam put his arm around her. 'I'm sorry. I'm just – this one's a tricky one.'

'I'm not staying for supper. Just one drink,' she said, looking up at him. 'I promise. I didn't know – is it a date?'

'Not sure,' Adam said. He touched her lightly on the shoulder. 'Wouldn't mind your advice, later. I'm looking for a sign either way before I make a move.'

Francesca came back with the drinks. 'I've just asked Mick if we can change the dinner reservation to three, Tess – why don't you have some food with us? We're eating. Go on, it'll be fun!'

Tess looked from Adam to Francesca.

'I think that's a sign,' she said.

'What's a sign?' said Francesca. She handed her her drink.

'Nothing,' said Tess.

'Go on!' Francesca said, nudging Adam.

'Yes, Tess,' Adam said woodenly. 'Go on. Please do join us.'

'Oh, all right then,' said Tess. She bit her lip, trying not to laugh. 'Since you insist.'

CHAPTER FIVE

Tess had been looking for some confirmation, a sign that, a month down the line, she had made the right decision moving back to Langford. She was due a good time, and that night was it. There was nothing her still-raw single state hated more than feeling like a gooseberry, but as they sat down she promised herself she'd leave early, citing preparation for the new job, leaving Adam to make his move. As darkness slid over the old building, and the lights behind the bar glowed at their backs, the welcome fire leaping in the grate, they sat down at a table and intently studied the menu.

'Mm,' said Adam, after that awkward pause that always joins the group of diners with menus who aren't quite sure what to say to each other. 'Looks great. I love the food here. It's the best.'

'Yep,' said Tess. She glanced down.

'You hungry?' Adam asked Francesca.

'Not sure,' she replied, seriously. She looked at the menu again, a curtain of hair falling about her shoulders. 'Deep fried local brie with cranberry sauce? Or chicken liver pâté with onion marmalade? What is this?' she said, laughing. 'Café Rouge circa 1997?'

Adam looked astonished, and Tess stifled a laugh, not

wanting to agree with her, but at the same time she felt a stab of loyalty. Almost as if, by dissing the Feathers, Francesca was dissing Langford, Adam and thus Tess's decision to live here. She caught this train of thought and shook her head. 'You can have a special,' she said, pointing to the board where '*Chicken Pie*' and '*Lasagne*' were starkly scrawled. Francesca looked at them, sadly, as if she'd expected more. Adam gazed expectantly at her. He seemed worried she might be about to drop dead of starvation.

'Hey,' he said. 'We can—'

'No, no,' said Francesca, hurriedly. 'It's fine! So.' She put down her menu and smacked the table. 'You two have known each other for – what? How long?'

'Thirty years,' Tess said at the same time as Adam said, 'No idea,' and they broke off, laughing.

'And you grew up here?' Francesca said. 'That's so cool. I bet it must have been a lovely place to grow up.'

'It was,' said Tess. 'Just – it's a lovely town. Small, friendly. Very . . .' she trailed off. 'We could pretty much do what we wanted, couldn't we?'

'Were you near each other?'

'Opposite houses,' Adam said, rolling his eyes. 'Tess and Steph used to throw mud at me over their garden fence. Lovely children. My mum . . .' He paused. 'Mum was always having to tell them to stop bullying me.'

'What a load of rubbish,' Tess said, feigning indignation to cover the pause that always happened whenever anyone mentioned Philippa.

'Do they still live there?' Francesca said.

Tess opened her mouth, but Adam said quickly, 'No. Mine – don't really know who my dad is, he was Irish and my mum met him at college in Dublin. My mum's dead. And hers,' he jerked a thumb in Tess's direction, 'moved to the seaside.'

Francesca laughed, awkwardly, at the contrast, and looked embarrassed. 'Sorry, I didn't mean to—'

'S'fine,' Adam said quickly. 'I was being – yeah.' He smiled at her. 'Anyway,' he said, turning to look at Tess. 'Langford is a beautiful town. Bit quiet sometimes, but I like it that way.'

There was a silence. All three looked down at their menus again until Adam broke the slight tension, gently touching Francesca's hand.

'How about you, then?' he said.

'Well, I've come here for peace and quiet, so that suits me fine,' said Francesca. 'Just some time somewhere new, some fresh air, chilling out, getting some perspective, walking, reading, you know.' She spoke slowly, and gazed into the fire.

'Sounds like a great idea,' said Tessa, sympathetically, whilst thinking at the same time, *Chilling out and getting some perspective? Who are you, Deepak Chopra?* 'Just a week or so, then?' she asked, smartly. 'How long will you be here?'

'Bit more than that.' Francesca dropped her mellifluous voice. 'I need to not be me for a while.'

'I know,' Adam was murmuring, staring into her eyes. 'But you're here now, and you couldn't have come to a better place.'

Tess wished she *wasn't* here, in the gooseberry costume she'd been afraid of donning. She cleared her throat, and said nothing, and as the silence between her two companions grew more intense, and they held each other's gaze, Tess wanted to hold up a banner:

IF YOU'RE GOING TO SNOG . . .

GET ON WITH IT!

Just as she was wondering if staying for dinner was a massive mistake, Mick appeared with a notepad, humming to himself, one bandy leg tapping out a rhythm on the floor.

'Ready?' he said, eyes flicking from Francesca to Adam.

'Oh, hello, Tess! Didn't see you there. Any reply from that advert yet?'

'None yet,' Tess told him. 'Thanks, though.'

'When's the new job start then? You looking forward to it?'

'Week after next, Mick,' she said.

Mick whistled through his teeth. 'Is that right?' He smiled kindly at her. 'Well. You done all right for yourself, haven't you? Langford College, eh.'

Francesca looked impressed. 'What, the residential place? Is that Langford as in Langford, here? I hadn't realized.' Tess nodded, ignoring the churning feeling in her stomach.

'That's the one,' Mick said. He shrugged his shoulders. 'Good to see you, Tess. Look at you and Adam here, your little husband, eh?' He grinned in delight. 'That's what she used to call him,' he told Francesca.

Adam rubbed his head with his fingers. 'Oh, God,' he said, in mortification.

'These two,' said Mick, jabbing his pencil in the air with delight. 'When they was little, well – you couldn't see the daylight between them! Like a little pair of Siamese twins. Her so dark, him so blond, riding their bikes down that lane there.' Mick's rich, slow voice was like the scene-setting narration at the beginning of a nature film. 'It were ever so sweet. We all thought so.'

'Mick,' Adam said firmly, coming up for air. 'Leave it.' He smiled shamefacedly across at Tess and she shook her head, smiling back at him in embarrassment.

'Aah,' Francesca said, and patted them both on the back. 'That *is* so sweet. Now, Mick,' she said, getting down to business. 'This roast with all the trimmings, what is it?'

'Chicken, did it myself this afternoon,' said Mick.

'Great,' said Francesca. 'I'll have just the chicken, and a green salad – *no* iceberg please – and some of that potato salad you made for lunch if you can lay your hands on any? And I want a glass of the Chablis – shall we just get a bottle?'

Adam and Tess nodded mutely at her. 'That's that, then!' she said happily, as Mick scribbled away and then turned to Tess.

'Er . . .' Tess said, at a loss. 'Er . . . Same for me?'

'No problemo,' Mick said, scribbling it down with a flourish.

'I'll have the fish and chips, please, Mick,' said Adam. 'And a pint of Butcombe when you've got a minute, but I'll have a glass for the wine just in case. Need a hand?'

'No, you're all right,' said Mick, and he walked off. Francesca turned back to them.

'That's adorable. So you were boyfriend and girlfriend?'

'No,' said Tess, a little bit too quickly. Adam glanced at her.

'No,' he echoed. 'Just – when we were little, five or six. That's what *some* of us –' he glared at Tess, before grinning at her – 'used to go around saying.'

'So the two of you never . . .' Francesca made a strange flapping gesture with her hands. Tess and Adam both stared at her, then at each other, in bewilderment.

'Joined a hand puppet society?' Adam said. 'No. We never joined a hand puppet society together.'

'You know what I mean,' Francesca said.

'No, I don't,' Adam said, shaking his head at her wickedly. 'What?'

'I don't know . . .' Francesca had the grace to look embarrassed. 'Had a little teenage romance when you were younger. I don't know,' she repeated. She looked at Tess. 'Come on, you must have thought about it, at one stage or another.'

'Not really,' said Tess.

'Er – no,' said Adam. He shook his head.

'So you never had a moment? You've just always been friends?' She shook her head. 'That's weird.'

They were both silent.

'It may be, but it is true,' said Tess eventually, aware she sounded very prim.

'Yeah, nosy girl,' Adam told Francesca, and she nodded.

'I believe you. Thousands wouldn't.' Tess took a sip of her

drink, and Adam did the same. As if realizing the conversation needed changing, Francesca said, 'So. It's always quiet around here, you say? No crazy rock festivals down the road or anything?'

'I don't knew about that,' Tess began, and then there was a loud noise, and the door to the pub across the bar flew open, banging loudly against the wall, and a middle-aged man burst in, palming his hair firmly onto his shiny forehead as he hurried into the bar.

'A'right, Mick!' he called loudly to the landlord, pushing a stool out of the way and knocking over a chair.

'A'right, Ron,' said Mick.

'Meeting's starting in five minutes, that all right with you?'

'No probs,' said Mick. 'Not many people in tonight, anyway, you can have the place to yours—'

'Save the water meadows!' Ron shouted suddenly, with enormous vigour. Francesca jumped; Tess dropped the fork with which she had been toying. Even the more stoic Adam blinked in surprise.

'All right, Ron?' he called. 'How's it going?'

Ron turned around at that. ''Ullo, Adam!' he said, coming forward. 'Good to see you! It's been a while, you all right?' He peered, mole-like, at Tess. 'Hullo there, Tess.' Tess held up her hand, and Ron's gaze moved from her to Francesca, and turned back to Adam. 'Right you are,' he said to him, clearly meaning, Go on, son. 'You coming to the meeting tonight?'

'No,' said Adam. 'We're just having some food.'

'Suggs is organizing it, Adam, didn't he mention?' Ron said firmly.

'Yes, he did.'

'You don't agree with them building over the water meadows then, do you? Letting that Mortmain woman get away with it again, eh?' Ron's voice rose, his nose twitched, as he waggled a finger – benignly – at Adam.

'You know me, I don't like taking sides,' Adam said easily.

He smiled at Ron, and just as Tess was looking at him curiously, Francesca said, in her charming way, 'Ron – it's Ron, isn't it?'

'Yep,' said Ron, non-committally.

'Sorry to be stupid, I should know this, but what exactly is going on with the water meadows? I only got here a few days ago.'

'You haven't heard about it?' Ron said incredulously, as if the idea that this wasn't front-page news across the country hadn't occurred to him. 'That's strange. You know the Langford water meadows, right?'

'I'm afraid not,' Francesca said politely.

'You never heard of them? That's—' Ron scratched his head, as if he could scarcely conceive of such a thing. 'Only the most precious bit o' land for about a hundred miles, that's all. There's more wildlife, more plants, more birds sighted *only on* the Langford water meadows than anywhere else in the country. And they want to fill it in, drain the land and sell it off so we can have a bloody shopping centre there!' He was shouting again now, his burr more pronounced than ever. 'That bloody Mortmain woman, she's got it all stitched up! What's she want the money for anyway? She ain't got no one to leave it to. And she thinks she can can ride roughshod over us all. Again!'

He held a finger up to heaven and his eyes looked skywards; he reminded Tess of a Roman statue.

'Wow,' said Francesca. She turned to Adam. 'Is that true?' she asked.

Adam nodded slowly. 'Yes,' he said. There was unease in his voice and Tess remembered what it was that had been bothering her; the truth about Adam and the bursary, how Leonora Mortmain had always been so unpleasant to him in particular ever since. 'Yes, I suppose it is true. But it's done, isn't it? The council's given initial early approval—'

'What does the council know?' came another loud voice

from behind them, and Adam stood up, laughing, his deep voice echoing around the pub. Beside them, Mick put down the tray of drinks and started laying out cutlery, as Adam hugged the bearded man next to Ron.

'You bastard,' he said fondly. 'I didn't know this was happening tonight.'

'Tess!' said the stranger. 'I didn't know you were going to be here.'

'Suggs!' Tess said turning round. She hugged Adam's best friend, squeezing him tight.

'Look at you, with two ladies, you smooth bastard,' Suggs said, sitting down happily next to Francesca. 'I'll join you, shall I? Meeting doesn't start for a few minutes.'

Ron was still hovering behind Tess and Adam. 'We need you to sort out the leaflets,' he said, tetchily.

'Andrea'll do that,' Suggs said easily. 'I haven't seen Tess properly since she got back. Mick, do me a favour and bring me a pint of the good stuff, will you?' Mick shook his head, smiling indulgently. 'Thanks, mine host.' Suggs leaned forward. 'You lovely ladies signed the petition yet?'

'No,' said Francesca. 'Just show us where, though. They can't do that, can they?'

'Looks like they are,' said Suggs, and Ron nodded. 'It's a right fucker. You'd think they wouldn't be allowed – the council wouldn't let it happen.'

'They have, though,' said Adam evenly.

Suggs turned to him angrily. 'I know you love them Mortmains, because that stupid cow paid for your education and you feel like you have to crawl to her, you little sucker.'

'She paid for you to go to *school*?' Francesca said, bewildered.

'Shove off, Suggsy,' said Adam, tugging his hair and looking uncomfortable, but Suggs ignored him.

'Enough's enough,' Suggs went on. 'There's a lot of people in this town who think she's gone too far this time.' He paused for dramatic effect. 'You know, the Mortmains have been shafting the good people of Langford for years and she's no better. There was Ivo Mortmain, Victorian feller, he got a girl from the town pregnant and then killed her father when he came to complain. Shot him in the face! And old Mrs Mortmain's father, he sold a whole bit of land by Thornham and they made it into horrible box houses, not fit for a pig to live in. That were fifty years ago! And she – she turfed out the old people in the alms houses by the church fifteen years ago, just because she wanted to sell them on.' He gripped the back of Adam's neck. 'Remember how angry your ma was about it?'

Adam grimaced. 'She went round to see her.'

'She did?' Tess said. Adam nodded.

'Well, exactly,' Suggs nodded meaningfully at him. 'His mother in a bate – you wouldn't want to see it.' He smiled. 'She stormed round there and tried to persuade her, but it didn't have no effect. Why would it? And now this. Well, we won't put up with it any more. It's time it stopped.'

'Hear, hear,' said Ron.

'Oh, right,' said Francesca, but Tess was looking at Adam, whose expression was set. 'What do you think, Adam?' Francesca said innocently.

'I'm not saying she's a nice woman, but I don't take sides,' said Adam. 'Sorry.' Tess and Francesca stared at him in disappointment. 'Excuse me a second,' he said, and got up and left.

By the time he came back, the pub was full to bursting with locals, and the mood was jolly if increasingly rowdy. Placards were being passed around, chairs were scraping on the floor, and at the front a sharp-faced woman was filling out forms, waggling a pencil at someone. Adam sat down.

'What was that about?' Tess started to say, but Adam held up his hand.

'Hey, sorry. Sorry, T.' He turned to her, and there was a

look of desperation, almost, in his eyes. 'Please, let's not go on about it. It's just the hypocrisy of it, that's all.'

'What do you mean?' Francesca cried. 'How can it be a good thing?'

'I've lived here my whole life,' Adam said with a twisted smile. 'I'm just saying sometimes there are ulterior motives to things. I'm not exempt, but it's not as simple as it seems, is all I'm saying. That development would give people jobs, it'd increase tourism. It might not be such a terrible thing.'

'But the water meadows,' Tess said, a catch in her voice. 'How can you say that?'

'Yes, and do you really want more tourism?' said Francesca, curiously. 'Don't you want to find other ways of sustaining the town?'

Tess loved her then, for not being a pushover. Adam looked at her, and nodded slowly. He scratched the back of his neck.

'You're right,' he said. 'Just – anyway.' He cleared his throat. 'T, how's the hunt for a flatmate going?'

'It's not,' said Tess. 'I don't know what I'm going to do.'

'Where do you live?' Francesca asked politely.

'Just past the church, towards the old hall.' Tess turned to her. 'I've got to find someone to share the rent, otherwise I'll have to move out.'

'What's the house?' Francesca said.

'It's a cottage really. It's tiny, but it's so sweet. It's called Easter Cottage.'

'How many bedrooms?'

'Two,' said Tess. 'In fact I—' Their eyes met across the table.

'Can I come round tomorrow?' said Francesca.

Tess looked at her. 'Francesca – you mean –'

'And if you find someone long-term, I'll move out straight away, we can put it in my lease. Promise.'

'Go on then.' Tess's shoulders slumped, and she breathed out, smiling at Francesca.

'Are you – sure?'

52

Tess looked at the beautiful girl opposite her, and ran over the evening thus far in her head. Then she looked at Adam, who winked gently at her, holding her gaze. She smiled at him, then back at Francesca, as the noise from the bar grew louder. She raised her voice.

'Never been surer about anything.'

CHAPTER SIX

One week later, Tess nodded at the portrait of Jane Austen, as she had taken to doing before she went anywhere, and stepped out of the front door of Easter Cottage. She looked gingerly about her, and then up at the sky. It had rained for the last five days, rained as she and Francesca lugged sodden cardboard box after box into the tiny little house which was now Francesca's home, rained all that evening as they hopefully opened the back door onto the tiny little garden, where Tess had fantasized that they'd have drinks; it rained the next day, when they stocked up on food, the day after, when Francesca bought a DVD player and huge flat-screen TV without telling Tess and Tess told her she'd have to take them back; the day after that, when they sat on the sofa all afternoon and evening, made mojitos, ate Pringles and watched *My Big Fat Greek Wedding* (great), *27 Dresses* (crap), *You, Me and Dupree* (which they thought was possibly the worst film ever made) and *Pan's Labyrinth* – well, the first five minutes, before agreeing that yes, it was probably a masterpiece, now was not the right contextual time to dive into said labyrinth, but they should definitely keep the DVD player and the huge flat-screen TV and watch *Talladega Nights* instead. And it was still raining the next day, when Adam took them to the pub on Easter Sunday for lunch.

Tess had the house. She had the housemate, she had some friends. It was spring. All she had to do now was start her job. Start the process of living her life here, in this town, seeing some sort of vista stretch out ahead of her. But still, on this, her first day in her new job, it was raining.

'Byee!' called Francesca, from inside the cottage. Tess turned round and looked back through the front door, which opened directly onto the cosy sitting room. There, lounging on the sofa, in an embroidered silk Chinese dressing gown, watching TV and munching on toast, was her new flatmate who, this time just over a week ago, she'd never met. Tess smiled.

'Byeee!' she called back. 'Francesca, remember to call BT again about the broadband, will you?'

'Sure, sure,' Francesca said reassuringly. 'Good luck! Have a great time!'

A great time. Tess shut the door behind her and opened up her umbrella. She wasn't sure about that. Her heart was in her mouth and she was tired, not having slept at all the previous night. She fingered the brochure in her bag, already heavy with textbooks and notes. Langford College had three components: year-long intensive A-level courses, in languages, History of Art, Classical Civilization, English and so on; the shorter options, intensive bursts devoted to one specialized area, anything from cookery to flower arranging to Roman Poetry, usually over a period of a few weeks; and then finally there were visiting professors who gave one-off lectures, an open-air private theatre down by the lake, lovely accommodation – all in the dramatic surroundings of Langford Hall, one of the best and earliest examples of neo-Gothic Victorian architecture, predating even Pugin.

It was a five-minute walk away, standing at the edge of the town in its own grounds. Her first class wasn't till three. 'The Splendour That Was Rome', a two-month course of four classes a week, culminating in a trip to Rome where she, Tess Tennant, would be leading ten people on a tour of the ancient city. And here she stood, on a wet, grey street, shaking with nerves, wishing she could run back inside her nice new cosy home and stay on the sofa with Francesca, watching DVDs all day.

No, she said firmly. A journey of a thousand miles starts with a single step. Who could she be today, to get her through this? Maria singing 'I Have Confidence' in *The Sound of Music*? Too chirpy. Meryl Streep in *The French Lieutenant's Woman*? Too . . . prostitutey. Lizzy Bennet. Yes, when in doubt, think of J. Austen on the wall and Lizzy Bennet. Calm, funny, her own person. Tess set off down the street with something approximating a spring in her step; if Lizzy Bennet was alive today, she reasoned, she could easily be Tess, setting off to teach Roman history to a group of retired posh people. Actually, she was more convinced Lizzy Bennet would be an ethical trader at KPMG, storing up a handful of assets in advance of any impending market collapse which she would then redistribute to deserving causes, but never mind. Twirling her umbrella, she tripped across the uneven cobblestones to the end of the street, where Lord's Lane met the high street, the main road that led out to the edge of town.

'Tess?' called a voice from behind her suddenly, and Tess swivelled round wildly. She was unsure where the voice had come from; that was the unnerving thing about living in Langford, she had realized. You were never quite sure who knew you and who didn't. In London, no one knew you. It was kind of nice. Sometimes.

'Tess! Yoo hoo!'

Walking along the high street towards her was a vaguely familiar woman, neatly dressed in a Husky jacket and headscarf.

'Tess! Ah. I knew it was you,' said the woman, smiling broadly, showing enormous teeth. 'I said to myself, I bet that's Tess!'

Diana? Carolyn? Jean? Tess asked herself wildly. *Something like that. God, it's on the tip of my tongue. Audrey? Jean? It's Jean, I'm sure it's Jean.*

'I'm doing your course!' the woman said, proudly. 'Present from Jeremy! Bless him.'

Jeremy . . . Jeremy and . . . who the hell was it? Tess racked her brains for the magic formula of garbled couples' names. Something and Jeremy . . . And then realization dawned.

Jan and Jeremy! Jan Allingham! Of course. 'You are? That's great! Hello, Jan!' Tess said, smiling brightly at Jan Allingham (for it was she), who held out her hand.

'Well, here you are, here we are,' said Jan, briskly patting her short, rigidly waved hair. 'We're going to be your first students, you know.'

Tess looked at her watch in alarm. It was just before eleven. 'The first class isn't till three,' she said.

'Oh, I know, I know!' Jan cried. 'I wanted to come a bit early. Get my bearings, complete the registration forms, have a look round.'

'Oh!' said Tess, weakly. 'That's very . . . That's great!'

'You enjoying being back then, dear?'

'Yes,' said Tess. 'It's great. Very excited about teaching, too.'

'You seen lots of Adam, then?' Jan asked, tapping Tess's arm. 'Shall we carry on walking?' she said, as she carried on walking. 'The two of you when you were little – so adorable.' Tess smiled politely. 'Isn't it funny, when I can remember you peeing into a potty! And now you're going to be teaching me!'

'You only moved here when I was a teenager,' said Tess firmly.

'Oh, well, details!' Jan cried happily. 'Now, who's this flat-mate of yours, that gorgeously glamorous girl, the one who I keep seeing with your Adam? Andrea's seen them together a few times, says they're quite the item.'

Tess nodded. 'Francesca. Yes. She's absolutely lovely.'

'So nice for Adam after *everything* –' Jan mouthed the word *everything*. 'It must be good for him.'

57

Since there was no answer to this but a short, sympathetic *Mmm*, Tess said, 'Mmm.'

'A nice steady girlfriend. And rich too. I heard she was a *banker*.'

They turned onto the high street, which was almost deserted, its shops dark and the houses forbidding, in the soft March rain. 'I don't think they're actually boyfriend and girlfriend—' Tess began timidly, but Jan interrupted her.

'Diana! Hellooo!' she called loudly, as a figure in front of them in a flared corduroy skirt turned around cautiously. 'Diana! It's me! You remember Diana, don't you?'

'Is that Tess?' said Diana Sayers, walking towards them. 'Hello, Tess.' From under a short, severe fringe she nodded briefly at Tess, who smiled back, unable to remember where or how she knew Diana. 'I'm taking your course, just off to have a look around and complete the registration forms, all that.'

'Oh! How nice,' said Tess, her mind racing. *Vicar? Baker? Candlestick maker?* 'That's—'

'Bit of a busman's holiday for you, isn't it, Diana?' Jan said, tapping Diana on the arm again, as if motioning her to move off like a carthorse. 'I'd have thought you'd have had enough of schools for a while!'

Of course. Diana Sayers! Mrs Sayers, the Langford primary school secretary. Adam's godmother. Philippa's best friend, she hadn't seen her for years, how could she have forgotten her?

'I thought it was probably about time I actually learned something now I'm retired,' Diana said gruffly. 'Sick of children. Don't care if I never see another one.'

'Aaah. That's nice,' murmured Jan, not really listening, and Tess bit her lip, trying not to laugh.

'Cross here,' Diana commanded, raising her left arm high in the air, and the little crocodile obediently crossed the road.

'Did you go to the meeting last week at the pub?' Jan said. 'Andrea's furious with me for not going, but I had to wait in and pick Jeremy up from the station. Some stupid golfing day, bloody idiot. She said it went well,' she added, inconsequentially. 'Ron's wonderful at organizing that sort of thing.'

'Oh, I went,' Diana said, nodding. 'Only briefly though. Andrea's started the petition, she's going to take it round the town. I thought we should probably give copies to people like your Jeremy, Jan, get him to pin it up in the office? I mean, Thornham's only a couple of miles away from here, they'll be affected if this bloody superstore goes ahead too.'

'I must say,' said Jan, ignoring her. 'That Family – I've broken with them. Simply broken with the Mortmains, and Carolyn Tey can waggle over to me with her big sad cow eyes all she wants and say, "Oh, Jan, I know Mrs Mortmain's *ever* so *grateful* to you for your support," when that damned woman wants the PCC to approve her horrible fence so she doesn't have to look at any ordinary people. But they're going to have to learn a lesson! We won't take it any more! Ooh –' she said, breaking off. 'I do like your shoes, Diana. Where did you get them? I've been looking for something like that. Something a bit smart, but with a plimsoll lining.' She emphasized the 'l's in plimsoll, so it sounded like *plllllimmmsollllll*. 'Can you walk far in them?'

'Good grief, Jan,' said Diana crisply. 'Do concentrate! We need to stand shoulder to shoulder on this.' She turned sharply towards them and said coldly, 'Until we do—'

'Goodness!' Jan called. Tess looked up; there in front of them were the stone pillars at the start of the drive. 'We're here – and look who's over there! Talk of the devil! It's Carolyn and Jacquetta! We said we'd meet for coffee, but I wasn't sure if they'd make it too! Tess, you remember Carolyn! I don't know if you'd have met Jacquetta . . .'

Of course Tess vaguely thought she might, once, have met Carolyn, but she knew better by now than to admit that she actually had no idea who she was. She felt as if she were in a parallel universe, that this Langford, full of scary ladies in Marks and Spencer Footgloves, had been bobbing outside her window, waiting to pounce on her for the last few days while she watched TV or made food or walked to the pub, sandwiched between Adam and Francesca.

Carolyn was a fair, pretty woman with rather faded looks and an anxious expression. 'Hello, dear,' she said, nervously, as if she expected Tess to bite her. 'This is very nice, isn't it. You know—'

'Jacquetta Meluish,' said her companion, standing tall and pushing her wavy dark gold long hair out of the way, slowly and deliberately.

'Oh, yes,' said Tess. 'Don't you work in that shop on the high street? The one with all the nice cake stands and notelets in it?'

'I *own* Knick-Knacks,' Jacquetta said, slightly tightly. 'Have done for ten years now.' She pronounced it *yiaahs*. 'I should tell you now, Tess, isn't it? – that I received a First in Greats, Some Years Ago. I feel it best to be honest now, from the start, about my Unfair Advantage. Aha-ha-ha.' She gave what Tess assumed she felt was a self-deprecating laugh.

Oh, God, Tess thought. She remembered with a flash of fondness Year Ten at Fair View, none of whom had ever given her this much grief. Yes, one of them had been found carrying a knife, but Tess had believed Carl when he said it was for cutting the twine on parcels. 'I'll go on ahead,' she called politely, as the knot of women behind her waved and carried on chatting, while she set off up the short drive to the house, the words, 'Really? This is your birthday present? Oh, he is wonderful,' 'I *know*, Richard said she looked *quite mad*,' and 'Well, of course, she complained to the diocese about him,' echoing behind her, and the dark, forbidding house with its turrets stabbing the cloudy sky ahead. Francesca, the sofa and the TV seemed a long way away.

A couple of hours later, as Tess's eye scanned over the list of her twenty new pupils, her heart sank. There were far more names on it than she'd expected to recognize; somehow the idea that she might actually be teaching people she knew hadn't occurred to her, much less that they'd be the parents of people she grew up with, or people her mother had served sherry to. Beth Kennett, the head of the college, a sensible woman in her late thirties, had explained it to her with a smile, handing her a cup of tea in the stately but draughty staffroom.

'We always get an influx of Langford locals this time of year, I don't know why. Perhaps they've been given it for Christmas. Derek always said it was most likely their New Year's resolution to do something different, plus they all want the trip to Rome,' she said, her eyes twinkling. 'But Andrea was saying they've all been rather excited about you, you know. You grew up here, didn't you?'

'Yes,' said Tess. She was still a little shaken from her walk in. 'God, I had no idea. It's been years—'

'Well,' said Beth kindly, 'you just have to let them know who's boss.'

Tess thought of Jan and Jacquetta. 'That's easier said than done.'

'Come on,' said Beth, a little briskly. She tucked her hair behind her ear, and jabbed a small finger onto the list of names. 'There's plenty of other people in the class too, you know! You've come from one of the toughest schools in South London. Wasn't there a hostage situation there last year? This should be a walk in the park!'

A walk in the park. Tess cleared her throat, now, and looked up, as a watery shaft of sun shone through the huge leaded window of the room. Her notes, which she had written and rewritten, and her lesson plan, lay in front of her, on the old wooden lectern. She loved this moment, when she had them in the palm of her hand, when she knew they were to learn all these wonderful things, hear about these amazing civilizations, that would transform the way they saw their own world.

She began:

> 'Thy hyacinth hair, thy classic face,
> Thy Naiad airs have brought me home
> To the glory that was Greece
> And the grandeur that was Rome.'

The class looked at her as she spoke; they had ceased to be Jans and Dianas and Jacquettas; they were a mass of faces, the majority unknown to her. They were hers.

'Some of you will know Rome; you might have been there already. I'm sure you all recognize the Colosseum, or know what a temple looks like. I know you've all heard of Antony and Cleopatra, or crazy Nero. Perhaps you've read *I Claudius*, or seen *Gladiator*. You know that Roman civilization is everywhere still among us.'

She paused. Her eyes ranged up, to the window.

'But what I hope this course will give you is a full understanding of the grandeur *and* the glory that was Rome, why it is so important to us still today, and how it shaped the modern world as we know it. Everything from the month of August to the word "comprehensive" to the way we vote, with a bit of *Star Wars*, some wine, the best speeches you'll ever hear and for some of you, a nice trip to Italy thrown in along the way.'

Tess unclenched her hands, which she realized had been scrunched up at her sides, as the class gave a small, appreciative laugh, their upturned faces watching her. Someone opened an exercise book; someone else uncapped a pen, someone cleared their throat. They were relaxing into this. Now it could begin; she looked around, wondering why she still felt uneasy.

Then the door opened. Tess looked up at the creaking sound, to see a silhouette ahead of her. A pair of eyes bore into her with dark intensity. Leonora Mortmain, dressed in black, her hand clutching a stick, began her descent into the bowels of the classroom, looking at no one. She nodded, unblinking, briefly acknowledging Tess's eyes on her, and Tess nearly reared back in shock – so wizened was the face in front of her, so emotionless and yet intense her gaze. Her progress was slow but steady, and gradually everyone turned around to see her, Leonora Mortmain, the most hated woman in the town, walking down the steps of her old family home, and when the class saw who it was, a couple turned back but the rest, horrified, began to mutter amongst themselves. Diana Sayers looked murderous; Jan Allingham shook her head. Slowly, Leonora Mortmain lowered herself into a chair in the front row, and nodded slowly, as if granting permission for the lesson to go ahead.

'She –' 'Why?' 'I can't believe –' Like reeds by a stream, the rushing whispering began, until Tess rapped on the lectern, and some of them jumped; not Leonora Mortmain, however. Tess clapped her hands.

'Silence, please.'

She had forgotten, too, the calm that came with being in charge of a class: she had no command over her own life but here, here was different. They were instantly quiet. 'Thanks. Now, let's begin. I want you to listen to this. I'm going to read you a speech, one of a series written by the greatest orator who ever lived. If you have an enemy –' she cast a quelling glance around the room – 'tackle him like this. If you want to make your case against them, say it like this.'

Holding up Cicero's *Philippics*, she began to read, her hands shaking only slightly.

CHAPTER SEVEN

Dear Tess,

Hi. I hope you got my message. I still have your old writing bureau in my attic, the one you stored there after the burglary. I'm selling the flat as we're buying a house and so I should like to give it back to you. Ticky and I are going to a wedding in Dorset next month. May I drop it off then?

I hope your new life in Langford is going well.
Will

Dear Tess,

Hi! How's it going in the countryside? Danced round any maypoles yet? How's the job? That's great news about the house, but who the hell is this random girl you're moving in with? Sorry about all the questions, I need an update!

It's all cool here. Cathy has settled in OK, I think it'll be fine living with her. Anil asked me out. We're going to the cinema next week. No big deal, he's nice so we'll see. Crazy John had a party upstairs with his crazy crackhead friends on Saturday, someone called the police and he got taken away! Can you believe it. Mr Azeem's got burned down last week, they think some lads did it.

The reason I was emailing as well is because Will aka Wuell phoned yesterday. He didn't know you'd left London. He was a bit surprised. Anyway, he said he'd tried your mobile and you hadn't answered, a couple of times. He wanted your address. And he says he wants to be friends. That was what he wanted me to tell you! He said he's going down to Dorset in a couple of weeks, he'll be in touch and maybe try and pop by with Ticky (that's her name, right?). I said nothing. Tess, I hope that's OK. Didn't know what else to do.

Also you still owe me £67 for the bills, remember. Sorry to chase.

Speak soon Tess.

Meena x x x

Hi Meena,

Long time no e and I'm really sorry I haven't been in touch properly. It's been really hectic here – started job two weeks ago, been trying to sort everything out and prepare all the courses and stuff. Apologies.

The job is going well. It's odd, going from teaching some bored 14 yr olds to all these super-keen people who've PAID to have you TEACH THEM. It's posher than I'd realized, standards are v high – I don't know if I'd have come here if I'd known, I'd have been too scared. But teaching people who want to learn . . . great.

Francesca is really cool, you'd like her. Except she's even messier than me, you wouldn't like that. She got made redundant so she decided to escape from London for a few months. She'd been here on a school trip and always liked it. I thought she might be a bit too Londony, but she's hilarious. She's got something going on with Adam, you remember my old friend Adam? They are 'seeing each other', but they're both being hilariously casual about it. MUCH LIKE YOU AND ANIL. That is SO COOL Meen – so the date was this week? Tell me how it went?

It's so lovely here, Meen, when are you coming to stay? Most days I come back from college and Francesca's here and we watch TV and slump on the sofa or I cook and potter around the house, or else go to the pub which is about five minutes away, with Adam and Suggs and people from college. I can go for long walks whenever I want, and it's getting lighter in the evenings and it's so beautiful. I'm happy here.

Last, not long till I go to Italy in June!!!! A whole week in Rome – only drawback is it's me and loads of crazy middle-aged people who ask questions the WHOLE time, but still, it'll be lovely.

Lots of love
Tess x x x x
PS Sorry, just reread your email. Will pay money back asap.
PPS And Ticky .... Ticky!!! Fucking TICKY WHO CALLS THEMSELVES THAT.

'Tess?' The white wooden front door, which swung alarmingly at the slightest touch, was flung suddenly open as Tess, who had been typing furiously at the computer, swivelled round.

'Oh, hi,' she said, as Francesca barrelled into the sitting room of Easter Cottage, a small but light room which doubled as a hall, storage area, sitting room *and* dining room. 'Where have you been? Wow.' She deleted the last line of her email to Meena, then pressed 'Send'. 'Look at all those bags!' she said, standing up, her heart beating. 'Wow,' she said again.

'I know,' Francesca panted. 'Done some shopping.' She dumped the bags carelessly on the wooden floor and slumped onto the sofa. 'I'm completely and totally exhausted, Tess.' She kicked off her gold flip-flops; constraints of weather and water never really affected Francesca's footwear choice, Tess had noticed. The flip-flops skidded next to Tess's school shoes; sturdy brown slip-on brogues, covered in mud.

'Where did you go?' said Tess, crouching over the bags. 'There's loads! How did you find the shops? It's a small town!'

'I wanted some retail therapy,' said Francesca. 'Some stuff for the house.' She held up a small blue cube. 'Look! Got this at that really cool shop up by the lanes, the one that sells Alessi stuff. It's a lamp.'

'Right,' said Tess. 'Wow, it's . . .'

Francesca was pulling other things out of the bag, Mary Poppins-like. 'A plate from Arthur's! Decoration for the side table!'

'What side table?' Tess asked, looking around her.

'The side table that I bought at the antique shop! The one next to the butcher's, after the car park!' Francesca was beaming. She pushed her hair coolly out of her eyes. 'This place is going to look amazing, once I've finished—' she halted. 'We've finished . . . er, doing it up.' She looked up at Tess, who was standing over her, her hands on her hips, and said breezily, 'It's marvellous. Great, isn't it?'

'Great, if you're paying for it,' said Tess, firmly. 'Francesca, I've barely got any money for, oh, I don't know. Silly things, like forks, and Pantene.' She took her hands off her hips, knowing she looked a little confrontational, and tried to let her arms swing casually by her sides, as though this was normal, as though it wasn't really, horribly tricky. Less than a month they'd lived together and she really didn't want it to be a mistake. She didn't want Meena to say, 'I knew it'd never work out. Crazy idea!'

She hated flatmate confrontations and was still amazed at how perfectly normal people could behave so strangely when sharing accommodation with others. Money. It was always about money. Will's hideously posh but otherwise polite flatmate, Lucinda, had suddenly announced that Tess should contribute to the rent when she was staying the night there, that they should keep a note of the days she stayed over and split the monthly rental three ways on those days. In their third year of university, Tess's friend Emma had perfectly calmly announced one morning that she thought Tess should pay her two pounds fifty for letting her borrow her silvery top the previous night. Francesca was kind of the opposite; Tess could feel herself turning into Lucinda or Emma.

Yesterday Francesca had said, without irony, 'Do you think we should just buy a proper dinner service? There's a lovely one I saw online at Selfridges. It's only a couple of hundred quid or so.'

Tess watched her new flatmate now. 'But it's—' Francesca began.

'Francesca!' Tess said, exasperated. 'I don't want a plate. Or a side table. Or a dinner service for eighteen people when we've only got three chairs! Stop spending money to make yourself feel—' She stopped, aware the words were too far out of her mouth. Francesca stared at her. There was silence in the little sitting room. The last of the day's light shone bravely through the dusty windows.

'. . . Sorry.' Tess cleared her throat. 'I'm sorry. That's really rude of me.'

'No,' said Francesca, scratching her neck with her nails; it left red lines on her pale skin. '*I'm* sorry. I'm crazy. I need to calm down and . . .' She blinked, suddenly. 'I just need to take it easy. Right.' She looked around her, as if 'easy' was just something she could physically pick up and start taking. 'I'll take this all back . . .'

Tess picked up the blue lamp, which was lying lopsided on the tatty old brown sofa. 'This is lovely,' she said placatingly. 'Why don't we keep this?'

'Oh.' Francesca smiled. 'OK. I love it actually. And the plate?'

'I don't need a decorative plate.'

'That's not the point,' Francesca said. 'Was it not William Morris who said, "Have nothing in your homes that you do not know to be useful or believe to be beautiful"?'

'I do not believe it to be useful or beautiful,' said Tess, putting her hands back on her hips.

'OK, OK,' said Francesca, snatching the plate out of her hands. 'I'll put it in my room. I'll – she narrowed her eyes. 'Where's your sense of fun, Tess? God, I bet you're a bossy teacher.'

Tess thought fondly of that morning's class on Virgil's *Georgics*, in which she and her students had talked about the world of the hive as parallel with the Roman Empire. They had a) read the material, b) answered the essay questions, and c) listened in rapt silence as Tess talked about Virgil's ideas of Rome and the countryside. Then, over coffee (Jan had made a walnut cake), all had discussed the relevance of the *Georgics* today to farming and the countryside. Andrea Marsh, who was not only the college's secretary (every employee at the college was allowed to take one free course a year) but the co-founder of the campaign against the water meadows *and* kept bees, was particularly interesting.

'The English bumblebee could be extinct in five years,' she kept saying. 'And no one knows why. If they'd listened to

Virgil in the fourth *Georgic*, it'd all be OK. If we didn't have these ridiculous ideas about twenty-four-hour shopping and eating huge strawberries grown in Chile in December and destroying our countryside to build brand new things –' she cast an angry look at Leonora Mortmain – 'then we might be OK. He knew that!'

But Leonora had said nothing. She reacted to nothing. She just sat still, until Carolyn Tey – who was devoted to her, a sort of lapdog – offered her a slice of cake.

'Do try some, it's quite delicious,' she'd said, her blue eyes bright with hope.

'No, thank you,' Leonora Mortmain replied. 'I have had enough.' She clamped her thin lips together. Tess wondered once again why she was there, as she didn't seem to be enjoying the classes – but how could she tell? Leonora never reacted to anything.

She'd been teaching for a fortnight, and she was still surprised by how much she loved it. It was a treat to teach a class that didn't lounge in its chairs, picking its nose, staring up at her with eyes full of near-psychopathic loathing. It was a treat for her to say, 'Who wants to start reading this passage?' and to see ten hands shoot up. It was a treat for her to watch the awkward Ron Thaxton, whom she had come to see was extremely shy, blossom in the class, talking fluently and articulately about Augustus, about battle strategies, his stuttering anger almost gone.

And then it was a treat for her to walk the ten minutes home, threading into town, her bag swinging from her arm, popping into shops here and there that sold things you actually needed, like a needle and thread, calling hello to people as she went. She was starting to recognize faces now, old and new. Some people remembered her from before, they asked how her mum and dad were, what Stephanie was up to. She thought of London now, of travelling back home, squashed on the tube, dodging the dog shit and the cracked pavements that had once tripped her up, the rain and the unfriendly faces. Tess hugged herself; it seemed so far away. She thought of Will, his huge face like a blank canvas, looming over her the night of Guy's wedding, as he said, 'But Tess, don't you see? We're not the same sort of people. We want different things.'

She had cried, she didn't understand what he meant. 'But I love you!' she had cried, clutching at his shirt – why had she done that?

'I don't think you do,' Will had said, removing her hand. 'You don't love my friends, you were bored the whole way through the reception. Lucinda's a really interesting girl, you could have bloody made an effort. You're so – rigid, Tess, it has to be on your terms or not at all.'

Tess shook her head, remembering it now. Dumped because she wasn't nice to a girl called Lucinda who wanted to charge her rent and who made a living from making stuffed animals. What a diss. But . . . was he right?

'Penny for them,' Francesca said softly, standing behind her. 'Hello?' Tess started.

'Sorry, I was miles away,' she said, and blinked.

'Are we all OK then?' Francesca asked. Tess nodded. Francesca patted her housemate on the arm. 'Fancy a glass of wine before I shoot off?'

'Sure,' said Tess, going through into the little kitchen, which looked out over the handkerchief-sized garden via a rickety old glass-paned door. She opened the drawer, looking for the corkscrew and glanced up at the sky. 'Hey, it's stopped raining!'

'It has,' said Francesca. She slapped her hands on the sides of her thighs. 'Spring is here, and I'm ready for romancing.' She looked up around her, her eyes sparkling. 'Isn't this weird? Us, here, in this house? Isn't it strange, completely bonkers?'

'Yes!' Tess said, smiling. She was pleased to see her so happy. 'Who are you getting ready to romance? Is Adam coming over?'

'He sure is,' said Francesca. 'We're going to try the pub at the other end of town, want to come? The Cross Keys, you know it?'

The door of the fridge swung wide open, knocking loudly against the wall, and they both jumped.

'It always does that! So annoying. Ow,' said Tess, putting the wine bottle firmly on the kitchen surface. 'That's a lovely pub,' she added, rubbing her hand. 'Right next to where we grew up. Adam's mum worked there for a bit.'

'What was she like, Adam's mum?' Francesca asked curiously. 'Adam never talks about her.'

'She was lovely.' Tess took out some olives, bought the previous day from the Jen's Deli on the high street where Liz worked. Jen's Deli catered for tourists wanting a picnic. The olives were three pounds ninety-nine for a small tub. She tipped them into one of the little painted bowls that sat on the kitchen mantelpiece. 'Ooh, I love this, don't you? I feel as if I'm in a picture book, living in my own little cottage.'

'You are living in your own little cottage,' Francesca pointed out. 'So am I.'

'Oh.' Tess took the nice new glasses out of the cupboard. Francesca lolled against the kitchen counter. She plucked an olive out of the bowl.

'Has Adam always lived there, then?'

'What?' Tess opened the bottle. 'Lived where? Here?'

'In that house,' Francesca said patiently. 'Did he never live anywhere else, after she died? Am I going out with a man who's never lived anywhere else?'

'So you are actually *going out* with him?' Tess said, trying to sound nonchalant. 'Oh, my God!' She swallowed, hastily, realizing she sounded like a teenager. 'So have you – I thought you two were . . .' She trailed off.

Francesca tossed her hair casually behind her back; Tess had noticed that, far from doing it to intimidate, she did this when she was feeling self-conscious.

'Ahm. I don't know. I suppose so. I'm seeing him.' She raked a hand across her scalp. 'We talked about it on the weekend. I don't know what *going out* means these days, do you? It's a bit juvenile, anyway. Like, sometimes it means one thing, and sometimes it means something else . . . you know . . .' She trailed off, and Tess was pleased to see she was blushing.

'You like him!' Tess hit her housemate on the arm. 'Oh, my God, how cool. And he likes you, it's obvious.'

'Is it?'

'Absolutely.' Tess thought back to the previous Sunday, when she, Francesca, Suggs and Adam had taken a picnic up to the ruins of Langford Priory, once the greatest monastery in Somerset before Henry VIII had given it a good going over. They had sat in the grass, perching on stones scattered around, looking down over the valley towards the town, and that's when it had happened. Tess had asked Francesca for a knife, and Francesca had leaned into the bag to get one, her hair falling in her face and, without thinking about it, Adam had reached forward and gently tucked her hair behind her ear, his big hand touching her shoulder afterwards. He said nothing, Francesca said nothing, but Tess had watched them, with affection and a pang of loneliness, realizing she was aware of something they weren't: that her oldest friend had fallen hook, line and sinker for Francesca Jackson.

She asked, a little shyly, 'Can I ask – when did this all . . . happen?'

'Oh – properly? Well, he came round to bring that spanner he'd promised? And he ended up fixing the door and then he stayed – and he stayed . . .' She blushed.

She stopped, and looked at Tess guiltily, though why, Tess wondered fleetingly – there was nothing to be guilty about, it was nothing but good news. Why shouldn't they have sex in the middle of the day, in her own home, while Tess was off wearing a sensible cardigan and shirt, teaching people about things that happened two thousand years ago?

'That's – it's OK with you, isn't it? It doesn't make you feel weird?'

'Of course it's OK with me!' Tess said. As she said it, she knew it wasn't, it was a bit weird. It was her flatmate and her oldest friend, after all. She'd just have to get used to it, and then it'd be fine. And if she practised looking as if it was OK, it would be.

'Oh, good,' said Francesca. 'I don't want things to be awkward.'

'Why would they be? He's not my boyfriend.'

'Exactly,' Francesca said.

The words, *No, he's my boyfriend*, hung in the air, unsaid.

'So are you hanging out in the day then?'

'Well, it was only Monday it happened. Sunday if you count the walk. So yeah, he came round on Tuesday too, and today – well, I'm seeing him in the evening so I – I wanted a distraction.' She picked at the side of her nail. 'And I went shopping.'

'So that's it,' Tess said, smiling. 'It's a substitute for shagging.'

'No!' Francesca smiled too. 'How rude. He's – oh, man.' She sighed, mistily. 'He is so gorgeous. You have no idea. I just feel like . . .' Her shoulders rose and sank again, and she gazed unseeingly past Tess, into the sitting room. Tess followed her gaze, almost desperately, hoping to see what Francesca saw:

A kiss in a sun-dappled glade.

A gorgeous man arriving at the cottage and sweeping you off your feet.

Mind-explodingly good sex . . . in the afternoon.

Instead, she saw:

The batteries from the TV remote control, which were always falling out (it had no back, mysteriously).

A stack of essays on Virgil and Rome spilling out of her cloth bag.

Her main school shoes, clumpy, sensible, covered in mud, lying next to Francesca's strappy gold flip-flops.

Francesca was like Dido or Thetis, lying on a day bed eating chocolates, a cloud of hair tumbling down her back, whilst handsome suitors arrived to pay court and ravish her. She, Tess, on the other hand, was a dwarfish teacher with a pile of marking to do, a hair growing out of her chin and footwear that even Mary Whitehouse would say could do with sexing up a tad.

'Drink?' Tess said, practically ripping the cap off the bottle of wine and upending it into her glass. 'When are you going out? You meeting him at the pub?'

'No, I'm going to his house to pick him up,' said Francesca. 'Haven't been there before. That's why I was wondering what –' she took a sip from her glass, and flicked her hair again.

'What what?'

'What his mum was like. If there's anything I should know.'

'If there's anything you should know.' Tess stared into the distance. 'Ahh.' She exhaled, through her teeth. 'Philippa. She was wonderful. That's all you need to know.'

'That's not very helpful.'

'I know. Sorry.' Tess thought back. 'I can remember her, really clearly, after thirteen years. She was just a wonderful person. It's a tragedy.'

'What exactly happened?'

'It was an aneurysm. She just – dropped dead in the street one day.' Tess swallowed. 'She was on her way back from the shops. Mum found her.'

'That's awful.'

Tess nodded. 'It was. Her, of all people. Philippa was – she was really special.'

'Like how?'

'Like – when we were little, she treated us like we were people in our own right, you know? She'd give you little presents for special occasions, nothing much, just personal things that were just for you.' There was the time when Tess was eleven, and had to have braces on her teeth for eighteen months, and Philippa had bought her a special two-year diary, to count down the days till they were off, and she'd scribbled little things in it. *'Only a year to go now!'* *'Who's that beautiful girl? It's young Miss Tennant, the one with the perfect teeth!'*

'Aah,' said Francesca. 'Nice.'

'She *was* nice. She –' Tess started, and then she stopped. 'She was lovely.'

'What happened to Adam's dad, then?' Francesca asked tentatively. 'You don't have to tell me, but he hasn't mentioned, and I sort of thought, was it something awful?'

'Could be,' Tess said, sipping her wine again. 'No one knows.'

'Knows what? How he died?'

'No,' said Tess. 'There isn't really a mystery there, I think he's just some guy who she had a thing with. No one knew really where Philippa came from, that's the weird thing. That house was empty for years, and then one day she just turned up.'

'Like Mary Poppins?' Francesca was smiling.

'Sort of,' said Tess, earnestly. 'Honestly, she never really told anyone anything about herself. Mum asked her once, why she came to Langford, and Philippa said, "I don't know myself, to be honest." And then she never said anything again.'

'No,' said Francesca, fascinated.

'Yep. And I've never understood it. Why did she come to Langford? Why? I mean – we were lucky she did, but –'

'It's interesting,' said Francesca. 'Wow.'

'Absolutely,' said Tess, though she felt a little guilty, giving up Adam's family secrets like that. She looked out of the window, wondering. Really, she supposed, she didn't know what the secret actually was, so how could she give it up? Adam himself didn't know where he came from. That was how it had always been.

CHAPTER EIGHT

One Friday afternoon, just before the first May bank holiday, Tess sat on the sofa, putting on her shoes and humming loudly so she couldn't hear anything that might be going on in the bedroom upstairs. She had been teaching all morning and was on her way out to get some food for their picnic. She, Adam and Francesca were going to the beach the next day and the fridge at Easter Cottage had never been quite so denuded. Two sex-mad grown-ups ate a lot, Tess had discovered. It was like living with termites and a team of Sumo wrestlers.

The noises that she had been pretending not to hear from upstairs grew unavoidably louder, a crescendo, and Tess banged her feet on the floor and started singing as she searched for her keys. Suddenly, almost abruptly, there was silence, and after a minute she heard footsteps on the narrow stairs, a slight stumble and then a muffled curse – as the owner of the feet narrowly avoided the stair with a missing chunk, especially hazardous without shoes.

'Hey there, you!' Adam called to her, still cheerful. 'Coffee?' Tess looked up at him, in disbelief, as he went into the kitchen. 'Is that Francesca's dressing gown?' she said, watching Adam pull the Chinese silk carefully around him as he put the kettle on.

'Why yes, and I think it's just lovely,' said Adam. He scratched his thick hair thoughtfully. 'She's given it to me.'

'So I can hear,' said Tess, unable to resist.

'Ha ha,' said Adam. 'Very funny.'

'It's not that funny,' said Tess, wishing she didn't sound so grumpy. 'Sitting down here listening to you two going at it hammer and tongs.'

'Tess!' Adam said mildly. 'Mind your own business.'

'My own business?' Tess stood up and laughed shortly, swinging her bag over her shoulder. 'Bloody hard to, when all I can hear is you two having sex when I'm trying to read in bed. I've had to buy earplugs!'

'No, you haven't,' Adam said, but he looked a little fazed. 'We're having a great time. I really like her, what's your problem?'

There was something ridiculous about him, standing holding the kettle, with the thin silk clinging to his legs, his tall, broad frame, as his hair stuck up comically on his head. A wave of fury washed over her, that he thought it was OK. That they both did.

'My problem?' Tess yelled. She shook her head wildly. 'My problem is I moved back here for some peace and quiet, and there's no fucking coffee in the jar before you look, because you two bloody drank it all, and there's no food in the fucking fridge because you've eaten it all, and when I'm trying to watch bloody *Antiques Roadshow* all I can here is you two, bellowing "Yes! Yes!" at each other, like you're watching a football match!'

Adam looked at her, as she took a deep breath and was silent, and he started laughing.

'Or – anything,' Tess said weakly, glad the tension was broken. She was being ridiculous. 'You know. *T4* and stuff. *The Wire*. Anyway, *Antiques Roadshow* is really good, I'll have you know.'

'Clearly,' Adam said, shaking his head, still laughing.

'Last week, they had a pensioner on it.'

'No. Amazing.'

'And she had a teapot Josiah Wedgwood designed himself. *Himself.*' Tess nodded significantly. 'It was worth over a thousand pounds. And that lady can now buy a new walk-in bath, for her husband Roger.'

'To think you once played strip poker with the under-eighteens Hampshire cricket team,' Adam said ruminatively.

'Sshh.' She drew a circle around her with her finger. 'Remember. It's in our –'

'– circle of trust,' he finished. 'Sorry, I forgot about our circle of trust.'

They were both silent for a moment, and then Adam said, again, '*Antiques Roadshow.*' Tess watched him, arms folded. Adam had a big, deep laugh, that seemed to take him over completely.

'Hey,' he said, eventually. 'I'm really sorry, Tess. I should have thought about you more in this. It's just – she's great.' He smiled. 'I really like her.'

'I know you do,' she said, pleased for him. 'Look, I'm just popping out to get some food and stuff –'

'I'll come with you,' said Adam. 'Seriously,' he added, as she looked at him in disbelief. 'Francesca's fast asleep and I need a new battery for the bike lamp, too. Give me five minutes. I'll just jump in the shower.'

'Er . . . OK,' said Tess. Adam grinned.

'Look pleased!' he said. 'I'll give you street cred, Granny.'

As they walked along the high street, Tess carried her wicker basket over her arm. Adam shook his head. 'I worry about you. You're turning into someone from Cranford. My godmother Diana doesn't have one of those, and she's . . . older than you. Plus they're completely unwieldy.'

'*O tempora, o mores,*' Tess said tartly and then regretted it.

'You think Cicero was saying we should give up plastic

79

bags and use wicker baskets, do you?' Adam asked, innocently. 'Don't show off your Latin with me, Tess. You know you'll lose.'

Adam's brain was a source of mystery to Tess; he never forgot anything, a quote, a story, an obscure piece of syntax. She taught Latin and Greek, and she often couldn't remember the word for 'ship' in either language. But she could remember what happened one summer ten years ago as if it were yesterday, or Stephanie's wedding, or Will's face as he told her he loved her for the first time ... Adam, she knew, had trouble remembering his own birthday.

It was curious, that tension that existed within him. She looked at him sideways as they walked along the street, he whistling, his hands stuck deep into his pockets. It was Roman, she supposed. Brilliant, practical, organized, neat – and yet chaotic, hopeless, romantic, kind at the same time. It was strange, she thought, that she, Tess, was now her teacher, and Adam, with all his brilliance – Adam was ... what was he? She blinked, recalling herself to the present.

'Er, I'm a bit sick of the deli. Cheese shop?' Adam said, pulling her out of her reverie. She smiled at him as she spotted Liz putting a leg of ham back in the window of Jen's Deli and looking up at the little high street in the sunshine. She waved at her.

'Stop it,' said Adam.

'Oh, get over yourself,' Tess said. 'She's in my class.'

'Your class?' said Adam.

'Yes, absolutely,' said Tess. 'She's pretty good actually. She's coming to Rome. I'm part of her self-improvement programme. Just like you were,' she added wickedly. Adam frowned as the bell sounded another lucky customer entering Mr Dill's Cheese Emporium. 'What do we need?'

'Well.' Tess tucked the basket – Adam was right, it *was* unwieldy – under her arm and counted off on her fingers. 'Stuff for tonight. Stuff for our trip to the beach tomorrow.

Hi, Andrea!' She waved at Andrea Marsh, who was crossing the road.

'Your window boxes are looking lovely,' Andrea told her, but unwillingly, as if it cost her to do so. 'Just going to see Miss Store, and I noticed them. Are they pansies?'

'Yes! So glad you like them – agh!' Tess swallowed, as a car drove past and Adam bodily dragged her up onto the pavement.

'For God's sake, be careful, T,' he said, crossly.

'See you at the meeting later!' called Andrea, walking on.

'Yes, absolutely,' Tess called after her. 'You going to that tonight?'

'What?' Adam said, looking back across the road. He was squinting at something. 'Oh, the meeting? No, don't think so.'

'But *everyone's* going,' said Tess.

Adam nodded solemnly. 'Who's *everyone*?'

'Well, you know.' Tess waved her hands. 'The people at the college – apart from Leonora Mortmain, of course – um, Ron, Suggs, Francesca –'

'No, she's not,' said Adam. 'We're staying in and watching a film.'

'But Adam –' Tess remembered how curious he'd been about the campaign, the night of the first campaign meeting. 'Suggs is organizing it. It's going to be—'

'Look how local you are these days,' he said, mocking her. 'Remember your first day back here, when you scorned the high street? Look at you now. Practically in bed with all the important people in town.'

Tess ignored him. 'Adam, we should all go—'

Adam held up his hand. 'I'm not going. Sorry. Let's get some cheese. And then let's argue about it some more.'

'I'm not *arguing*,' Tess said, even more patiently than he. 'I am merely pointing out that –'

She swung the wicker basket behind her, as a soft male voice said, 'Ouch.'

Tess froze, and looked up at Adam, who was gazing over her shoulder as if he'd seen a ghost.

'Hi – God. It's you. Forgot your name, sorry,' said the voice.

'It's Adam,' he said, and stepped a little closer towards Tess.

'Of course. Tess's old friend. Well, hi. I'm Will. Hi, Tess.'

She turned round mechanically, like a doll spinning on a music box.

'Hi, Will,' she said.

The last time Tess had seen Will was in January, at their friend Henry's birthday drinks, at a pub on the New Kings Road. Tess had gone for one drink only and had waved, in a friendly, brisk way at Will on her way out, weaving through the crowded pub, heady with the scent of expensive perfume, cigarette smoke wafting in from outside, and lilies in huge vases on the bar, the smell of decay lingering behind their sweetness.

Will was holding hands with someone behind him; through the thick press of bodies around her she couldn't see her face, but she knew it must be Ticky. Tess had smiled again at him, rolled her eyes as if she were fantastically busy and pushed past him mouthing 'Bye' as she fell out of the pub onto the pavement. There she had stood miserably in the sudden cold, her shoulders stooped, feeling like a total outsider. She hadn't fitted in there, never would.

Now, she looked up at Will as he stood, tall and godlike on the high street. She remembered with a rush of recognition, like hearing a song that reminds you of a summer holiday, a curious feeling of alienation, of being different, an oddity, that came with being with Will.

'Hello,' Tess said, determined to be friendly and mature. She had practised just such a scenario with Meena in their flat – Meena!

It all came flooding back to her, now. The email! The bureau – oh, shit, that was why he was here.

'Will, how are you?' she said. She leaned forward and

kissed him on the cheek, as Adam stood behind her. Gently he prised the wicker basket out of her hand, and put it on the ground. 'And you must be Ticky,' she added.

From behind Will stepped a tall, thin, fair girl, with the longest legs Tess had ever seen, enormous green eyes which bulged out from her tiny face. She was wearing what looked like a turquoise romper suit.

'Hi!' she said, slightly flatly, raising one hand. 'I'm Ticky. It's soooo great to meet you.'

Will, who was still gazing at Tess, nodded. 'Hey, yous,' he said – Tess had forgotten how soft his voice was. 'You OK, hon?'

'Super!' Tess said, practically shouting.

'Did you get my email, and the message? I'm sorry to just turn up here without warning, you know. But I did really want to give you back the bureau.'

He pronounced it 'rally' and 'beeyurrrohw'.

Tess glanced from Ticky to herself as if mentally comparing their appearances. Hers (shortish, averageish, horrible black clompy shoes, top and cardigan – *an old sage cardigan with big roomy pockets, oh, the inhumanity – and oh, dear God, was she really wearing an A-line skirt?*) with Ticky's (on-trend playsuit, honey-coloured limbs, soft blonde hair, cherry-red Havaianas). She gave a tiny groan, and Adam glanced at her.

'Oh, the bureau!' she said loudly. 'I'm so sorry, I didn't get in touch with you. Of course!' She leaned in what she hoped was a nonchalant way against the nearest thing, which happened to be the wall of the cottage next to Mr Dill's, the cheese shop. Unfortunately it was a little further away than she'd calculated, and she fell against the old stone with a thump, jarring her shoulder bone as she did so.

Will shook his head. 'It's fine,' he said, smiling kindly, and put his fingers together. Watching him, Tess realized that he looked a bit like David Cameron; how had she not noticed this before?

'So,' said Adam, from behind her. 'What are you doing here? What – er, what a nice surprise,' he added quickly.

'Ah – we're on our way to Lucinda's wedding,' he said, as if Adam would naturally know who Lucinda was. 'It's in Dorset, at her dad's place, really beautiful. We're staying at the Tailor's Arms with loads of friends.' Ticky lolled against Will as he said this. 'So – we thought we'd stop off here for a pint, and give you the bureau. Pit stop!' he finished. He looked round, trying to sound enthusiastic. 'Lovely town, I must say. You live near here?'

'Yes,' said Tess, mechanically. 'Just round the corner.'

'Ah.' He rocked on his feet. 'And – great. So, everything OK with you then, hon?'

If you call me hon again I will bite off your head and store it in the bureau after you've gone. 'Yes, great, thanks.'

'Really?' Will said, as if he knew this was rubbish but was keeping up the pretence.

'Will was worried about you, when you didn't reply,' Ticky ventured suddenly, her voice rusty with misuse; she herself looked surprised that she'd spoken. Tess's hands curled into fists; she tried to breathe. 'He thought you were probably still—'

'This all sounds lovely,' came Adam's voice behind Tess. He slipped his arm round her waist. 'Where are you parked? Shall we show you the house, and we can unload the bureau?'

'Great,' said Will, looking with surprise at Adam's hand on Tess's hip.

'Tell you what,' said Adam. He smoothed back her hair, and kissed Tess's forehead. 'Darling, why don't you carry on and go to the grocer's before it shuts, and I'll take Will and – I'm sorry, I don't know your name.'

'Ticky!' Ticky said brightly. 'It's short for Candida.'

'Of course it is!' Adam said, nodding enthusiastically. 'Very nice to meet you. Well, I'll take Will and Ticky to the cottage and we'll get the bureau inside. Sorry,' he said, turning to

Will. 'You know us country folk. The shops round here shut at five, I'm afraid, and we're going to the seaside tomorrow. Need to get stuff in.'

'Oh, absolutely,' Will said, nodding through his astonishment.

Adam took Tess's other hand, and kissed it. 'That OK with you, sweetums?' He turned to Will. 'She hates it when I call her that, don't you!' He squeezed Tess's waist.

'Sure do,' said Tess, stepping into the role with an aplomb that surprised her. 'Well, that sounds great, my little cutie-pie.' She moved towards Adam, and made kissing sounds at him. He silenced her by grabbing her, dipping her and kissing her on the mouth.

'Sorry,' he said, turning back towards Will and Ticky as he flung her upright again. 'Wow. We're just still really in that honeymoon period, aren't we, my love? Grrr.' He slapped Tess's bottom.

'Grrr,' said Tess, slapping him back. 'My God, yes!' she cried gaily. 'We're at it all day, I'm pleased to say!'

There was a silence. Adam cleared his throat and looked at the pavement, trying not to laugh. Will and Ticky stared at them, clearly rendered speechless: this wasn't in their plan, it was clear. 'Gosh,' said Will eventually, clearly not sure what else to say. 'Nice one guys.' He cleared his throat. 'Let's get going then, shall we? Car's parked just here –' he pointed down the road – 'and off to the side.'

'Then I think you're in Tess's street,' said Adam. 'Bloody marvellous.' He turned back to her, solemnly. 'OK, sweetums?' he asked, his eyes sparkling. 'Try not to miss me too much. I know I'll miss you.'

'What about Francesca?' Tess said, trying not to smile at him.

'I'll just make sure she's OK before we start unloading. Francesca's my sister,' he told Will and Ticky firmly. 'And she's ill. She's very ill.' They looked alarmed. 'Er – with the flu,' he amended hastily. 'So I'll just go and warn her not to come down while we're carrying the bureau in. The chill might kill her. And – er, she might be infectious, so also you should keep away from her and not talk to her, if you see her.'

'Yes,' said Tess, marvelling at the fecundity of his imagination. 'We've only just been given the all-clear ourselves. From the . . . clinic. So – er, bye then,' she said. 'Great to see you, Will. And Ticky.'

'Absolutely!' Ticky said with something like enthusiasm, banging her hands together. 'Rally great.'

'Yes,' said Will, nodding ponderously. 'Look, Tess – this is all fab, you know? Seems super for you, just – yah.' He stepped back, nodding, his eyes half-closed.

'Give my love to Lucinda,' said Tess. 'Hope the weekend's fun. Sorry to dash off. I'll see you later,' she added, to Adam.

'Mhhm,' Adam said, with gusto. 'Shall I just meet you in the pub in twenty minutes or so?'

'Lovely,' said Tess. 'Perfect, in fact.'

He took her hand and kissed it. She clutched his hand back, inexpressibly touched by the gesture, and he shook his head and smiled at her.

She should have known as she walked into the Feathers a little later, her basket laden with food for three, that they'd be there; should have known that Will, totally intrigued, would want to stay for a drink before they set off again. He had a kind of prurient curiosity; she'd always found it rather contradictory, that he could be so concerned with wearing the right tie, and presenting the right face to the world and yet also so fascinated with the mundane, private details of people's lives. How much things cost, how often So-and-So had sex, how big X's new house was. She hadn't noticed it, till it was almost over between them, of course. Harmless, yes; kind, patrician, with his curling upper lip and cufflinks; impressive, probably. Tall and strong, the kind of man who would protect you –

yes, undoubtedly, apart from the time that pitbull had barked at them in the street and he'd pushed Tess in front of him.

As Tess walked through the bar to the terrace outside, directed there by Mick's jerk of the head, and found the three of them sitting companionably, looking out over the great view across the valley towards Thornham, its church tower golden in the afternoon sun, she almost nodded to herself at the inevitability of it all, then remembered, with a start, the part she – and her new boyfriend – had to play.

'Hello!' she said, feigning a brightness she did not feel. 'How nice!'

'Well,' said Will, standing up, his hands slapping the wooden table. 'We thought it'd be nice to check out your new local pub. We've got ages to get to Dorset.'

Pointless to tell him that it wasn't her new local, that she'd lived here all her life, known it longer than she'd known him, this view, these hills, the old city wall down to the left, covered in ivy; and Adam, standing next to him, watching him with amusement. Will never remembered what she'd told him. He'd visited her parents, he knew they'd taken early retirement and lived by the sea, but it wouldn't occur to him to remember anything beyond that.

Channel one of the nice ladies of Langford, she told herself. Jan Allingham would know how to cope with this. Tess put her basket down on the table. 'Who needs another drink?' she asked, hoping against hope that the answer would be 'Oh, no, thanks. We'll be on our way now!'

'I'd love another pint of Butcombe's,' Will said. 'Thanks very much.'

Ticky smiled up at her, slightly vacantly. 'Just a sparkling water for me, thanks, Tess.'

'I'll get them.' Adam jumped up, and pushed her ahead of him into the shady corridor. 'Hot air balloon,' he said, briefly. 'Just remember, hot air balloon. Over Bristol.'

'What?' Tess said, quite bewildered.

'No time. Hot air balloon. Oh, and it's been a month.'

'*What?*' she said again, exasperated, but Adam pushed her back out onto the terrace.

'They'll be gone soon,' he said into her ear. 'Go!'

Ticky patted the bench. 'Your house is wonderful,' she said, with the charm of the privileged. 'It's so *cute!*' She smiled, displaying dazzling white teeth, as Will lolled beside her, his hand carelessly draped between her thighs. 'I love it.'

'Thanks,' said Tess, sitting opposite them. 'I like it.'

'We got the bureau in, no worries,' said Will. 'Looks jolly nice in that little sitting room.'

She turned to him gratefully. 'Thanks, Will. And – look, thanks a lot for bringing it all this way. It's really sweet of you.'

'No problemo,' he said, with hearty gusto. 'I'm – uh – I'm glad you're all sorted now. Seems to suit you, out here.'

'Thanks,' she told him. 'It does. I love it.'

'Well, that's really good,' he said, staring intently between the slats of the table. 'And you and Adam – that's, yep.'

'And it's so romantic.' Ticky interrupted her reverie. 'Just so sweet, I love it.'

'What's so sweet?' Tess said, blankly.

'How you got together. His birthday present. That's so sweet of you. I'd love to do that.' She edged closer to Will, snuggling against him, and swinging her legs over his so she was almost sitting on his lap, like a little girl on Santa's knee.

'Do what?' Tess said. They looked at her curiously. 'Oh!' she exclaimed, realization flooding through her. 'Sorry! The hot air balloon.' Bloody Adam, what was he thinking? 'Yes, it was a lovely way to spend, er – to spend his birthday.' His birthday was in the next couple of weeks, wasn't it? Or was she dreaming?

Happily, Adam appeared then, carrying a tray.

'We're just talking about the hot air balloon,' Tess said.

'Oh, of course,' Adam said, setting the tray down on the table. He wiped his hands.

'That's just *fantastic*,' said Ticky. 'So – *impetuous*, for a first date.' Adam looked at Tess.

'Yes, I suppose so,' he said. 'But when you know, you know.' He paused.

'You've known each other since you were –' Will gestured towards the ground – 'yay high, what took you so long?'

'It's a good question,' Adam said. 'I don't really know.'

He bit his lip and flicked a glance at Tess.

'Me neither, sweetums,' she said, but the name was starting to grate, now.

'I forgot to ask you what you wanted,' he said. 'So I got you a pint as well. I know you love a bit of bitter. Hah.' He laughed, nervously.

Bitter. She *hated* bitter, almost as much as she hated aubergines. 'Oh,' she said, narrowing her eyes as she took the drinks off the tray. 'Thanks.'

'You?' Will asked. 'You like bitter? I thought you never drank beer. You always said it made you, er – full of wind.'

There was a silence. Ticky swung her legs back and nodded sorrowfully at Tess, as if acknowledging a dreadful truth no one else was brave enough to admit.

'Hey,' Adam said, raising an eyebrow. 'Tess does a lot of things these days she didn't used to.' He cleared his throat, realizing this was maybe a bit too much.

Tess kicked him under the table and took a deep breath, letting the scent of wood smoke and country air fill her nostrils, calm her down. Then she looked at Will, almost impassively. His hair was ever so thick; rudely so, corn yellow, almost ginger, it stuck out from his bowed head, veering alarmingly towards her. She saw, as if it were a scene from someone else's life, a film, her hands running through that hair, the pleasure she once felt at being with him, in his rush-matted, neutral flat in Fulham, how correct and safe and *proper* she

89

always believed she was as his girlfriend, when they were a unit, a neat unit of two. She shook her head, trying to recall this person she had been then.

They had discussed Aristophanes's speech in Plato's *Symposium* that morning in class. The *Symposium* said that humans were originally two people joined together until the gods, fearing their strength and their speed, had ripped them apart. So that humans are condemned to spend their lives merely one half looking for that other half and when they find the other half, they can finally be together with them for ever. Tess loved that idea, had always loved it. But was it true? Was Will, this person she had pinned all her hopes on, that other human? She couldn't believe it now. Ticky was that person to him, it was absolutelyobvious. And she – she breathed out, raggedly, not sure she could go on with this charade, and suddenly felt a cool hand on her forearm.

'You OK?' Adam said in a low voice, as if it were just the two of them, as if Will and Ticky weren't there, and she felt herself say calmly, 'Fine.'

He squeezed her wrist, quickly, his thumb on the under-side of her skin. 'Yes.' He turned back to the others. 'Well, cheers,' he said. 'Great to see you both.'

They sat in silence again and drank their drinks, and Tess glanced at him, her mind racing.

'Thanks, thanks a lot, bruv,' she said, as they walked back down the high street later that evening. 'I owe you.'

Adam stepped back and held his hand up. 'No worries, g'friend,' he said. 'It's his loss.'

Tess stared at him. 'Are you drunk?'

Adam shrugged. 'A bit, maybe. I did have four pints. I thought they were never going to leave! I'm sorry, I know he's your ex.'

'I know,' Tess said, glaring down at the paving slabs,

watching her feet step on each crack. 'I know. He's so different from me. He looks –' she trailed off.

'He looks like a member of the Bullingdon Club on his way to a reunion,' said Adam, his tongue loosened by alcohol and release from stilted conversation. 'I didn't think people like that still existed.'

She wanted to be cross, but she couldn't be. 'You're right,' Tess said. 'He *was* a bit like that. I don't know, I just never saw that in him . . .' She paused. 'He wasn't – I don't know. He wasn't a bad man. He isn't a bad man.'

'Never really knew what you saw in him, if I'm being honest,' Adam said simply. 'Sorry again. That's rude.'

'It's OK,' she said. 'I . . . I think I was looking for something. Something that wasn't there.'

'I have known you for a while now, you know.' Adam poked her in the arm. 'He just never seemed –' He shrugged. 'Oh, well.'

There was silence; it was a chilly evening, and the high street was virtually deserted. 'You coming back to ours?' said Tess.

It was an obvious question – they were nearly home, and Adam's house was the other end of the town. 'Um, if that's OK,' said Adam.

'Of course it's OK,' said Tess. She laughed. 'I liked it when you told them we were going to a Sandals resort for our holidays. Will's face.'

'I liked it more when you told them you liked it when I spoke to you in a Russian accent,' Adam replied. 'God only knows what they think now.'

There was a silence again. Tess said in a small voice, 'It was – good to see him. But . . . I don't really care what they think.'

'Good,' Adam said. 'Neither do I, Tess.' They carried on walking for a little while. 'Listen, T –' he said.

But at the same time Tess suddenly burst out, 'I don't know why I went out with him.'

91

'Right,' said Adam. 'I have to say . . .' He trailed off.

'Two years, too,' Tess said, faltering. It seems like a dream now, she wanted to say. But it wasn't, because a few drinks with him again and she could see now what that time with Will had done to her. He was so . . . oh, she'd never really seen it before, but he was a little pompous. So sure he was right and reluctant to hear her point of view, as though she was a stupid little girl. He spoke slowly, and when she tried to interrupt him, he simply carried on talking. And the sex – what sex. At first – and she cringed to think of it now – she'd rather liked his professorial, grown-up way of treating her, had found it rather a turn-on that he was so formal, reserved, buttoned up. Now, when she thought of how she'd tried to get him to want her more, tried to excite him, it made her want to disappear, as fast as possible, into the ground. And she'd begun to think that was normal, that it would *always be like that* . . . She looked down at herself with disgust. He just hadn't fancied her, that was all, and why would he? He was hanging on in there till something better came along, something Ticky-shaped, with honey-coloured limbs and hair and friends in common and . . . Ugh.

'Penny for your thoughts,' came Adam's voice in the darkness, startling her. Tess laughed, hollowly. 'Come on,' he said. 'What's on your mind?'

'You don't want to know,' Tess said bleakly.

'Come on,' said Adam. 'It's me, T. I've just spent the evening pretending to be your boyfriend.' He said, in a thick Russian accent, 'We have no secrets, Misha.'

Oh, I was just thinking about the last time I had sex with Will, and he stopped halfway through and said, 'Can we just stop this? Let's just go to sleep, shall we?' and then picked up the FT *while I lay there, naked, next to him . . .*

'Seriously,' Tess said, kicking a dandelion out of the way as they turned into Lord's Lane. 'You really don't want to know. And I don't want to tell you.'

'Is this the Dealbreaker that you won't tell me about? You are turning into a bit of a librarian, I have to say,' said Adam smugly.

Tess stared at him with loathing, all former understanding and maturity between them gone. 'What?' she practically cried.

'Well, T. All that chat to Will about the course you're teaching. And all that stuff about Ancient Rome. I mean, no one likes all that better than me, but when you started going on about how the hole in the roof of the Pantheon was twenty-seven feet in diameter – well. Even I was a bit bored. I thought Ticky was going to fall asleep.'

Tess took her hands out of her cardigan pockets. 'What the hell, Adam?' she yelled. 'Not this again. Don't you find that interesting?' Adam shook his head, smiling at her. 'Well, you should,' Tess told him tartly. 'The Pantheon, it's the greatest building ever! *They still don't know how it was built!* And – boring Ticky, it's hardly a difficult subject, is it? She's about as interesting as a – a slice of brown bread!' She pointed over her shoulder, as if Ticky were there. 'Before it's even become bread!' She cast around her. 'Like – when it's flour! No, when it's wheat! She's like a field of wheat! Even more boring than that, like a – a –!' She ran out of steam and stared at him. 'I can't believe you said that.'

Adam opened the door; she wondered, in the back of her mind, why he now owned a set of keys. 'Tessa. I'm not having a go at the person who built the Pantheon, OK? I'm just saying, there's a time and a place,' he said, smoothly, waving tacitly to Francesca, who was sprawled on the sofa clutching a box of toffees, her long brown hair glowing against the electric blue of the Chinese silk dressing gown. She raised her eyebrows, waved at them with one hand, and popped another toffee in her mouth with the other. Adam took off his coat. 'And the time and the place were not necessarily then.'

'Sup?' Francesca mumbled indistinctly. 'Howas the jink?'

'Awful,' said Tess, bitterly. 'He's an idiot, she's an idiot, I can't see any reason why I was with him all that time, and, by the way, according to Adam not only am I really boring, but I'm turning into a sodding *librarian*.' She kicked off her shoes.

Francesca raised her eyebrows again, as Adam moved over to the sofa and took her hand; he flicked each of her fingers, gently, looking down at her, and kissed her gently on the lips.

'Librarians are great, my mum's a librarian,' Francesca said. 'It's not that. I think it's more that you're turning into an old lady.' She nodded, as if she was glad she'd found the point of what Adam was getting at. 'Mmm.'

'Yes,' said Adam. 'That's it.'

Francesca slid a toffee into his mouth, her thumb catching his bottom lip. Adam's eyes glazed over.

Tess, still standing by the door in her bare feet, felt as if she might have been a novelty act they were keeping in a cage, like a female Elephant Man. Elephant Lady. Who has some interesting information about Roman temples. She sighed, wobbily, feeling the beer swilling around inside her. 'I'm going to bed,' she said, her voice aching, and it sounded as though she was merely grumpy. 'Night.'

'Night,' Francesca called.

'By the way, thanks again, Adam,' Tess yelled as she stomped up the stairs.

'Any time, T,' Adam said. 'Night, pet.'

There was silence from the sofa, as the TV talked to itself, and Tess closed the door to her room and leaned against it, staring blankly at the white wall opposite. What was happening to her? She felt as though was playing her own version of Snakes and Ladders, or some other board game. Someone who'd taken one step forwards, two steps back. From downstairs, she heard soft laughter and a low moan. Tess buried her head in the pillow, and finally let herself cry.

CHAPTER NINE

The trip to Italy was the central plank of the Langford College Classical Civilization course. Around half the class were going; it justified the high fees and it emphasized that which could not be said out loud – that this was a course without qualifications, with a nice holiday at the end of it. Of course, it would be nice, no, desirable, to come out of it with a working knowledge of Rome and her Empire, and the miracle that was fifth-century BC Athens, but if you were aiming to be the next Erich Segal or Sir Kenneth Dover, you wouldn't come to Langford College.

It seemed to be coming around incredibly quickly. One moment it felt as if Tess had been back for just hours; after Will's visit she realized it was nearly four months since she'd returned to Langford. The feeling of shiny newness she'd had was starting to leave. She was in a routine.

But Langford was so beautiful, this time of year. How could she have lived in the city for so long, knowing what spring was like in the countryside? Sometimes, Tess felt almost drunk on its beauty. The frothing cow-parsley in the hedgerows, the birds that sang outside her window in the morning, the bright green of the lanes, cowslips and primroses and everything in bloom, the riotous signs of life bursting forth everywhere. In the town, people opened their windows and let down the striped awnings of their shopfronts; pots filled with geraniums appeared outside the pub, and the tables and chairs. Dark green bunches of asparagus were everywhere in the shops; cool, sweet winds blew through the backstreets, into dark rooms dusty from the winter. The town was coming alive again; she felt it, Tess felt it more than anyone.

'Are you doing something different with your hair, dear?' Jan Allingham asked Tess, a week afterwards, as she was wiping down the whiteboard. The class had broken up and her students were dispersing slowly, grey and ash-blonde heads grouped together, clutching their textbooks and notepads, talking earnestly, nodding to one another.

Tess turned around, the cloth in her hand. 'Me? No, nothing. Literally. It's far too long. I must get it cut, actually.'

'I did wonder.' Jan bobbed up and down on the balls of her feet, and touched her top lip with her tongue. 'It's grown really fast, hasn't it!' She smiled at Tess. 'And that's a lovely jumper.'

'Thanks!' said Tess, touched. 'I bought it—'

'Is – is it from Marks?' Jan said. 'I think I have it in blue.'

'Yes,' said Tess. 'It is.'

'Great class today, Tess, thank you,' said Andrea, popping up behind Jan, while Tess clutched at her hair and looked down at her jumper. 'So interesting. I can't wait to tackle my essay on Dido. Marvellous stuff!'

Next to her, Diana Sayers rolled her eyes. 'Come on,' she said. 'I said I'd walk home with Carolyn. She'll be waiting.'

'Carolyn?' said Andrea. 'Carolyn *Tey*? Huh.' She shook her head.

'Ooh, Andrea,' said Jan.

'What's wrong with Carolyn Tey?' Tess asked, curiously.

'Nothing, dear,' said Jan. 'Andrea's just being *a bit childish*, that's all.' Tess followed her gaze out over the old polished floor of what once had been the Great Hall of the house, and saw Carolyn helping Leonora Mortmain out of the door. As usual, Leonora Mortmain carried no books, no notepad. She didn't do any of the coursework, she didn't answer any questions or contribute to any debate. She just sat and stared at Tess, almost unblinking, with a dark-eyed intensity written on her still, hawk-like face that Tess could neither become used to nor fathom.

The other members of the course were half locals, half actual real people, as Tess had started to think of the other hapless students who were unconnected with Langford. And the majority loathed Leonora Mortmain, her superiority and coldness, her seemingly callous determination to rip the heart out of the town. Carolyn Tey, whose father had been her local solicitor, was practically the only person in the class who would talk to her. But Carolyn was a dreadful snob, as Diana was always pointing out. Wasn't her father the person who, fifty years ago, bought old Mr Crispin's place Apple Tree Cottage, and renamed it Apple Tree House? People had long memories here.

'Childish?' Andrea exploded. 'Childish, is it, Jan Allingham, to care about what happens to your bloody town? I don't think so! The planning meeting's next Monday, and you know what she's trying to do? That woman? Move it to when we're all supposed to be in Rome, on our trip and send her solicitor along instead! She's said she has a minor operation on the original day. My eye. So either we cancel the trip, which is all paid for, or we miss the meeting.' She fingered the poppers on her quilted jacket. 'Honestly, I don't like to speak ill of anyone, but that woman –!' She paused, and said petulantly, 'Why's she coming on the trip anyway?'

'She's on the course, like you all are, she presumably wants to see Rome.'

'I don't believe it, I'm afraid,' said Andrea. 'She wants to cause trouble. And ruin everyone else's fun.'

Beside her, Diana nodded in sympathy, and Jan, who was rather bossy but liked to think of herself as fair to her fellow man and woman, looked thoughtful, as if she wasn't quite sure what to say next. Tess clutched her cloth, not sure if it would be rude to go back to wiping the board, as the rest of the class milled slowly out. Deep down, though, she couldn't help but agree with Andrea. Why was Leonora Mortmain coming to Rome?

'Well,' Jan said, after a pause. 'I very much like your jumper, dear. I might have to get another one, in green.'

'Oh – thanks.' Tess patted the jumper awkwardly. She wasn't any good at accepting compliments, and indeed she wasn't sure this was one, really, since it was a fifty-five-year-old woman telling her she wanted to copy her style. Still, it was sweet of her. 'Remember, next week I want those last essays about Augustus in!' she called to the retreating backs of her pupils, glad of the chance to change the subject.

'Bye, Tess!' Liz called, slinging her bag over her shoulder. 'Great class. Maybe see you in the pub over the weekend?'

Tess found Liz's friendly behaviour daunting. 'Sure!' she called back. 'Thanks, Liz!'

'Well, I'm off.' Diana appeared, winding a silk scarf around her neck. 'Thank you, Tess, that was very interesting.' She glanced at Jan and at Andrea, who was still muttering mutinously next to them. 'Carolyn's obviously gone on. I'll walk out with you, shall I?'

'Oh, thanks,' said Tess, gratefully. She grabbed her bag.

'We've got committee tomorrow,' Andrea was saying to Jan. 'Are you still coming?'

'Of course I am!' Jan cried indignantly. 'Andrea, we need to stand shoulder to shoulder! Not face each other as enemies, like . . . that Roman general, at the gate! Oh, I've forgotten his name.'

Tess rolled her eyes and followed Diana towards the door. 'I saw Adam last week,' Diana said unexpectedly, as they walked down the drive, Diana pushing her bike. 'He told me he spent last Friday being your paramour.' Tess smiled.

'He told you that?'

'I'm his godmother, Tess. I do occasionally speak to him, you know. The old boyfriend turned up then, did he?'

Her tone was sympathetic. Tess said, 'Yes. I owe Adam, big time I owe him.'

'That's what friends are for, I suppose,' said Diana, in a curious voice. 'Do you miss him?'

'Adam? I—'

'No, Tess! I meant the old boyfriend.'

Tess considered for a moment, the only sound around them the dripping rainwater of the recent shower along the driveway, and their steps towards the main gate. 'Miss him? Not really. I miss the other things.' She gestured with her hands, rather awkward at saying this to Diana Sayers. 'You know.'

'Well,' said Diana, with her simple, disarming honesty. 'Isn't that nice? Not to miss him.'

'Oh,' said Tess, taken aback. 'Yes. I suppose so, yes.'

'So, how are your parents?' said Diana, switching topic abruptly. 'I must ring your mother, it'd be lovely to see them.'

'I'm going down week after next, that's funny,' said Tess. 'On the Saturday, just for the night.'

'Isn't that Adam's birthday?' Diana said. 'He was talking about it the other day. Said he was going to have a barbecue, up at the cottage.' She cleared her throat. 'It's good for him to have people round. I worry he doesn't . . .' She trailed off, wrinkling her forehead.

Tess remembered, with slow horror, that Adam had mentioned the barbecue to her the previous weekend, not once but twice. But, in the way that two sides of your brain can happily know that you're doing two totally separate things and never does one talk to the other, now she realized with horror she'd booked the train tickets down to Devon, and happily agreed with Francesca that they'd go to Adam's birthday together ... Damn.

'Oh. God, that's so annoying,' Tess exclaimed. 'The tickets are booked – I have to go – God! Why don't I think!' She tapped herself on the forehead.

'Don't worry,' Diana said, in quelling tones. 'It's Francesca Adam was worried about, you know.'

'Yeah ...' Tess began, knowing that her not taking Francesca would be a big deal; he treated her a bit like a child, sometimes. When he wasn't shagging her, that was, she thought meanly. She opened her mouth to try and explain this but then, from out of nowhere, a black Jaguar drove silently past them. Tess and Diana both craned their necks to see who was in it.

'Well, I never,' said Tess. 'What's Mrs Mortmain doing in that incredible car with that man?'

He was a large man, sleekly tailored in an effort to hide his burgeoning stomach, and he stroked his black hair back from his face as he leaned forward towards his fellow passenger, smiling ingratiatingly at her. She, however, sat upright, her mouth set.

'Oh, Tess,' said Diana, with a sigh. 'He's Jon Mitchell, the developer. He's the one who wants to buy the water meadows. He owns Mitchell's. That chain of DIY stores.'

'My goodness!' cried Tess. 'That's him?' She watched the car disappear, and then said, darkly, 'I don't know how she lives with herself, that woman. I really don't.'

'It's easy to have principles when you don't have to apply them,' said Diana softly. Tess spun round to look at her.

'What do you mean? You can't say you agree with her? With – what she's trying to do to the town?'

'Tess, the last new shop to open here was a tea shop, called Ye Tudor Tea Shoppe,' said Diana, and there was a note of sharpness in her voice.

'So?' said Tess, who liked Ye Tudor Tea Shoppe. It had

100

waitresses in old-fashioned uniforms, and everyone spoke to each other in a hush. 'It's Langford! What's wrong with that?'

'What's wrong with it is that there's no community hall here, and it costs four pounds to buy a pint, and if you grew up here and you want to buy a house, forget it, because a two-bed cottage costs about three hundred thousand pounds, and there are coach parties wandering the streets practically twenty-four hours a day,' said Diana. 'Look, I run a B&B in the summer, I'm as guilty as the rest of them. But we live in a *community*, not a heritage site, and I can't one hundred per cent blame Mrs Mortmain for trying to breathe a bit of life back into the town, even if it is going to end up driving some of the tourists away.' She paused. 'Don't tell the others, but I don't care if I never see another tourist again.' She gestured out, towards the water meadows. 'I'd rather there was a supermarket and a John Lewis out there. I'd be able to get some decent curtains, for starters. And my godson and his friends – they'd have jobs, for another thing.'

Tess had never heard the usually reserved Diana talk like this before. So she thought Adam didn't have a job because there wasn't an out-of-town shopping centre here? Tess didn't know what to say. She looked out towards the disappearing car, the gates of the college. 'I – I just don't see why it has to be on the water meadows. And why we can't act better as a community, that's all. It's nice living here,' she said weakly, thinking of what she'd left behind. 'It's safe and cosy and – and nice.'

Diana gave her a strange look. 'Nice? It'll be dead in a few years if we're not careful.' She shook her head. 'Forget I spoke. I don't know what I'm talking about. Just tired, I expect.' She collected herself, almost as if she was aware she'd said too much, and then got on her bicycle. 'Bye, Tess,' she called, leaving Tess in the middle of the driveway, holding her bag of books. She watched her go, bemused, and then set off back to Easter Cottage.

Tess told Francesca about this conversation, as Francesca mashed up the ingredients for mojitos in a large mixing bowl. 'Well, she's right, I don't think all that tourism is good for the town in the long run. But who knows what the future holds,' Francesca said, licking mint and sugar off her fingers. 'But I'm telling you, when my six months is up, I'm not going back to work in the City, that's for sure. Not that there'll be any jobs there anyway.'

'No?' Tess handed her a glass, watching her curiously from the doorway of the kitchen.

'No way,' said Francesca. 'Mmm. That's nice. I'm staying right here. Trouble is, there's nothing to do round here if you're not a tourist or someone who wants to study stupid things like History of Art or Roman Civilization . . .' She smiled. 'I'm *joking*. But there is nothing else to do. So actually, I did something about it today.'

'Really?'

'Yep.' Francesca's eyes sparkled. 'I'm helping Ron and Andrea with the campaign, volunteering. You know I actually trained as a lawyer.' Tess nodded. 'Long before I got sucked into the evil world of finance. I'm looking at the legality of what they're proposing to do, because I'm sure there's something fishy going on.'

'Wow.' Tess clapped. 'That's brilliant. Er – have you told Adam?'

'No. Why?'

'Don't know why,' said Tess. 'It's just – he's so weird about the campaign. Have you noticed?' She felt as if she were betraying something as she said this, but it was true.

'He's weird about it because he's behaving like an adolescent,' Francesca sounded firm. She poured a large slug of rum into the bowl. 'You know, I love Adam.' She paused. 'I don't mean like that. I –' She smiled, mistily. 'I really like him. But he's got to grow up. Fine to stay here all your life, but not fine to use it as a stick to beat other people with when they dare to disagree with you about anything connected with Langford.'

Francesca had a way of saying things which summed up what Tess wanted to say so perfectly but couldn't articulate without using five times as many words. Tess laughed. 'I'd love to hear you say that to him.'

'I have,' said Francesca, and she smiled her cat-like smile. 'He knows I'm right, he just doesn't see it yet. But he will.' She nodded and for some reason Tess shivered, as if a goose had walked over her grave. 'I've got him where I want him. He just doesn't realize it yet.'

'Oh, Francesca –' said Tess, not sure what to say next, because she knew Adam well, so well, knew how stubborn he was, how little he liked being told what to do, manipulated, which was why she thought he was such a bloody-minded idiot, still living in his mother's house, still working shifts at the pub and the museum. 'Please don't get your hopes up with him. He's . . .' She said frankly, 'He's never going to change. He's so stubborn.'

Something flickered across Francesca's lovely face, but she said nothing. Tess got up. 'What are we having tonight?'

Francesca looked blank. 'What do you mean?'

'Well, as well as the mojitos,' Tess said. 'Not that they won't be lovely . . .' She trailed off.

'Dunno,' said Francesca. 'I haven't *cooked*, if that's what you're thinking. I've made cocktails and it took bloody ages. You could have a bit of appreciation for what I've done, thank you very much.'

Tess ran over to her and hugged her, feeling her bony arms, her hand on her back. She was fragile, she thought, she'd be so easy to crush. 'I do have appreciation for what you're doing. I just assumed – completely insanely, obviously, that you'd made supper as well.'

'No,' Francesca said. 'My plan was, we get trashed and then do karaoke with these cool new karaoke DVDs that I ordered from Amazon.'

'Great idea,' said Tess. 'And we can have the rest of that shepherd's pie I made yesterday. I've got some peas in the freezer.'

Francesca rolled her eyes, opened her mouth as if she would say something, then shut it. She smiled at Tess. 'Bless ye, old lady. Come on. Give me your glass.'

CHAPTER TEN

Jan Allingham was in a flap. She was usually a rational woman, with an unshakeable faith in humanity, but when an event occurred to test this faith, she was conversely distressed out of all proportion.

She hated being late, even if it was only by a couple of minutes, and she was going to be late. If someone said ten o'clock, they meant ten, not five past ten. It was one of the things that drove her absolutely mad about her dear husband Jeremy, though time – thirty-five years of marriage – and wisdom – fifty-five years on God's green earth – had taught her to accept with as good a grace as possible things like Jeremy's breaking of his solemn vow that he would pick her up from the garden centre outside Thornham at twelve thirty. No, she had learned simply to smile and say, 'Don't worry, dear, thank you for coming.' Conversely, of course, he was always absolutely furious if she was over a minute late to pick him up from anything – with the righteous indignation of the truly guilty.

It was thanks to Jeremy that she was going to be late for the committee meeting of the Save the Water Meadows Campaign. Bloody Jeremy, who had said she shouldn't get involved, that it was asking for trouble, that it was putting other people's backs up. Accept the inevitable, he'd said, looking at her over his copy of *The Times* that morning.

'It's going to happen,' he said, his ruddy face creasing into lines as he munched his toast. 'It's inevitable, I'm afraid, dear. Market forces.'

Jan didn't care about market forces. She whisked some cling film over the remains of the Galia melon pieces she'd had for her breakfast. 'What's that got to do with anything?' she demanded, pushing the fridge door shut.

'It's got to do with the council and the Mortmains and a whopping great company that's used to having its own way, that's what they're used to.'

'Leonora Mortmain's an evil old woman,' said Jan, pettishly.

'That's the trouble with you lot,' said Jeremy, putting down his paper. The phrase *you lot* infuriated his wife. 'You think because she's old and grim-looking and eccentric that she has no real power. She's one of the most important landowners around here, she wields enormous influence. Just because she's a woman and she hasn't invited you all round for tea and cakes doesn't mean she doesn't know what she's doing. She's an impressive woman, I'll give her that. Intelligent, too.'

Jan paused in her wiping down of the draining board. 'How do you know that?' she said, curiously.

'Met her a few months ago when I had to value a couple of the cottages down towards the water meadows,' said Jeremy. 'Had a bit of a chat, actually. I told you.'

'No, you didn't,' Jan said, exasperatedly. 'You had a bit of a chat? With Leonora Mortmain? Typical you, Jeremy, that you don't even think to mention it.'

'Well, I did, and she was rather interesting. I reckon she was quite a gal in her time.' Jan frowned. 'Honestly, love. Something quite special, I bet she was popular with the . . .' Jeremy recalled himself. 'Anyway, her family's lived round here for three hundred years, did you know that? Used to play in the meadows when she was a little girl, with the gardener's son, or the vicar's son or something,' said Jeremy reflectively, picking up his paper again. 'Got quite misty-eyed about it, in fact.'

Jan couldn't imagine black-clad, iron-jawed Leonora Mortmain as a young girl, let alone one who did anything as fanciful as playing in fields. 'Look,' she said, whipping Jeremy's breakfast plate smartly away from under him, much to his surprise. 'She ought to know better. I didn't move to Langford to spend my final days in a suburb of an out-of-town shopping centre. I moved here – we moved here,' she amended hastily, 'so we could live in a beautiful, historic town and enjoy all the amenities.'

'Greg wants it to happen,' said Jeremy, grabbing another piece of toast and defiantly buttering it on the tablecloth. Greg was Jeremy's junior surveyor, who was rare in Langford, in that he'd lived there all his life. 'Says it's just what we need. Bit of reality. Plus he's right, we don't have a decent DIY shop round here for miles.'

'Greg's talking rubbish,' said Jan firmly. 'So are you, Jeremy. I know we need more jobs in the town, and it's too expensive, and everything, but we don't need that. Don't take a sledgehammer to crack a nut.' She thumped her hand dramatically down on the walnut kitchen surface, and looked out of the window of the bungalow towards the spire of St Mary's church.

The Allinghams had moved to Langford from Southampton, seven years previously. Their youngest daughter Jenny had finally left home, and Jeremy had been offered a job in the local chartered surveyor's office, four days a week, by an old friend who was retiring. It was to be his last job before he himself retired, and the plan, as far as he was concerned, was to spend more time playing golf and reading Robert Ludlum thrillers. In a decent place, where there was a decent pub within walking distance.

Jan had different ideas, however. She had, along with many children around the country, come on a school trip to the town and the Roman villa when she was a girl, and had fallen in love with the place. It had seemed to her, mired in suburbia, the height of Englishness, for her outwardly practical demeanour concealed – as is so often the case – an intensely sentimental, romantic soul. That, plus an unshakeable faith that what was right would always prevail, made her an optimist of the most terrifying order. Here, untrammelled by ugly modernity, was a place so unchanged that Charles I might well recognize the town that had hidden him, at great danger to itself, from the Roundheads. Here, too, was a high street down which Jane Austen had walked, where she would still feel at home. Living here was like a dream come true for Jan. Yes, of course, one had to live in modern times, but she had her hessian 'Langford's Own Plastic Bag' bag for shopping at the farmers' market, didn't she? And didn't she get the bus everywhere she could, instead of using the car, and didn't she recycle everything, even though it meant driving the green box down the road as the recycling truck never seemed to make it into the cul-de-sac?

'It's the realities of the modern global economy,' said Jeremy, taking his plate back firmly, and putting the paper down on the table. 'If you want to be able to fly to Rome to waft around looking at old dead statues, you have to accept there are downsides.'

'Look, I've got no problem with the modern global economy,' said Jan, who had spent many years working for a luxury cruise company and was well aware of 'market realities', as the firm had been wont to call them just before they hiked up the prices. 'And that's rubbish, Jeremy, I'd go to Rome by coach if I had to, that's how we went to Italy for our honeymoon, remember? It's more that I don't believe for a second this is going to help the town.'

Jeremy turned over a page of *The Times*. 'Ah,' he said, in placatory tones. 'Twenty-three degrees in Rome. When are you off?'

It infuriated Jan when Jeremy patronized her like this. She had worked as long as him. Just because she was a woman, and a woman in her fifties who liked a tea shop and who fussed a bit – she knew she did, she tried not to – why should that mean that her opinion was risible? Her opinion and so many other women like her. It was sexism, that was what it was. She bit her tongue, as she had done so often in their marriage. 'For every one job it creates, there'll be four tourists who don't come to Langford because they're put off it by this horrible development, and that's potentially far more jobs lost, not to mention what a violation of planning laws and everything else it is.' She was getting worked up. 'And I hate that attitude, Jeremy, that one that says it's either or, that either you're a fuddy duddy who's clinging to some old tradition and can't see the modern world around them or else you're a dynamic thrusting young individual. It's rubbish. This is about community!' She banged her hand on the surface again. 'It's about the heart of the town! It's about . . .' She ran out of steam and looked at her watch. Damn it.

Jeremy said, after a pause, 'I thought we drove to Italy for our honeymoon. We didn't get the coach, did we? I had the new Austin. Green. Nice car, that was.'

'That,' said Jan awfully, picking up her bag, 'is not the point, Jeremy. I have to go to my meeting now. Goodbye.'

The conversation with Jeremy – who was a fool, she had to remind herself – had made her late, and now she would be late for Ron and Francesca, the dear girl, who was so sweetly offering to help with the campaign. Jan hurried out of Watermeadows, the sweetly inaccurate and inappropriately named cul-de-sac where she lived, walking briskly towards the pub. She cut behind the warren of backstreets that formed the old heart of the town, where the lanes twisted and curled and where many a visitor to the town had found himself ending up by the old town walls that led down to the meadows, rather than the high street. Jan was a local though, of course, and it was with no little pride that she knew how to navigate her way through the maze, coming out at the back of the garden to Leda House, Leonora Mortmain's home. The garden was huge for a townhouse; though she was trying something between a walk and a trot, Jan glanced up as she always did, at the rose that climbed up the back of the house, and took in the sweet smell of the garden stocks in the air.

Jeremy's words rang in her ears. What was he doing, chatting away to Leonora Mortmain, and not mentioning it to her? For starters, she'd do anything to see inside Leda House (apparently, there was a Fabergé egg in the drawing room!). The idea of a teenage Leonora Mortmain, gambolling in fields with the butcher's son or whoever, was ridiculous. It struck her then, and she slowed down, that it was probably something to do with the fact that she just didn't seem like the kind of person who'd ever been a child. Much less been happy, been in love, got drunk, kissed someone she shouldn't. Unimaginable, really! Jan thought of Jeremy suddenly with a smile, she didn't know why. She turned the corner, onto the high street.

It was only five minutes past ten when she arrived at the Feathers, but they were five minutes too many. Mick was outside, wiping down the blackboard.

'Hello, Jan,' he said, standing up. 'You here for the meeting? Francesca's just arrived.'

'Yes,' panted Jan, practically running towards the door. 'See you later, Mick.'

Inside, she found Ron, Andrea Marsh and Francesca, sitting around a table at the back of the pub. She bustled towards them.

'Gosh. I am sorry, honestly. It's been a bit of a hectic –'

Ron looked up, and Jan stopped as she saw the look on his face.

'Council just called, Jan. It's all over.'

'What do you mean?' said Jan, her breathing short. She put her hand on the table.

Ron's face seemed to have aged twenty years in one day. 'That old – that woman signed the agreement yesterday. Council's approved it. The Mitchells have offered to finance some community park or something, so they've given planning permission for the shopping centre to go ahead. They start draining the land next month.'

Andrea gave a huge sniff; Francesca patted her hand. 'I'm calling them this afternoon,' Francesca said, drumming her pen on the table. 'This isn't over, Jan. I'm telling you.'

Jan smiled at her. 'Of course it's not,' she said, steadying herself on the table and catching her breath. 'We'll fight it, and we'll win.' She raised herself up, with a proud expression. 'Won't we?'

But somehow, she didn't believe it was true. It would take a miracle, and that sort of thing just didn't happen.

CHAPTER ELEVEN

A couple of days after the council had approved the application, the changes it would bring were already being felt. Tess noticed it as she walked to the college and saw people standing outside their front doors talking to neighbours, or little knots forming on street corners. The posters up in Jen's Deli and the cheese shop, the sign outside the pub, they were still there: but they each had a thick black line through them. In the window of the Feathers that directly faced onto Leonora Mortmain's house there was a sign: 'HAPPY NOW?'

Andrea Marsh crept around with a face as long as a broom handle and Ronald Thaxton was a broken man. Langford was small enough that all of the main players were well-known, and Tess was in the deli one day with Francesca, sitting at one of the tiny tables squeezed into the shop, when a man came up to them.

'Is there really nothing you can do?' he said to Francesca. 'I heard you were a lawyer, is the application all in order?'

He was about forty, rather sturdy and traditional-looking, wearing a battered old Barbour, and a neat, short blue tie.

'Here's your coffee, Tess,' said someone, putting a tray down.

'Thanks,' said Tess absent-mindedly, not looking up but

watching Francesca for her response. Francesca smiled, her most scary smile.

'I'm afraid it is,' she said. 'The council is being extremely difficult about it, but it is all in order. I'm still—'

He interrupted her, putting his hand on the wobbly painted metal table. It lurched alarmingly to one side. 'Forgive me,' he said. 'But has anyone been in touch with English Heritage, or someone similar? Those water meadows are without equal in this part of the country. They can't just drain them and concrete them over, there must be a law against it.'

'You'd think,' said Francesca, nodding up at him. 'But I'm afraid not. Morely and Thornham have rich reserves of flora and fauna too, and since Langford's the town, their reasoning is that it's the one that can best support expansion.'

Tess, aware that someone was watching them, looked over and realized the person who'd given her the coffee was Liz. She was standing next to Claire, who was also in her class at school, a girl around the same age as her and Liz.

'Hi!' Liz said, waving. She wiped her hands on her apron. 'Do you need anything else?'

'No, thanks.' Tess shook her head, almost impatiently, turning back to the stranger.

'But that's absolutely ridiculous!' the man snorted. 'I'm sorry, but –'

Francesca frowned at him. 'It's not my fault!' she said, not unreasonably. 'I'm on your side, remember! But that's what they've said. We're appealing, of course we are –'

He stood up straight. 'I'm so sorry,' he said, looking at her with an expression of remorse. 'That's incredibly rude of me.' He held out his hand. 'Guy Phelps. I own George Farm, just the other side of town.'

'Yes, of course,' Francesca said, as if she was well aware of George Farm and all its doings. She took his hand. 'Francesca Jackson,' she said. 'And this is Tess Tennant,' she added, indicating Tess next to her.

'Nice to meet you.' Guy Phelps shook Tess's hand enthusiastically too, but returned his gaze almost immediately to Francesca and Tess went back to eating her carrot cake. 'Well,' he continued, as Francesca smiled politely up at him, 'I'd better be off – thanks again,' he finished, though he hadn't thanked her before.

'Nice to meet you,' said Francesca.

'Let me know if there's anything I can do, won't you?' he said.

'Thanks,' said Francesca. She looked at Tess. 'I'm sure there will be at some point. See you soon.'

'She youw shoon,' Tess added, her mouth full of cake.

As Guy Phelps departed, touching a finger to an imaginary cap, much to both girls' delight, Francesca turned to Tess and said, exasperatedly, 'Tess!'

'Wha'?' said Tess, wiping the crumbs from her lips.

'Do you have to eat cake like a three-year-old? Or the Count of Monte Cristo? After his prison spell?' she added, indistinctly.

'What about the Count of Monte Cristo?' Adam said, appearing at the back of the shop where they were sitting. 'Who was that bloke? Hi, Liz.' He waved at Liz, who waved back. 'Hello, you.' He bent down and kissed Francesca's head.

'Something Phelps,' said Francesca. She paused. 'He was just saying about the planning permission.'

'Oh,' said Adam.

There was a silence. The previous night, Adam and Francesca had had a massive, and noisy, row about lots of things, including Francesca helping out with the campaign. Francesca had told Adam to get his head out of his arse, and Adam had told Francesca it was none of her business, he'd lived there all his life and she didn't know what she was talking about. It had ended in bed, but it still hadn't been right this morning. So Tess said, not wanting to get into it again, 'What's wrong with the way I eat cake?'

Francesca looked at her and sighed. 'Oh, God. Look at you.' She waved a hand around the table, where Tess's cake was liberally sprinkled. 'When I remember I first thought you were this terrifying sophisticated intellectual, with this brilliant classy capsule wardrobe and that lovely hair –' She flicked Tess's hair back from her face, and crumbs scattered everywhere. '"This is what people in the country are like",' I told myself,' she added, not looking at Adam, who sighed, whilst Tess looked appalled, and brushed her face with her hands.

'What are you saying?'

'I'm saying,' said Francesca wearily, 'you've turned into a hobo.'

Tess was outraged. This was fatigue and boyfriend issues talking, not common sense. She wasn't a hobo! Sure, she hadn't worn heels for a week, no, a month, well, a few months (was it really that long?). And sure, she hadn't had her hair cut for a while, but *Jan* liked it! And why did she need to when she could just trim the split ends herself, which was actually quite an addictive activity when you were listening to *The Archers* or something? After all, who was she dressing up for? The nice ladies of her class? Francesca? Adam? Exactly. She looked down at her sensible shoes, and noticed with a wince that her jeans were covered in mud at the ankles.

Embarrassment, and a dawning sense of realization, crept over her, hot and certain. When was the last time she'd washed these jeans? When was the last time she'd even ironed anything? Or plucked her eyebrows, or put on mascara, for that matter?

She looked up at Francesca. 'That's so rude,' she said, but there was a note of uncertainty in her voice.

'I agree,' said Adam. 'She looks fine to me, you always do, T.' He patted her on the back, reassuringly, and this, somehow, depressed Tess even more.

'Thanks,' she said.

'No problems,' Adam said, staring with intensity at Francesca. 'No problems. At. All.'

Tess was a reasonable person, but there was only so much mooning over Francesca in one day she could take, and since they'd also had the window cleaner round that morning, and she had spotted him gazing lovingly through the glass at Francesca while she combed her hair, she was a bit sick of people falling over themselves (quite literally in the window cleaner's case) to point out how ravishing Francesca was and what a horrible old grub she was. She stood up.

'I might go back and do some work before the class,' she said. 'It's only ten days till we go now.'

'Is it really?' said Adam. He frowned. 'I keep forgetting. T – so I'm not going to see you on Saturday at the birthday barbecue, am I? You're still going to your mum and dad's?'

'Sorry,' she said. 'Really sorry. But I haven't been to see them for ages, I completely screwed up . . .'

'That's so annoying,' Adam said, standing. He held up his hands. 'I mean because you won't be there, not that you've screwed up,' he said, as she opened her mouth to apologize again. 'Remember my sixteenth birthday?'

'Course I do,' she said, laughing.

'What happened?' Francesca asked, propping her elbows on the table. She loved a story about Adam and Tess and their Langford youth.

'Oh –' Adam turned round. 'We went up to London for the day, and we went to Piccadilly Circus, and then we found this boozer in Soho that'd serve us, and I got completely drunk, and then we went to see *True Romance* in Leicester Square – God knows why they let us in, there's no way we were old enough, Tess was only fifteen as well.' He scratched his elbow and chuckled. 'T, do you remember where we went afterwards?'

'Covent Garden,' she said promptly. 'And we had another drink in a pub and then went to the Rock Garden and had burgers and we thought we were *so cool* . . .'

'And then,' Adam said, smiling at Francesca, 'do you remember you were saying how you can't believe bits of

London join up with other bits when you first go there, because it all seems separate?' She nodded, turning her face up towards him. 'We walked across the river to Waterloo and got the train home and I was so sick when I got home. I've no idea how we got there – I wouldn't know the way now, either.'

Tess chewed a fingernail. 'It's true.' She suddenly had an enormous pang for London. 'Oh, my God,' she said suddenly. 'Daniel Mathias dumped me after that day, do you remember? He thought we were a couple!'

'Did he?' said Francesca.

'He was an idiot, though,' said Adam.

'No, he wasn't,' said Tess.

'He kept a comb in his back pocket. And he actually used Brylcreem.'

'OK,' Tess conceded. 'Maybe he did.' She gave a small snort at the memory. 'It made snogging him a bit tricky. Like, you'd grab hold of him, and your hands would slither down to his shoulders and leave greasy marks on his shirt, and he'd get really cross.'

Francesca and Adam laughed, the tension gone.

'Very true,' said Adam. 'You owe me for that, at least, as well as owing me a birthday drink.'

'Absolutely.' Tess ran a hand through her hair, awkwardly, remembering Daniel Mathias's Brylcreem.

Adam said, 'Hey. What are you doing next weekend?'

'Packing for Italy. And I told you, I'm going to London on Sunday,' said Tess. 'To see Meena for the day.'

'So that's Sunday,' Adam nodded, solemnly.

'I've just thought of something,' said Tess. She looked at Francesca, who was getting money out of her purse. 'Yes.'

'What?' said Francesca.

'Next week. Us three. Evening out in London town. I love it.' She clapped her hands together; it would kill two birds with one stone – she could take Adam out for a birthday drink in style, AND it gave her a week to get her shit together before she went back to London. Wear a top she'd actually ironed, perhaps. Perhaps – daring – try out some of that crazy stuff they were wearing in the Big Smoke she'd heard about, called Make-Up.

'Where will we stay?' said Francesca.

'Easy,' said Tess. 'We can stay at my old place – Meena's away on the Saturday night, that's why I'm seeing her on Sunday. I'll check, she won't mind.' Francesca looked unsure about this, so Tess added hurriedly, 'Her new flatmate's an old friend of ours, Alex. I'll sleep on the sofa, you two can have Meena's room. Honestly, we're always having people to stay there. *Were* always having people to stay.' She looked at the pair of them. 'Are you in?'

'I'm definitely, one-hundred-per-cent in,' Adam said, rubbing his hands together. 'Can we find that pub again?'

'No,' said Tess. 'I'm sure we can do better than that place. Francesca?'

'I'm in,' said Francesca. 'Yes, we *definitely* can do better than that place.'

'You weren't there,' Adam said defensively. 'It was brilliant.'

Francesca rolled her eyes. 'I'm sure it was . . .' she said.

'I might have three T-shirts printed,' said Tess, excitedly. "*Adam's Birthday Piss-Up '08.*"'

'You'll be wearing all three,' said Adam. 'But you go for it.'

'Absolutely,' said Francesca, looking pointedly at Tess's crumpled top. They smiled briefly at each other, but the tension was still there.

'Tess, dear, may I ask you something?' Carolyn Tey asked her timidly, the next Thursday after their class was over.

'Yes, of course,' said Tess. 'What's up?'

'Well – do we need to bring any books with us? On the trip?'

'I was going to ask you the same thing,' Jacquetta said, graciously.

'Up to you,' said Tess, trying not to smile. 'There'll be talks from me every day depending on what we see, so bring a notebook as I've said. But it's your choice if you want to bring something to help you – a reference book or something, any of the ones we've recommended.' She stood up, stretching her neck and her arms. 'Is that OK?'

'Sure,' said Jan briefly, and zoomed off. 'See you on Monday. Bright and early,' she called over her shoulder.

'Bye!' called Carolyn, scampering after her, and the classroom was empty. Almost empty – Tess looked up, and to her surprise saw Leonora Mortmain rising slowly to her feet. She hadn't noticed her before; she usually left almost immediately after class.

'Do you need a hand?' Tess said, hurrying over.

'I am fine, thank you,' Leonora said, calmly standing. Tess looked at her, thinking how old she seemed these days. It must be hard, being the most unpopular woman in town, and she realized she barely even knew her.

'Is someone coming to pick you up? Shall I walk you home?' Tess asked.

'You?' Leonora Mortmain said, staring at her in astonishment. 'My housekeeper will be here any second. Please, do not trouble yourself.' She sounded absolutely horrified.

'Right, then,' said Tess, wishing she wouldn't stare at her like that. 'Um – are you looking forward to the trip to Rome, then?'

'Moderately,' Leonora said. She walked stiffly towards the door, looking around her. 'They are not supposed to pin things to the wall. This is a listed building.' She turned back. 'Do you know the difference between a gerund and a gerundive, by the way?'

'Yes,' said Tess, taken aback. 'The gerundive is – er, well, it's a sort of verbal adjective. *Amanda*,' she said weakly, grasping at the example they always taught. 'To be loved.'

'Yes.' Leonora Mortmain held up her hand. 'I suggest you

use that knowledge next time then. Your translation of the Catullus poem today was wrong. I look forward to Rome, but not if your teaching is to be peppered with schoolboy errors. Good afternoon.'

'Mrs Mortmain?' a nervous voice called, distant in the hallway. 'Hello, are you there?'

'Right!' said Tess under her breath, as the old woman disappeared from sight. 'How lovely! So glad she's coming!'

She looked up and around the cavernous classroom which had been the drawing room when the Mortmains were in residence, lit in diamond patterns by the leaded windows. She picked up her stack of books and walked to the door.

On her way she walked past something and then stopped. It was her own reflection, caught in an old, mildewy mirror by the door, and she stared at herself in dismay. Tess was not particularly fascinated by beauty preparations, the mystery of the hair salon, or a new breakthrough in nail technology, but she used to like it well enough. When she lived in London, Tess had loved going into department stores, trying on silly make-up she wasn't going to buy, and having the occasional splurge – when her teacher's salary would let her, that is. By the time she was thirty, she'd realized what she could wear (hourglass-shaped tops, belts, denim skirts and leggings) and what she couldn't wear (maxi-dresses, anything smocky or flowing was particularly cruel to her). She had a style, based on the fact that the junior maths teacher at Fair View had once, *once*, fleetingly said in the pub that she looked like Audrey Tautou. She had slept with him, obviously.

How had it come to this, that she didn't even recognize herself in a mirror? Sure, it was nice that she didn't have to make an effort now she was here in Langford, but was it really that good for her? Perhaps it was as a direct result of living with Francesca. She deliberately wasn't like Francesca. 'Look at the new Bayswater!' Francesca had shouted on Monday evening, poring over a copy of *Elle*. 'Oh, my God, I love it, don't you?'

Tess had been balancing fondant fancies into a pyramid shape on the cake stand. 'What on earth is a Bayswater?'

Francesca looked at her as if she were a lunatic. 'Bag. A Mulberry bag. Are you mad?'

'Yes, I'm totally mad,' Tess said. 'I'm insane, for not knowing what a Bayswater is. Look, have a fondant fancy,' she said, advancing into the sitting room, gingerly balancing the cake stand.

Francesca watched her progress with something like dismay. She closed *Elle* and shook her head. 'Look at you. You really need a night out, Tess.'

Tess didn't agree. It was stupid, all of that obsession with clothes and facials and body lotions that smelt nice. She'd moved here to get away from all of that. It was silly and it got in the way of other things: being a real person, having thoughts in your head, caring about things like the water meadows. But then, Tess thought confusedly, Francesca did both. But Francesca was also pretty mad herself. She shook her head and shivered again, in the cold room, walking out into the hallway. She didn't like Langford Hall, never had done. There was something oppressively Gothic about it. Perhaps Jane Austen had got the inspiration for *Northanger Abbey* there. Oh, no, it wasn't built until 1846 and she died in 1817. Perhaps she should go and check the dates in the museum. It'd be nice, she could pop into the Tea Shoppe afterwards, they did a lovely Eccles cake. And she needed some suntan lotion for her trip to Rome. Factor 45, best be on the safe side – and insoles for her shoes, the chemist next door did a nice range ...

Tess checked herself. Good God, Francesca was right. She did need a night out. A haircut, and a night out.

CHAPTER TWELVE

'What do you mean, you're not coming?'

'I mean, I'm not coming. End of discussion.'

Tess could hear Adam clearing his throat. 'Francesca,' he said, quietly. 'But we – I –'

'Look,' Francesca's voice was harsh. 'I don't see the point of me coming for this one night just so we can pretend everything's wonderful, when it's not and it hasn't been for days now. Weeks, even!'

'It's fine, you're just—'

'Don't patronize me, Adam,' she said. 'You're the one who's making it like –' her voice cracked, and out in the sitting room, Tess winced. She got up, and went into the kitchen, clearing the remnants of lunch away. She wished she couldn't hear. She was sick of hearing it.

'I know this week's been difficult –' she could hear Adam saying impatiently. 'I know you've been working really hard on the appeal as well, but Francesca, it's supposed to be fun, a night out, come on –'

'That's exactly what I mean,' Francesca shouted. 'That's why I'm not coming. Do you seriously, *seriously* think you and I are simply going to forget that we've barely said a nice word to each other for two weeks and –' she put on a fake cockney accent – 'set off for a jolly night out in London town? Get real, Adam. I can barely stand to look at you, let alone . . .'

Her voice trailed off.

'That's it, then?' Adam said. He was calm now. He opened the bedroom door; in the kitchen, from where she could see the stairs opposite Francesca's bedroom, Tess jumped back, guiltily, as if she were eavesdropping. She looked at her watch in agony – they were going to miss the train if they didn't leave now, come on . . . She put her hand to her mouth, in anxiety, and then said, 'Adam – Francesca – we really need to go.'

She'd said that five minutes ago, and this is what had prompted the conversation currently taking place. She picked up her bag and went to the door, and she heard the murmur of hissed conversation, before the bedroom door slammed and Adam came running down the stairs, his face white, and his brown eyes black.

'Are we going?' he said, curtly, as if she were the one holding him up. Tess stared at him; he was fierce, his features set; she didn't recognize him.

'Yep,' she said, holding up her bag. 'Um – Francesca –'

'No,' he said, holding the door open for her. 'She's not coming. It's – yeah. Right, got everything?'

'Yes,' Tess said.

He grabbed her back, almost as if by force, and set off down the road, marching so fast she had to run to keep up with him. 'We're late.'

'Yes, I know we are,' said Tess. 'But we'll make it at this rate, if we march very fast like Roman soldiers and don't enjoy ourselves *at all* – Adam, are you OK?'

'Yes, thanks,' said Adam. 'It's just – it's over with me and her. Yeah.' He stopped. 'I have to say, I'm pretty relieved.' Tess's mouth dropped open, and he turned to her and smiled, tightly. Seeing the expression on her face, his softened. 'Sorry.'

'No,' she said, putting her hand on his arm, knowing how

upset he must be. 'I'm sorry.' She stopped. 'Look, do you want to just –'

'No, way,' he said. He took her arm. 'It's my birthday night out on the tiles. We might have to revise a few of the plans, but we can still go ahead with the original one, eh?'

'Absolutely,' she said. She squeezed his arm, and there was silence as they walked briskly, turning right behind Leda House towards the station.

'She said I was a loser,' Adam said morosely, after a couple of minutes. 'She said I was pathetic.'

'Oh,' said Tess. She didn't know why, but she bit her lip, trying not to laugh. He turned to say something else, and caught her expression.

'Are you *laughing*?' he said, in disbelief.

'No – not much – not at all,' Tess said. 'It's just – I don't know.'

'What the fuck!' Adam said, striding on ahead.

'Sorry,' said Tess, trying not to smile, and catching up with him. 'It's just the way you said it, Adman. You *sounded* like a bit of a loser. Just a little bit.'

'That's what I mean,' Adam said, turning to her. 'It's fine from you. It's fine when you tell me I'm being a complete dick. But it's not fine from her.'

'Why?' asked Tess, trotting to keep up with him. They were approaching the station.

'Don't know,' he said. 'I don't know. Oh, man,' he said. 'I'm so stupid. Why did I –'

'Why did you what?'

'Nothing,' he said. 'Nothing, doesn't matter now.' He sighed.

'Well,' said Tess, as he jabbed the buttons on the ticket machine with the ferocity of one trying to defuse a nuclear bomb, 'well – this is going to be a super-fun night, isn't it.'

But actually, it was. Though the odds were stacked against it, it was one of those nights. It just was. They arrived up in

124

Waterloo as the evening sun was streaming through the great glass case of the station concourse; they stood beneath the clock for a moment, getting their bearings.

'Is it strange being back?' Adam said.

'Yep,' she answered him.

Adam dodged out of the way, to avoid a couple barrelling through them, dragging some huge suitcases. He stepped smartly back beside her, and she thought how strange it was to see him in the city, this bustling, heated metropolis, where there were more people here at the station than probably lived in the whole of Langford. She looked at him anxiously, but he didn't seem to be on the verge of a yokel-related panic attack.

He turned to her and said, 'So, what shall we do?' He shook his head. 'London, eh? Can't remember the last time I was up here.'

Coming up for five months in a small country town and Tess realized she still thought of herself as a Londoner enough to find it unbelievable that someone couldn't remember the last time they were here. How did people live, who weren't used to living among all this? Didn't they find everything else small by comparison? She caught herself, and realized how silly it was to still think that way. She remembered how unhappy she'd been, how London had been this place of cold grey streets and piss-stinking alleyways, long dark nights and constant rain.

Not now, not in early summer, not this night with Adam by her side. She patted his arm. 'What shall we do? You're joking, aren't you? We're not tourists, we're locals. Well, I am. Well, I was. You need a plan if you're going to have a good time here. No sense in going out without research. First rule: have a plan.'

'And do you have a plan?' Adam asked, opening his eyes wide. 'God, I hope you do. We could just go and find that pub, of course.'

He said this nonchalantly, like he wasn't bothered either way.

'We're NOT doing that,' said Tess. 'It's your birthday evening plan. OK. Check it out.' She held out a piece of paper, and they bent over it together.

1. *Drinks: Lamb and Flag, Covent Garden*
2. *Dinner: Great Queen Street, Longacre*
3. *Afterwards: The French House? Karaoke?*
4. *After that: Beaujolais? The Phoenix?*
5. *After that: Bar Italia.*

Adam looked up, slightly horrified. 'T, I'm not doing karaoke.'

'It's just a plan,' she told him. 'It's subject to change. Don't worry . . .' She pulled her hair out from her coat.

'Where's the Lamb and Flag?'

'Covent Garden. It's really old. Like, bits of it are Tudor old. It's great.' She looked up. 'Especially if the weather's nice, we can stand outside, it's always pretty crowded. OK?'

'Sounds great,' said Adam, relieved.

'Right!' she said, smiling at him. 'Let's go.'

'I like your new hair, by the way,' Adam said, as they walked through the station. 'It's nice.'

The previous day, Tess had finally gone to Fringe Benefits on the high street, for a cut and blow-dry. She smiled almost shyly at Adam.

'Thanks!' she said. 'It's part of the new me, I'm sure you've noticed.'

'I have, actually,' he said, much to her surprise. 'You've smartened up a bit. It suits you. Not so scruffy looking.'

'Er, right,' Tess said, leading him towards the exit for the South Bank. 'Thanks for that.'

'No worries,' Adam said. And then he added, with all the charm of men, 'It must be weird for you, living with someone like Francesca. She's so gorgeous all the time.'

'Well, exactly,' said Tess, as they walked through the tunnel that led up to Hungerford Bridge. 'I got used to walking around with a bag on my head, you know, because she's so gorgeous like you say. It's just easier that way. For me and other people.'

Adam looked at her. 'Oh, sorry. I only meant –' He slapped his forehead. 'I'm an idiot. I didn't mean it like that, I meant that she's really –' he searched for the words – 'really *obviously* gorgeous.'

They were climbing up the stairs to the bridge that crossed the Thames, and tourists, theatregoers, jugglers and homeless people were pushing past them. Tess stopped, shaking her head. 'Do you listen to yourself sometimes?' she said.

'Er – why?'

'Men!' Tess shouted loudly, as people around them looked at her in alarm, and Adam took her elbow, hurrying her across the bridge. 'You are incredible, you know that?'

'What?'

'Jesus, Adam!' Tess said, the wind blowing her hair in her face. She wedged it firmly behind her ears. 'Look, I know I'm not like – like, some ravishing beauty, like Claudia Schiffer, and I know Francesca is, but – give it a rest, will you? God, the way men think it's fine to just say stuff like that!' She gazed over to the other side of the river, growing nearer as they marched furiously in tandem.

'I didn't—' Adam began, but Tess put her hand up to his mouth.

'Sshh,' she said. 'Don't say anything more, otherwise you'll end up saying, "You're quite attractive, for a troll," and then I'll have to leave.'

'I wasn't going to say that,' said Adam. He paused. 'Sorry, T.'

'Fine,' said Tess. They stopped, looking across at the city, as they walked through the air towards it. The river was grey and choppy; clouds scudded across the sky, and off to the west, behind the Houses of Parliament, a rose-pink sunset flecked out towards them. The city lay ahead of her, still light, still full of possibility, and she hadn't realized how good it would be to be back until that moment. She had left London nearly five months before, grey and tired of the rushing, selfish life she'd seen all around her, rejected by a man she'd thought she'd loved. Langford was her home now, she knew that, the pace, the friendliness, the people, the fact that she could go out in a shirt made of a sack and no one would think it was weird, or that she could get genuinely excited about plant pots, or cushion covers, or jam. She shook her head as one of the windows on the old Shell-Mex building winked at her in the setting sun. It was only now, really, she wondered if she might have left something behind here, too.

The Lamb and Flag was Adam's kind of pub – no nonsense, good beer. But it was too crowded, and they clutched their drinks outside, wedged in a triangle between the wall, some Americans who'd just arrived in London and some Queen fans down from Hemel Hempstead who were about to go and watch *We Will Rock You* (and were very excited about it).

'You're always saying people in London aren't friendly,' Adam said as they squeezed their way past people in the tiny Dickensian passageway taking them out to Floral Street. 'They were nice.'

'They were American tourists, bruv,' said Tess. 'They actually used the word "Londontown". And some people from Hemel Hempstead. Of course they were nice. They're not from London. Sorry. Londontown.'

'Oh,' said Adam, smiling. 'Sorry, sis.'

She smiled back at him, as they turned into Longacre.

Great Queen Street, just along from Longacre, was unadorned, crowded and friendly. 'This isn't full of tourists.' Adam said, as they waited for their table. 'And it's –' he looked a little relieved – it's nice.'

Tess looked around the room. 'No, you're right,' she agreed. 'It's more –'

'People you might want to talk to.'

'What do you mean?'

'Well, not stuck up, all poncey and posh and Londony la-di-dah.'

Tess nodded, looking over at Adam with his soft plaid shirt and slightly sticking-up hair, his eyes alight with pleasure as he gazed round the room. She'd forgotten how much more low-level glamorous people were in town, even somewhere like here, which wasn't a 'scene' place. Girls in skinny jeans and stylish floral tops, necklaces dancing as they leaned forward to say hi to people, pushing their hair behind their ears. Men smiling, checking their hair in mirrors, adjusting ties, slapping each other on the back, hugging people. She thought of the Feathers, as she watched Adam's gaze take it all in. Ron might be nursing a pint in the corner, that old guy who always seemed to have a sore patch on the back of his hand would be quietly hacking away by himself, a couple of anniversary couples sitting quietly in the back, and maybe Suggs and Mick chatting at the bar . . . She looked around the restaurant, full of tasteful colour, life and energy, and knew it was good to be back.

'I booked a room at Claridge's,' Adam said, suddenly, into their silence.

'What?' Tess said.

'That's why I was so cross with her. I've got a room at Claridge's. I didn't know what to do about it.' He turned to her and said quietly, 'It was going to be a nice surprise for her.'

Her heart went out to him. 'Claridge's?' He nodded. 'Oh, Adam.' She looked up at him. 'You are so sweet.' She didn't know quite what to say, she loved them both, so she patted him on the back. 'D' you really think it's over?'

'Yes,' he said sadly: 'I really do.'

'If she'd known –' Tess reached out towards him. 'She'd have –'

'I told her about the hotel.'

'You did?'

'Yeah. She said –' He trailed off.

'Yes?' she prompted him.

'She said I needed to sort myself out, that I was a fraud.' He said it quietly.

'Well, that's horrible,' said Tess. 'You're not a fraud, anyway. You're the least fraudulent person I know.'

He looked at her, a strange expression on his face. 'I sometimes think you don't know me very well.'

'Come on!' Tess said, laughing. 'I know you better than anyone!'

Adam looked as if he was going to say something else, but instead he said, 'Well, it doesn't matter. It's over.'

The waiter bought the menu on a single sheet of hand-written paper, and Adam drank from a tumbler of wine.

'Can you cancel –' she began.

'Called them while you were in the loo, earlier,' he said. 'No.' He shrugged. 'It was stupid of me to do it. I was just trying to make things right, it's been so bad between us these last couple of weeks.'

Tess said, curiously, 'What do you think went wrong?'

Adam scratched his head and grimaced. He patted the table firmly. 'Well, it's a combination of things, but – uh, yeah. It's pretty much – yeah.'

'Yeah what?' said Tess gently, in her best don't-scare-boys-and-they'll-tell-you-stuff low voice.

'Pretty much my fault, yeah,' Adam said, nodding. He looked up and smiled, that dangerous, sexy smile that she knew so well. 'I always do it, I know how to make them like me, but then they get to know me and –' he pushed his hand firmly down on the table, a small controlled gesture – 'then they see that I'm not the nice uncomplicated bloke they thought I was.'

'Oh, that's not true,' said Tess, thinking, *Gosh, that's so true.* The waiter came back with some more wine and took their orders. Tess was surprised at Adam's self-knowledge, and said so.

'Come on, Tess;' he said, laughing at her. 'I'm not saying I'm this interesting complicated tortured person either. I'm just saying – they have this idea of me and the reality is more complicated. And more dull.'

'How?'

'They think I'm a nature-loving country boy with a nice smile who misses his mum and hates the Big Smoke, and that's true, and then they think to themselves, Hang on, but his mum died over thirteen years ago, what the hell's he doing?' Adam's smile grew more rigid: 'And then they ask a bit more, and they say, "But he's never really done anything. Oh, he got a place at university, he never took it. Oh, he was supposed to be this Classics genius, and instead he's working three nights a week at a pub and giving out tickets to old ladies in a museum."'

'They don't think that,' said Tess.

'They do, Tess,' he said, putting his hand on hers. 'And you do too. I know it.' She shook her head at him. 'Because it's true.'

How did you say to someone you knew and loved so well that you agreed with their worst critics? That knowing them so well merely made you despair of them more, because you could see both their potential and the rut they'd got themselves into?

Tess didn't know what to say. He was right. She drank from her glass. 'You could go to teacher training college, perhaps?' She wanted to help him, and she didn't know how. 'Finish your degree?'

Adam put up his hand. 'Look,' he said, calmly. 'You don't have to advise me. There's just stuff I have to work out.'

'I'm only trying to—'

'I know what you're trying to do, and don't. I can't explain it, it's my problem, it's within me and I have to sort it out.

131

So just don't. Let's have a chilled evening and forget about it, about Francesca, about all that, shall we?'

His tone was still light; Tess rarely saw him furiously angry, but she knew him well enough to know when to leave it. 'Fine,' she said. 'Just – Ad, if you ever need me –' she put her elbows on the table – 'you know.'

'I know, T,' he said. He gripped her wrist. 'Thanks.'

The starters arrived and they clinked glasses again; as if a switch had flicked the mood was suddenly lighter between them. 'We haven't done this for ages,' Tess said, feeling happy. 'Had dinner, the two of us.'

'You're right,' said Adam. 'Thanks, T. This is great. And listen, instead of going to Meena's, why don't we just go to the suite?'

She blinked rapidly at him, faux-batting her eyelashes. 'Oh, Mr Smith. Claridge's? Wow! You're so *stylish*.'

'Oh, eat your dinner, you awful girl,' he said, switching the plates around so the asparagus was in front of him. 'And don't drink too much. You know wine on beer makes you insanely drunk.' He raised his voice slightly. 'Remember that night in Spain when we were fifteen and you tried to kiss that flamenco dancer, and he pushed you over and you fell on a cactus?'

Tess glowered at him and dipped her bread in her soup. 'God, I loathe you,' she said, as one of the diners at the table next to theirs stared at them both in astonishment.

CHAPTER THIRTEEN

Since Adam was obviously about a foot taller than Tess, and since they had spent a lot of their time in pubs since they were teenagers, she had long ago in their adolescence been given a special drinking dispensation. This was called 'The Ringer', and it basically meant Tess could ring a bell (usually imaginary) and order Adam another drink and a chaser at any point during the course of the evening.

That night, the Ringer was probably where it all started to go wrong.

'What do you want to drink?' Adam asked Tess, when they got to the French House after dinner. It was after ten thirty and both of them were slightly the worse for wear.

Tess leaned her elbows on the bar and stared up at the drinks, the clamour of the tiny, crowded room ringing in her ears. It was a warm evening, and the doors were flung open out onto the Soho street. Inside was organized chaos; old men in pork-pie hats nursing pints, a gaggle of students who were well on the way to being drunk; and four girls dressed in vintage, upholstered clothes, their glossy hair set in waves, red lipstick perfectly in place.

'Yes, what can I get you?' the woman behind the bar said briskly, flinging a glass in the air and catching it with one hand.

Tess nodded. 'The Ringer,' she said firmly. 'You need to have the Ringer. I'm too drunk.'

She leaned forward and tapped a plastic cocktail stirrer at the glass the barmaid was holding. 'The Ringer,' she said, slightly indistinctly.

'Never heard of it,' the barmaid said, unimpressed.

'Sorry,' Adam stepped in hurriedly. 'My friend is using code. What she means is, can she have a gin and tonic, a shot of tequila and a pint of –' He scanned the list. 'What beer do you have?'

'Adam, they're not going to have Butcombe's here,' Tess said. 'We're in London.'

'And a pint of Stella,' Adam said, ignoring her.

He carried the drinks to a ledge adjacent to the bar and set them down. 'Cheers,' he said. 'Londontown.'

She raised her glass. 'Londontown.' He drank his shot, and she drank her gin and tonic.

'That was nice,' he said, picking up his pint. His eyes were alive. 'OK, we're on stage two!'

'Stage three if you count the pub,' Tess said. 'Stage four if you count the train.'

'You're being pedantic,' said Adam. He raised her glass to her mouth. 'Drink up.'

'OK.' He tilted the glass so the liquid slid down her throat, and nodded encouragingly.

'I'm just glad – no offence, I like Meena loads,' he said. 'But I'm just glad we're going back to Claridge's, somewhere we can walk to, not somewhere we have to peg it for the last tube.'

'It's actually pretty central, compared to some places.' Tess was defensive of her old home.

'I know, and it's great,' Adam said. 'Always really loved coming to see you there. But just – I always remember running for the tube and it taking ages, and everything. Always took ages to get anywhere in London.'

'It doesn't –' Tess was going to embark on a long repudiation of this, until she realized that she was supposed to agree with him, now. It was two minutes to the Feathers in Langford from her house. 'Well,' she said, into the momentary silence, 'you're right, staying at Claridge's is definitely going to cut our journey time home. We can stay out as long as we want.'

Adam raised two fingers to the barmaid. 'Two more shots, please.'

'No way,' said Tess.

'Come on,' said Adam, who was definitely enjoying a second wind. 'We're in London, baby! It's my birthday! We're staying at the coolest hotel in the world!'

'Yeah,' said Tess, scrunching up her face. 'We're young, free and single, and ready to mingle!'

'Yeah, that too!' said Adam. The drinks arrived, and he clinked his new shot against hers.

'Cheers,' Tess said. 'Here's to the Ringer.'

'Yep – Tess, thanks,' Adam said, serious for a moment. 'I didn't think it was going to be like this but – it's fun, isn't it?'

'It's always fun, being with you,' Tess told him honestly, and their eyes met fleetingly, and they were silent, amidst the hubbub of the pub. Someone brushed past them; it was as if something changed then.

Adam drew a deep breath. 'Well, you know how I feel about that,' he said, and his voice was hoarse.

He looked directly at her. Tess looked at him, and it was as if they were the only people in that crowded, hot room. 'Can I ask you something?' he said.

After a second, she nodded, her heart hammering.

'What was the Dealbreaker with Will?' he said. 'Can you tell me now?'

Tess groaned, relief coursing through her. 'It's embarrassing.' She cleared her throat, leaning towards him. 'Only if you tell me what the Dealbreaker with Liz was.'

'OK,' he said, blinking heavily, and she knew he was slightly drunk. 'Man, this is evil of you. OK.' He exhaled, and lowered his voice. 'Well . . . she cried.'

'She cried?'

'After we'd –' Adam looked around, to see who was close to them and whether they were listening. 'After we'd had sex. Well, during, really.'

'Oh,' said Tess. 'Like, properly?'

'Yep,' said Adam, sombrely. 'It was awful. Tears streaming down her face. I thought there was something wrong, so I – er, stopped, and she started crying even more, and begging me to carry on so I started again but –' he rubbed the back of his neck – 'it kind of kills the mood. Someone like, sobbing – and not in a good way. While you're trying to . . .'

'Bang them,' Tess said promptly. 'Blimey, did she say why?'

'She said she always did it, especially if she was feeling a bit emotional,' said Adam. 'That's why – sort of why I didn't call her again.'

'You know what?' Tess told him. 'That's fair enough.' He nodded gratefully.

'What about you?'

'What?'

'Come on, Tess,' Adam said. 'You know. What was it with you and Will? What was the Dealbreaker?'

She hesitated, then looked frankly at him. 'Well –' she began. 'He –'

'*Hej!!*' someone yelled behind them, and pushed them to one side, and a band of enthusiastic Swedes, wearing blue and yellow, burst into the tiny room. One of them, a man, breaking free, grabbed Adam by the arms, pulling him away from Tess. '*Hej*, my friend!' he said. 'Good evening! We won!'

'That's great. Won what?' said Adam, stepping back, still staring at Tess, but smiling.

'Yes! Thank you!' the man told him, squeezing his shoulders and sliding past them to the bar, where he merged into an amorphous blob of blue and yellow once more, and shouts of '*Skol!*' rang out.

The two friends, pushed apart, stood looking at each other, and then, as if acknowledging it was ridiculous, it was all ridiculous, they laughed, each mirroring the other.

'Londontown,' Adam said, shrugging his shoulders. He held up his drink again and she touched her glass to his, her adrenalin subsiding. Tess felt heavy with something. Was she drunk? What was happening? Or rather, why wasn't she more surprised? But the moment passed, though things had already changed, into a succession of drinks, of hilarious conversation with excited Swedes – who, it turned out, had won a big football match that afternoon, against Russia – some singing, led by one of the old men in a pork-pie hat, and then being almost bodily turfed out of the pub by the increasingly enraged barmaid.

They walked slowly through Soho in the warm May evening, till they got to Kingly Street. Tess didn't want to get back to the hotel. She wanted to delay the moment; she didn't know why, only that she knew something was in the air, and that this evening would soon be over. And she didn't want it to be.

They stopped under the Liberty stone bridge.

'Do you know where you're going?' said Adam, looking up and around him. 'I don't know where the hell we are.'

'This is Liberty,' said Tess, a little sadly. 'It's my favourite shop.' She gazed up, into the black leaded windows which stared blindly onto the dark street.

'Is it?' said Adam. 'Why?'

Tess had always loved Liberty, because of the fabrics, and the clothes, and the jewellery, and the Art Deco coolness of it all. But there was one reason above all.

'The staircase,' she said. 'It's carved wood and there's a little frog between the first and second floors.'

On their first anniversary, Will had bought her a necklace from there. It was a huge, heavy, show-stopping thing, in cut glass and ribbons, and though she could rarely wear it, she loved it. She swallowed at the thought.

Adam laughed softly as she said this. 'A frog, really?' He gazed down at her. 'T, what's wrong?'

'Nothing,' Tess said, brushing away a tear. 'Just Will. He bought me something here. Stupid idiot.' She hated herself for crying like this; why, when she hadn't thought of Will for weeks?

'Oh, darling,' Adam said, his low voice so kind, so comforting. 'Don't cry.' He put his arms around her. 'Please don't. He's not worth it. He's an idiot. Trust me.'

'I know,' Tess said, wishing she could just stay like this, her head on his shoulder, his arms around hers.

'Why are you still letting him get to you?' His voice was muffled in her hair.

She wasn't, really. It was the image of herself he'd left her with. 'What I really hate him for is –' She swallowed. It was so hard to say, to tell the truth.

'Come on,' he prompted gently. He rubbed her back and she knew, remembered she could tell him everything and anything, ignored the warning bell that was sounding . . .

'I hate him, because he made me feel so unattractive,' she said in a small voice.

'What do you mean?' Adam stood back. He leaned over her, his dark eyes glittering in the dark street. 'He was horrible to you?'

'I was trying to tell you earlier. That was the Dealbreaker. For him. He –' Tess knotted her fingers together and looked down, at the black street. 'He didn't want me. After a few months, he – we didn't – argh.' She winced. 'I don't want to say.'

'It's me,' Adam said. 'Come on. You can tell me anything.'

She looked into his eyes and knew it was true. He nodded,

encouraging. She said, quietly, 'I thought he wasn't into sex. That perhaps it was just what happened to people, you know. We stopped –' She looked up, imploring him to understand. 'I tried – I tried these awful, embarrassing things to get him to want me. Oh, God. And then – now, he's with that – that blonde sex-toy on a stick and I – I'm this cardigan-wearing troll and I feel – I feel . . .'

Emotion flooded over her, emotion and alcohol fumes, and she began to cry. Adam put his finger under her chin, gently.

'You're beautiful,' he said. 'You always have been.' He kissed her cheek, where a tear was rolling down her skin. 'Don't cry, Tess,' he murmured. 'I hate it when you cry.'

She raised her face to his, a question on her lips. He closed his eyes slowly, then opened them. Their faces were millimetres apart. She could feel his breath on her lips, her eyelashes almost touching his skin as she stared at him, at the face she knew so well. She didn't recognize him all of a sudden: she blinked, slowly, closed her eyes and parted her lips.

And he kissed her. His hand pushed her hair away from her face, the way it always used to; she felt his fingers on her scalp, on her skin. His lips on hers, his chest pressed against hers suddenly, as she put her arms around him, under the bridge in the quiet street, and kissed him back.

'I knew that was going to happen,' he said, when he eventually broke away from her. He put his hand on her shoulder, his thumb on her neck. 'This evening, Tess, didn't you?'

That was the thing – she'd forgotten she didn't have to change herself for him, to moderate anything. 'Yes,' she said simply. She reached up, and kissed him again.

'I didn't plan it like this, though,' Adam said. 'I mean –'

'Getting dumped by Francesca so you could come up to town without her,' said Tess, and then she wished she hadn't.

But he said mildly, 'That's weird – that seems a million miles away, now.'

Langford seemed a million miles away too, Tess thought, as Adam took her hand. 'You know which way to go, don't you?' he said, as she crossed Regent Street and led him into Mayfair.

Neither of them knew what was going to happen when they got to Claridge's, but it didn't matter then, there. They walked past the Art Deco Vogue House, into Brook Street.

'It's quiet, isn't it?' Adam said, clutching her hand. 'It's Saturday night, you'd think it'd be busier.'

'I know,' said Tess. 'It's like it's just you and me.'

'Sometimes I think it's always just been you and me,' Adam said. He stopped, and turned to her.

'It has,' said Tess. She said quietly, 'But Adam – us knowing each other so well – that's not a reason.'

'Don't you think so?' He looked at her curiously. 'Ah, I think it is. We know each other so well, we knew this was going to happen, we just needed to get out of Langford for it to happen.'

'That's what you said before,' she told him, putting her hand gently on his cheek. 'All those years ago, and—'

'It was different then, we were babies,' he said, almost impatiently. 'We're grown-up now.'

'Are we?'

'Yes, we are,' he said, bending over and kissing her again. 'Being here – in London –' he squeezed her hand and raised it, to encompass the street, the blinking lights of New Bond Street, the quiet of Hanover Square – 'I don't see you as my oldest friend, that girl I grew up with, who I had that summer fling with years ago, who only wears muddy boots and teaches Jan and Diana the Classics.' He smiled, pulling her towards him. 'You're the girl who's the funniest person I know, who I can tell anything to, who's *real*, not fake, who's so beautiful and she doesn't know it.' He ran a finger down her cheek. 'I can be myself with you, you can be yourself with me.'

That summer fling.

She bit her lip, she didn't know what to say. They walked for a little while, in silence, past great grey townhouses and wrought-iron railings. She felt as if she were in a film, in a dream.

'What if I don't know who I am, though,' she said, smiling weakly. 'If I don't know how to be myself any more?'

'I know,' he said seriously. 'I know you. But it's completely new. I know you.' He kissed her again. 'And I want you. Tess – don't you want me too?'

That was how Adam had persuaded her the first time, all those years ago, in the meadows, after his mother had died. The first time – her first time. She had cried over him for six months, when she realized it *was* just a summer thing, a way to ease the pain he was feeling that could never really be eased. Of course she wanted him; she always wanted him, his intoxicating smile, his ready laughter, his low voice, his dark eyes, his kind heart – but he didn't know her the way he thought he did, because he didn't know just how much he'd hurt her, how he'd rejected her. Adam still thought she was his old, jolly friend, albeit with a nice new haircut, and how could he say that when she didn't know who she was, what she was doing?

They were still walking, they were almost at the hotel. But then, as if confounding her fears, he stopped and said, 'This doesn't have to be a big deal, Tess. But you know I want you.'

'Me too,' she said.

'So – let's just have fun tonight. Don't worry about it.' He breathed out, slowly, watching her tensely, as though he was worried he'd gone too far, and she remembered how good it was to be with him, how much she did want him, how she'd hidden that away. Just for one night . . . just once more . . .

'Yes,' she said, almost urgently. He gripped her hand, and she broke free from his grasp, putting her hands on his face, and kissing him, enjoying him, remembering how good he felt. 'OK, you're right.' She smiled. 'We're grown-ups now, after all, aren't we?'

'Damn right,' Adam said, matching her smile, and they ran up the steps of Claridge's, into the cool, elegant lobby, as the night porter smiled at them indulgently. He probably thinks we've been together for ages, Tess thought. Perhaps he's wondering if tonight's our anniversary.

Perhaps he's not wondering anything at all.

'We've booked a room,' Adam told the concierge behind the desk. 'Adam Smith, one night.'

'Yes, sir,' said the concierge, tapping furiously. 'Let me just see if there are any messages –'

Tess tensed for a moment; fear gripped her, she didn't know why. Adam's warm fingers squeezed hers as they held hands. The phone rang and the concierge, distracted, picked up the keys, and then picked up the phone. 'Hold, please,' he said brusquely. He leaned forward.

'That's all fine,' he said, and Tess relaxed again. 'Room three three eight. Thank you, sir.' He went back to the call and they were alone again, the only other people in the lobby, and it was quiet, but a comforting, reassuring quiet. They smiled at each other like schoolchildren.

In the lift, they sat side by side on the tiny, elegant sofa, holding hands, almost formally, and then Adam leaned over once more and kissed her softly on the lips.

'This is a wonderful night,' he said. 'Darling Tess.'

She smiled at him, her heart swelling with joy.

The doors opened; Adam looked up, and turned to the left. Down the corridor, their feet silent on the plush soft carpet, they walked, until they reached room 338. Tess was nervous suddenly; the perfection of it all, the suddenness too. But, as if he knew, Adam rubbed her back as he fumbled for the key, and the slight touch of his hand calmed her down and she felt a lifting of her mood, a clearing of the clouds. She was here, he was here, it was amazing. They laughed as he struggled with the lock.

'We must look like crazy people, with just these little bags,'

Tess said. 'Everyone else with Louis Vuitton cases for weeks and then us.'

'There's no one else to see us,' said Adam. 'It's just you and me, remember?'

She smiled at him, her hair falling in her face, and he pushed it back and kissed her again as the key turned in the lock and they almost fell into the room.

'Adam?'

In the darkness, a voice.

'Adam, darling?'

There was a rustling sound, as they stood in the doorway, frozen, and then a bedside lamp came on, throwing a soft glow across the room, and revealed Francessca, on the bed in a fluffy towelling robe, her hair glowing in the gloom, her face flushed with sleep. She blinked at them.

'Hi – Tess?'

'Hi,' said Tess, mechanically. 'What are you—'

Adam's voice cut across hers. 'Francesca, what are you doing here?'

Francesca curled a strand of hair around her finger. She looked at Adam, and said slowly, 'I made a massive mistake, darling.' She rubbed her eyes and knelt up on the bed. 'I'm sorry. I got the train up a couple of hours ago. I wanted to tell you, I'm sorry.'

'Francesca –'

There was a catch in her voice. 'Can you forgive me?'

Adam pulled away from the door towards Francesca. He stared at her; suddenly, Tess didn't know what he was thinking. All she knew was, she had to get out of there. Waves of something – of shame, guilt, emotion, love, attraction – were washing over her, but for now there was nothing to be done. *Let's just have fun tonight.* It was the same as always, nothing had changed. Her mind started clicking into gear, flipping over possibilities. She felt for her jacket. Was the key to Meena's still in there? Yes, it was.

At least this time she'd got out before she'd gone in too deep. It would have been a disaster, sleeping with Adam. She cleared her throat.

'Look –' she began. 'I'll take off, then.'

'No,' said Adam, turning towards her. 'T –'

Francesca watched them both, blinking, as if she were waking up little by little. Any moment now, and she would start to wonder . . . Tess shoved her hands into her pockets. 'I'll get a cab to Meena's outside,' she told Adam firmly.

'But it's miles away.'

'It's not,' she said, trying to sound patronizingly sure of herself, when he was right, it was miles away, but she was glad it was miles away, the more distance the better. 'I can't stay here.'

'Yes, you can,' Adam said. Francesca cleared her throat.

'Adam,' Tess said, under her breath, trying to keep her voice steady. 'What are we going to do, share a bed, the three of us? That's just weird.'

Adam shook his head. 'I'll go to Meena's. You stay here, with Francesca. I don't want you –' His hands dropped to his sides, helplessly. He had no claim over her, and he knew it.

'You don't know where it is,' said Tess. 'And she's expecting me to be there, anyway.' She looked up at him imploringly and then stepped a little further into the room. 'Bye, Francesca!' She waved. 'Short but sweet. Speak to you tomorrow.'

'Yes,' said Francesca, smiling at her excitedly. 'I'm sorry about all – all this. I'll talk to you tomorrow. I've been waiting for you for ages! What on earth have the two of you been up to?' She rolled her eyes behind Adam's back, as if they were both complicit in Adam's uselessness, and Tess could have hit her, then.

But it wasn't Francesca's fault, it wasn't anyone's. It was . . . just one of those things.

'It's just one of those things,' she said to Adam, in the doorway again.

'Yes.' He nodded. 'I think you're right. Look –'

'See you when I get back,' Tess told him. His eyes widened. 'When you get back?'

'Yes.' She nodded. 'I'm going to Italy, remember? I'm away for a week.' He looked at her – was it relief in his eyes, or something else? She winced at how much it hurt, and then patted the doorframe, unable to bring herself to touch him. 'I'll talk to you soon, yeah?'

'Um – yeah,' Adam said.

'Adam –' Francesca's voice came from inside the room. 'Aren't you going to put her in a cab, for God's sake? She can't walk the streets on her own at this time of night.'

'I'll be fine,' Tess called out, at the same time as Adam said, 'She says she'll be fine.'

She turned and looked at him. Yep, she was right. He was the same old Adam.

'Thanks,' she said, unable to keep the anger out of her voice, and she walked towards the lift.

'I'll be back in a minute,' she heard him call softly to Francesca, and then he was running after her, down the corridor.

'Leave me alone, Adam,' she told him, opening the heavy door onto the staircase; she didn't want to wait for the lift.

He followed her, as her feet tripped on the stairs. 'Don't go like this, T,' he said. 'This is all a big mistake, I'm sorry –'

She carried on running down the stairs. 'Thanks. I know it is.'

'Hey,' he called down to her, increasing his steps as she was getting away from him. 'This is hard for me as well, you know. I didn't realize she'd be here . . .'

She stopped, on a landing, and looked at him. Both of them were breathing heavily. 'Two girls in one hour is pretty good going, even for you,' she said sarcastically, wishing she could bite her tongue. 'And lucky for you, one of them's waiting all ready for you, naked in a hotel room, and the other one's off, so you don't have to do anything. It's all done for you. Just like it always is.'

'Don't be a bitch, Tess,' Adam said. Her eyes widened and he shook his head. 'Sorry. I don't mean it. Just stop living in the past.' He amended himself. 'Don't – let's not say anything we'll regret.'

'Don't call me a bitch,' she said, venom in her voice. 'And don't say I'm living in the past, Adam. Don't. There are lots of things I could call you, and I don't.'

'OK, go on then,' he said, clenching his teeth. 'You're always right, aren't you? Always bloody right. Tell me.'

'I'm not going to tell you,' she said, turning and running down the stairs again, the endless square spiral – when would she reach the ground, when would she be out of here? They reached the lobby, and a slumbering night guard looked up and smiled as they stormed past him, through the revolving doors, out onto the pavement. Adam caught her by the shoulder, and she cried out in alarm and stumbled against the black railing. He grabbed her, stopped her from falling.

'Sorry,' he said. 'Tess, I didn't mean—'

'You never mean it, do you,' Tess said, wrenching herself out of his grasp and facing him, her eyes blazing. 'You didn't mean to kiss me tonight. You didn't mean to come off your bike. You didn't mean to fuck up your A levels and never hold down a job for more than three months.' She could hear herself, saying these hateful things, but she couldn't stop. 'You didn't mean all sorts of things, but they happened anyway, and no, of *course* you're not responsible, are you? It's never your fault, is it?'

'Go on,' Adam said, and he jammed his hands into his pockets and moved slowly towards her. 'Go on, say it.'

'You didn't mean to sleep with me the first time, but you did.' Her voice grew softer; her throat hurt, she wasn't going to cry. 'You didn't mean to get me pregnant, but you did. You didn't mean to forget on the day I had the abortion, but you

146

fucking did, Adam, *you did*. And you didn't mean to go off with Sally a week later on holiday but you did.' Her voice was cracking. 'Tell, me, Adam. What was the Dealbreaker with me, eh? What was wrong with me? When was the moment – the moment you looked down at me and thought, "Nah, gone off her now, doesn't matter if I treat her like crap."?'

She spat out the words, tears streaming down her face. They dropped on the pavement.

'There wasn't a Dealbreaker with you.'

'Of course there fucking was,' she said, laughing heavily. 'There must –' She wanted to say, there must have been some reason, some reason why you didn't want to be with me, what was it?

'I'm sorry. I'm sorry about it all. About the abortion,' he said, his kind eyes frowning, looking deep into hers. His arms dropped back down to his side. 'I'm sorry I made you go through it alone, I'm really sorry that it happened at all.'

A car lumbered slowly past, breaking the still of the Mayfair night. She stepped away from him.

'Tess –' he called after her. 'Please – please, listen. I'm sorry –' But she ran to the corner of New Bond Street without another word, afraid of what more they might say to each other. And this time he didn't follow her.

A cab swerved violently to the kerb. Tess climbed into it, gave the driver Meena's address, and settled back into the comfortingly hard shell of the seat. She stared out of the window, into the London summer night. She thought it might have started raining, but it was her eyes, brimming and bleary with tears. It was almost exactly thirteen years since that summer, and though it seemed like a lifetime ago, and though Adam had clearly forgotten almost all about it, she had forgotten nothing. She remembered it all.

Thirteen Years Ago

Neither of them knew it was going to happen. She would look back and marvel that she could have woken that day with no idea of what lay ahead of her. That she could start the day as a – a child, really – and end it in Adam's arms, his hands clumsily stroking her hair, the two of them clinging to each other, exhilarated, exhausted.

Her mother was cross with her that day; Tess had accidentally broken a cup, two plates, and a vase, by throwing a spoon at Stephanie over breakfast. It had hit the dresser that stood in the corner of the crowded kitchen. It was bad luck, it wasn't her fault. Well, not all her fault; she wasn't the one who'd started it, it was her sister who'd jabbed the fork into her leg. It wasn't fair being the youngest, it was very unfair, in fact.

'You're nearly eighteen!' her mother had said, her face contorted into an agony of suppressed anger. 'I really, really do not understand what's wrong with you!'

'But she started it! And she's older!'

Her mother was harassed almost to a point past sanity. 'I don't care. I do not care. You should be ashamed of yourself. That was Grandmother's plate, she was given it for her wedding. Broken into a hundred pieces. Are you happy now?' Emily Tennant was shouting at her now, the pent-up anger of the humidity and stultifying heat releasing itself. Her face was red and shiny. A greasy tendril of hair flapped out from behind her ear.

'I'm sorry, Mum,' she said, genuinely contrite in the face of her mother's rage. 'I didn't mean to, and she was the one –'

She was going to say, 'She was the one I was aiming for,' but she halted, not convinced this would be the answer her mother was looking for.

'I've got the Mynors coming round this evening, and the man coming about the curtains. Can't you find something to do today? Because I really don't think I can stand you and your sister going at it all day long.'

'Sure, sure,' she said, watching her mother's tense face in alarm. 'Oh, Mum – I am sorry –'

'Doesn't matter,' her mother said, stifling a sob. 'Just – go away!'

She did, without a backwards glance. She ran to the door, pulled it open, ran out into the sunshine without saying goodbye, her heart heavy, her teenage sense of outrage already melting away into guilt, and sorrow, and a resolve to bring something back for her mother. An ice cream? A book? Her eye wandered as she caught her breath. Diving down the warren of medieval side streets and through a gap in the houses she suddenly caught a glimpse of fields, of the countryside beyond, a flash of enticing green. She would slip quietly through the streets, out through the gap in the ancient city walls, down the stairs to the water meadows. An apple and a book, that was all she needed, she'd pick some flowers for her mother on the way back. She jumped in the air excitedly. Everything was OK again, the memory of Mum's face as she picked the coloured shards of china off the floor but a distant memory, with the extreme callousness of youth.

'Hello there, you. What mischief are you up to now?'

She jumped, and turned around guiltily. 'Adam! My God, you gave me a fright.'

'Exactly.' He smiled, and took her hand from her mouth. 'If you weren't up to something awful,' he said, mock-slapping her fingers, 'you wouldn't be looking quite so guilty. What is it?'

'Nothing,' she said. 'I'm just escaping home, that's all. Mum's furious with me. I've been horrible.'

'I bet you haven't.' There was laughter in his voice, but a note of sympathy too. She heard it. 'I was just off for a walk,' he said. 'Got some reading to do. I was heading down to the water meadows. Um – fancy coming with me?' He looked down at her; he was so tall these days, and she felt so little; when had he grown so much, outstripped her, turned into this tall, broad-shouldered man? Where was the eight-year-old Adam, who could annoy her so much by dressing up in her pink ballet tutu? The last few months, since Philippa had died, had permanently changed him, and it was only now, coming across him by accident, that she saw it clearly. Who was this stranger, practically a grown man, in front of her?

She hesitated.

'I could do with the company,' he said, shrugging.

'Of course,' she said. 'I was going that way anyway.'

'Really?' He smiled. 'Great minds think alike, I suppose.'

'Absolutely,' she said, smiling too, and they set off together as the early morning sun crept up and over the roofs of the town, flickering through the silent streets.

Even today, years later, Tess could remember how much she'd wanted him. So perhaps she shouldn't have let him, but she wanted to. Wanted to feel his arms around her, his body on top of her. To touch him, comfort him, when she didn't know what else to do after what he'd been through. And so when they were lying side by side on the rug he'd brought with him, in silence, listening to the wood pigeons coo dolefully in the trees at the edge of the park, feeling the blazing, lazing summer warmth steal over them, she did not move when he leaned over her, nor was she that surprised.

His hair flopped into his face, shading his features as he hung over her.

'Are you OK?' he said, his hand stroking her leg. She could feel the warmth of his palm on her skin, through her thin cotton dress.

She wiggled a little, her hair fanning out in the grass, and smiled up at him. 'Of course I am. Are you?' She stroked his face, wanting to make everything better, wanting him to feel better.

'Sort of.' His fingers moved more slowly, he was staring down at her. 'Easter, I mean, it seems – a lifetime ago.'

'It was,' she said quietly.

He shook his head, as if he didn't want to remember. Remember everything that had happened afterwards.

At Easter, at her mother's birthday party, only a week before Philippa died, Tess had kissed him, or rather let him kiss her. They had been upstairs in the corridor, just the two of them, as music blared out from the garden and downstairs was filled with old married couples. They had both had a bit to drink, but not loads, and Adam had pulled her out of the corridor into the spare bedroom, pushing her hair back from her forehead, and kissing her passionately, so they fell on the bed and only leapt apart when they heard footsteps on the stairs. She had enjoyed it, even though it should have felt wrong, or weird, this boy who was now a man, her oldest friend. And then Philippa had died, and it had been forgotten, of course, buried in the rush of grief and despair that filled the next few months. She wanted to reach out to him, had wanted to help him. She didn't know how. Until now.

Now, it was curiously undramatic. As if it was totally normal.

She looked up at him again. His expression was strange, not the Adam she knew. And she liked him, this new person.

She didn't know what they were doing; she wasn't sure he knew either, only that it felt right. And that's when Adam kissed her.

He moved her arms so they were above her head, pinning her hands there, so he could run his hands over her body, over her breasts, kissing her stomach, her breast bone, her nipples – she could feel the scratchy hairs on his face, rasping against her skin. She cried out when he pressed down on her.

'I'm sorry,' he whispered, stroking her face. 'Oh, Tess. I love you, Tess.'

She loved him too, she always had done. He wouldn't let her move until he came up for air and they moved together, and she opened his trousers and took him in her hand and stroked him till he groaned. And when he finally pushed inside her, it hurt, but only for a moment, and then it felt great. As if he was plugging something, filling her up. They hardly made any movement in the field; he rocked his hips urgently against hers, and she welcomed him in, till he came inside her, his cry strangled as if she was hurting him. Then silence.

And it was as if she had been snapped back to reality and they were two teenagers again, one in a half-undone dress, her knickers in the grass, the other with his trousers discarded, his pants around his knees, breathing heavily against each other, rocking again, just the two of them, as his breathing subsided and she stared up at him.

'Hello,' he said, pushing the hair off her forehead.

'Hello,' she answered. 'Adam –'

'I've been wanting to do that for a while now,' Adam said, with an attempt at composure, and then a smile broke out over his face, the one she knew so well, and he shifted his weight from on top of her, and covered her mouth with kisses.

It was scorching hot, deadly quiet in the grass where they lay. She was wondering what they had just done. It felt so private, just between them. She couldn't have imagined, have foreseen, the result of that one summer's day.

'You and me –' he said, stroking her body with one hand, running his fingers up to her neck, over her breasts, between her legs.

She rolled over so she was on her side, facing him. 'Me and you.'

'You and I, really,' Adam said, and she leaned over him, and kissed him.

'Know-it-all,' she said, in between kisses.

'I mean –' he said, almost shy. 'Can we do that again?'

'Now?' She laughed softly.

'Now . . . and later on. And tomorrow.' He smiled his beautiful Adam smile.

'I'd like that,' she said.

'Me too,' he said. 'Or rather, and I.' He was lying on the ground, looking up at her, a curious expression on his face. 'Thank you,' he said, and he kissed her fingers. 'It's – you make me feel better, make me think it's going to be OK. Thank you.'

She should have listened to him, properly listened, beyond the sweet words and the easy smile. She should have remembered what Adam was like but why would she? He was her friend, he was in unimaginable pain, and she wanted to be with him. She always had. By the end of the summer, she was nearly eighteen, and she was meeting Adam nearly every day, sometimes at his house where Philippa's things were still everywhere – her tagine dishes, her embroidered kaftans, a hair clip, piles of her books. Or they would go down to the water meadows. They didn't talk; they sank frantically into each other's bodies, Adam with an urgency, a desire to forget that Tess soon found disturbing, because she realized she could not reach him, could not help him, and that this, whatever it was, was not helping him, really, either.

153

After that first time, they used condoms. But it was too late. Before she went to university that autumn, Tess had found out that she was pregnant. And she knew exactly when it had happened. She didn't tell anyone, except Adam, and only when she had booked herself into the clinic for an abortion. She told him, standing in the garden of Philippa's cottage, the late September sun shining on her face, and watched with a numbing sickness as something she supposed was panic crossed his face, to be replaced by relief.

'It's fine,' she had told him. 'I'm sorting it out.'

He had moved towards her, but she kept her distance. The relief on his face was like a knife through her heart. But what had she wanted him to do? Sweep her off the ground, tell her he was here for her, they should stay together, keep the baby? No, no way. She was eighteen and she was going to university; her life was ahead of her, and she had to do this, have it taken care of, and then go to London, leave Langford.

It was such a long time ago now, her memories of it were obscured, as if slatted blinds fell across long parts of that summer and autumn, blocking out some bits, highlighting others. The waiting room at the clinic was a soft pale pink – she remembered that and felt it was strangely thoughtless, pink for a girl, blue for a boy. Why couldn't it have been a more clinical colour, a sensible grey or a pale mint green? She had spoken to her mother the next day, from the telephone in her halls of residence, and she remembered her mother chatting inanely away about Adam and how good it was he'd gone on holiday. She had no idea about any of it. Tess still remembered creeping back upstairs to bed, curling up as tightly as possible, thinking perhaps she would never, ever get over the misery she was feeling now. After a few days she told herself she was stupid, of course she would. But she never quite did. That summer never quite left her.

*   *   *

154

The cab was passing Clapham Common, a ghostly grey expanse of nothing, the leaves of the trees black in the weird yellow light from the street lamps. Tess stirred. Perhaps that was how she felt about Adam now, too. Memories that were distorted, that stretched too far back for there ever to be a clean slate between them, an honest friendship.

She heard his voice again, breaking into her thoughts, telling her that she was living in the past. 'You're right, I have been,' Tess whispered to herself. 'But at least I've *got* a past. And a future.' She lifted her chin, staring out of the window, narrowing her eyes, determined not to cry again. It still hurt her so much when she remembered.

PART TWO

'I'm only thinking of my pet theory about Miss Honey-church. Does it seem reasonable that she should play so wonderfully, and live so quietly? I suspect that one day she will be wonderful in both. The watertight compartments in her will break down, and music and life will mingle. Then we shall have her heroically good, heroically bad – too heroic, perhaps, to be good or bad.'

A Room with a View, E.M. Forster

CHAPTER FOURTEEN

No one had told Tess about the jasmine in Rome. All over the city, just before June, it bloomed, sparkling white on green against the old rose-pink buildings, like fairy lights, gleaming in the moonlight of the quiet streets, throwing an invisible cloak of perfume over the city. Everywhere she went, the faint, sweet smell of jasmine hung in the air; sometimes they would turn a corner and it would hit them again, the wall of an old palazzo covered in it. The scent was intoxicating, it was almost spicy, not too heavy, absolutely delicious. It was not like anything else, anything at all, it was fresh and seductive; and she was transfixed by it.

And so, one Monday afternoon when the jasmine was just unfurling, a group of weary travellers arrived in Rome, led by none more weary than Tess herself. The minibus, which had met them at the airport and weaved through the afternoon traffic, along the ancient Appian Way, past the ruins of the Baths of Caracalla, through the old ochre walls of the city, now disgorged its cargo onto a shady street in Trastevere. It was that most unwelcome time of day in European cities for the traveller, when evening has not yet arrived and the heat of the day is still immense. Coupled with the fumes and sweat, and the sun still beating down, it feels as if the cool of night-time will never come.

Limbs aching from the cramped bus and from lack of sleep, Tess clambered off first, waving each of her fellow passengers out as she counted them. 'Eight, nine. Ten, including me.' Someone tapped her arm. 'Yes, Carolyn?'

'Tess, dear. Is breakfast included at the hotel?'

On the relatively short journey from the airport Carolyn Tey had asked when they would arrive, how hot it would be, and whether she needed to dress for dinner. Tess clutched her copy of *Orgoglio e Pregiudizio* and counted to three. She said, calmly, 'I'm sure it is, but why don't we double-check once we're inside. Now, if you'd like to follow me –'

'Oh, dear, cobbles,' said Carolyn. 'I do hate walking on cobbles. I keep thinking I'm just about to fall over. Don't you know what I mean?' Tess nodded, trying to look interested. 'I don't mean you, dear,' said Carolyn. 'You're much too young to worry about that sort of thing. Andrea, isn't it funny, walking on cobbles?'

Andrea Marsh, who looked hugely offended at being identified as 'old enough to worry about falling over on cobbles' nodded coldly, and walked on, followed by Ron, who was fixing his cap firmly to his head. It looked like a relic from a driving club in the fifties.

'Dear, dear, dear me,' came a mellifluous voice from behind Tess. 'How far, do you know, my dear, to *l'hotel*?'

'It's around the corner,' said Tess, struggling to keep it together.

'Oh, my,' said Jacquetta Meluish, fanning herself. 'Oh, these pretty streets, through which we walk.' They were twenty metres from the bus. 'We should, I daresay, stick together? Lest one of our *gruppa* become unencumbered.'

Jacquetta had not vouchsafed a word during the previous two-month course, but in the ninety minutes since their arrival on Italian soil had transformed into a living breathing expert on all things Italian. Tess looked wildly about her.

'Albergo Watkins,' Jan called, from the front. 'Is that what it's called? I thought it was supposed to have the moon or something in the title.'

They were gathered around the huge, panelled front door, which had two enormous disc handles attached to it. Stuck on the front was a chipped sign:

Albergo Watkins
For stay pleasant

*

'It's only got one star,' Andrea said suspiciously. 'I thought we were staying in a four-star?'

'Oh, no, no,' said Tess. 'I don't think that's a star. I think it's . . . an . . . asterisk.' She nodded, trying to convey an authority she did not feel. 'It's decorative. Not indicative. Ha-ha!' She laughed semi-hysterically and knocked on the door. 'Well, let's see what they've done with Albergo di Luna, shall we?'

The door creaked open; they filed in, blinking in the sudden dark. Leonora and Diana were the last in. Looking at the man holding open the door, Tess blinked again.

'*Buona sera,*' she said. 'Are you –' she looked down – 'Signor Capelli?'

The man was not friendly. '*No,*' he said. '*Signor Capelli e . . . Kaput.*' He clapped his hands together, in a gesture of alarming finality. '*Benvenuti.* Well-come. Ladies.' He spoke English slowly, with great emphasis. 'To. Our Hotel. Ladies.'

Ron cleared his throat. 'Er – hello. Excuse me.'

'Ah. And *Signore.*' The man bowed.

'What happened to Albergo di Luna?' Tess asked, feeling more and more as if she were in a strange modern play.

'*Caput.*'

'Yes, but –' Tess said, wishing she were not being watched by the pupils of the Classical Civilization course. 'I booked ten rooms – here –' she batted her hand against a piece of paper – 'at the Albergo di Luna. Not at the Albergo Watkins, whatever this place is.'

'Is the same.'

'What?' said Tess.

'*Nuovo . . . com'e si dice . . .* It is new owner. New name.'

A large, fat fly flew right in front of Tess's face; she brushed it away.

'Oh, dear,' said Diana Sayers. 'I do so desperately need the *loo*, Tess. Could you ask –'

'So do we have the rooms?' Tess said, ignoring her with a stab of guilt.

With the illogicality she had forgotten about in Italy, the atmosphere suddenly changed. The man clapped his hands again, this time with a smile. 'But of course!' He clasped Tess's fingers. 'Welcome to new hotel!'

'Er –' said Tess. 'Thanks!'

The ladies – and Ron – around her heaved a sigh of relief. The fly buzzed past Tess's ear this time. She batted it again, trying not to get irritated. 'Right, then. Let's get the bags out of the van and sign in – and see our rooms, OK?'

'Yes, yes,' said the man in soothing tones, as if these were dull, bourgeois concerns. 'I show you rooms now, yes? And bags come in moments.' Much to Tess's secret delight, he now clapped his hands again, and at this command a youth appeared, incongruously attired in a too-large bellboy outfit, and scuttled out into the street.

'I am Pompeo,' announced the man, in much the same tones as Kirk Douglas in *Spartacus*. 'Welcome, come with me, to our hotel.'

Two flights up, with the ladies and Ron trailing behind him, Pompeo flung open a door. Striding into a dark room, he stood in front of a shuttered window, and gestured towards it with the back of his hand.

'And now,' he said, like a magician with a rabbit in a hat. 'Hello to Roma.'

He leaned over, and pushed the shutters open – the wooden slats swung away, and the light flooded in; a row of buildings

162

beyond them, rose-coloured and slathered in jasmine, green and yellow rooves nestling in the afternoon sun; a white Baroque church in the distance, and there, just through a gap, the trees fringing the green Tiber river, and next to it, the Castel Sant' Angelo and the cypress trees, black in the afternoon sun. Tess leaned out and breathed in and the stress, the strain of the last few days seemed to melt away. She could smell the jasmine, she could even smell coffee, something sweet on the air. Outside on the street, two men were arguing, in Italian, and even that to her, now she was here, sounded sweet.

'Is OK?' Pompeo asked.

She turned around; she was smiling. 'It is more than OK. It is lovely. Thank you.'

As Tess brushed her hair later that evening, looking in the mirror, she sang, quietly happy. She was here, and she was determined to enjoy herself. London seemed like a bad dream. Francesca's beautiful face, her ravishable body, Adam's expression; all gone. That miserable cab ride to Balham that had cost her thirty-five pounds; sleeping on the sofa in the tiny sitting room of her old flat, like a stranger, the dry papery toast Meena had made her for breakfast when she'd arrived back, to find this snivelling wreck of a girl in her bed. Tess's misery hanging over her like the clouds outside on that grey morning – all gone. Her hangover, her confusion, her volatile sense of self-worth, which should never, ever again be linked to whether some man found her attractive or not! – all gone. She was in Rome! It was time to put all that behind her, to live a little, live her own life, instead of either living through Will, as she had done in London, or living the life of an eighty-year-old afraid of getting a chill as she had been doing since she moved back to Langford. The scent of jasmine came to her again, through the open window. She laid down her brush and stepped back, looking at herself. She touched some dark lipgloss to her lips and stared into the mirror. There were circles under her eyes, brown and smudged.

They were downstairs, waiting for her, a slice of middle England in the heart of Italy, and what she really wanted to do was run away from them. She wanted to wander by herself through the city, sit in a little restaurant with a *pizza bianca*, a glass of red wine and breathe out gently, then go to bed and sleep for hours, possibly days.

No, she told herself. That's no good. You're here, you made the decision to come here, now get on with it. But lurking in the back of her mind was the thought that had been there since she'd left Adam on Saturday night. That she had made a mistake in moving back to Langford, that she was trapped in a stasis of her own making, old before her time, unattractive, closed off to the world. The image of Francesca on the bed haunted her. She was so attractive, so sexy, she looked like a girl who knew what she wanted, knew how to fall in love, how to break hearts and how to inveigle her way into hotel rooms. Tess was not like that, she knew it, and though kissing Adam had woken her from her chintzy, tea-shop slumber, his almost instant rejection of her had sent her crashing back down to earth with a cold, hard bump.

Tess adjusted her pale blue linen dress and pulled her mushroom-coloured shawl over her shoulders, picked up her bag and turned back to face herself. The girl in the mirror watched impassively. Her dark blue eyes were grave. Outside, she could hear Ron saying, 'Yes, nearly time to go, I did say I'd be here on time,' rather loudly. It made her smile. The eyes smiled too. She nodded at her reflection, squared her shoulders and went out of the sunshine-filled room, shutting the door behind her.

CHAPTER FIFTEEN

There were ten of them. Tess mentally divided them into two groups, Older and Younger, though she had read the Age Discrimination Act when she joined Langford College and knew thinking like this was illegal. The Older group consisted of Diana Sayers, Carolyn Tey, Andrea Marsh, Leonora Mortmain, Jan Allingham and Jacquetta Meluish (who had now told everyone that she'd studied at the British Institute in Florence when she was A Young Gel).

The Younger were the two girls – well, women – around Tess's age, Liz from the deli and Claire Cobain. They were much less trouble than the Older. On the flight to Rome, Tess had found out that Liz had moved to Langford only nine months ago, having left her job as a theatrical agent. She was reading scripts freelance, as well as working at Jen's Deli. Claire was on a sabbatical from work. She was reading *Eat Pray Love* and *Men Who Can't Love: How to Recognize a Commitmentphobic Man* (she made copious notes in the back of her paperback edition).

And then there was Ron, the only man.

For their first meal in Italy, Tess had picked a little pizzeria not far from the hotel, in the heart of Trastevere. She didn't expect it to be a late night, because Tuesday, their first full day in Rome, was going to be a long one: the Forum and the

Colosseum. As they walked through the quiet backstreets in a little crocodile, Tess – still determined to enjoy herself – listened, with growing amusement, to the power play unfolding behind her.

'I haven't been to Rome for years and years,' said Carolyn Tey happily, as she trotted next to Leonora Mortmain, who was walking slowly but surely, magnificently upright, with a stick. 'Isn't it lovely?'

'Of course, I've been here fairly recently,' said Jacquetta unnecessarily. 'John and I have some very old friends who live here.' She sighed. '*He's* a professor at the university, and *she's* absolutely wonderful, a painter. She had an affair with Francis Bacon, you know.'

'Really?' said Diana Sayers, doubtfully. 'Are you sure?'

'Oh, yes! He was absolutely mad about her. Used to draw her. *Naked*.'

'That is fascinating,' said Leonora Mortmain neutrally.

'I know,' said Jacquetta. 'But I haven't seen them since . . .' She trailed off. John had disappeared somehow, whether by design or accident, permanently or temporarily Tess didn't know, and Jacquetta was rather mysterious about it.

'I spent quite a lot of time in Rome when I was a student,' said Ron, waiting till the last moment to stake his claim. 'So of course I know it quite well.' He looked nonchalantly around. 'Very nice to be back.'

'Well, for me there's nothing like Rome in summer,' said Jacquetta, firmly.

'Me neither,' said Carolyn, somewhat uncertainly.

'I haven't been to Rome since my honeymoon,' said Jan, catching up with Tess. 'So I must say this is extremely exciting! And I'm hungry. Tess, what's on the menu for dinner tonight?'

'Pizza,' said Tess. 'Proper Roman pizza.'

'Oh,' said Jan, trying to mask the disappointment in her voice. 'How extremely nice.'

'Trust me,' said Tess, laughing. 'You'll love it. It's not like any pizza you've had before.'

They were walking down a narrow cobbled street, flanked by two-and three-storey buildings in orange and ochre. Red geraniums in window boxes hung precariously from iron holders, the jasmine ran riot everywhere, its dark green leaves the colour of the shutters. People were coming alive for the evening, the shops were open again. Men stood on street corners, snugly buttoned up in padded Husky jackets, the Romans' idea of what temperature constitutes warmth, and the Britons', being two completely different things. They passed two men talking animatedly, one jabbing his index finger upwards, precisely and with great force, his mouth wide open as he described some great drama while his companion nodded in world-weary agreement.

A red Vespa had been left against a wall just past them; a young man, a cloud of black hair framing his handsome face, came out of a house and swung one leg over the machine. He looked at Tess, his dark eyes neither questioning nor rejecting, he just stared at her, and then rode off, veering away from an old lady carrying some blue plastic bags down towards them.

'What's down there?' Jan asked Tess. 'It seems to come to an end.' Tess came to with a start and followed Jan's pointing finger.

'Down there? The Tiber,' she said, happily. 'We cross into the historic centre, it's called the Centro Storico – there, across the Ponte Sisto. That's how we'll get to the Forum tomorrow.'

'So we're not in the centre?' said Jan, sounding rather disapproving. 'Oh.'

'Yes, that's a shame, I hope we don't have to walk *too* much,' said Carolyn. She turned to Jacquetta, who looked rather unsure.

'We are much more centrally placed than if we'd stayed in an hotel by the Forum, or the train station,' said a voice behind

Tess. Leonora Mortmain waved her stick at them, and went on, 'In fact, in Trastevere – literally, "across the Tever", the Roman name for the Tiber, we are actually in one of the better areas.'

No one said anything to this, but Liz and Claire, the more polite rear of the crocodile, said, 'Oh!' and smiled in gratitude. The others did not.

'Well,' hissed Jan, stomping beside Tess, as they turned into a little piazza where there was an awning with the sign '*La Primavera*'. 'I still really have no idea what *she's* doing here, Tess, do you?'

Tess smiled and nodded non-committally which, over the next few days, would become almost second nature to her. As the waiter appeared, a tall, genial man with a pointy beard, she said hello and uttered the phrase with which, again, she was to become extremely familiar.

'Ho una prenotazione – per dieci persone.'

'Yes,' said the waiter, ushering them back outside, where there was a long table set; under a vine-covered awning. 'A booking for ten persons. Is here.'

'Oh, it's so marvellous!' said Jacquetta, clapping her hands. 'Look at the dear little pots hanging above the oven! I'm in heaven!'

'Where's the loo, Tess dear?' said Andrea.

The waiter smiled at Tess, almost sympathetically.

'Jan, *you* go here, dear.'

'No, I don't mind, honestly, Diana. *You* go here. My hip is almost fully recovered and if I start to feel a twinge, I can just get up and move around.'

'Oh. Right. Now, Carolyn, where are *you* sitting?'

Tess had to agree with Jan; she, too, had no idea what Leonora Mortmain was doing here. Though her name had been on the list since February, Tess had never really thought that she would actually come. She wasn't someone you could imagine in any other setting than that of Langford, with her black clothes, slow gait, imperious bearing, cold stare. Yet here she was, in a backstreet pizzeria in Trastevere, sitting next to Tess (though Tess knew that was because no one else would sit next to her), gnarled, beringed hands clutching her ebony cane, expression set, her mouth almost exactly a straight line.

Tess realized two things: that she had never really had a conversation with Leonora Mortmain, not since she was a teenager, and that she was much older than she'd thought, close up, as it were. She was so incongruous, here, even amongst this gathering. As the fluster of sitting down eased and the group arranged itself, she turned to the old lady and smiled, in a 'well, here we are!' way, but Mrs Mortmain blinked slowly, looked down and then up, totally ignoring her. With a heavy heart, Tess wondered ignobly if she'd have to sit next to her for every meal. It was going to be a long week if that were the case.

After they had ordered the meal (and after Jacquetta had asked for an Italian menu rather than an English one, saying she actually found it easier to understand the original than the translation) and after the wine had been put on the tables, the mood relaxed somewhat. No one was sure who was to play what role yet, as is always the way with holidays; and though Tess was their leader, she was young enough to be their daughter.

Diana, who had earlier snapped at Andrea about the room allocation, turned to her and said, 'I've been meaning to ask, Andrea – did you ever make that trip to Norfolk Lavender when you were visiting your sister?'

And Andrea, very much mollified, said, 'Oh, thanks for remembering, Diana. Well, no –' turning to Tess's end of the table with what could only be described as a snarl. 'It was when the campaign was keeping me so busy, so I rather had to rush back.'

'What a shame,' said Diana, loudly.

Ignoring this, Leonora Mortmain turned slowly and said to Tess, 'Was your mother a fan of Thomas Hardy?'

'Um, I don't know,' said Tess, alarmed. 'Why?'

'Your name,' said the old woman slowly. 'I should have thought that was obvious from my question. Excuse me.' She moved her glass away from her neighbour's and took a sip, oblivious to her – it was Jan – look of scorn.

'Oh,' said Tess, enlightened. 'Well, I'm called Tessa, not Tess. I hate *Tess of the D'Urbervilles*, actually.'

'Really?' Leonora swivelled towards her.

'Yes,' said Tess. 'Total drip, if you ask me.'

'A drip?' said Leonora, as if she'd never heard the word before. 'What do you mean?'

'I mean I never liked her. I don't know why schoolgirls are always swooning about her and her horrible life. It's like Melanie versus Scarlett in *Gone with the Wind*. Who wants to be Melanie?'

'That novel,' Leonora told her sternly, 'is not a book with which I am familiar.'

Tess sighed inwardly. If Leonora Mortmain thought *Gone with the Wind* was a bit fresh, she'd better not ask her what she thought of *Lace*, let alone *Life with my Sister Madonna*, which she and Francesca had recently devoured. 'I mean that I don't want to be like her. Girls shouldn't want to be like her,' she said. 'They should want to be like –' she searched for inspiration – 'Well, like Jane Eyre. She was independent, she fought for herself in a time when that was almost impossible. Well, perhaps you'd want to be a bit cheerier than Jane Eyre, she did get married in grey, after all.' Leonora eyed her with something approaching alarm. 'Tess of the D'Urbervilles –' she dropped her hands to her lap – 'she just lets things happen to her,' she said.

'Yes, I see what you mean,' Leonora Mortmain nodded. 'I do,' she added quietly. 'How interesting.' She had large hands for such a small woman. Her long fingers played with the bread in front of her, squashing it into the oilcloth covering

170

the table. 'You say that a woman should live for herself, not in the shadow of others.'

Tess looked at her. 'Yes,' she said, wondering what she meant. 'Though I admit, sometimes it's hard to know whether you're doing the right thing in going for it, or simply being pig-headed, whether you'll ruin everything.'

'What does your friend Adam think about that?' asked Leonora Mortmain.

Tess was genuinely startled. She put her wine glass down on the table and held it steady, as if a tremor had just disturbed them. 'Adam?' she said. 'No idea, why should it m-matter what Adam thinks?'

The old woman was watching her, and there was something indefinable in her eyes. Tess heard herself, and realized she must have sounded rude. 'Well,' Leonora Mortmain said. 'It must be interesting, for the pair of you, having grown up together, with the same passion for the Classics. You may recall I gave your friend a scholarship to that effect.'

'Oh. Yes, of course,' said Tess warily, thankful again that it hadn't been her who'd been so blessed, for Leonora Mortmain's behaviour towards Adam had been bizarre. She had closely followed – and had never been pleased with – his progress through the excellent public school he had been sent to and when, after his mother died, Adam had given up on university she had been actively rude to him. She had written to him, angrily severing all ties. Tess remembered one afternoon that summer at Adam's house, the clutter of Philippa's uncleared life around them, lying on the floor naked together, breathing heavily. She had pulled a shower of papers onto the floor with them, one of which was this letter. He had told her what was in it, smiling ruefully, and they had laughed at the spitefulness, the pointlessness of it: what business was it of hers? He'd lost his mother! Why should he care what old Mrs Mortmain thought?

'My point,' Leonora Mortmain was saying, 'is that you,

with your ability, have risen further than Adam, with his. And given his gift for the Classics, it seems a little strange. He has never left Langford, and you have. He has never done anything which—'

Tess interrupted her. 'Mrs Mortmain, I'm afraid –' She saw Adam's kind face, his ruffled hair, his tall frame as he ambled beside her, and she couldn't bear it. 'He is my best friend,' she said. The old woman lowered her lids and looked at her. There was a pause.

'Again, I see what you mean,' said Leonora Mortmain. 'You are rather like me. I have thought that before.' Her hands fiddled in her handbag with the little book she always carried around, a slim old volume in faded buttercup cloth.

Tess looked at the book, to see what it was, but Mrs Mortmain snapped her bag shut in a fury. 'Like me?' Tess said, collecting herself, trying not to sound horrified. When she and her sister had been little, they used to play a game: who is most like Mrs Mortmain. It was designed to scare the other one as much as possible. If Stephanie could hear this conversation now, she'd laugh her socks off.

Tess was horrified, but merely said, 'Oh! Oh, really.'

'Yes,' Leonora Mortmain said calmly, but she did not elaborate further. One hand was still clutching the cane; with the other, she smoothed her red paper napkin over her lap, as if it were finest linen. 'Did you know his mother? Philippa?'

'Yes, of course,' said Tess, surprised. 'I grew up next door to her.'

'You went to school with her, did you not?' Leonora Mortmain licked her lips, her eyes focused on something far away in her mind. 'Ah, yes, you did.'

Tess looked at her. 'No, Mrs Mortmain – I grew up with her son. Adam is my age.'

'I know that,' Leonora Mortmain said crossly, as if Tess had just insulted her. 'Of course I know that. Please – give me some more water, if you would.'

Somewhere, a church bell rang, a twanging, strange sound, and the first of the pizzas arrived, scented with thyme and oregano, and the party relaxed after the rigours of the day. And then someone cleared their throat, loudly.

'Well, cheers, everyone,' said Ron, half-standing up, a little awkwardly. 'Here's to – the holiday!' and they all – apart from Leonora Mortmain – raised their glasses, and so the moment passed.

But later that night, as Tess was lying awake in bed with the shutters a little open, watching the black shadow of the trees play out against the silver light on the wall, she remembered the conversation. How strange Mrs Mortmain was. She, Tess, reminded her of herself! How awful. She pressed her hand to her heart, it must be indigestion, she told herself. OK, it was awkward between them, but she would never, ever stand by and listen while anyone was rude about Adam. Especially Leonora Mortmain. He was her oldest friend. And there, in the darkness, she closed her eyes and thought of him, how much she loved him and wanted to protect him. And suddenly everything else that had been worrying her seemed many, many miles away. Which it was. And a good time to put it all behind her. Which it was. Finally, in that strange room in a strange Roman hotel, Tess slept.

CHAPTER SIXTEEN

On that first morning in Rome, as she led her group across the Ponte Sisto, the bridge that led from Trastevere into the heart of the city, Tess thought of Mr Eager in *A Room with A View*, quoting the *Punch* cartoon. 'What did we see in Rome?' an American child asks her father. 'Oh, yeah. Guess Rome was where we saw the yellow dawg.'

It was a hot, cloudless day. Listless Senegalese men spread fake designer bags out on rugs, or threw spinning holographic circles up into the air and caught them, mesmerizing a small group of Italian children. The river sliding slowly by below the bridge was a soupy grey colour, fringed with trees, shredded plastic bags caught in the branches and rustling in the wind. In the distance, she could see black pines and the white marble of St Peter's and across the bridge lay the heart of the greatest empire ever, and to her the most beautiful city on earth.

She had spent a happy month here when she was at university, and she still remembered it well; she wanted the others to love it as much as she did. But she was too busy making sure Jan and Carolyn weren't too far ahead, and that Leonora Mortmain hadn't fallen too far behind, that they were going in the right direction, that everything was in place, this first morning of her first teaching holiday.

'Up there is the Vatican. And the Castel Sant' Angelo,' she said, pointing upstream. 'That's where Tosca threw herself off.'

'Oh!' squawked Jan. 'How horrible!' She shuddered.

'It didn't *really* happen,' said Jacquetta graciously. 'Don't worry.'

They were over the other side of the bridge. Tess clapped her hands. 'We're heading into the centre now, and going through the old Jewish Ghetto. The streets are pretty confusing, so we need to stick together,' she told them, feeling like a nursery school teacher. 'No wandering off and looking in windows at anything. We'll never find each other. OK?'

'Yes,' they all chorused. 'Right, let's go.'

They were walking towards a ruined stack of white marble pillars at the end of the road, the remains of the Teatro di Marcello. 'This is what I love about Rome,' Tess said. 'You can walk along a normal street and right slap bang in the middle is a theatre built by Julius Caesar.'

'Wow,' breathed Liz, standing next to her. 'That's amazing.'

It was amazing, Tess thought. She patted Liz on the arm, and cut behind the theatre, the rest of the group following her in the sunshine as they threaded their way towards the Capitoline Hill.

There are people who say the Forum is the greatest archaeological site there is, and Tess was one of them. For her, it wasn't that it was the best-preserved – it wasn't, as anyone who's been there could tell you. A great deal of imagination is required to put yourself there, in the shoes (or sandals) of a young senator in Imperial Rome, hurrying along the Via Sacra on his way to the Curia, the Senate House through the busy Forum, its streets stuffed with the booksellers and soldiers, slaves carrying litters, merchants of all kinds hawking their wares, the food stalls bursting with delicacies from all corners of the empire. Today though, the pillars of the great temples are often all but demolished, grass grows over the house where the Vestal Virgins lived, stones lie randomly about, hardly anything is marked, tourists stand around in bemusement, not quite sure what they should be looking at but – but . . .

'If you apply a little imagination,' Tess told her group, gathered at the Rostra at the far end of the Forum, 'you can see it all. Here,' she said, looking around her and smiling, because she was so glad to be there, 'is where Mark Antony spoke about Julius Caesar, after he'd been stabbed to death by his own colleagues, on his way to the Senate House. Close your eyes.' She did the same. 'Just close your eyes and imagine.'

She could see it in her mind's eye, as clearly as she ever could. She opened her eyes again; they were looking at her, slightly bemused.

'I think I've got something in my contact lens,' Andrea said, after a pause.

'OK,' said Tess, climbing off the stone on which she had been standing.

'I can imagine it,' Claire said, eagerly. 'Only – it's a bit like *Gladiator*.'

'That's fine!' said Tess, pleased. 'Better than nothing.'

'I can too, then,' said Ron.

'These weren't ruins,' Tess said. 'These were temples to wealth and prosperity. Like sky-scrapers in New York. Or stately homes in Britain.' She put up her hand to shield her face from the sun, which was rising higher in the sky. 'Come over here . . .'

They walked behind the temple of the Vestal Virgins, overgrown with wild pink roses, to the edge of the Forum, where the Colosseum rose up in the distance.

'Look at the Arch of Titus. It shows the slaves carrying the huge menorah from the Temple of Jerusalem. No one knows what happened to it, it was the holiest object in the temple and it was vast, ten feet wide – and where is it now?'

'Where is it now?' Diana repeated blankly.

'Don't know,' Tess said softly. They breathed in, in awe. 'No one does. It disappeared when Rome was sacked by the Goths. But it must be somewhere.'

'It's hidden in the Vatican,' said Ron, nodding definitely. 'Read a book about it a couple of years ago.'

'Wow,' said Jan. 'Really?'

'Oh, yeah,' said Ron, as Andrea looked at him in admiration and Leonora Mortmain turned away in annoyance. 'If you knew some of the stuff those people had nicked over the years ... Oh, yeah.'

'Someone's been reading too much *Da Vinci Code*,' said Diana, not unkindly.

'No smoke without fire, Diana,' Ron said snappishly, jumping off the edge of the mound of grass on which he was standing, next to the great arch. 'No smoke without fire.'

It was in the Campo dei Fiori that it happened. At the north end, where they were sitting having coffee and tea, weary from a day's traipsing around a city in a way that no twenty-mile run could match. Leonora Mortmain looked exhausted, and sat quietly in the shade, her wide-brimmed hat hiding her face, a cup of tea by her side. Even Jacquetta was a little subdued, though she still managed to tell several people who were listening that Giovanni, a very dear friend of her and John, had lived on the other side of the Campo. The fruit and vegetable stalls that crowd into the square in the early morning were packed up and gone, a few desultory oranges and strips of wet lettuce on the ground the only sign that it had been there.

Drinking her lemonade, suddenly Tess remembered that the eastern side of the square had some ruins of another theatre, the Theatre of Pompey, which was where Julius Caesar had been stabbed in 44BC. She couldn't recall exactly where they were though, or even if they were visible to the naked eye these days. Looking at the dishevelled and tired group, she knew she couldn't ask them to wander over there on the off chance.

'I'm just going to look for something,' she said, getting up, the blister on her foot throbbing as she did. 'I'll only be a minute. Stay here.'

They all nodded mutely, like children, and Tess walked swiftly through the busy square, filled with tourists, Italians lounging having coffee, walking their dogs, the queue outside the bakery as long as ever. She turned off, onto a little square which was called the Piazza del Biscione. She was sure the foundations of the theatre were here.

Suddenly, there was chaos. She was flung by what seemed like a huge force, against a wall, and felt a sharp scraping pain on her right arm as she did. She looked up, totally disorientated, as a moped sped past her, followed by a dark-haired man running after it, shouting and swearing.

'Aspetta! Aspetta! Uno ladro, aiuto!'

He bumped into her as she stood up, and ricocheted off her, so that she fell against the wall again, crying out in pain. The moped had disappeared. An Italian lady appeared from the square, also running, out of breath. She shook her fist at the young man and they both shouted at each other, asking questions. He scratched his head, she waved her hand in the direction the bike had taken. A crowd of idle onlookers gathered. Tess gripped her arm and stood up, leaning against the wall and wincing, and the man turned to her and much to her surprise, said in an American accent, 'Hey. Are you OK?'

'Yes,' Tess said. 'Just my arm – ouch.'

He took her hand and twisted her arm towards him, while the woman looked on.

'What happened?' Tess said, screwing up her face as he brushed grit off her arm. The skin was torn, the graze was long, grey and bloody.

'Some guys on a moped, they stole this woman's purse,' he said. 'I was trying to catch them, till you got in my way.'

'Well, I'm sorry about that,' said Tess, feeling as if it was her fault. She winced as he gripped her upper arm.

'You haven't broken anything, but your shoulder's gonna hurt tomorrow.' He patted her arm, and smiled down at her briefly. 'I'm Peter, by the way.'

'Tess.' Tess struggled up and shook his hand, grimacing. 'Ouch,' she said as he gripped her hand.

'Oh, wow. I'm sorry.' He looked at her, his dark eyes full of concern.

'It stings,' she said, not wanting to sound as though she was making a fuss. 'Is there a –' She could hear shouts coming from further down the tiny street and looked up.

'Hey!' Peter said, following her gaze. 'It's him! They caught him!'

Suddenly a mob – that was the only word for it – of angry citizens appeared, pushing and shoving a young man at their centre, who was being held by the shoulder. *'Questo! Allora! Carabinieri!'* they were all variously shouting, while the young man wailed, his face a picture of distress.

'What's wrong with him?' Tess said. The mob started to fade away. Someone went off to call the police, someone to pick up the bike, and still more people simply just hung around.

Peter stepped forward and asked someone a couple of questions. 'He's hurt his arm too,' said Peter. 'Bumping into you must have sent him off course.' He turned to her and smiled. 'That's pretty awesome. You caught a thief! Good job.'

Tess looked at him properly for the first time and realized he was really quite – no, extremely – good-looking. He had looked and sounded totally Italian, but he was dressed in a curiously non-committal way – jeans, trainers, a white shirt and a soft grey V-necked pullover. She met his smile, trying to toss her hair. 'No problems,' she said, a little breathily.

'What are you doing here, anyway?' he said, as the sound of the police's sirens grew nearer in the tiny streets. She wondered if her group, ensconced in their guide books and cups of tea, would hear it, and if they did would ever think she was at the centre of it? No. 'You on holiday?'

'I'm – sort of,' Tess said, rubbing her arm again. She pushed herself away from the wall and shook her head, wishing, not for the first time, that she had long, Francesca-like siren tresses.

'*Signore, questo uomo e il ladro, e vero?*' a voice said from behind them, and Peter turned around and started talking back to the assembled Carabinieri officers.

'*L'eroina, e questa ragazza,*' Peter said. 'You're the heroine,' he told her, as the tall, portly, handsome Carabinieri stared at her appraisingly. 'They will need to take your details.'

Though she was now convinced that her ladies and Ron would be wondering whether she'd been sold into the white slave trade, Tess had to stand there for a long few minutes still while she and Peter gave their names, addresses, filled out a form, and were questioned variously by several Carabinieri, as well as some of the bystanders who were taking an involved approach to this affair. The accused was in the car, still crying piteously, handcuffed to a morose Carabinieri officer. He was very young, Tess thought, looking at him. What was he hoping to do with the stolen bag? And if she'd been a second later, would he have still crashed and hurt his arm, or would he have got away? She touched her throbbing shoulder, out of some kind of perverse empathy.

'I have to go, Tess,' said Peter, as he turned back from the police. 'But you should go to a *farmacia* and get something for your shoulder. Some Deep Heat stuff, it'll freeze otherwise.' He stared at her thoughtfully. 'Hey. You have great eyes.'

Tess snorted. 'Come off it.'

'What?' he said, not understanding her. 'I mean it,' he said. 'They're dark blue. Very intense.' He shook his head. 'That's so incredibly – I do not believe I just said that.'

'Well, you did,' Tess said, secretly deeply flattered.

Peter looked down at the ground, then up at the sky. He

exhaled deeply. 'Oh, jeez. Look, I was going to ask you something,' he said.

'What?'

'I was going to ask –' He shoved his hands in his pockets, and Tess stared at him curiously. 'Oh. OK.' He cleared his throat. 'So, can I ask you a few questions, some time? How long are you in town for?'

Her face was blank. 'A few questions?' She shook her head. 'Why on earth would you want to do that?'

'I'm a journalist,' he said, smiling. 'I live here. I'm not a psycho, I promise. I'm doing a piece on tourism versus the locals in Rome. This would be great to include. This incident.'

He had a way of saying definite sentences that meant Tess had to listen carefully to what he said each time.

'Tourism versus locals,' she repeated.

'Yeah,' he said slowly, as if she were a bit stupid. 'You know what I mean? How a city can survive with its own identity when it's under siege twenty-four seven. Would that guy make a living stealing bags if there weren't so many handbags to be stolen, all stuffed with new euros and cameras and all that crap?'

'Huh,' said Tess, watching him. 'I'd say he just shouldn't be stealing handbags in the first place.'

Peter scuffed his trainer gently against the wall. 'Sure. But all that stuff about what makes a city great is ultimately what kills it, because it draws the tourists to it. Then they suck the life out of it. Don't you think? It becomes a shell.'

Tess knew something about this. She had also spent the whole day looking at shells, in the company of a thousand other tourists, and they were the building blocks of modern civilization. 'I don't agree,' she said, though she'd been thinking about this a lot lately. She looked at him. 'I think a town needs the old and the new to combine. Work together.'

She was thinking of Langford, would it be nothing without its Jane Austen Centre, its funny gift shops, the visitors' book with Beau Brummell's signature?

'That's crap,' he said. 'I think. You have to look forward, that's how all the great cities were created. Forget the past.'

'You sound like a dictator,' said Tess. 'That's Albert Speer's plan for Berlin you're talking about.' She clutched her map tightly, and showed it to him in her fist. 'I'm not saying all cities do it well; I think Florence and Venice, they have too many tourists. But this is a pretty good mix, isn't it?'

She waved her hand, dropping the map as she did. It fluttered to the ground and he followed her gaze across the Campo dei Fiori as they stood at the far corner. She crouched on the ground to pick the map up, looking around her. The tourists with visors and bumbags – the Americans. The anxious, thin ones striding across the open space with their noses in their Dorling Kindersleys – the British and Swedes, sometimes Germans. The washing hanging in rows from the windows of the rusty-coloured palazzi, the man singing as he folded up his vegetable stall, the women bustling away from Il Forno, the bakery at the other end, bags of warm soft *focaccia* and *pizza bianca* wrapped in greaseproof paper swinging by their sides. The smell of coffee and jasmine, always in the air. This was why she loved Italy; it seemed real, all of it, no matter how touristy, crowded, theatrical it might be. She breathed in and out, forgetting who she was with, relaxing, drinking it all in for one brief, total moment.

'Perhaps you're right,' he said at her elbow, after a pause. He bent down, and handed her back the map and something else. 'Here's my number. You should give me a call, I really do want to ask you some questions. Human-interest angle, the girl who was caught up in a mugging, that kinda thing.'

'Weelll –' she said, not sure how to respond.

'Come on, it's only a few questions,' he said brusquely. 'It'll take a couple of minutes and then you can go back to – who are you here with?'

His eyes looked her up and down in his decisive way,

which she highly resented. It was as if she were a piece of meat: was she old, young, pregnant, married, up for it, frigid?

'None of your business!' she heard herself say.

'Wow –' he said coolly. 'So you're here on a dirty weekend, isn't that what you Brits call it?'

'I'm not telling you,' she said, equally coolly. 'Who are you here with?'

'I'm on my own now,' he said, raising an eyebrow.

'Really,' Tess said. 'You live here – alone?' She didn't believe him.

'Well, I do now,' said Peter.

'Ah, Gregory Peck in *Roman Holiday*,' she said, smiling. 'Filing copy late, playing cards with your buddies, living a louche Yankee journalist's life.'

'I am now,' said Peter.

'"Now"?' Tess said.

'Eventually, she gets it,' Peter replied, amused. 'You're not great at taking a hint, are you? I was married. To an Italian. That's why I live here.'

'Oh,' said Tess. He nodded gravely.

'But she left me. Three months ago.'

'She left you?'

'Moved back home to Naples with her ex.'

'God – I'm sorry,' said Tess. 'I've been stupid, I shouldn't have –'

He held out a tanned hand. 'Hey. It's OK. Turns out she was a terrible cook. What's the point of marrying an Italian if she can't cook?'

'Er –' Tess wasn't sure if he was joking or not, and she was about to ask what he meant, when suddenly a voice behind her called out, 'Yoo-hoo! Tess!'

She turned round. Jan Allingham was peering around the corner, her hands clutching the wall like the little boy in *Cinema Paradiso*.

'Tess, dear, are you all right? Only we heard the sirens, and

183

you'd been gone so long, and Jacquetta said she thought she heard *gunshots*, so Andrea started to panic and I offered to come and find you.' she trilled. 'Here you are!'

'Oh, man alive,' Tess muttered under her breath.

'Ah,' said Peter, stepping back and leaning against a wall. 'On tour with your moms,' he said softly. 'I see.'

'It's not like that,' Tess said childishly. 'I'm a Classics teacher, thank you very much, and these are my pupils.' But this sounded even more ridiculous, somehow. She turned to Jan. 'Are you all OK?'

'Yes!' said Jan, almost wildly. 'Except Leonora, she –'

Tess started wildly, she always forgot about Leonora Mortmain, the black-clothed viper in the bosom of the group. 'What did she do?'

'Told Ron he was a member of a lunatic socialist fringe,' Jan said briefly.

'Oh, dear God,' said Tess. She turned back to Peter, who was standing there with a sardonic look on his face. Her eyes met his, briefly. 'I have to go,' she said.

'Sounds like it,' and his dark, fathomless face relaxed a little into a smile. 'Please call me so we can talk some more. Press date's not till Friday, so I have a few days.'

'You're very direct,' said Tess.

'I have to be,' Peter said. 'It's my job. Plus, what's the point in wasting time? If you want something, you should go for it.'

'Oh,' she said, considering this. She nodded. 'You're probably right, you know.'

'I am totally right,' he told her, grinning. 'You miss the story if you don't go for it. Of course, I went for it with Chiara, and I was totally wrong about that, but – hey.' He gestured with his hand, almost laconically. She watched him, transfixed, as did Jan, open-mouthed. 'I'm here, aren't I? I could be back in the States writing articles about the steel industry for the *Pittsburgh Post-Gazette*. It's not so bad. Gimme a call.'

'Well –'

'Or – just if you get bored. You should enjoy yourself a little while you're here, too.' He looked at her directly, held out his hand and she shook it. His clasp was strong.

'Look, sorry again about – er –' she said. She felt she ought to apologize for being so rude, but she didn't quite know what for. 'Sorry about your wife.'

'I forgive you. You're not the Bosnian guy who banged her,' he said, and his handsome face creased into a smile. 'It's OK. Nearly OK.' He nodded at Jan, who blushed, and then nodded at Tess. She stared back at him helplessly. 'Hey – good police work. I hope your shoulder feels better.' He glanced at her arm. 'Speak to you soon, Tess,' but he was talking to thin air, for Tess had hurried back into the Campo, Jan bustling in her wake.

CHAPTER SEVENTEEN

Hi, Tess. Hope you're having a good time. All good here. Very quiet town without all those people you're looking after. See you when you're back. Adam

It probably *was* quiet in Langford, without all those people. It was certainly very loud here, in Rome, shepherding them around the city all day. Loud, hot, chaotic, relentless, and unsatisfying. In the shower back at the hotel, Tess stood still, letting the cool water run in rivers over her head, resenting Adam intruding here. She didn't want to think about him. She forced her mind elsewhere.

It was Tuesday; six more days to go. She had never imagined she would remember with any fondness the Fair View Year Ten day trip to Bath, where one of her class had stolen a biscuit from the motorway service station (and been caught by security), another had jumped out at an old lady behind a statue in the Roman Baths (she had angina), and three others had simply disappeared, turning up two hours later insensibly drunk by the bus station (two of them were sick on the coach journey back), but she was wrong. At least that had only been a day long. And teenagers were annoying, but you could yell at them and then it was over. This . . . oh, dear. The fussing! The amount of time it took them all to cross the road! The incessant questions and faffing around, about the menu, the drinks, the entrance fee, what was happening next! Even the two younger members of the group, Claire and Liz, seemed to be aping the behaviour of their elders: she had heard Claire say to Liz, 'I must buy some Footgloves when I get back home. They seem so *useful*, don't you think?' Tess had stared at her, almost in horror, and Claire had looked a little surprised when she'd seen the expression on her face. 'Maybe,' she'd amended. 'I'll try some on.'

Standing naked in the shower, feeling the water run over her body, the dull ache of the muscle pain in her shoulder felt almost erotic, exotic, after today. She stepped out of the shower and dried herself with a towel. Her shoulders and arms were flushed with the sun. She remembered that American man, and what he'd said. 'On tour with your moms.' How rude. How annoying!

How right he was.

His card was in her purse. *Peter Gray*. Such an American name for such an Italian-looking man. She found him vaguely disconcerting; there was something dangerous in his dark, almost hooded eyes, his staccato manner, the very directness with which he conducted himself. Tess was used to a depressing cross-section of English men, who stammered their way through a variety of half-truths, took passive-aggressivity to a new level of art form, who spoke of equality but were mostly terrified of women.

She had talked about this a lot with Francesca, that arch-realist. Standing by the window, rubbing cream into her arms and shoulders, Tess found herself thinking about Adam and Francesca, she couldn't help it. What was going on in Langford? Were they properly back together? She hoped they were both OK, Francesca especially. She still didn't understand what had happened with her and Adam on Saturday, but she was realizing, with the benefit of a good night's sleep and a change of scenery, that that night in London was not the start of

187

something new. It was the line being drawn under something old. A teenage romance – that's what it was, with all its tawdry, heartbreaking, familiar drama. He had called it a summer fling, and it had hurt her, but he was right. That's all it was, with a sadder than usual ending. She had never really come to terms with its conclusion: the abortion, the wall of silence afterwards, the start of her new life at university and never discussing it with anyone there, because the one person she would have told about it was the one person she couldn't talk to.

It was easy to think clearly here. Easy to have perspective. Tess looked round the room, at the mirrored sliding cupboard doors, where the clothes she had hung up fluttered in the evening breeze, at the faded, half-hearted etchings of Roman ruins up on the walls – of the Baths of Caracalla and the Colosseum, at the shiny caramel-coloured linen coverlets on the narrow single beds. It was anonymous, and there was comfort in that anonymity.

She applied the Italian version of Deep Heat which she'd bought from the pharmacy, wincing slightly, and as she did ran through, with no enthusiasm, a potential seating plan for the evening. She had quickly learned that her group was like a teenage girl – needing constant ministrations and reassurances, but basically pliant if told what to do in a firm way. Tess sighed at the thought, casting one more look at her phone to see if there was another message, before stopping herself. *She* was the teenage girl, if anything. They were in Rome! She had prevented a theft! They were in the cradle of civilization, it was spring, anything could happen! She drew out a piece of paper from her notepad, picked up her pen and started scribbling.

They were having dinner that night in a traditional trattoria just off the Piazza Farnese and when they arrived, Tess's first impression of gloom was quickly overtaken with delight. It was a truly Roman restaurant, from the polished barrels stacked up around them and the black-and-white posters of films and autographed pictures of local celebrities tacked up on the walls, to the simplicity of the dark wood contrasting with the red-and-white checked tablecloths. As the group stood, huddled in the doorway, a woman bustled up to them, gesturing frantically for them to take their seats around the long table at the heart of the low-ceilinged, cavernous room.

'*Sono Vittoria*,' she added, jabbing her finger into her breast-bone. '*Benvenuti!*'

There was an awkward pause as each member of the group started to shuffle towards a seat, trying not to look too alarmed at who was next to them. Jan, Diana and Carolyn instinctively drew together. Jacquetta hovered at their edge. Ron, as ever, tried to look remote and forbidding, and succeeded in neither. Leonora, of course, stood at the back, tapping her stick lightly on the ground.

'Mind out there, Carolyn, excuse me if I squeeze past.' 'I don't mind going in next to Jan, Diana!' 'Where are you going, Mrs Mortmain? Oh, right. I'll just . . .' 'Claire, can I sit next to you?'

'Stop!' Tess called out, as Jan had almost edged halfway along the side of the table against the wall, clutching her bag determinedly. 'I've done a seating plan!' There was total silence. She smiled. 'I thought it'd be a good idea,' she continued, not giving up. 'I'll do a new one each night. We can chop and change, exchange ideas on what we've seen, and I'm going to ask you all what your favourite part of the day was, whether that's a fact or a sight or just something that struck you! Righty ho!'

An English couple filed past them, on their way to a table further back in the restaurant, and the husband said with relief to the wife, 'Good God. I'm glad I'm not with them, aren't you?'

Tess pretended not to hear this. 'OK!' she called out. 'Ron –' she pointed towards the middle of the table. 'You're here, all right? And next to you – yes, Leonora, if you don't mind going there.'

Ron scowled; Andrea, Diana and Jan inhaled sharply, but Leonora Mortmain sat steadily down in her seat, not meeting anyone's eye. She lifted her bag onto the table, withdrew the little book she always carried around with her, and calmly opened it, as Tess carried on talking.

'. . . Jan here, Jacquetta here, next to you, and I'm here, Liz, yes, you go there. Right!' She looked around the table again. 'Shall we sit down?'

'The sooner we do, the sooner we can eat, and the sooner we can be out of here,' Ron said, with an attempt at humour. It fell sadly flat; the rest of the group looked at him in horror. All except Andrea, whom Tess had long suspected nursed something of a *tendre* for Ron. She tittered nervously, and Ron looked up defensively, to be greeted with her rather watery smile. He breathed in loudly through his nostrils. 'Aaah. Menu?' He handed a plastic card to Leonora Mortmain, who took it in silence.

'Great!' said Tess, over the settling silence, ignoring the throbbing in her arm and shoulder. 'This is nice, isn't it.'

They brought red wine and water, bread and olive oil, and then a variety of starters: stuffed courgette flowers, thick with creamy goat's cheese and drizzled with thyme-infused honey, grilled vegetables, bruschetta with borlotti beans, and thin, pink strips of prosciutto, sliced by hand from a cured leg of pork on a table nearby. They munched their way through, passing things along to each other, being deliberately polite.

'I didn't know you'd lived in Brighton, Ron? How interesting. We were in Southampton for years, you know.'

'So, your family's from Leamington Spa, Claire? Do you go back there often?'

'That's very interesting, Jacquetta. Very interesting!'

Tess thanked Bacchus more than once for the gift of wine, which smooths over many things, and by the time the main courses had come, the company was positively relaxed. Plates of lamb and veal, heaped high with rocket and potatoes and waxy, garlic-scented white beans, were set down on the table and everyone dug in, exclaiming over the taste of the succulent grilled meat. Vittoria stood nearby, smiling indulgently at them. It had been a long, hot day, and to be here was a balm. Tess watched in pleasure as the group relaxed, chatting politely, talking about what they'd seen, asking each other questions. She didn't know why she was even surprised, however, that Leonora Mortmain did not join in, did not talk, and did not make any effort. She sat at the end of the table, by the door.

'Do you have to go back to the police station for what happened today?' Jan asked. 'Awful, that was. You poor thing.'

'I know,' said Tess. 'No, I don't, thank goodness, they took my number and they said they'd call me if they needed anything more.' She stirred in her chair.

'My cousin was in Rio once,' said Carolyn, unexpectedly, 'and someone ripped her earring from her ear. Tore it into two flaps.'

'No!' Jan screamed, as the others looked appalled.

'Yes,' said Carolyn, alarmed by her own voice. 'I know, isn't it horrible?' She looked around her now, and at Leonora Mortmain. 'Ever since then . . .' She shuddered.

'That's not going to happen,' said Tess firmly. 'That was just bad luck, that's all. It could happen on the streets in London, for goodness' sake.' They all looked at her in terror. 'Anywhere. It could happen in Langford!'

Carolyn gave a low moan. 'Don't say that,' she said. 'How awful.'

'It could,' said Tess, turning to Carolyn. 'It could happen anywhere. Not necessarily having your earrings ripped out of your ears, but – similar,' she said mischievously. Carolyn looked terrified, and Tess said hurriedly, 'But the fact is it won't. The chances are astronomical. So there's no point worrying about it.'

'Philippa was mugged, quite badly, don't you remember?' Diana said suddenly, to no one in particular.

Tess, who had been breathing in, smelling the coffee, started: 'Philippa? When?'

'Oh, quite soon before she died,' Diana said. She clicked her teeth together. 'Random violence, like you say. Horrible. Right in the middle of Langford.'

'There you go,' said Carolyn, pleased, before realizing how she sounded. 'How awful,' she added contritely.

'It was in the lanes behind your old houses, where your parents lived too,' Diana said. 'Nasty business. They never caught him.' She looked down at the table, and Tess remembered, memory seeping back again, how Diana and Philippa had been so close; Philippa's closest friend, really.

Tess said slowly, 'I'd forgotten that. What happened?'

'What happened?' Diana looked up. 'I don't know. She was coming back from Thornham, on her bike, and it was dark – it was February, I think? Anyway, she got off and was pushing the last bit of the way and someone came up behind her and pushed her over. Stamped on her hand, she broke a finger, and he took her bag. He had a knife, too.'

'She twisted her ankle,' Tess said, remembering it suddenly.

'*He* twisted her ankle,' Diana said grimly.

'She was in hospital. Adam had to pick her up.' She stared at her empty coffee cup. Someone was jangling a fork against their plate, like scraping wind chimes in a breezy sky. 'Poor Philippa.'

'They said it was nothing to do with her death, but I don't know,' Diana said. Her severe face was set, her grey fringe a perfectly straight line. 'You're knocked over, threatened with a knife, stamped on by some little shit and then two months later you drop dead from a brain haemorrhage? I'm sure they're connected.'

'Me too,' said Andrea. 'For what it's worth. And I can't believe they never caught him. But that's the thing, you don't know what's round the corner. Everything can be lovely and cosy, and then next moment – bam.' She slammed her hand on the table.

The noise from the fork got louder. Tess looked up, to see Mrs Mortmain now sharply tapping the fork on her tumbler. Next to her, almost unconsciously, Jan laid her hand gently over the older woman's shaking fingers. Leonora Mortmain looked at her, in utter shock, and then she shook her head.

'Sorry,' she said, much to Tess's surprise.

But Diana Sayers watched her, with something like contempt on her face.

'I just don't think that sort of thing happens in Langford,' Leonora said eventually, shaking her head querulously.

'Neither did I,' Diana said. 'But it did. Anyway, that was – how long ago?'

'Thirteen years,' said Tess, after a moment's hesitation. Funny, when she thought of Philippa, who seemed so real to her still, she couldn't believe it was that long ago. Suddenly she could see Adam, whose face had seemed so remote to her these last few days; not the Adam she'd left behind in Claridges last Saturday night, but her oldest friend, his light brown hair, kind face, urgent, sweet smile, the way that back then, they had no secrets, no worries. That Adam – he seemed awfully far away to her, now.

'I mean, perhaps there was a reason for it,' Leonora said slowly, deliberately. 'It seemed to me that Philippa – Smith? Was that the name she used? She had some rather unsavoury associates.'

'What on earth does that mean?' asked Diana quickly. 'What a ridiculous thing to say. She was mugged by a nasty thief, she wasn't in the Mafia!'

'Shhh,' said Jan, as the waiter hovered nearby.

But Diana was furious. 'I'm sorry, that's incredibly offensive to Philippa,' she said. 'She didn't bring that on herself. You know that, better than most people.'

'Really?' Leonora Mortmain gently put her lips together, and raised her eyebrows a fraction. 'I didn't know her as well as you.'

'No, you didn't,' said Diana pointedly. Tess stared at her, she had never seen her so full of fury. 'And you ditched her son, too, when he most needed help. If I was you, I'd keep my opinions about Philippa to myself.'

There was an icy silence. Tess, transfixed with horror, came to with a start to find someone plucking at her elbow; it was Carolyn, asking if they should get the bill. Tess said yes, and realized Diana was watching her, glowering under her fringe. Tess met her gaze and grimaced apologetically, as another memory surfaced: Diana and Tess's mum, after the funeral, arriving to clear out Philippa's cottage. Adam shouting at them, the awful rows they had about what to keep and what to throw away and in the end, them leaving him to it, as he refused their offers of help, alone in that house. She had spent that summer among Philippa's things; she wondered where they were now – probably still in the attic somewhere, her clothes eaten away by moths, the books turning to dust, when she herself was still so alive in all their minds.

Strange, these things that she only thought of when she was away from the town. She looked around the table, at these faces that were becoming so familiar to her, looked at them again as if she was seeing them for the first time. Was Jan the bustling, bossy, organizational freak she made out she was, or did she also have a sensitivity with which Tess wouldn't have credited her? Diana – she had always seemed so scary, but was she really that person, or someone warmer, sadder, with a more interesting past? Middle-aged women get a raw deal, Tess was starting to realize. Middle-aged men can run companies, put on weight, clap each other on the back and do what the hell they like, but middle-aged women aren't allowed to be anything more than ciphers of something rather amusing. They're not allowed to have hopes and dreams and keep secrets, or be empire-builders, confident and strong. They either have to be flapping and fussing or dry and disapproving—

'Tessa?'

Her head snapped up. 'Yes?' she said, coming out of her reverie.

'How do you say, "Can I have a Coke?"'

As they were finishing their meal and coffee was being ordered, there was a sudden commotion. A dog rushed into the restaurant, barking loudly, followed by its owner, who had let go of its leash. It was a mongrel dog, not huge, but large enough to push chairs out of the way and dislodge an unused table as it ricocheted, full of energy and panic, through the restaurant. The diners were alternately shocked and amused when he shot like a bullet through the doors.

'Look!' Ron cried, as the dog leapt past him.

'Stop him,' someone said quietly. 'Please, stop him.'

'Oh, he's just a little thing,' said Diana briskly. 'Nice little chap. Wonder what he's doing.'

'Stop him, please,' said the voice again. Tess looked back to the table to find it was Leonora Mortmain. Her eyes were huge, she looked as if she had aged ten years in ten seconds. 'I do not like dogs,' she said, scrabbling to get to her feet. It was unsettling to see her so discombobulated. 'Please. Stop him.'

'You don't like dogs?' said Diana, amazed.

'I hate them.' She patted her hair. 'I hate them.' There was a silence around the table; Leonora Mortmain gave a shallow sigh. 'I shall go back to the hotel now,' she said, finally struggling to her feet. She tapped her stick on the ground smartly and leaned on it, pushing stray grey locks of her hair back into place with a shaking hand. Behind her, the owner and his pet were reunited, with much wailing and many imprecations, and both fell into the street again, the dog dragging the man impatiently by the lead. Tess half stood up, but Leonora shook her head. 'No. Mr Thaxton, would you be so kind, could you escort me home?'

There was a slightly stunned silence. Tess loved Ron in that moment, for the polite way he got to his feet, nodding. 'Of course,' he said, only slightly reluctantly. 'My pleasure.' Andrea glared at him imploringly, but Ron took Leonora's arm and they left the restaurant, going out into the night. Tess could hear laughter from the street, see the orange light from the candles on the tables outside and she thought again how incongruous Leonora Mortmain was, here, how she should instead have been touring Rome with Mr Casaubon from *Middlemarch*. Had she ever been young? Had she ever yearned to hurl herself out of the restaurant into the warm, jasmine-scented evening, feel her bare feet on the cobbles, run across the ancient river into the heart of the city, ride a moped, drink wine till dawn?

Tess shook her head. Of course she hadn't. She gazed out at their retreating figures and thoughtfully chewed her fingernail.

'Isn't it true,' Jacquetta Meluish said, recalling her to the present, 'that there was a bookshop in the Forum? I seem to remember, when I stayed here with a dear *professore* friend of John's –'

Diana Sayers raised her eyes to heaven. Andrea nudged her. The two younger girls smiled politely, and Carolyn Tey assumed an expression of rapt interest.

'Are you all right, dear?' Jan Allingham said suddenly, leaning over to Tess. Jacquetta stopped in surprise.

'Me? I'm fine,' said Tess.

'You look rather tired,' said Jan.

'She does, doesn't she?' said Andrea, leaping on this gap in the conversation. 'You've had a long day, dear. Perhaps you should go back to the hotel too.'

'We've all had a long day,' Tess said, laughing.

'Yes, but we haven't been flung against the wall by motor-cycling muggers,' said Diana. 'That shoulder's going to bloody hurt you tomorrow, you know.'

Tess didn't want to tell them that it already was. She smiled, touched that they cared, but knowing that she couldn't leave them, take off back to the hotel, or even anywhere else. *You should enjoy yourself, too*, the American had said.

'Oh, well,' said Jan. She patted Tess's arm. 'We'll be back home soon. Home! I mean back at the hotel.' She laughed. 'Oh, look at me, here five minutes and I'm calling it home!'

Jacquetta said, 'I always think of Rome as somewhere where one could happily live. That's what I was saying, about John's friend Alberto, who was professor of music . . .'

Tess cast one last longing look out of the door, as the vibrant blue light of evening turned slowly into night.

CHAPTER EIGHTEEN

Ron was waiting for them when they arrived back at Albergo Watkins, sitting in the tiny makeshift bar-cum-lobby. He was clutching a beer, with one leg thrown out in front of the other, one arm resting on the back of the wooden settle that lined the wall. The receptionist was studiously ignoring him.

The effect Ron was aiming for – unruffled international traveller who hangs out in hotel lobbies – wasn't quite convincing. He looked rather cross and, as they all came back in, turned to them with something like a snarl, leapt up and then carefully put his glass of beer back down on the table.

'That woman –' he said, advancing towards them, his grey eyes wide open. 'Tess, don't put me next to her again this holiday. Otherwise I want a refund. I am not doing that again. I'll sue.'

'Ron shouldn't eat rich foods in the evening, you know,' Jan whispered loudly to Andrea. 'They make him ever so cross.'

'It's none of my business what he eats in the evening, thank you, Jan,' Andrea said.

Tess, who had a pack of legal information as well as Health and Safety, First Aid and travel tips up in her room, none of which she wanted to have to use, blinked at Ron in alarm.

'Er,' she said. 'OK, Ron. I'm sorry – she asked and I thought you'd be OK. Oh, dear,' she said, seeing he really did look upset. 'What did she say?'

'Things,' Ron said, grinding his teeth and pacing.

'Ooh, what kind of things?' said Andrea, her sharp little face alive with potential outrage.

'She told me –' Ron said, stiffly. 'She – oh, that woman. She told me that I should write and apologize to her for the things I'd said. Otherwise there'd be consequences. Consequences!' He gave a snorting laugh, which dissolved into a fit of coughing. 'Cool as a cucumber, we're walking back through the streets, all nice as you like, I'm trying to be polite and she says that.'

'*Write and apologize?*' Andrea said incredulously. 'After what she's done?'

'That's not all,' said Ron, pacing up and down. 'That is not all.'

At that point a German couple slowly opened the front door and stepped into the lobby, where they were prevented from advancing any further because of the bottleneck of aghast onlookers listening to Ron. Tess gently moved Liz and Jacquetta out of the way so the couple could move past. She watched them abstractly, admiring their European-ness, the woman with her frameless neat glasses, shiny cropped blonde hair, the man tanned and athletic, she in crisp linen, he in a shirt and pressed trousers. They were so very different from the ragged mob standing in the lobby with her.

She pressed her fingers to her temple, wanting to stay calm. 'What else?' she asked.

'She said –' Ron cleared his throat. 'Actually, can you give me a minute?'

No one quite knew what he meant by this, so no one moved.

Ron closed his eyes and flared his fingers upwards, so his palms faced outwards, like a mystic sage. 'I meant, can you leave me and Tess, please? I need to tell her something.'

'Oh,' said Andrea, disappointed, but Diana Sayers motioned to her to be quiet. Andrea looked at Ron, who looked back at her and nodded, a look of silent understanding, and she suddenly switched. 'Right, see you upstairs,' she said, and pushed Liz, Claire, Jan, Jacquetta and Carolyn towards the stairs.

'What is it, Ron?' Tess said, moving towards him. Silence fell in the lobby, and the woman behind the desk looked up, bored, twitched her thick Prada glasses and went back to her crossword puzzle.

Ron scratched his head and bared his gums, breathing in so the air whistled between his teeth. 'Oh, goodness,' he said. 'I don't know how to say this, that's all.'

'Say what?' Tess asked, unaccountably scared by his grave demeanour. He was silent. She said gently, 'Ron, come on, tell me.'

'She's cracked in the head,' he said eventually.

'Who?' Tess said stupidly.

'Mortmain. Her.' He could barely bring himself to say the name. 'Leonora Mortmain.'

'What do you mean?'

'I meant what I said just now. But there's more to it than that. Sh-she's – sommat's wrong with her, I don't know what it is. I think seeing that dog set her off.' He scratched his head again. 'Rude bitch,' he said, with a flare of his anger again. 'Sorry.' He looked down.

Tess felt fear strike into her heart, she didn't know why. 'Ron,' she said, as if to a child. 'Tell me what she said.'

'It's hard to say,' Ron said frankly, his eyes meeting hers. 'She's got something on me, for starters.'

'What's that?' Tess said.

'She knows about something.' Ron rubbed his face with his hands, in some kind of agony. 'I bribed a man, fellow on the council. Way back, years ago, Tess, right? I wanted to open a cinema, little picture house.'

'That would have been nice,' said Tess, encouragingly. Ron's face was creased with distress.

'Would have been. Would ha' been great for the town, always wanted a cinema when I was a boy, growing up there. But I stuffed it up, didn't I? Gave a bung to someone on the planning committee, he was bent as they come. They got him for a whole bunch o' stuff, and they found out about me.'

'Oh, dear, Ron –' Tess said, upset. 'That's –'

'It was bloody stupid of me, and I thought no one knew,' Ron said, grimacing. 'I got a sentence, suspended, paid my fine, thought it was all done. But she's found out. How's she found out?'

'I don't know,' Tess said. 'I honestly don't know, Ron, but you mustn't –'

'Argh,' Ron said again, a low angry noise. 'I hate her. She was enjoying it. She said, she said all that stuff about how I had to apologize to her. That everyone on the committee, the one against the building works, we should all apologize to her. We've harassed her, 'parently.' His voice was bitter. 'She said she'd make sure everyone knew what I done. That I should give up the campaign. She's ruined the town, doesn't even care –' He looked up at her. 'Do you think less of me? Bet you do, now you know. What people are going to say . . .'

Tess put her hand on his arm. 'Course I don't,' she said, patting his shiny nylon shirt. 'Come on. You mustn't let her get to you. She won't say anything, and who'd believe her? What else did she say?'

'It's hard to say,' he said simply. She nodded encouragingly. 'OK,' he said eventually. 'She doesn't like you. She's going to complain about you to the school when we get back.'

Tess nodded imperceptibly, though she felt sick. 'Right,' she said. 'Any particular thing?'

'That's what I mean. She says you're a bad influence.'

Tess laughed, almost with shock.

'She was just saying it as if it were normal, you know, as

we're walking back through the streets, and it's this nice evening and I say, more to get her off the subject of my troubles and all, I said, "Isn't it nice havin' Tess showing us round Rome, she always was a nice girl, even when she was little, Frank and Emily must be proud of her."' He looked embarrassed. 'Anyway, that's by the by. So we'd just turned off that main square onto a side street, and it's very dark all of a sudden. She stops and stares at me, but not at me, like at someone else, and she says, "She's a bad influence." Just like that.'

Tess shook her head, and gestured to him to carry on. Her throat felt thick, as if a piece of bread were stuck in it. Ron was in his stride now. "A bad influence, and they was right, I shouldn't have come." So I says, "Who's they?" and her voice is all shrill and everything and she says, "Never you mind that, I'm going to make sure she don't do one of these trips again." And then she says –' Ron cleared his throat – 'she says, "I don't remember him any more." Like that. She was crying. Trying to at least. My blood ran cold, I tell you.'

'"Him"?' Tess said sharply, so loudly that the receptionist looked up from her book again, making a moue of bored curiosity with her mouth.

'That's what she said,' Ron told her, with relish. 'That's why I think she's cracked in the head.' He shivered a bit. 'I asked her what she means, and she shakes her head and says, "No one remembers." And then she laughed! She sounded mad. High-pitched and everything, and I knew she wasn't listening to me.' He said, almost calmly, 'It was like she was talking to someone else, someone who wasn't there.'

'Blimey,' said Tess. She put her hands on her hips. 'Well –'

'She don't like you,' Ron finished, almost triumphantly. 'She really don't like you.'

There was lots that didn't make sense, and Tess was not sure enough of Ron's testimony to give in to the sinister feeling of unease uncoiling within her. She remembered Leonora on their first night here. *You are rather like me*. Well, she obviously didn't think that today. She pulled herself together and said, in her most normal voice, 'Listen, Ron, I think she was probably tired. Don't worry about it.'

He looked at her. 'She wasn't tired.'

'She's an old lady, Ron –' Tess wanted to give her the benefit of the doubt. 'And she's not the easiest of people, let's face it. In fact, it's pretty hard to feel sympathy for her. But she's here on her own, she doesn't have any friends, and she's had a long day. I think the wine got the better of her.'

'She only had a glass.'

'Look –' Tess said, squeezing her arm with her hand, forgetting how sore it still was.

'Your shoulder OK?' Ron said.

'It's all right. Just a bit tender.' She winced, and it made her remember. 'It's been a long day for us all, that's what I think. So – can you do me a favour? Don't mention this to anyone. The last bit, I mean, as well as the first bit. I don't want them thinking Leonora's gone mad.'

Ron looked unconvinced. 'Course I won't,' he said, gloomily. 'But I think she *has* gone mad,' he said.

Tess patted his arm in what she hoped was a friendly, conspiratorial way, not a patronizing, shut-up-and-give-it-a-rest way. 'Perhaps she has,' she said, with gallows humour. 'But she was a bit weird to start with. Let's monitor it ourselves, shall we?'

'It was those eyes,' Ron said, unwilling to let it rest. 'Her eyes, they looked so spooky.'

Tess was suddenly very, very tired. 'Right,' she said, nodding and feeling that perhaps Leonora was right, she was a terrible tour group leader, but for the moment if she didn't go to bed she would simply curl up on the fake marble floor of the lobby and pass out. 'I'll watch out for the eyes and – and Ron, thanks.'

Ron nodded briefly, like a soldier. 'My pleasure.' He stepped back, bowing his head as a farewell gesture, and climbed up the stairs, leaving Tess alone.

She stared around her, taking in the large, attractive Victorian painting of the Colosseum that hung on the wall by the stair-case. Around the base of the huge structure, possibly the most recognizable image of Rome, well-dressed ladies and gentlemen promenaded in a genteel fashion, as the dark, brooding circle rose above them, giving no hint of the torture and relentless slaughter that had taken place there. Again it struck her how funny it was, that they had spent the day parading round these old ruins, saying 'Ooh' and 'Aah' and not really thinking about the reality, the fifty thousand people who could be accommo-dated there, the bloody games that lasted from dusk till dawn where on one day alone five thousand animals could be killed, and many gladiators too. Staring at the refined figures circling the old amphitheatre, Tess was reminded of one fact: that the Romans had, by dint of rounding up countless rhinos, hippopotami, tigers and lions, purged the more dangerous corners of their empire of bloodthirsty animals who posed a threat to them. She shook her head. This was civilization, too, but it was a strange kind of civilization.

'Sir Frederick Fortt,' she said, reading the name of the artist at the bottom of the canvas. The receptionist looked up again.

'Mees Tennant,' she said, her lovely, low voice caressing the consonants of Tess's name. 'Tessss Tennant?'

'Yes,' said Tess, shrugging her shoulders wearily, wondering what fresh hell awaited her with her messages.

'Theeese are for you. *Che bellissimi fiori!*' she said, and she reached down to her side and picked up a bouquet of roses. She thrust them at Tess unceremoniously.

Tess took them. They were roses, palest pink, scented, tied with a thin blue ribbon to which a tiny envelope was attached, and the scent of them took her breath away. The receptionist smiled at her conspiratorially.

'You have an admirer here, in Roma!' she said.

'I very much doubt it,' Tess said, thinking of her conversation with Ron, but she laughed. *'Grazie, signorina.'*

'Grazie, e buona notte.'

She climbed the stairs, tiredness gone, fingering the crisp white card, her fingers fumbling with the keys so she could get into her room and open the envelope.

Hope your shoulder feels better. Come have a drink with me tomorrow after dinner, and I'll show you the real Rome. No tourists! Via del Mascherone off the Piazza Farnese. You should enjoy yourself too, while you're here.

Ciao

Peter

CHAPTER NINETEEN

Almost exactly twenty-four hours later, Tess's leather thong sandals slapped quietly on the oily black cobbles, her heart beating a tattoo in time with her feet, as she crossed the dark Piazza Farnese, heading towards a side street off the square. Her responsibilities were over, another day was over. They had seen the Pantheon, the Ara Pacis, some more ruins. They had wandered round Rome in the heat till their feet begged for mercy, till Tess was sick of the sound of her own voice, of being the leader, in charge, the focus. At last she was alone, carefree, with the cooling air of a Roman evening on her bare skin.

She stood in the centre of the piazza, and turned slowly around, breathing in, her eyes closed, and when she breathed out again, she was no longer Tess, the sensible Classics teacher who shepherded people around all day, who was muffled up in a scarf and tank top against the chill of a late spring and draughty English buildings, who watched someone like Francesca with awe. She was a girl in a black jersey dress with a coral-coloured shawl and the glow of a few glasses of wine and a limoncello inside her, hurrying across a darkened square to – what? What was waiting for her?

She breathed in again, the now-familiar smell of jasmine filling her lungs. She turned off the square, into the Via del

Mascherone, the dark bulk of the Palazzo Farnese towering over the narrow street. A couple were kissing passionately in an alcove of the palazzo; they ignored her as she hurried past, the man reaching behind the woman to pull her closer towards him. When she reached Peter's flat – a stone building three storeys high, with a dark green front door visible in the light from the street lamp and a blue moped parked outside – she rang the doorbell. There was a jangling sound, far in the distance, then silence. A moped zoomed past her and she turned, as if embarrassed to be caught doing this. It was another couple, their dark hair fanning out behind them. The woman was driving, the man clinging onto her, one hand round her waist, the other on the back of her neck at the top of her spine in an oddly proprietorial hold.

Tess rang the bell again, flicking the card from the flowers Peter had given her – which had the address on it – against her fingertips. It made a scraping sound in the sudden quiet of the street.

Still nothing.

Perhaps the address was wrong? Perhaps he'd meant another day . . . Perhaps . . . And she realized, then, how silly she'd been, building her hopes up all day, getting excited about something as ephemeral as this. It wasn't real life, it was a fantasy!

One more try: Tess rang the bell, feeling foolish now. If this was the life she wanted to be living he would appear now, apologizing, he was on the phone, in the shower, wherever.

Outside the beam of the street lamp it was oddly dark on the street, no light from the palazzo or the black wall of the garden behind it, and Tess was glad, because she thought she was probably blushing as she finally turned and walked slowly towards the river. She might as well go back to the hotel now; no point in rejoining the others over drinks. She'd felt stupid enough about her exit from dinner anyway; her responsibilities were over for the day, but as she rose from the table in the restaurant, clutching her napkin, she had told what she knew sounded like a vastly over-concocted half-truth about a friend who lived in Rome with whom she wanted to catch up. She'd tried to make them believe the friend was a she . . . She wasn't sure how many of them had believed this.

Tess walked along the cobbled street towards the Ponte Sisto, her heart heavy at the thought of crossing the bridge back to the hotel. It was becoming clearer to her how completely, stupidly ridiculous she'd been. She looked at her watch; it was a quarter to twelve and perhaps it was for the best. They were going to Pompeii the next day. It was going to be a long day. She needed to look out her guide books – oh, and her socks, to wear with her walking sandals, which were starting to rub. No, she didn't care how stupid it made her look – who was going to notice, anyway?

'Tess!'

Wearily, Tess started to list things in her head she ought to check again before the morning, and so she almost missed the voice that called again, 'Tess! Hey, honey! *Tess!*'

She looked back in amazement. There, standing at the edge of the bridge, one leg resting on the very same bright blue moped she'd just seen, was Peter. He waved frantically, gesturing to her to come over to him. She turned and walked towards him.

'I'm sorry,' he said, as she approached. 'I can't take this thing on the bridge.' He was panting. 'God, I'm sorry. A minute later, and I'd have missed you.'

'Yes,' she said, parting her lips and smiling at him. 'I – hi!' She'd forgotten how good-looking he was, his almost black hair shining in the moonlight. 'I went to your flat – I must have got the wrong –'

She sounded really prim, she knew it, apologizing like an idiot.

'No, it's my fault,' he said earnestly. 'That's where I was going. To your hotel to write you a note. I don't even have your cell.' She shook her head. 'I got caught up on a story. Embassy reception for the Queen of Norway.' She blinked. 'It's true,' he said gravely, but he was smiling. He ran his hands through his hair and then rubbed them together. 'So. You still want to do something?' She nodded. 'I promised you I'd show you Rome, didn't I?'

'Yes,' said Tess. 'You did.'

He patted the seat, and handed her a helmet. 'Put this on, then,' he said. 'We're going for a ride.'

She shook her head, and started laughing. 'I – I barely know you!' she said.

'Don't be so British.' He held out his hand, smiling. 'I'm Peter.' They shook hands. 'You're Tess. I'm your host, now jump on and let's go have some fun.'

The night was young – well, actually it wasn't, but she was in Rome, after all, the air was fresh and suddenly, Tess Tennant was sick of thinking things through, wondering about everyone else except her, chewing her nails over an embittered old woman, struggling to keep the peace, trying not to think about Adam, about back home, about everything. This was the bridge. She could choose to cross over to the other side if she wanted, or she could stay, and try being the person she wished she was. She looked into his treacly black eyes, and smiled.

'Deal.' She took the helmet from him. 'What do I do with this?' she asked, holding it awkwardly. He looked astonished. 'I mean, is there a strap or a trick or –'

'You put it on,' Peter said. He jammed the helmet over her hair. 'You don't need to overthink it. Just put it on and let's –' he swung one leg over the Vespa – 'let's go.'

Don't overthink it. He was right. As he revved up the engine and they started to move off, Tess caught hold of him, wrapping her arms round his waist and holding on for dear life; wasn't there a system, an easier way of doing this, she thought? There must be . . . But no. You just clung on to this almost complete stranger for dear life as everything became a blur, and streets whizzed by, terrifically fast, and then gradually, as the desire to scream loudly receded, you looked up and the blur started to take shape. Now they were zooming down a long straight road, with narrow pavements that occasionally gave out onto small piazzas with tables and chairs, cafés with laurel bushes dividing them from the street ... Shops with elegant elaborate old black frontages with gold lettering, white marble Baroque churches crammed in amongst the ochre buildings, all whizzed past in a flash and she looked around her, then looked up between the buildings at the inky night sky, wondering how she got here, until they turned into a side street and Peter gradually slowed down to a halt.

'Here we are,' he said, helping her down. 'You OK?'

Tess shook out her hair and looked around her. 'I'm fine,' she said, smiling. 'First time.'

'I'm glad it was me,' he said, mock-serious. 'C'mon, let's go get a drink.'

'Where are we?' Tess said.

'Right by the Spanish Steps,' Peter said. 'But we're going to a bar nearby first, is that OK?'

She didn't know where they were and, for the first time in days, she wasn't in charge. 'That sounds absolutely great.'

They walked through a grid of thin, narrow streets. Off the main street through Via Condotti, with its designer boutiques all shuttered up, lifeless dummies in the windows, in minimalist blacks, blues and greys, expensive handbags laid out on glass plinths like holy icons to be worshipped during the daytime. They cut one block down and an uneasy silence settled upon them. It was quiet, no cars, few people, and Tess started to wonder if she'd made a mistake, if being a free spirit was so great or whether it was better to be tucked up in bed back at the hotel with the Barbara Pym she had just started.

But then Peter said, 'Here we are. OK, what would you like to drink?' and Tess realized they were standing outside a tiny little bar, with a few tables in the front, and peering inside, she made out a long, low, orange-lit room whose walls were crammed with black-and-white photos. Above the door it said, '*ENOTECA DI GIORGIA*'. There were a couple of people outside, smoking, and a few more inside.

'Shall we go in?'

'Oh, no,' said Tess, who was from a country where any outside eating and drinking was viewed as a luxury rather than a right. 'Let's stay outside. It's a lovely night.' She looked down the street. 'Via Bor – Via Borgononola,' she said, stumbling over the syllables.

'Via Borgognona,' Peter said. 'One of my favourite places, this street.'

'What's down there?' she said, for there was noise and light and milling people in the far distance.

'The Piazza di Spagna, where the Spanish Steps are,' Peter said. 'And the tourists. Didn't I promise you I'd take you there? Here is a little more . . . Roman.' He pulled his hands out of his pockets. 'What would you like to drink? I'll go inside.'

Tess thought for a second. 'Could I have . . . is it OK if I have a glass of . . .' She paused. 'No. Um . . .'

'Hey,' said Peter. 'I'll get it, as long as it's not heroin. Come on, it can't be so bad.'

Tess nodded. 'What I'd really like is a glass of something fizzy. Prosecco.'

'No problem.' He disappeared, emerging a few moments later and sitting down next to her. Tess was listening, rapt, to the two men at the next table, both old but rather distinguished-looking businessmen, resplendent in beautifully cut suits, who were smoking incessantly and talking rapidly in low, smooth voices. They looked up suspiciously at Tess, one of them appraising her coolly, arrogantly. The other flicked the ash from his cigarette into a foil ashtray, and dispatched the rest of the treacly liquid in his glass.

'You OK?' Peter said, pushing a small paper coaster towards her.

Tess shook her head and smiled. 'I was just thinking how Italians aren't how they seem to be. Back home, if you're Italian that means you must be a kind-hearted, apron-wearing, gesticulating person. You know? It's so clichéd. That all you do is make pasta and sing opera. Not –' she raised her eyebrows a fraction – 'be like that.'

The two men got up to leave, throwing some money on the table. '*Buona sera,*' the first said to Tess, emotionless, and they walked off.

'My father-in-law,' Peter said, 'was a local councillor in Naples.' Tess raised her eyebrows again. 'I know,' he said, smiling. 'Quite a job. Quite a job. And even in this crazy city, when the refuse strike was happening and no one knew what was going on, and the traffic was getting worse and worse and the tourism had all but dried up, every day, he'd come back to Chiara's mother for lunch – pasta, meat, coffee – and a siesta. Every day. And you know what?' He smiled. 'He was one of the sanest men I've ever met. Had his priorities straight.'

'Chiara – that was your ex-wife, right?'

Peter nodded. 'We're not divorced actually.'

'Oh.' Tess didn't know how to arrange her face at this information. 'Right!' she said breezily. He smiled.

'Comes through pretty soon though, an annulment from the Church. It pays to have an uncle who's your local priest, it would seem.' His smile was twisted, and he looked down at the table.

'I'm sorry,' said Tess, not knowing what else to say.

'Hey, that's OK,' Peter told her. He drank. 'So, how about you? Who's the person who screwed you over?'

'No one,' said Tess, alarmed. 'How did you know that?'

'I didn't, though you just told me as much,' Peter said. 'I was just making polite conversation. So who is he? Or she. No judging.'

'He,' said Tess. 'He is – oh, I don't know. He is –' The drinks arrived at that moment, and she took hers gratefully. 'Cheers. Thank you. Here's to you.'

'To you, and your holiday in Rome,' said Peter, almost formally. They drank, and Tess felt the chalky, sharp bubbles fizz deliciously in her throat, and she smiled.

'Oh, it's lovely to be here,' she said impulsively.

He laughed. 'Away from your ladies? Yes, the mysterious holiday, and I still don't know why you're here. Who was he?'

'He was . . .' Tess laughed, but then she was silent for a moment. 'I'm not sure *who* he was, to be honest.'

'What does that mean?' Peter said. 'You went out with the Phantom of the Opera, is that it?'

Tess took another sip of her drink, feeling the bubbles in her throat. She closed her eyes briefly, listening to the soft chatter from inside the bar, the lovely sound of Italian.

'He was called . . . Will,' Tess said. She shook her head. 'Gosh. A year ago, I thought we were all set, that we didn't have a totally perfect relationship, but that – hey – who does? I thought we'd be together for ever, we'd been together for two years or so. And then . . .' She narrowed her eyes, trying to remember what it had been like, being with Will. But she couldn't. It was like she had been another person, her London self who didn't have any wellies and who always blow-dried her hair. And who felt slightly numb inside all the time.

'And then . . . ?'

'Then I moved back home and . . . and . . . my oldest friend – he's called Adam.' She looked up at Peter, and met his gaze, then she shook her head. 'This is stupid. You don't want to hear all this.'

'Actually, I do,' he said. 'I like hearing about other people's lives, it's my job. And it means I don't have to think about my own crappy life for a while. Carry on.' He waved his drink at her, as though he was conducting, and then waved to the waiter who was standing in the doorway, watching them. '*Un'altra bottiglia, per piacere.*'

Tess put her drink back on the table. 'The thing is, I don't want to talk about it.'

'So maybe just tell me the rough outline.' His voice was kind. 'It's easier to tell a stranger, after all.' He looked at his watch. 'And it's kinda late. My time of day. Tell me.'

She laughed again, her voice low in the darkness. And then she told him about Langford, about the new job, about the holiday, about everyone who was on the holiday. He was a good listener – but he was a journalist, she would tell herself afterwards, he was paid to listen.

Still, she liked him, nonetheless. She liked the way he laughed as she told him about the ladies, the Older and Younger camps, and about Langford. She liked the way he chewed his lip when she told him about Leonora Mortmain and how disquieting she found her. She liked the smile on his face as she told him how much she loved teaching them, being here and seeing all these things. She liked his bitten nails, and the way he drummed his fingers on the rickety metal table, softly, while she talked. She liked his curiosity about her, about why she was here, what she was like, what she liked. It was nice, on the simplest level, to be with someone who wanted to know about you – who you were, what you did, and who was interested in what you say. That, in itself, was enough to make her feel a little sad.

But she shrugged it off, and they fell into a companionable silence, while she stared unseeingly into her glass. She was in Rome, in a café with a mysterious stranger. She felt as if she were coming alive again, waking up after a long, long sleep. Tess shivered to herself.

'Are you cold?' Peter said.

'No,' said Tess. 'I was just thinking.' She looked at him. 'Can I ask you something?'

He nodded.

'Have you seen your wife since she left?'

He looked a bit surprised, but shook his head. 'No. Well, once, but she didn't know it.'

'When?'

'I went to Naples last month,' he said. 'I had a story to do, I was writing about Berlusconi making his first visit there and promising to sort out the refuse. But I went to her parents' apartment, to find her.' He breathed out through his nostrils. 'Because – man. She wouldn't return my calls, my emails, texts, nothing.'

'You didn't know where she was?' Tess said, alarmed.

He said, 'Yeah, I knew that. I knew she'd left me, gone back to Leon – that's the guy, she was with him when we first met, two years ago.'

'Where did you meet?'

'At a UN thing in New York. She's a translator.' He lifted his face to the sky, and moved his head from side to side, so his neck clicked. 'She was living with him, but we got together and – then we got married, a year after we met.'

'Wow,' said Tess. 'That's fast.'

'Too fast, it would seem,' Peter said grimly.

'Oh,' Tess said. 'But you fell in love. You weren't to know.'

He laughed. 'You're an optimist, aren't you? I should have known, I think. Someone who's with a boyfriend already and happily cheats on him with you isn't someone you should one hundred per cent trust.'

'And this is Leon?'

'Yeah. He's Bosnian.'

'Right.'

'He's an asshole.'

'He sounds it.'

Peter's voice grew softer and softer. 'So I go to her mother's place. I just want to talk to her, for her to talk to me, you know?' He shook his head. 'To treat me like a human being, not a dog, or something you'd kick in the street, like a used

Coke can. But I got there, and I stood in the street, it's right by the music academy there, and there's some guy playing the violin in the apartment across the street, and I looked up and – there she was. In the window, with Leon.'

'What – what was she doing?' Tess said, fear in her voice.

He said slowly, 'She was laughing.'

'Oh,' said Tess.

'She had her arms round his waist and she was laughing at something he said. And that's when I knew it was over.'

'You knew then?'

'Yeah,' he said. 'You know . . . you can convince yourself about a whole bunch of crap when you're in it. It's going to work out, that thing they do doesn't matter, relationships are hard. But when you see the woman you love with someone else . . . and the way she looks at him, she never looked at you like that . . . well.' He drained the last of his drink. 'No one's going to give you that piece of information. You have to see it for yourself.' He put the glass down on the table. 'No matter how much it hurts.'

Impulsively, Tess reached out and lightly touched his hand. His eyes opened, and she blinked, settling back swiftly in her seat. 'I'm so sorry,' she said, genuinely sad for him. 'I know what you mean, I think.' She thought of Adam's hands on her body, of Francesca's luscious, cool voice in the darkness of the hotel room, the way he drew back from Tess when he heard it. How much that had hurt her, and that was, she told herself, nothing compared to what Peter must have felt.

His dark eyes met hers again, and she was unable to prevent herself saying, 'She's mad, your wife, anyway. Leaving you, I mean.'

Peter grinned. 'Why?'

Perhaps it was the jasmine, or the Prosecco, or Italy in general. Tess said, 'She just is. I've only known you two days. But trust me.'

He turned to her swiftly. He caught her arm, and looked

at her, shaking his head, his eyes searching, his face illuminated only by the soft light from the café.

'Tess,' he said. 'Wow –' He stared at her curiously, and she back at him, biting the tip of her tongue between her teeth, not knowing what to say now to him, wishing she'd kept quiet. But suddenly the tension cleared; he laughed. 'You're hilarious.' He covered her hand with his. 'Thank you. Well, the same is true of you.' He patted her arm. 'It really is.'

'Thanks,' she said softly.

They stared at each other for a few moments, and the dark street seemed to entirely melt away, as if they were the only people around. 'OK,' Peter said after a few moments. 'How about I show you some more of Rome, before I drop you off?'

'Sure,' said Tess.

'What do you have tomorrow on the itinerary?'

'Pompeii,' she said. His eyes widened.

'Really? You guys are packing it in, aren't you. So we'd better go.' He took some euros out of his trouser pocket and put them on the table, shaking his head as she made for her bag. 'This is my treat. Come with me.'

CHAPTER TWENTY

They walked up the road to the Piazza di Spagna, and as they emerged on the square – really more of a long, asymmetrical oblong – Tess gasped. The Spanish Steps were huge, wide, taller than the buildings flanking them, floodlit, leading to a vast church perched high above. Though it was after one a.m., there were still people sitting, chatting, talking.

'This is proper tourism,' Peter said. 'You should see it during the day. Horrible.'

Tess gazed up at the steps and the huge pink Baroque church at the top, at the tourists and the locals chatting, walking gently through the palm trees in the middle of the piazza, at the warmth and humanity gathered together. 'I like it,' she said. 'I've always liked it.'

'You would,' said Peter. 'You're not nearly elitist enough for a Latin teacher. I'll give you the tour, though you probably know it all.'

'I haven't been here for over ten years,' Tess said. 'And everything I know about Rome happened in BC time. I don't know the rest.'

'OK!' he said, looking pleased. 'So it's called the Spanish Piazza because the Spanish Embassy's over there –' he put his hand on her shoulder and pointed – 'and Keats died in that

218

house there –' he swivelled her round a little, gesturing to a rose-pink house next to the steps. 'And this is where all the smart nineteenth-century tourists used to stay, around here, before it got taken over by fat people in coach parties who want to go to McDonald's. Over there,' he said, pointing to the far corner of the piazza. 'Mostly Americans. I admit it. Sometimes I hate my countrymen and women.'

'At least they've made the effort to come in the first place,' said Tess, gazing up at the church. 'Better than staying at home and having no interest in the world around you.' Peter's grip on her shoulder tightened.

'I know, but why come if you're just going to blindly follow some crazy lady with an umbrella around like a sheep for a week? What's the point, when you don't see anything with your own eyes, because you're too busy looking at it through a camera, so you've got something to take back and show the folks at home?' She laughed, mostly out of surprise at the anger in his voice, but when she turned round, she realized he really meant it.

'Sorry,' Peter said. 'I guess when you live in another country, you only see the worst of the one you left behind. And you want to be identified with the place you live, not where you're from. Sounds stupid.'

'No it doesn't,' said Tess. 'Doesn't at all. Don't you miss it, though?'

He jumped a little. 'What, living in the States? Sometimes. I miss my friends. I miss other stuff about it.'

'Like what?'

'Well – I don't know. Lately –' He scratched the back of his neck. 'I've been here two years, and I love it. But my editor rang me up yesterday, about a job back home.'

'Wow,' said Tess. 'Where?'

'San Francisco,' Peter said. He nodded. 'Yeah. I always wanted to go there, too. West Coast correspondent. It's a pretty cool job. I'm going to interview with them over the phone.'

Tess felt slightly betrayed, she didn't know why. This wasn't part of her *Roman Holiday*-esque fantasy, the gorgeous American man hopping on a plane back home. 'Don't you like it here?'

'I love it here,' he said, and he smiled at her. 'I'll probably end up staying here anyway, the job is way out of my league. And I kind of feel like I was meant to live in Rome. But we'll see.'

They turned and started walking, away from the gentle tide of people walking towards the steps. 'OK then,' said Peter. 'If we're doing the proper tourist trail, let's tackle the big one. The Mount Everest. The tackiest thing ever built in a town like this – it should be the set for an Elton John concert, not in a sidestreet in Rome. Come on, let's get on the bike.'

It was only a short ride through the tiny sidestreets of the Centro Storico. Tess was amazed to see so many people still out, despite the hour; Italians, mostly, couples walking arm in arm, elegant women in brown and grey and black, men with jumpers thrown casually over their shoulders, young men in groups, young women talking animatedly, their heels clattering on the pavements, all out for a late-night *passeggiata*. They stopped in a dark alley, and Peter kicked the stand on the moped out and locked it. Tess stood next to him, shivering slightly in the sudden chill of the night. She raised her arm to look at her watch, then stopped. She didn't want to know what time it was now, she didn't care. It was late. Too late. She should have gone to bed ages ago. Tomorrow was – oh, tomorrow was to be worried about tomorrow. She'd feel awful anyway. She had to remember, though, to—

She felt a light hand on her shoulder, and turned around in surprise.

'We're here,' said Peter. And he took her hand, and they walked down a tiny sidestreet, towards a great white light, where the sound of rushing water grew louder as they approached. 'Keep on walking,' he said. 'We have to walk round, so you can see it from the front.' He put his hand over her eyes, and guided her, slowly. 'Up these steps. Avoid the stall selling charming plaster casts of the Pope and the Colosseum. Just here, oh, I'm sorry –'

Tess yelped as she stubbed her toe on a marble bollard.

'OK. It's time. Behold,' he said, taking his hand away from her eyes. 'The Trevi Fountain. Where Vegas comes to Rome.'

Tess gasped, she couldn't help it. She had been to Rome several times, starting with when she was a teenager on a school trip, and she must have come to the Trevi Fountain then, and other times since. Yet she had no personal memory of it, more a composite, and she didn't know if that was real or based on *La Dolce Vita*. Not until now.

'It's hilarious,' Peter said.

'It's wonderful,' she retorted. He looked at her, surprised.

'You really think so? I think it's awful.'

Vast, alarmed-looking horses and athletic but slightly indolent-looking gods stood over them, as the floodlit bright blue water crashed against the huge white marble edifice, which was carved as if it were rock and stone, with botanical accessories. Tess laughed with delight. 'How can you say that. It's brilliant. Look –' she grabbed his hand. 'Look at that seagull, looking really confused, next to that marble plant. It doesn't know if it's real or not.'

Peter smiled and squeezed her hand, not releasing it. 'Maybe you're right. It's pretty nasty in the day, though.'

'But we're here at night,' Tess said, turning to him, smiling happily. 'And it's lovely.'

There was a silence; a comfortable silence, and Tess thought again how easy it was to be with him, this virtual stranger. He held onto her hand, as they stood at the side of the fountain, watching a few teenagers play at its edge, a couple talking seriously, an old man walking steadily past, eyes averted, as if its very gaudiness offended his eyes. One of the teenagers screamed in outrage, as another took something off him and ran away, laughing. Tess turned to Peter, curiously.

'You never asked me any questions,' she said, suddenly. 'I thought you wanted to ask me some questions, about the mugging.'

'I did,' he said. 'Oh – yes, that's totally right.' He looked a little chastened; she wished she hadn't said anything. 'We should do that.' He released her hand, and ran his fingers through his hair. The moment was gone, she realized, cursing herself. She'd ruined it. 'So – what are you doing tomorrow night?'

'I didn't mean –'

'Hey, no!' Peter said. 'What are you up to, maybe we could have a quick conversation about it, or maybe –'

'Well, we get back from Pompeii late afternoon, I think, and we're just doing our own thing tomorrow evening, I didn't want them to worry about having to get back and change for supper so we'll just have something casual.' She paused. 'So, I'm kind of free.'

'Right.' He was rummaging in his pockets, and didn't look up. Tess swallowed, and put her hand on his arm.

'And then Friday's free too. All day. I'm by myself all day.'

'A free day,' said Peter. 'That is interesting. So – it's a free day.'

'Yes,' said Tess.

'Meaning –'

'We can do whatever we want.' Her eyes met his.

'Can we?'

'Not necessarily you and me,' she said, tapping him on the chest. 'But –'

He caught her hand and held it. 'I'm serious,' Peter said. She looked at him, curious.

'What do you mean?'

'This,' he said, and he bent his head and kissed her.

Usually, there is some sign that the hero and heroine of the scene are about to start kissing, Tess thought. But here, none – well, he was a boy, she was a girl, they were in Rome, it was a late night in summer . . . but other than that . . . Oh. She really was out of practice at recognizing the signs.

She closed her eyes briefly, and Peter put his hand on the back of her neck and drew her towards him. It was late, and quiet, and the only sound was the crashing water from the fountain, and the only movement the water falling against the floodlit white carved rocks of marble. His chin scraped hers; she could feel his tongue, gently pushing into her mouth. His lips pressed on hers, and he pulled her towards him, fervently, his hands on her hips.

'It shouldn't happen here,' he said, after a while, pulling away from her and breathing deeply. His fingers touched her shoulder bone, moving the strap of her dress off a little so he could kiss her skin. 'This place isn't the place where it should happen.'

She smiled. 'I don't mind. I like it.'

'You are such a lil' tourist.' He was kissing her collar bone now, moving up to her neck, his lips tickling her, his stubble scratching her. She sighed, catching him to her. 'So I'll see you tomorrow night, then?' he murmured, the pads of his fingers stroking her skin.

'Yes,' she said happily. 'Tomorrow.'

'You're not going right now, are you?'

She looked at her watch. It was just after two. She looked back at him, at his dark eyes, glittering in the light from the fountain, his wicked, kind smile that she knew so well, she felt, yet which was so full of promise, so exciting.

'No,' she said, grinning. 'Not *right* now.'

'How long have I got?' he said, running his hands through her hair, over the back of her neck.

'Oh . . . about five minutes. Max,' she said, smiling. And

223

she kissed him back, pulling his head towards her, wrapping her arms around him and, for the first time since she'd got to Rome, Tess Tennant started feeling less like an old schoolteacher and more like a young woman.

CHAPTER TWENTY-ONE

Going to the ruins of Pompeii, a summer home town for rich Romans destroyed by the eruption of Vesuvius in 79 AD and preserved beautifully in volcanic ash, so that generations of tourists can troop round its wide, spookily empty streets and pay five euros for a small bottle of water, is not a day trip away. It might be, if you are a hardy type who doesn't mind getting up at six a.m. to supervise a group of truculent grown-ups in getting to the station and on the right train for Naples at seven a.m. but otherwise it is just too damn hard. And yes, arriving at Naples, the craziest town in Europe, is a little taxing, but you just have to go with the flow because something weird is going to happen to you, even if you're only there for twenty minutes. As Tess discovered.

It was peculiarly unfortunate that the group of child pick-pockets selected Carolyn Tey to rob of some euros in her moneybelt, and even more unfortunate that a taxi driver, enraged when they said they didn't want a cab, that they were only looking for the Circumvesuviana train station, the train line that went to Pompeii, should squeeze Carolyn's bottom, of all people's, and ogle her quite so suggestively. As Diana said, when they were finally on the local line and Carolyn lay, prostrated across two seats, gasping with hysteria,

'I don't usually ask for that kind of thing, but I do wish he'd picked me instead of her.'

Tess was only thankful that Leonora Mortmain had said she was not coming today. She was probably right to give it a miss. 'I am not being buffetted from pillar to post to go to Pompeii and back in One Day,' she had said. 'It is a ridiculous idea. I shall stay in my room, and they may bring me luncheon on the terrace.'

Travelling on this line, which skirted the Naples coastline, going down to Sorrento and Positano, those beautiful coastal resorts, had long been a dream of Tess's, and what a dreadful disappointment it turned out to be. The line was slow, the trains were hot and dirty and covered in graffiti, the landscape was impoverished, industrialized and uninspiring. The sea was miles away. They chugged in muggy silence, looking out of the greasy, graffiti-covered window, and Tess started to wonder then if this was a good idea.

At ten thirty they disembarked from the train, and by eleven they were wandering round the ruins of Pompeii, and it suddenly became a good idea. The streets were wide and empty, the stepping stones the citizens used to cross the roads were still there. The bawdy drawings of Priapus with his enormous member – painted as good luck, to ward off evil spirits from the house – briefly revived their spirits. It was their third day of sightseeing, and Tess felt able, as she led them around, to cross-reference with a couple of other places they'd visited. The little stalls, with two holes in the counters for amphorae that would have sold food, right next to a grand nobleman's mansion, next to a brothel, next to another stall selling wine: Tess always loved how jumbled up it all was, like the Forum. It wasn't like suburbia as she knew it, rows and rows of identical houses, where a corner shop was a good five-minute drive away. Everything was together here: rich and poor, good and evil and, in the distance, a dark, sloping shadow, the mass of Vesuvius, covered even today in a dark cloud.

'It seems so far away, they must have watched it erupt and thought they were going to be OK,' said Liz, as they stood on the Via del Vesuvio and looked north towards the volcano.

'They did,' said Tess. 'And that's why so many people died, and so quickly.' She rubbed her eyes.

'Hey, are you all right?' said Liz curiously. 'You seem awfully tired, if you don't mind me saying so! Are you coming down with something?'

'I didn't get much sleep,' Tess admitted. 'Totally my fault. I'm exhausted. Bit of an early start, too.'

Liz nodded. 'You're telling me. Oh, well. You can sleep this evening. And tomorrow.'

'Ye-es,' said Tess. She rubbed her ear.

She didn't know if she was going to see Peter that night, or even tomorrow. She wanted desperately to see him again. Her mind was totally alert: she couldn't stop thinking about him. She was fizzing with excitement about seeing him again, despite her grogginess and lack of sleep. What was it about him that was so completely appealing? It wasn't just his extraordinary good looks, nor the way he made her laugh. Nor the way she could tell him anything. It was – oh, a combination of all of those, but more the feeling that it was like a sign, a weird karmic thing that had brought them together. Despite having signed a witness declaration form at the Polizia the previous day before supper, a laboriously long process, she was certain that was the last she'd hear of the moped mugger. The pain in her shoulder was almost gone, too: it was, honestly, she felt, as if that was all imaginary, just a ruse to get her to meet Peter. As if, after years of Will's coldness and Adam's mind games and then months of wearing clompy shoes and not shaving her legs and feeling totally unattractive, as if she had been sleeping, and he had come to wake her up.

'You make me feel like a natural woman,' she sang quietly. 'Here, we're going to the Visitors' Centre for lunch.'

227

'And then home?' Carolyn asked hopefully.

'Bit more to see, and then home!' Tess said perkily, girding herself and picking up a tray. 'Ooh, pasta salad. Lovely!'

It was a long, long day, and when they eventually got back to the hotel in Rome the pinched feeling behind Tess's eyes felt more like a vice, and her feet were killing her, the blister on her toe resembling something like an open sore. She staggered up to her room in the late afternoon heat, trying to be polite to poor Carolyn – no, unfortunately she didn't think there was any point in filing a report with the police on the Incident in Naples – and Jan Allingham – no, she didn't have any hairspray, but there was a pharmacy opposite, they would have some. Thank you. Goodnight.

She opened her bedroom door, kicked it shut with her foot, flung open the window and then fell face forwards onto the freshly straightened and turned-down valance, feeling the silky, shiny new sheets under her nose and chin.

'I love you, bed,' she muttered, and closed her eyes, her legs sticking off the edge of the bed, and she passed out in seconds.

Minutes later – or was it hours? Days, it could have been – Tess awoke, to the sound of banging, she thought in her head. Blearily, she looked up, then turned over so she was on her back. What was it? She looked up, her eyes adjusting to the darkness, and then realized she had no idea where she was, or what time it was. She blinked, breathed in, saw the open window, realized she was in Rome, and looked at her watch. It was eight o'clock – must be eight o'clock at night. Yes. Pompeii. The train ride back to Naples in the carriage smelling of urine . . . She ran her hands over her face, feeling the slimy grime and sweat of the day settling in her pores . . .

There was that noise again, on the window. It was more like a splatter, not a bang. Tess sat up, her head spinning, and looked towards the open window, as if expecting to see a swarm of frogs, merrily jumping up and down and throwing themselves wetly against her shutters. She got up and, with a slightly wobbly gait, for she was still half-asleep, leaned out of the window, which is when it hit her.

Something cold, fleshy and wet landed on her face. She screamed, her mouth obstructed by whatever it was that she thought was attacking her, and fell back onto the bed. From a distance, she could hear someone, calling, 'Tess! It's me! Hey, are you OK?' Her hands flew to her face, shaking, her reactions delayed by fatigue and recent sleep, and removed a clump of wet paper towels, which had been soaked in something . . . she sniffed it. Wine?

'Eh?' she said aloud, in the darkness of her room. She hauled herself up from the edge of the bed, and leaned gingerly out of the window again, holding up her hands. 'Don't throw any more!' she called incoherently into the leaves of the trees outside her window. Then she looked down, onto the pavement.

There, standing on the pavement with a metal bucket in his hand, was Peter, looking up at her, concern etched on his face.

'Shit,' he said, as Tess dabbed ineffectually at herself. 'Did I get you? I was only trying to get your attention, I wasn't even sure you were there . . . I couldn't risk throwing stones, I did that once before and it broke a window clean through.'

'Peter?' she said, dumbly. 'Hello? Is that you?'

He smiled up at her. 'Hey.'

'Hey,' said Tess, rubbing her brow, where she had been hit particularly hard. 'What the –'

'I was just wondering if you wanted a drink,' Peter called up. An old lady passed him on the street, muttering at him, and gesturing at him; he stepped out of the way.

'So you wait outside my room and then hit me in the face with paper soaked in – what is this?'

229

'Prosecco,' he said. 'I got a bottle of it.' He held up the bucket, which she could now see was an ice bucket. 'I remembered you like it.' He sighed, and started laughing. 'This hasn't gone well, has it?'

Tess laughed too – she couldn't help it, it was infectious. 'I'll come down,' she said. 'Give me five minutes.'

'Have you eaten? I have an idea.'

'No, and I'm starving,' she said.

'That's great.'

'Peter –' she called.

'Yes, Tourist Tess?'

'I'm so tired I can barely stand.'

'That's OK. We're going to be sitting.'

'Oh.' Tess smiled down at him. 'Oh. OK. Um – I'll see you in a sec.'

'Hurry up,' he said, and she could hear the laughter in his voice as she stepped away from the window.

Thirty minutes later, at the top of the steps leading to the Janiculum Hill, where the streets of Trastevere are even more cobbled and steep than usual, Peter and Tess sat on a bench overlooking the city, each eating a pizza and drinking the Prosecco in the wine bucket.

'This is possibly my favourite meal so far in Rome,' Tess said, chewing happily. She turned to him and shivered, hardly able to believe he was next to her, that this was happening, this lovely, handsome, kind stranger was real.

'You haven't had pizza yet?'

'I have,' said Tess. 'But every time I've eaten so far, it's mostly been with a group of people who are tugging your arm and asking what the Italian for parmesan is, or where the loos are, or when we're leaving, or – having mental breakdowns and acting totally weird. I haven't just –' she turned and smiled at him – 'just sat and eaten some food and chatted.'

He tucked a lock of her unruly black hair behind her ear,

and smoothed his finger over the bone beneath, tracing a path down to her neck. 'Poor thing.'

'I'm not complaining,' she said softly, breathing in, luxuriating in his touch, letting the feeling it gave her to feel his fingers on her skin sink in. She rubbed her eyes. 'I am complaining, and I should shut up. I'm just tired.'

'That's my fault.'

She looked out at the grey-blue sky fading into night, the glowing ochre city beneath them, the pizza box on her lap, his hand on her shoulder. 'How can you say that, Peter?' she said, smiling. 'This is the best bit so far.'

'It gets better,' he said, moving along the bench so he was next to her. He kissed her gently, sucking her bottom lip and biting it tenderly, his hand on her neck. Behind them a couple passed by, talking fast in Italian, not breaking off at all to wonder at two people kissing on a bench high above the city. She loved that about Rome. No wrapping herself up in layers, the feeling of sun on her shoulders, the feeling of Peter's lips on hers. She felt she was coming alive again. No one to care, no one to answer to . . . for this night and tomorrow, anyway.

'I'm on holiday,' she said, happily.

'You've finally realized,' he said, kissing her neck.

'No, I mean – I'm free tonight and tomorrow. It's my holiday within the holiday.'

'So you are,' he said, his eyes glittering at her in the dark. 'So you are. Well, what are you doing tomorrow?'

'I don't know,' she said, suddenly shy. 'I was going to –' Her hands knotted themselves together in her lap. 'I don't know,' she admitted.

Peter sat back and looked at her. 'Come back to my apartment. Tonight. We can spend the day together tomorrow.'

'No!' said Tess, laughing. 'I can't do that.'

'Why not?' he said seriously. 'What's stopping you?'

'I –' Tess looked out over the twinkling scenery of Rome, laid out like a set design in front of her. 'I don't know you.

And I have to get back tonight, to make sure no one's died, or run off, or something.'

'Go on.'

'And –' She blinked, her eyeballs aching as they had been all day. 'I'm really, really tired.'

'That's pathetic.'

'I know,' said Tess. She shook her head, looking at him, and took a deep breath. 'Yeah, it is. You're right. And – hey! They'll be OK if I don't go back, they're not babies, are they.' She paused. 'But still.'

'You're worried you don't know me.'

'No, it's just I'm tired,' she said, laughing. 'Honestly.'

'How can I prove to you that I'm a good guy,' said Peter. His hand rested on the bare skin of her thigh, and she shivered. He clapped his hands. 'Let's play a game, shall we?'

'OK,' said Tess, uncertain.

'OK.' Peter stroked the collar of his beautifully pressed shirt – he was always immaculately dressed, Tess noticed, like a true Italian – and held up the index finger on his right hand. 'So I tell you one thing about myself. You –' he held up the index finger on his left hand – 'you tell me one thing about yourself.'

'Right,' said Tess. 'That's easy.'

'Only rule is,' said Peter, 'you can't have said it to anyone else before. Doesn't matter how stupid it is. You just can't have told anyone else before. OK?'

Wow. 'OK,' Tess said.

It was warm up on the side of the hill, as the evening grew later and the lights of the city dimmed one by one. Tess was still bone tired, but she was totally comfortable, sitting here as a soft evening breeze, like a gentle spirit, played around her hair, her shoulders, in the trees of the park behind them. 'You go first,' said Peter, nodding at her.

'Well –' Tess wasn't sure of the parameters. This was hard, like writing a message on a colleague's leaving card hard. You had to be pithy, but interesting. Reveal something, but not too much. 'All right,' she said eventually. 'One of the worst dreams I've ever had is when I dreamt I had a band of thick black pubic hair around my neck.'

'That is really horrible,' said Peter, in admiration. 'Disgusting.'

'I know,' said Tess, pleased that he was horrified. 'I don't know why it's so horrible. It just is.'

'That's a good start.' He cleared his throat. 'So my one is, when I was ten I peed just a little bit in my dad's beer when he wasn't looking and he drank it.'

'That's awful,' said Tess.

'Yeah.'

'Did you ever tell him?'

'No,' Peter said quietly. 'He died four months later, of a heart attack. I thought it was my fault. For years.'

'And you couldn't tell anyone?' He shook his head. 'You poor thing.'

'Yeah. It wasn't good.' Peter rubbed his hands together. 'So – your turn.'

Tess took a sip of her drink. 'One of my pupils cheated in an exam and I didn't say anything. Because she'd been ill and I really liked her and she had a tough life.'

'How did she cheat?'

'We had one half of the GCSE students – that's the name of the exams – sitting the test in the morning and the second half in the afternoon, and she saw what the set text was in the morning over someone else's shoulder when she was sitting a different exam.' Tess blinked. 'So she could go and look up the text in her lunch break and learn it properly and then ace it.'

'What could have happened to you? If they'd found out?'

'I don't know.' Tess looked down at her hands. 'Sacked, probably. They closed down the department the next year anyway. The funny thing is, I still think it was the right thing to do.'

'Really?'

'Sort of,' Tess said. 'She did A levels, she's from a rough estate and her family's completely messed up. She's going to university. She might not have done without it.'

'But she cheated.'

'But she'd been ill with a tummy bug and she hadn't revised properly.' Tess's voice trembled. 'So – yeah. I don't tell anyone that.' She shook her head. 'It's got to be your turn now.'

'OK.' Peter nodded, looking out over the city. He looked down, picked up the bottle, poured the remaining liquid into their glasses. 'Man. OK. When I moved to Rome, I –' He shook his head. 'Wow. I knew she was having an affair, soon after we got married. I just had this feeling. So I followed her. I followed her for about two weeks.'

'Seriously?'

He nodded. 'Seriously. And I was right.' He rubbed his eyes. 'And it made me feel so pathetic. Scurrying around like a rat, watching out for her all the time, hiding behind corners – that's why sometimes I think I have to leave, go back to the States – Rome's good for that, hiding behind things, dashing down sidestreets.' He smiled bitterly.

Tess hated watching him like this. 'Did you see her?'

'I saw her. I heard her—' he broke off. 'That's when I stopped.'

'You *heard* her?' Tess was incredulous. 'With him?'

'I followed her to a hotel, some place out by the Borghese Gardens. I wasn't sure what room, I walked along the corridors.' He cleared his throat. 'Then I heard her.'

'What was she doing?'

He stared at her impatiently. 'Tess, I know what sounds my wife makes when she's having sex, even if it's not with me.'

'My God.' *My wife.* He still called her his wife.

'It's pathetic.' He drained the glass and dropped it into the ice bucket. 'It's so – pathetic. You hate yourself, more than anything. I just went home and sat on the edge of my bed for hours. I didn't say anything when she got back. Didn't say anything for another two months.'

'Wow.'

'It was pathetic,' he said again, and then frowned. 'Shit, I can't even think of words to describe it, and I'm a journalist. That's what it did.'

She patted his hand, holding it on her leg, stroking it. 'That's not you. That's her. That's *awful*, Peter. You don't deserve someone like that.'

'Oh, is that right.' He was morose. 'I deserve someone worse than me. Someone who secretly films people having sex and then watches it back.'

'No, someone better than that!' Tess said. 'Much better than that. Someone who makes you behave like that, who drives you to that – they're not worth it.'

The skies over the city absorbed the light, so that the clouds above them were almost purple. He shrugged his shoulders. 'Whatever you say. Your turn.'

'Well,' Tess said. 'We're certainly racing through the issues, aren't we? OK.' She swallowed. 'I put – oh, man, this is bad.'

'What?!' Peter looked up, interested.

'Well –' Tess explained. 'My big sister Stephanie, she was always friends with me and Adam, my best friend. And when we were teenagers, she told me she liked him. But I didn't want them to – *do* anything. I wanted him to myself. As friends, you know.'

'So what did you do?'

'Well, Stephanie said she was going to go over and ask him out.' Tess could still remember the day, as clearly as if it were yesterday. Stephanie, two years older than her and supremely confident, thin and unconcerned with what other people thought, blithely standing up after breakfast one day in the summer holidays. 'I'm going to ask Adam out, now,' she'd said. As if it was nothing. No big deal.

'Come on!' Peter slapped the bench. 'What did you do?'

235

'I – oh, my God.' Tess buried her face in her hands. 'I picked my nose, really casually, and I put a bogey on her hair. I sort of patted her head, like, "Good luck!" so it was at the front of her hair. And then she left – he lived across the road. And she came back about five minutes later and she never mentioned it again.'

Peter was staring at her. 'You are evil.'

'I know.' Tess shook her head. 'I know, there's nothing I can do about it.' She took a deep breath.

'You must have really liked him.'

'Oh,' Tess scratched her neck. 'It's just he was my best friend, you know? In my awful selfish teenager mind I didn't want it getting in the way.'

'What happened to him?'

'He's still there,' said Tess. 'Yeah, still there. We're still friends.'

'That's cool.'

'Yes, really cool.' She looked at him. 'So, your turn.'

'I'm not sure we should be uncovering any more. OK though,' he said. He looked at her, as if appraising her. 'OK. Whew.' He took a deep breath; it was quieter now, later, it felt as if they were the only people in the park. 'I wrote my mom letters, from a handsome suitor. When I was like sixteen. Telling her she was beautiful.'

'What?'

'She was just really sad all the time. And crying. She was really lonely.' He wrapped his arms tightly around himself. 'I can't believe I did it. I wrote her like, four, five times.' He said it as if he were reciting a lesson. 'I can remember it totally clearly. I said I was someone in the neighbourhood, that I thought she was a very pretty lady, that I really liked her but I couldn't tell her who I was.'

'You're joking,' Tess said. 'That's – that's amazing.'

'Well, it's weird.' Peter drummed his fingers on the bench. 'I think it made her happy, that's the crazy part. I really think she fell for it.' He rolled his eyes. 'She started dating, taking us to the beach in the summer. She married my stepdad like, three years later. Like that had anything to do with it –' He put his hand out. 'But sometimes I think people need to hear someone likes them, even if it's not true. It's good for the soul. Carry yourself differently.'

Tess nodded. 'It's true,' she said fervently, amazed by him. She put her hand on his. 'It is good for the soul.'

'I think it's weird,' said Peter. 'When I look back on it. But remember –' he smiled – 'I thought I killed my dad, too. It's very Oedipal. So that's it. That's the biggest secret of my teenage years. Phew.' He breathed out. 'What's yours? Or is the thing in the hair or the weird dream, is that it?'

There was silence. Below them, the sound of ambulance sirens rose up from the roads along the Tiber, and a church bell rang somewhere; she could hear, very faintly, music floating up from a piazza, at the bottom of the hill. It was polka music, a violin, a piano, a tambourine.

She heard herself saying, 'I had an abortion. When I was eighteen. I didn't tell anyone. Apart from the – him, the boy.'

The music grew a little louder. 'OK,' said Peter.

Tess nodded. 'It's a long time ago, now.'

'I'm sure it is,' he said. He rested his hand gently on the back of her neck, his fingers stroking her hair. 'Do you still see him?'

'Like I said –' Tess took a deep breath – 'we're still friends.'

'Ah.' Peter lowered his head slowly. 'Oh, man. Right.'

'And it was a long time ago,' she said. 'Very long.'

'I'm glad you told me,' he said. 'Thank you.'

She breathed out, and drank the rest of the liquid in her glass.

'It's not a big deal,' she said. 'It was. It's not any more. It was years ago.'

He moved his hand so it was on her shoulder, and pulled her towards him.

'It's great up here, isn't it?' he said, as if he knew the subject was closed. 'Just the two of us.' He kissed the top of her head gently. 'You must be really tired.'

It was so long since someone had cossetted her, cared about her like that, it brought a lump to her throat. She *was* tired. She snuggled her head closer into his shoulder and stared out over the city. 'I am,' she said. 'But I'm glad I'm here.'

'Good,' he said, his fingers squeezing her shoulder. She cried out a little. 'Oh, shit, is that the bad shoulder?'

'It's much better now,' she said. 'Honestly.'

'Look at you, in the wars, going to Pompeii and back, baring your soul to me, on less than four hours' sleep.' He stood up and pulled her to her feet.

'I had a couple of hours this evening,' Tess pointed out. 'Before you woke me up by throwing a wet ball of loo roll in my face.'

'Loo roll – God, I love your accent,' he said. 'Sorry, I'll only say it once, but it is adorable. You are adorable.' He kissed her, running his hands gently over her back, touching her shoulder soothingly. She relaxed into his embrace, feeling her hair blowing slightly in the wind. They stood on the hilltop, not caring if anyone could see them. She couldn't remember the last time she had felt this comfortable, this content. Perhaps it was fatigue. Perhaps it was Rome. But she loved it.

They walked hand in hand back down towards her hotel, stopping to kiss every now and then, and when they reached the bottom of the treacherous steps that led down to her street, Peter took her hand.

'I'm going to give you an invitation,' he said. He kissed the inside of her palm. 'Come to my apartment tomorrow, for breakfast. Go in and get a good night's sleep.' His hand was on her collar bone, moving down to the cotton of her T-shirt. He pushed it aside just a little, and kissed the soft exposed mound of the side of her breast. She gasped, in pleasure and shock.

'How does that sound to you?' Peter said eventually.

She stared at him, her eyes searching his face, looking for why this didn't make sense, but she couldn't see it. 'It sounds wonderful.'

'It will be.' He smiled wolfishly at her. 'Tonight was wonderful. Now go inside. And sleep, beautiful girl. *A domani.*'

'Goodnight,' she said almost shyly, kissing him on the lips and opening the door to the hotel, as if such an assignment was totally normal for her. He waited outside, watching, until the door closed, his face disappearing as it did so.

Pompeo was on reception. He cast her a polite but cursory smile. Tess wanted to hug him. Her heart was beating so fast, like a crazed battery-powered monkey beating a drum, it almost hurt. *I've had the most wonderful fantastic evening, Pompeo,* she wanted to yell. *I think I'm falling in—*

No. No. Get a grip, she told herself.

'Lovely evening,' she told Pompeo gaily as she gripped the bannister, swaying slightly with excitement. 'Perfect for drinking Prosecco and sitting outside.'

'OK,' said Pompeo, his handsome fleshy face a study of disinterest. 'That's so good. Goodnight.'

Disappointed, but still humming with excitement, Tess ran up the stairs. Never mind what Peter said – she doubted she would sleep well, now. She didn't care, though. She would take off her clothes and put on her pyjamas, and she would lie in bed and time would pass and then morning would come and then – then she would see him again. It was almost too good to be true.

CHAPTER TWENTY-TWO

I'm going to see him, she told herself. *I'm going to feel his hands on me. He's going to kiss me, we're going to have sex, I'm going to watch him on top of me, me on top of him, our bodies together . . . he's going to do these dreadful things to me and I can't wait.*

Tess hurried across the bridge, hugging herself, her weary, blistered feet reinvigorated after a surprisingly good night's sleep. A choppy, playful breeze whirled her shirt up into an umbrella around her bra; she slapped it down, embarrassed. It was another glorious day in this glorious city, and she was full of love for the world, because not only was it a glorious day and she was on her way to see Peter, but it was also a free day.

Free! It said so, on the itinerary, in black and white, she was free today, they all were, to do what on earth they liked. Jan and Diana were going to the Botanical Gardens: Carolyn was going to 'read' (which Tess thought meant she would probably stay in her room with the door locked, terrified to venture out unless accompanied by a joint SAS/Mossad crack team); Jacquetta was going to 'see how she felt' and go where the mood took her. And Claire and Liz were putting on their nicest dresses and going to the ultra-glamorous Hotel Russie, for a cocktail and possibly some lunch. Ron and Andrea had both mysteriously said, separately, that they were going 'out for the day'. Leonora Mortmain had only said that she was going to walk across the bridge to find a painting of which she was particularly fond, in a church near the Pantheon. Tess had said, 'Are you sure, Mrs Mortmain? You look a little pale—'

'I'm very well, thank you,' Leonora Mortmain snapped. 'Please. I know what I'm doing.'

But she, Tess, was going to an apartment over the river, to have breakfast with a gorgeous, funny, mysterious American man, and hopefully spend the whole day having sex. Perhaps she should be visiting the Ara Pacis, or some out-of-the-way church, but she wasn't. Perhaps she should be . . . oh, she didn't care. It was a beautiful, bright day, in the world's most beautiful, friendly, intoxicating, gorgeous city, and it felt, as she crossed the bridge, her sea-green sundress rustling around her, as if it was all there for her, as if anything was possible, as if life could never be any other way than this.

She rang the bell next to the large green wooden door, strangely nervous though she didn't know why. Perhaps it reminded her that she'd only met Peter a few days ago. How strange to think of it, for it seemed like ages, and she felt completely different. She knew him now, too. There was lots still to learn about him, but she knew him. And every time she learned something new about him, she liked him even more.

He's like the jasmine on the wall here, she thought. Completely intoxicating. Through her mind extremely briefly flashed the thought of what Jane Austen's expression on the wall back at Easter Cottage would be if she could hear Tess thinking things like that, but she pushed it to the back of her mind.

'Hey, Tess. It's the third floor. Come on up,' Peter's voice said, crackling static over the intercom, and she jumped a little, then pushed half of the great door open eagerly.

The dark passageway was cool after the heat outside. It gave onto a small white courtyard, full of plants. She bounded up the stairs, her hand running over the smooth wooden rail. The interior was old and beautiful, white and black tiles on the floors, the staircase black wrought iron. Third floor, come on, don't lose your breath, she told herself, and slowed down a little. Just as she got to the second floor, another huge oak door opened and a voice said, 'Hey!'

Tess jumped back. It was Peter, in a white shirt and chinos. 'You said third floor,' she said, accusingly.

'This is the third floor,' Peter said. 'Your math is terrible. One,' he said, pointing at the ground floor. 'Two. *Three*,' he said, mock-slowly.

'No,' said Tess, trying not to pant with indignation. 'Crazy American fool. *Ground floor*,' she said, pointing to the front door. 'First floor. *Second floor*. Here.'

'That makes no sense,' said Peter. 'You come from a stupid country.'

'So do you,' said Tess. 'That's another thing. Why, when you write out dates, do you go month, day, and then year? It should be day, month, and then year. It makes no sense. Because –' She ran out of steam, and stood, watching him.

'Do you want to talk about US / UK dating systems?' Peter said, his hands in his pockets. 'Or do you wanna come inside and have breakfast?' His eyes ran over her.

'I want some breakfast,' Tess said. She put her hand on his shoulder, and slid it around his neck, and then she kissed him hello. 'Please.'

He looked at her from under hooded eyes, his mouth twitching. 'You'd better come in then.'

The hall was tiny, but they went into the living room, and Tess handed Peter some coffee she'd bought at a little shop by the piazza in Trastevere. 'For you,' she said.

'That's really great,' he said. 'Because I don't have any

coffee, and it was going to have been a major problem. You are a great girl, Tess.' He kissed her again, and they stood in the centre of the room, their bodies pressing against one another tightly. Tess broke away, and looked around her properly. 'Wow,' she said.

It was a big room. Two huge windows, with wooden shutters, ran the height of the ceiling from which muslin curtains hung, wafting gently in the breeze. She wandered over and looked out, over the garden of the Palazzo Farnese, across the river to Trastevere, the Janiculum Hill, the north of the city, across to the Vatican and beyond. Everything was terracotta and golden under the blue sky, flecked with the black-green pine trees, and white marble ruins. She stood there for a moment as he watched her, taking it all in.

'A room with a view,' Tess said dreamily to herself. She could hear bells ringing, chatter from down in the square, the smell of heat and cooking and tarmac that was early-morning Rome. The high ceilings had plaster cornices, the walls were a light lavender grey, covered in framed black-and-white photos, and one wall simply lined with shelves that were crammed with books and magazines. A dark wooden dining table, strewn with paper, receipts, mugs and pens, stood at one end of the room. In front of the biggest French window there was a rug, a fluffy cream seventies thing and at the other end of the room there was a sofa, some chairs, and a TV.

'This is great,' Tess said simply. 'It's just great.' Peter came up behind her, and wrapped his arms around her. He kissed her neck, her ear, her shoulder.

'Thank you,' he said. 'I don't usually have people – since Chiara I don't –' He broke off. 'That's crass. I'm sorry. It's just I was concerned about you coming here, before.' She could feel his heart, his warm body against her back. 'No one has, since she left. And it's OK. It feels . . . good.'

'It's a great place, Peter.'

'I'm glad. I'm glad you like it.' He stopped. 'I'm sorry. That woman.' He shook his head. 'She's irrelevant now. Let me get you some food. Some coffee.' He sighed a little, and kissed her again. 'What do you want?'

She turned around in his arms, and put her finger to his lips, smiling into his dark eyes. 'I want you,' Tess said gently. 'I want you.'

He shook his head, smiling gravely but sweetly, his breathing ragged. He kissed her neck, her ears, his hands running up and down her arms, and then he lowered her to the floor, peeling her dress off, slowly, smiling, and made love to her on the rug, touching her, kissing her, all over. When he eventually put on a condom and slid into her, she thought it would feel different, strange, because she remembered only then that it was the first time after Will, but it didn't, it all felt completely right. They moved together, on the hard floor, and he raised himself up to look down at her. They both came quickly after that, and she lay underneath him, tickling the hairs on his chest and stroking his shoulders, not wanting him to pull out, staring up at him, wondering how she could have been so lucky. They didn't say anything. She thought it was because they didn't need to.

Eventually he got up, tossing her a large, squashy cushion from the sofa, and a throw, and he disappeared into the kitchen. Tess drew the throw over her body and lay there, looking up at the high wooden ceilings, the ancient fan that buzzed above her, feeling no inclination to move, watching the sun shine into the room in wide white stripes.

Peter reappeared a couple of minutes later, carrying two mugs, some things on a plate, and a green bottle, glistening with dew. He raised it towards her.

'I thought we might have a toast. And some food.'

He came and knelt down beside her, and set the plate – which had salami, cheese, and some bread – down, and the mugs. He leaned forward and kissed her, and she stroked the back of his neck.

'You are almost too perfect,' she said. 'This is too perfect. Hah!' She propped herself up on one elbow as he opened the bottle, then stooped to kiss her again, run his hand over her shoulder, her arm. She stroked his dark hair back from his face, revelling in the caramel-coloured skin, the lines around the eyes, the mole on his cheek. 'Are you a made-up person, Peter Gray?'

'I swear to you I'm not,' he said, smiling. He poured the sparkling, fizzing liquid into a mug which said 'Princeton '94' on it, and handed it to her. 'It's just nice to – yeah. Doesn't matter.'

He lay back down beside her, pulling her into the crook of his shoulder, and clinked his mug against hers.

'Nice to what?' Tess said, tentatively.

'Nice to have someone to do this stuff for. Someone like you,' he said, and kissed her hair. 'How do you like your holiday now?'

She laughed, low in her throat. 'A lot better. Thanks to you.' She held the mug on her stomach, listening to the slow fizzing of the liquid, and she could feel him smiling against her hair. His fingers stroked her ribcage, her breast, under the cotton throw.

Tess felt completely relaxed, but wholly alive. *Oh, my God, I love you,* she wanted to shout. *Thank you, thank you, thank you for coming into my life. Thank you, Roman gods, for Peter Gray. I don't know what I've done to deserve it, but thank you.* She wanted to turn to him and say it, simply say it out loud. *I love you.* It was crazy, she knew it. *I don't want to go home. I want to stay here, in Rome, in this apartment, with you.*

She didn't realize it, but she was falling asleep, and as Peter's fingers carried on stroking her, her eyes closed. Peter gently took the mug out of her hand, and placed it on the floor, curling up against her, and they slept. It was not yet quite eleven in the morning. At midday, a cannon sounded, and all the church bells in Rome, it seemed, rang out, some clanging loudly and joyously, some trilling sweetly, carried across from the hills around the city into the open window, and she stirred in his arms, opened her eyes, smiled and fell asleep again.

They did not leave the apartment until after three. Finally, showered and refreshed, they stepped out, hand in hand, onto the street. Peter pulled the great wooden door gently behind him, and as he did Tess looked round, to see if anyone could see them. Yes, her and Peter, this super new, fantastic, wonderful, amazing twosome. Could other people see what they knew, that they had spent all morning and early afternoon, in the sitting room, on the floor, on the sofa, in Peter's bed, having sex, fantastic sex during which he made her cry out, during which he touched her and licked her until she screamed with pleasure? Could people tell they had been drinking, chatting, laughing, coming together more and more closely as the minutes turned to hours and time ticked by? It was the Prosecco, she told herself – but it was something else, too. The opposite of just a summer fling.

They were walking back to Tess's hotel in the early evening, slowly wandering through Trastevere before she met her group for dinner, and they walked in silence, happily, until they reached the Ponte Sisto. Its grey cobbles seemed to shimmer in the heat of the late-afternoon sun. Peter held her hand and they walked slowly across, and as they went Tess watched people walking past her. The tourist couple – were they American? – both in stripey tops, he with a camera around his neck. The dynamic-looking man and woman, both in business suits and dark glasses, walking fast, incongrously eating ice cream. They overtook an older man in a floral shirt, with a dog on a lead. The sun shone down, and Tess looked at Peter, who smiled at her.

'Well – that was probably my ideal way to spend a Friday,' he said. 'Don't you agree?'

'Definitely,' she said. She kissed him, and sighed a little. 'I feel like I've been on holiday. A holiday from the holiday.'

His lips were gentle on hers, his fingers warm on her skin. She breathed out a little, sighing again as she did. He kissed her more urgently.

'Don't sound so sad,' Peter said eventually.

'I'm not – well, you know –' Tess wasn't sure how to play it, all of a sudden, as if crossing the bridge brought her back into reality. In her mind she saw Diana's notebook, Jan's sun visor, Carolyn's querulous face. 'It's just that this is so great. And now . . . I have to go back to normal life.'

They were at the end of the bridge.

'Tess,' Peter said, turning to her. 'I know we said, holiday romance, but you know –' His hands were soft on her skin. 'Do you know what I'm thinking?' He kissed her gently on the forehead, and she closed her eyes slowly, happiness seeping through her.

'Yes,' she said, 'I was thinking something like that, too –'

'Tess!' someone called. 'Is that you? Tess?'

Tess and Peter sprang apart, and Tess narrowly avoided a young girl on a bike. 'Oof, sorry,' she said, leaning against the edge of the bridge to regain her balance. She looked down towards the Piazza Trilussa, which led back towards the hotel. There was Andrea Marsh, waving her arms and looking agitated.

'She's having a – a something!' she called. 'Ron – she's saying Ron is—! Tess, do come — quickly! Oh dear me!'

Tess looked at her and shook her head. 'What?' She jumped down onto the pavement. They were separated by a busy road; the traffic whizzed by her, as Peter stood behind her. 'What's happened?' she called. But Andrea's voice was partially obscured by the traffic.

'Leon— gone mad!' she said.

'Leon?' Peter said, from behind Tess, and Tess whirled round.

'Leonora Mortmain,' she said. 'The one I told you about, the old one – oh, my God, Peter, what's she –'

By the tiny fountain, the other side of the road, stood Ron, holding his hands up in an angry gesture of denial. He looked flustered and awkward, and in front of him, shaking her head, shaking it again and again, was a small figure in black, leaning on a stick. Leonora Mortmain.

'Come over with me,' said Tess desperately, as the incessant traffic miraculously stopped for a few seconds. They ran across the worn-out stripes of the crossing, towards the shouting couple, Andrea next to them.

'You're cracked!' Ron was shouting. 'Bloody cracked in the head, that's what!' His nose was scrunched up, and one eye was twitching. 'I ain't listening to you no more, you lying old bitch!'

'You killed her!' Leonora Mortmain screamed at him, her cracked, old voice hoarse. 'You took her away from me, and then you killed her!' It was a terrible sound; Tess stopped in her tracks. Tourists walking past them also stopped.

'Is she OK?' a woman with an Irish accent asked Tess gently. 'That lady? She's OK?'

'Yes, thanks,' said Tess, not believing herself. 'I think she's just a bit . . . confused.'

'She followed us from the hotel,' Ron said loudly. 'Tess, she followed us. She's mad!'

Andrea was standing at a distance, wringing her hands. She stepped forward, then, putting her arm gently on Ron's. 'Doesn't matter, Ron,' she said, with a calm Tess had not seen her possess before. 'Look, Mrs Mortmain,' she said, her jaw slightly protruding. 'What's the problem, eh? Ooh, watch out.'

A moped swerved past them – they were still, strictly speaking, in the road – and Andrea clutched the older woman by the arm. 'Get off me!' Leonora Mortmain cried, her hoarse voice like the screech of a bird. A man walked past with a dog, just an ordinary mongrel, smaller than a labrador, and it gave a soft growl. She jumped, pursing her lips, her eyes blazing wild like a little child's.

'I hate dogs,' she said. 'I hate dogs.' She stared at Ron. 'You know I hate dogs.' She fiddled with her hands, her fingers writhing against her stomach, and then she looked up, suddenly, and said, 'You took her away, didn't you!' She glanced around, as if suddenly realizing where she was. 'Where is he?' she asked, her eyes swivelling alarmingly fast.

'Where's who?'

Her face was a rictus of lines. 'Philip. Where's Philip?'

Tess misheard her. 'Philippa? Oh, Mrs Mortmain—'

'Not her. Not her!! I don't want her. I said Philip! Where is he?'

'Who's Philip?'

The old woman stamped her stick impatiently on the ground. '*Philip!* I keep asking, where is he? They keep saying he's coming . . . and then he doesn't. He doesn't come.'

Another moped shot past, this time sliding so close that Andrea gave a little scream as it stroked her skirt. Ron pulled her towards him, and Leonora too, but it was too late. The old woman's eyes opened wide, for the final time.

'You *are* just like me, like me,' she said, staring at Tess with a look of blazing annoyance, almost hatred. And then her mouth clamped shut and she sank, slowly, to the ground, still staring at Tess until her eyes finally closed.

CHAPTER TWENTY-THREE

A couple of years ago, Tess had watched a programme about the restoration of the famous statue of David by Donatello, which was taking place in the Bargello Museum in Florence. The restorer was a young woman who, for eighteen months, had done nothing but gently clean the surface of the metal, so the young man's beautiful body, poised between puberty and adulthood, was gleaming and soft perfection once more. She had worked with total dedication, the result being that each day she cleaned less than three square centimetres. And it would be worth it, she explained to the camera, for something so precious.

Tess was reminded of this all through that awful night, though she didn't know why. Afterwards she thought it was a sign, perhaps, of how contradictory Italians are. So seemingly willing to surrender to chaos, and yet so extraordinarily organized, patient, kind, unsentimental. The ambulance that drove them to the hospital – as she sat, staring blankly, Peter asking questions in Italian, Mrs Mortmain's tiny, stiff body lying on a stretcher – drove like a thing possessed, even though the hospital was only a couple of minutes away, the driver waving, cursing, even banging the windscreen. She had heard the ambulances' sirens all week, ululating around

Rome. It seemed completely unreal that she should be in one now.

Thank God for Peter, she kept thinking. He had called the ambulance, he had asked them to explain what was going on. He was clearly terrified too, but she didn't know what she would have done without him. He translated for her as they raced through the streets.

'She says your – Mrs – lady – she's had a stroke, probably, a kinda big one, but they need to see what damage has been done.' He patted her hand. 'It'll be fine. I'm sure. The hospital's –' He pointed, down to the river. 'It's right there. The Isola Tiberina.'

Tess had noticed, as she was crossing the Tiber a couple of times, an island in the middle of the river. 'There's a hospital there?'

He pointed again. 'Yep. It's very old. Been there since, like, Roman times I think. But it's really good.'

'Great,' she said, though it wasn't, really. 'So it's –'

'Literally two minutes away, Tess. It's going to be fine.'

She wished he wouldn't keep saying that. It wouldn't be fine. It wasn't fine.

Ron and Andrea had gone back to the hotel, to tell the others. Not knowing what else to do, as the ambulance arrived Tess had quickly rung Beth Kennett, the college principal, to break the news to her. The usually calm Beth had not been very reassuring.

'Oh, God. It's not just it's happened to someone,' she said. 'It's that it's happened to *that* someone. Shit.'

'Sorry,' said Tess, not knowing what to say. She hadn't done it on purpose, caused one of her charges to have a massive stroke. She watched as Mrs Mortmain was loaded onto a gurney and a crowd gathered around her, the afternoon sun beating down on them.

Beth sounded desperate. 'Oh, God,' she said again. 'Who's her family? I'd better call them.'

Tess paused. 'Well, she hasn't really got any.'

'There must be *someone*. She can't have no one in the world,' Beth said.

'I don't know . . .' Tess said. She felt as if she were being rude, highlighting the victim's lack of family. 'She was quite – er – solitary.'

Beth sounded brisk. 'No husband? Why's she called "Mrs"?'

'She always was,' Tess said. 'I don't know.' She realized just how much she didn't know. 'She didn't marry. I think. Actually, that's a point. I don't know who the next of kin is at all.'

'Well, that's what I mean,' Beth Kennett said. 'There must be someone. And we need to tell them.'

Tess had watched as the ambulance driver slammed the door. He gestured to her, and Peter motioned her towards the ambulance. Tess thought for a second. 'Carolyn Tey would know. I'll ask her. She'd know how to get hold of Jean, anyway.'

'Jean?'

'Her housekeeper.'

'God, it's like another world,' said Beth, breathing out with something between a splutter and a sigh. 'Fine. Can you let me know? I'll need to talk to her. Damage control, apart from anything else. And we need to discuss what you do next, how you bring them all home, her home too, depending on what her family says, if we can get hold of them. How awful. Keep me posted, Tess. You poor thing.'

The sudden kindness in her voice made Tess wobble a bit, as the shock of what had happened, the heat, the lack of sleep, all started to catch up with her. She nodded, unable to speak, and then realized that merely meant silence. 'Thanks,' she croaked.

'*Andiamo!*' the driver had called. '*Signorina, basta, basta!*'

Tess said her goodbyes and climbed into the back of the ambulance. She caught a last glimpse of the bridge, the tourists swarming around the fountain again, almost as if this had never happened there. The vehicle sped off, and she jolted a little. Someone put their hand on her leg and she jumped.

She looked up: it was Peter. She clasped his hand.

'Thank you,' she said, trying to sound brave. 'I'm glad you're here.' She looked out of the window at the scenery rushing past, trying to make things out, but everything was a blur.

The hospital was extremely old, but the wing where the ambulance took them was relatively new, with period seventies decorations oddly contrasting with marble statues of priests in clerical outfits. It was staffed by nuns. They were not kind, but they were efficient, showing Tess and Peter to a row of seats, telling them to wait. And wait and wait. They sat in a long, long corridor that seemed to go on for ever, down towards who knew what. It was very quiet, strangely so, as if the presence of the nuns subdued everyone, patients, doctors, those waiting for news.

Peter was silent. He held her hand, stroking her leg again.

'You should go,' Tess told him several times. 'I'll be fine, here, honestly.'

'No, you won't,' said Peter truthfully. 'I'll go if you want me to go, but I can speak to someone, if anyone ever appears to tell us what's going on . . .'

'It's fine, someone'll be here soon.' Tess moved his hand off her leg, again.

He smiled at her. 'I don't like doing nothing.' He got up, with the confidence of the American in an international situation, and set off to find a nurse, a doctor, anyone who might be able to help them.

Realizing they had been sitting down now for the best part of an hour, Tess got up too, and went outside, out onto the old bridge. She dialled the phone again, thanking the Lord once again that in a rare moment of efficiency – for such a crisis as this – she'd entered all her companions' numbers in, before the trip. 'Hello?' she said.

'Who's that?' a reassuringly familiar voice demanded.

'Jan, it's me, Tess. I thought I'd dialled Carolyn's number. Is she there?'

'No, she's downstairs. How is she? Where are you?'

'I'm at the hospital, and we're waiting for news.'

'She's still alive then, is she?'

Tess paused. 'As far as I know . . . yes, she's still alive.' It was so odd, her mouth framing these words. 'Has Carolyn got through to Jean?'

'She's rather upset,' Jan said.

'Of course,' said Tess, gritting her teeth.

'Diana's doing it,' said Jan.

'Diana?' Tess was surprised. 'She's got Jean's number, then?'

'She said she knows who to contact.' Jan sounded just the tiniest bit put out. 'I have to slightly say, Tess dear, it has been Chaos here for the past hour. Anyway, order has been restored. I did actually think that Diana might slap Carolyn. She got rather hysterical. Anyway, she's made the call. Jean will know what to do, she's a sensible woman.'

Tess had only met Jean Forbes a couple of times, but she knew this was true. She stared up past the hospital, out to the early-evening sky. 'I hope so,' she said. I feel wholly responsible, she wanted to say, but she didn't. 'Well, keep me posted, if they get hold of anyone.'

There was murmuring in the background; Tess could hear Jan's excitable tones, muffled by something – a hand? – over the phone. Then a voice said, 'Tess? Diana here.'

'Oh, Diana,' Tess said, relieved. 'Great to—'

'Is she still alive, then?'

'Yes,' said Tess. 'She's still alive. Listen, did you—'

'Don't worry about it at this end,' Diana said. 'Got through to them, Jean knows, she's told Clive Donaldson.'

'Clive—?'

'Eddie Tey's successor.' Tess remembered him. 'Solicitor. Handles all the Mortmain business in Langford. They've got another set in London, proper posh lot but for the moment he'll know what's best. There are things they have to do in a situation like this.'

'Things like what?' Tess asked.

Diana said, without preamble, 'Look, I can't explain all that now. You'd better go, Tess. Goodbye.' And the line went dead. Tess went back inside.

'Where did you go?' Peter was standing there with a doctor, a smart-looking woman in a white coat. 'This is your lady's doctor.'

'*Buona sera* –' Tess began, knowing a conversation with medical lingo in Italian was beyond her. '*La vecchia femina* . . .'

'Good evening,' said the doctor, in a low, scarcely accented voice, giving her a swift look. 'I am Francesca Veltroni, I am Signora Mortmain's doctor.'

'Hello,' said Tess, shaking her hand. 'Dr Veltroni – how is she?'

'I am afraid the prognosis is not good,' said the doctor. She pronounced each word deliberately, carefully, separating *not* and *good* with a glottal stop. 'Signora Mortmain has suffered an extremely serious stroke. She is not conscious. *Penso che* –' she paused. 'I think she will not recover from this, Miss –' and she looked down at her notes – 'Miss Tennant. But we will know more in the morning, I think, about how stable her condition is.' She raised her delicate eyebrows at Tess, who looked uncertainly at Peter, standing next to her. He was nodding, taking it all in. Gratitude to him washed over her. She smiled at him, and he smiled back, gave her a wink.

'You can go back to your hotel,' Dr Veltroni said. 'You are nearby?'

'Just in Trastevere, a ten-minute walk.'

The doctor nodded. 'That is con –' she hesitated over the word – 'convenient. I would, if I were you, go back to your companions tonight, and please try to sleep. Tomorrow, we look again at Signora Mortmain. Perhaps the situation will be better.'

'Dr Veltroni, should she stay here? Or go back to England?'

'She is in a stable condition,' Dr Veltroni said. 'As I have said, we will know more in the morning. Of course she can stay here. But her family might want to take her home, to make alternative arrangements for her care.'

'That's just it,' said Tess. 'There are no alternative arrangements.' She smiled at the doctor, thinking of the scared group back at the hotel, the mortally ill woman in the room next door, Beth Kennett pacing in her office at Langford College, and she tried to quell the rising tide of panic, to summon all her strength to deal with it all, now. *I don't know what to do,* she thought, as both Peter and the doctor, strangers a week ago, stared expectantly at her. *They are all relying on me, and I don't know what on earth to do.*

CHAPTER TWENTY-FOUR

Night was falling when Tess and Peter finally emerged from the hospital. They had seen Leonora Mortmain, tiny in her starched white hospital bed, with the yellow light from an outside lamp flooding the little room where she lay. Her hands were resting on her chest, and her lined face in repose was curiously strong, the cheekbones high and defined. It was shocking to see her like this, passive, laid out on the bed where anyone could walk past and see her. She was wearing a pale blue hospital gown. Her shallow breathing rattled in the echoing room.

'She will not remember you,' Dr Veltroni said. Her tone was comforting, though Tess wasn't sure that was what she intended.

They were standing now in a quiet little square in front of the hospital. Tess had not really got her bearings, and she looked around her, realizing once again she was on an island, in the middle of the river. The hospital was behind them, a church in front of them. An ancient white marble bridge led back to the centre.

'That's the oldest bridge in the city,' Peter said. 'Ponte Fabricio. It was built even before Caesar. There – there's a cool fact for you.' He wrapped his arms round her and she rested her head on his shoulder. 'Oh, honey. This isn't the time I had in mind for you. You OK?'

'Yes,' Tess said. 'Yes, fine.' She shook her head, wishing she could sink into his arms and stay there in the twilight. 'I'd better get back, though. I need to see if everyone's all right back at the hotel. See what's happened with finding Mrs Mortmain's nearest and dearest.' She spoke the last word bitterly.

'You don't like her, do you?' Peter said. Tess's eyes flew open.

'No,' she said eventually, leading him away from the hospital, so they were in the middle of the piazza, where only a couple of straggling tourists remained in the dusk. 'I don't like her. Sorry, but I think she's an evil woman.'

Peter shook his head. 'Tess, that's awful.'

'I know.'

'No, that's an awful thing to say,' Peter said, shaking his head.

'I know that, too,' Tess told him.

'What's she done to you? You don't know what made her that way.'

His tone was light, but there was a serious note behind it, and Tess was serious too. 'She's – not been very nice, to most people. That's the trouble. That's why I don't know what to do.'

'How so?' Peter folded his arms, and sat on an old iron bollard. 'What's she done that's so awful?'

'Well . . .' said Tess. 'She's made a lot of enemies. She thinks she's better than everyone else in the town. In Langford. Where I'm – they're all from.'

'Why does she think that?'

Tess shrugged her shoulders, looking around her. 'I wish I knew.' She told him briefly about the water meadows, and the planning permission that had been granted. 'I think the timing of this holiday is unfortunate, from that point of view,' she said, chewing the corner of her index finger. 'There are people here now who fought her every step of the way on those plans, and they're very cross with her.' He nodded, his intelligent dark eyes watching her, but she didn't feel he understood. 'It's their town, you know. Their home. They've grown up there, they've raised their children there, or they've chosen to live there and she just doesn't seem to care. Like – where are you from?' She realized she wasn't sure. 'Upstate New York, yes?'

'Long Island,' Peter said. 'Lot of good dental work and collagen there. Not many water meadows.' He said the last sentence with a terrible English accent, and she realized how foreign it all was to him, of course it was. 'But hey, my mom's Italian, and the village her parents are from, up near Turin, the mayor tried to put up a statue of Berlusconi last year, and he had his legs broken.' He nodded. 'Both of them.'

She loved him for trying. 'It's silly, I know. But she is – honestly, she's not a very nice person.'

'You said she was evil.'

Tess threw up her hands. 'OK, OK! Perhaps she's not . . . *evil*. She's just hard to like, that's all.'

'That's better,' said Peter, standing up and putting his hands on her shoulders. 'Actual evil, that's really bad. You don't know, something could have happened to make her that way.' He paused. 'Something that changed her.'

His face was serious. She stroked it, and drew his mouth down to hers, kissing him. 'OK,' she said. 'I understand.'

He drew back a little and stroked her hair. 'Do you want me to come back to the hotel with you?'

Tess really did, but she knew it probably wasn't that great an idea, to rock up back at the Albergo Watkins with a hot young man by her side – she knew the rumour mill would have been started already by Ron and Andrea and she didn't need any more fuel added to that particular fire. Plus, she was afraid, suddenly, afraid that all this – real life, is that what it was? – would get in the way of what had been, till Leonora

Mortmain dropped to the floor in front of them three hours ago, something almost perfect. She didn't want real life getting in the way of this. Not yet. Let it be in its own bubble, just for the moment.

'No, that's OK,' she said. 'I'd better go back on my own. You understand.'

'I do, but call me if you need me,' Peter said. He clutched her wrists. 'You are beautiful, Tess.' His expression was intense. 'So we'll go our separate ways on the bridge. I'll call you tomorrow, shall I?'

'Yes, please,' she whispered, wishing then that he was coming back with her. He kissed her, his hand under her chin, and walked away, up over the bridge. Tess turned, heading south, back to the hotel, to the rest of her life.

'Tess, there you are!' Carolyn Tey was sitting in the lobby of the Albergo Watkins, clutching a tissue, her faded pink face stained with tears, her fluffy blonde hair even fluffier than usual. Jacquetta sat next to her, patting her hand, fluttering her long lashes in time to the hand-patting, as if she were on autopilot. 'Oh – oh, dear, how is she?'

Tess patted Carolyn's shoulder as she made her way towards the bench, under the painting of the Colosseum. She knelt on it with one leg, feeling a bit dizzy all of a sudden, and the bright strip lighting of the lobby making her eyes hurt. At the desk, on the phone, was Diana Sayers, and next to her was Jan. Relief flooded through Tess as she realized, then, what she already knew, that Diana and Jan were sensible people, strange in some ways, yes, but sensible to a degree. And that was what she needed at the moment.

'She's not great, I'm afraid,' Tess said. 'The doctor says tomorrow will tell us more. She's not in any pain. But she is unconscious.'

'The doctor, did he say it was ca – caused by anything?' Carolyn said.

260

Tess looked up; Andrea Marsh and Ron were standing at the bottom of the stairs, side by side. They looked back at her, fear in their eyes.

'She. The doctor is a she,' Tess said. 'She's called Francesca,' she said unnecessarily, and she started as she realized the connection. Francesca . . . What was her Francesca doing now, back in rainy Langford on a Friday afternoon? It seemed a million miles away. 'She didn't say it was caused by anything. She said Mrs Mortmain was quite frail, that was all.'

'Poor girl,' said Diana, who had put the phone down and was striding across the lobby. She patted Tess on the back and Tess was touched to realize she was talking to her. 'What a day. No more news?' Tess shook her head. 'She's still hanging on, then?'

'Diana!' Jan protested, scandalized. 'Oh, my goodness, you can't say that!'

'Well, is she or isn't she?' Diana said calmly. 'I don't mind either way, but on balance, we don't want our holiday ruined by a fatality, do we?'

Tess laughed, partly out of shock. 'Did you get hold of Jean Forbes?' she asked.

'Yes,' said Jan. 'She's talking to the Mortmain's solicitors. She – oh, she said—'

Diana interrupted her suddenly, looking at Tess with concern. 'You look washed out, Tess, if you don't mind me saying so. It's been a long day. Have you eaten?'

What with the long morning sex session on the floor, the Prosecco, the walking around, the medical emergency and then the hours of waiting, Tess realized that she probably hadn't eaten anything all day, beyond a few pieces of bread and cheese at Peter's. 'No,' she said. 'And I'm starving. I might go out and—'

'Don't worry,' said a voice behind her, and she turned to find Liz and Claire standing in the doorway, holding a white package. 'We went to the bakery on the Campo dei Fiori. We

261

got some stuff, because we didn't know what everyone would be doing tonight. We thought you might be hungry.'

Tess stared at them gratefully. 'I love you both,' she said.

'No worries,' Liz said briskly. 'Thought it was something we could do to help.'

'Come out onto the terrace,' Diana said. 'Eat it there, we'll get some wine sent up, too. What a day.'

'What a day, oh, my days,' said Jan, following behind her. She touched Jacquetta on the shoulder. 'You coming, dear?'

'In a minute,' Jacquetta said heavily. 'I'll just make sure Carolyn is all right –'

'I'm fine,' said Carolyn, dissolving into tears ago. 'I – I'm fine . . . Oh, dear, it's all so awful, isn't it?'

Tess stared at her, not sure how to respond. She was in charge, and she didn't really know what to do, how to lead them, what was the right thing to say. 'Come on,' Claire said, guiding Tess slightly by the arm. 'We can discuss what we're going to do up there. It's a lovely evening. Let's try and catch the rest of it.'

They sat outside on the hotel's tiny terrace, where the jasmine was entwined with ivy and the sounds of the city wafted over them, as if on a breeze. In the morning, they knew, decisions would have to be made, but nothing could be done now, and Tess relaxed a little. They talked late into the night about anything and everything, laughing, smiling at each other's stories about awful jobs, about disastrous dates, about friends with children, their hopes for the future, and so on. It was a strange end to a strange day, and Tess realized, for the first time, how nice it was to talk to someone her own age, out here.

'You were always a bit scary, in class,' Liz told her, emptying the last of the final bottle into Tess's glass. 'I didn't really feel I could come up to you and say, "Hi! Wanna go for a drink?"'

'That's awful,' said Tess, thinking of how she'd never really talked to them before, or even wanted to. They were her own age, they'd both left London recently, and she hadn't noticed, or cared. And how she'd complained it was hard to make friends in Langford. She was . . . well, she was stupid.

'Well, it's good to talk to you now.' Claire yawned and stretched, and Tess did the same. 'Although the circumstances aren't ideal.'

'No,' said Tess soberly. She yawned again, and pushed the greaseproof paper that had held her sandwich away from her. 'I suppose I'd better go to bed. We'll know more tomorrow and we need to decide then what's going to happen.'

'If we go home early, you mean?' Liz said, kneeling up.

'It's up to you all, really,' said Tess. 'We're leaving on Monday, it's three more days. I need to talk to the insurance company about what people can do if they want to go back tomorrow.'

The two girls nodded. 'And how you get her home.' Claire stood up, gathering the paper and bottles together.

'What?' Tess was momentarily distracted, looking out across the rooftops, the starry sky, listening to the faint sound of ambulances racing along the main road next to the Tiber.

'Her. Leonora Mortmain. How you get her home. You're in charge,' Liz said, patting her on the shoulder.

'I am.' Tess nodded, and a chill ran through her again. 'Yes. I guess they'll tell me tomorrow, and then I'll have to decide what to do next.'

But as it turned out, she didn't need to make the decision. It was taken out of her hands.

By nine thirty the next morning, Tess was long up, showered and dressed. She had had breakfast and was due to go with Jan, Andrea and Ron to the hospital, to hear how Leonora had been during the night: she supposed that meant whether she had survived the night. Tess was just gathering her things together in her bedroom, as the morning sunshine played in the trees outside her window. The birds sang, almost raucously. She hummed to herself, trying to buoy herself up, as the sound of a car blocked out the birdsong for a moment. A car door opened, then slammed. Surely, she told herself, if she was dead, they'd have called her, Tess, already? They wouldn't wait for her to get to the hospital? Perhaps it was good news – if that *was* good news, for someone in that situation – she didn't know.

She went over to the window, shutting it. The car outside drove away and she heard footsteps up the stairs. It was quiet again. Tess looked for the birds in the trees, but she couldn't see them. Picking up her keys and her bag, she shut the door behind her and went downstairs. She was the first person there.

'Typical,' she said, out loud. 'If I don't boss them around, they just don't –'

But then the front door creaked open, and a man with a bag slung over his shoulder walked in.

He stopped dead in his tracks when he saw her.

'Tess,' he said. She stared at him, at this tall, strangely familiar man, shaking her head, and then she realized who it was. As if she was seeing him for the first time in her adult life. Her mouth fell open.

'Adam?' she said, her heart beating in her throat. 'Adam, what the hell are you doing here?'

'Tess. My dear.' Adam smiled, with his mouth and not his eyes. 'It's wonderful to see you.' He stared at her bleakly, his expression unreadable. He was a man, she thought, a grown-up, how had she not seen it before?

Behind her, someone said, 'Ah, you're here.'

Behind Tess, Diana came down the stairs quickly, and hugged him. She clutched his arm, her mouth set, and Tess could see, through her astonishment, that she was trying not to cry.

'Why – what's going on?' Tess said. 'Adam – what are you doing here?'

'He's the next of kin,' Diana said softly. 'He's the one you were looking for.'

Adam spoke then. 'It's true, Tess.' His low voice echoed in the polished hall, but he was speaking only to her.

She shook her head. 'I don't understand—'

He interrupted her. 'There's something you need to know,' he said. He cleared his throat.

'The one I was – the one I was looking for?' Tess said, parroting Diana's words. She shook her head and turned back to Adam.

He nodded slowly.

'Look. There's something I've never told you, Tess.'

'What?' Tess said, moving towards him. 'Adam, what is it?'

'Tess – she's my grandmother.'

'Who is?' Tess said stupidly, though deep down she knew what he was going to say, knew it because she should always have seen it.

She looked up at him then, into his face, to find the expression in his eyes did not match the cool indifference of his voice as he said, 'Leonora Mortmain is. She's – yes, she's my grandmother.'

CHAPTER TWENTY-FIVE

There was silence in the lobby, cloaking them all. Tess stared at him, shaking her head again.

'What?' she said eventually.

'I'm her grandson. Her only relative. As it turns out.' He smiled tiredly.

'How long? I – I mean, when did you find out?'

'When Mum died,' Adam said. 'She was her – mother. Is her mother.'

'Leonora? Mortmain?' said Tess, in utter disbelief. 'Adam – are you *sure*?'

'Yes,' he said, smiling at that. 'I'm afraid I am sure.'

He put his bag down on the floor, and rubbed his face with his hands.

'But when –? Leonora had a *child*?'

From between his fingers Adam spoke. 'It's a long story. Can we talk about it later?'

'Good idea,' said Diana, as Tess gaped at her. 'You must be exhausted, Adam. When did the flight leave?'

'Just after six,' he said. 'I went to Heathrow last night and slept on a bench in the lounge. It was the first flight I could get.'

'Did you get any sleep?'

'A little bit,' he said, squeezing her hand. 'Right, so –'

Jan appeared at that moment, fiddling with the belt on her cardigan, with Ron behind her.

'Oh, hello there, Adam,' she said, without any surprise. 'Thank goodness you're here. You got a flight OK? Oh, this stupid bag, it won't do up. Ron, where's Andrea?'

'I told her,' Diana said, whispering loudly at Adam, as if Jan weren't there. 'Sorry.'

'People are going to have to know.' Adam shrugged his shoulders. 'She can't keep it a secret now, surely.'

'Hello, Adam, mate,' Ron said, staring at him. 'What you doing here?'

'It's a long story,' Adam said, bobbing his head slightly, his lips tight together. 'You all right?'

'Yes, pretty good, but this is a bit of a shocker, isn't it? When d'you get in then?'

'Just now,' said Adam. 'Oh, hello, Andrea.'

Andrea bustled down the last flight of stairs. 'Adam Smith? Is that you? What are *you* doing here?'

Tess did not move. She didn't know what to do, what to say. Perhaps it was the repetitive questions, perhaps it was the shock, perhaps it was realizing that Smith wasn't his surname at all, most likely, and that that was the very least of it all, what his name was.

'You'll need to check in,' she said to Adam. 'Um – you're coming to the hospital with us, right?'

'I suppose so,' he said. 'Yes, I am.'

She didn't know him, she realized, this stranger. He was a stranger, that was it. He wasn't the Adam she'd grown up with, he was someone else. He had been, these last ten years, only she'd been too blind to see it. She pushed aside thoughts of the last time she'd seen him, of his lips on hers, how it had felt like some kind of homecoming to her. But she didn't know him at all. All this time, carrying that around with him . . . She stared up at him and smiled quickly, as if to tell him it was going to be OK, but he just looked blankly back at her and she backed away, as if he had bared his teeth.

Tess hugged the folder containing all her information to her, like a shield. 'Well, I can explain on the way. Dump your bags. I'll wait outside, guys.' She turned and walked out, pulling the door to behind her, and out on the step she breathed in deeply, drawing the morning air into her lungs, though it was painful and her chest felt constricted, as if something were sitting on it.

Adam – sweet, slightly useless Adam, her oldest friend, her companion through most of her life – he was someone completely different. Things that didn't add up now started to creep afresh into her head – how he had lived on next to nothing all these years, why he wouldn't move away, his curious, almost cultivated diffidence, indifference to life. His generosity, his bouts of silence, of self-loathing. He had paid for the abortion and never told her where the money was from. The memory flew back to her now, out of nowhere, and Tess looked up to the spotless blue sky and put her fist at the base of her throat, as if trying to move whatever it was that was sitting there, making it so hard to breath. Events, ideas, stories, all of them started to flow through her mind, around and around, like a carouse, and she could feel her breathing getting deeper and more rapid . . .

Enough. Now was not the time. The door opened again.

'You all right, Tess?'

'Of course,' Tess said.

'They should be out in a moment. Adam's just leaving his things.' Diana Sayers cleared her throat briskly, and slung her sensible brown handbag over her shoulder. Tess stared at her.

'How long have you known?' she said, turning away from her again and staring up at the sun, trying to keep her voice casual. 'About Adam. And Philippa?'

'Ah,' said Diana. 'Always known. I mean, Philippa told me a couple of years after she moved to Langford. We were very close, you know.' Her voice trembled and she gripped the clasp on her bag, as if for support. 'All this – it just makes me think of her, all alone. How she was so – so much better than most other people. She was my –' She swallowed back tears. 'She was my best friend.'

'What happened?'

'When?'

Tess's mind was racing. 'How did she have a baby?'

'Mrs Mortmain? I don't think anyone knows.' Diana blew her nose. 'She never told Philippa, that's for sure. Philippa came to Langford looking for her, just as soon as she was told who her mother was. She was eight months' pregnant. She was desperate. And Leonora Mortmain refused to have anything to do with her.' She nodded, correcting herself. 'That's not fair. She gave her the cottage. But it was right at the other end of town, and she told her she had to keep it a secret. That she didn't want anything to do with her.'

'But – but why?' Tess said.

Diana's severe features creased into a smile. 'I don't know, Tess! She was – she is – a pretty difficult woman.'

'So she never told—'

Diana interrupted. 'Philippa told me, I think that's it.' She said suddenly, as though blurting it out, 'You don't know how hard it's been, not telling anyone all these years. Knowing how that woman treated her.'

There was so much Tess wanted to know, to ask, but she just said, 'Oh, Diana, I'm so sorry.'

Diana sniffed. 'I'm fine.' She rooted around in her handbag, inelegantly blowing her nose on an ancient tissue. 'It's Adam who's not going to be fine. Right,' she said, looking at Tess, as if aware suddenly of who she was.' Are we off?'

The door opened and Jan stepped out, peering over her prescription sunglasses at the pair of them. 'Oh, hello. Diana? Shall we go?'

'Where's Adam?'

'I'm here,' said Adam, opening the door wider still. He looked up at the cloudless sky, then at Diana and at Tess. He was holding some papers; they rustled as he clenched them in his fist. 'Shall we go?' he said.

Tess realized he was talking to her, and that she was the one in charge. She said, 'Yes, good idea. We can walk, it's only five minutes or so. Let's go.'

'Want us to come?' said Andrea, who had appeared behind them.

'No, thanks,' said Tess, looking at her white face. 'Don't worry, Andrea. We'll be back soon. Why don't you and Ron go and get a coffee in the square. Tell the others where we've gone, will you?'

'Right, let's be off,' said Jan, bobbing on the balls of her feet. 'Sooner we go . . . and all that.'

Adam stared at her. 'We'll be fine, just the three of us, I think, thanks, Jan,' he said, and Jan stepped back, against the tree, as if she'd just been put on the naughty step.

'Oh,' she said. 'Oh, right then. Adam.'

'Did you bring the papers?' Diana said in a low voice, as they turned down a cobbled pedestrian street. Ahead of them, an old woman threw a bucket of water over the stones, whistling as she went back inside. Tess watched her.

'I did,' said Adam. He was walking more quickly than them, Tess noticed, as if he wanted to set a faster pace. 'I don't really know – I bought some ID. My birth certificate, too. In case we need to arrange – sign something – oh, God, I don't know.'

Diana patted his arm. 'S'OK, Adam,' she said slowly. 'It's going to be OK.'

'It's not,' Adam said, as if Tess weren't there. 'And now it's out, and everyone will know –'

'They had to know sometime,' Diana said. She glanced across at Tess. 'People had to know. Leonora was always going to die at some point, Adam my dear. So perhaps—'

'She's not dead,' Adam said shortly.

He pulled slightly ahead of Diana, who fell back into line with Tess. Diana said nothing and they continued in silence until they reached the end of the road, where Adam paused. Tess was so in thrall to his leadership that she didn't understand why, until she remembered she was supposed to be showing him the way.

'We cross the bridge here,' she said. 'It's on that island, in the middle of the river.'

'Wow,' said Adam, gazing across at the hospital, and then up at the rest of the city, as the river wound away from them and the white marble and black trees shimmered in the heat. 'It's beautiful, isn't it.' He sighed. 'Oh, God. This is fucking strange.'

Tess put her hand on his shoulder, but he moved away again and walked off.

Stumbling slightly as they turned in to the hospital, Tess looked sideways at Adam, knowing she had to be a friend to him, more so than ever, but totally at a loss as to how to do it. Her phone buzzed, and she reached into her bag to get it, knowing she should turn it off before they went inside. It was from Peter.

Thinking of you. Hope it's OK. I have something to ask you this morning, come and see me or I'll call you later. P xx

Dr Veltroni was on duty again, thankfully. She shook Adam's hand seriously, and said, in her beautifully low, slightly hesitant voice, 'Sir, you are the next of kin?'

'Yes,' said Adam. He nodded. 'I am her grandson.'

'You must sign these papers, here.' She waved a hand to the reception desk behind them, where Italian bureaucracy had free rein. 'But first you will want to see your grandmother, yes.'

'Yes,' said Adam, shaking his head; Tess wondered if he realized he was doing it. Dr Veltroni looked at him curiously for a second, then at Tess, and at Diana.

'She is not very good this morning, I am sorry. We do not see any change in the patient. So – I'm afraid we must discuss these options, when you have seen her. Mr –' She held out her hand politely.

'Smith,' said Adam. 'It's Smith.'

'Mr Smith. I do not think your grandmother will recover. As I said to this young lady and the young man yesterday, we know more this morning.'

Adam turned to Tess, his eyes narrowing, and opened his mouth, then closed it, shook his head and turned back. Dr Veltroni went on, 'You have to decide some things, we must discuss some things, about whether she will stay here or you will take her back to England. I am sorry. This is my truth.'

Adam nodded again and Tess clutched the back of the chair she was next to. Diana cleared her throat and said, 'Excuse me, doctor. Does that mean – she's going to die?'

'Of course,' said Dr Veltroni. 'Because she is old, firstly. Because she has had a big stroke, second. And so she will be in this state –' her long fingers sliced a flat line through the air – 'now, and I am sorry. She will not get better.'

There was a silence. Dr Veltroni looked expectantly at Adam. He shrugged his shoulders blankly and looked at Diana.

'I'd better go and see her, then.'

Tess waited outside while he went in; she felt it was best if he saw her alone. She and Diana sat in the corridor, the air close, the whirr of a ceiling fan and a buzzing fly the only two sounds. They didn't say anything, they were waiting. When Adam came out of the tiny room after a few minutes, he was talking to Dr Veltroni and his expression was unreadable.

'So I'll call up the hospice back at home and see. And then let you know.'

She nodded. 'But it is your decision, of course, Mr Smith.'

Diana and Tess stood up as they approached; Tess raised

her eyebrows, questioningly, at Adam. He said, 'We're just discussing what to do next. She can stay here, or she can come home. There's some responsiveness, so they need to make sure she's given the right care.'

'You mean there's a chance—' Tess said, but he interrupted her.

'I don't know. I need to think about what's going to be easiest. For us, for this good hospital here that has too few beds. For the hospital back home.'

There was a terrible silence. Diana broke it by saying, 'Adam, she's your grandmother.'

'She's not,' Adam said lightly. 'Grandmother isn't the right word for it. I'm her next of kin.' He looked up at the ceiling and breathed in and then out, as if he was trying his hardest to maintain his composure. 'I need to do the right thing. For her, but mostly for Mum. Dammit. And then it's over. Doctor – can you show me the forms to sign?'

He turned his back on them and went into the office. Tess looked at her watch. It was not yet midday.

They waited for him, shuffling and silent on the hard wooden bench. When Adam emerged ten minutes later, Tess said, 'What do you want to do now?'

She wanted to see Peter – the thought of falling into his arms, of feeling his warm, comforting body against hers, his hands stroking her hair, was incredibly tempting. Peter would know what to do. They were all strangers in this foreign land, at the mercy of receptionists, waiters, doctors, policemen. He was part of the city, he knew the streets, he was at home here and though she had met him – was it really only five days ago? She smiled at the thought – she knew him. Knew him better than she knew Adam, it turned out. Was that really true?

'I don't know,' Adam said. He looked at Diana.

'I'm going back to the hotel,' Diana said. 'Find Jan, and the others. Work out what we're going to do.'

273

Tess knew she should go back too, but she couldn't face it just yet. She said, 'I'll be along later, I think. We need to have a meeting, discuss what happens next.' Diana raised an eyebrow, and Tess went on, 'Can you round the others up, I'll be back in a couple of hours.'

'Where are you going?' Adam asked.

Tess turned to him. 'Oh, just for a walk,' she said simply. 'Just stretch my legs a bit.'

'I'll come with you, if that's OK.'

'Sure,' said Tess quickly.

'Seems a shame to be here and not see anything of Rome.'

Diana looked at them, a strange expression on her face. 'Right, then,' she said. 'I'll be off. See you both later.'

'Yes,' said Tess, hating herself. 'See you later. Right . . . Adam, let's go.'

As they stepped out onto the north side of the hospital island and crossed the bridge onto the Centro Storico, Tess stole a glance at Adam, wondering what to do. She had been going to call Peter, but she couldn't now. She couldn't ask Adam anything, either, as he clearly wouldn't answer.

He stretched his arms out wide, rolling his shoulder blades, then blinked rapidly. 'Where are we going?'

'Where do you want to go?' Tess said.

'Coffee,' he said suddenly. 'Some coffee would be great.'

'Let's go to the Campo dei Fiori,' she said. 'Get you some breakfast. Sit in the sunshine.'

Then they could walk up past Peter's apartment, and she could at least look up to the windows, see the bookcase, a tiny piece of that light, airy room. That would give her the strength to deal with what came next. Then she had to work out what they were all going to do. And how she could help Adam, if she could help him . . .

They strolled in silence, along the Via Giulia, where the traffic eased off and the jasmine hung heavy in the air.

'What a beautiful smell,' Adam said, breathing in. 'Smells

like the honeysuckle we used to have at home, do you remember?'

She had forgotten, but now she remembered. The memory washed over her like a flood. Philippa's wild, colourful walled garden, a little sun-trap on the edge of the ancient town, stuffed thick with flowers, all madly competing to outdo each other in size, colour and scent.

'Yes, of course,' Tess said, smiling in wonder. 'I remember now. Yes, it's just like it.'

'And the stocks,' said Adam. He stuck his hands in his pockets. 'All those Romans with their summer villas down in Pompeii and Naples. I wonder what their gardens were like.'

Tess looked at him, at the absurdity of the situation, and she began to laugh. 'Yep,' she said, as they crossed the street.

'What?' said Adam. He stared at her, uncomprehending. A scooter whizzed around the corner, making her jump, and he put his hand on her arm. She suddenly thought of Leonora Mortmain, her angry face knitted together with confusion and bile. *Where is he? . . . Where's Philip? . . . He doesn't come.*

'You,' she said. 'You and your Classics brain, Adam, that's all. Look, we're just getting to –'

They were approaching the Piazza Farnese, which led onto the Campo dei Fiori, and she looked up at Peter's building, to the second – or third if you were him – floor, blinking in the sunlight. As if he'd be there, leaning out of the window, calling out her name, like Romeo and Juliet in reverse.

There was a loud bang, and she jumped again. 'You're jittery, aren't you?' said Adam. 'It's just that door shutting over there, look –'

He pointed at the entrance to Peter's building, and she followed his gaze. The old door had slammed shut and there, on the doorstep, was Peter. Without meaning to, she raised her arm, and then put it down again, but he saw her. He stared at Tess, his dark eyes enormous.

'That's weird,' Adam said. 'He's looking at you. He's waving, like he knows you.'

Tess, rooted to the spot, watched as he approached. 'Yeah,' she said. 'I know him.'

'Hi,' Peter said. 'Tess –'

He looked at Adam. Adam looked at him. 'Hi,' Adam said eventually, gripping Peter's hand. 'I'm Adam, I'm . . .' He trailed off. 'I just got here this morning, and . . .'

'Yes, of course,' said Peter, as though he totally understood. 'It's good to see you.'

Tess felt she had to explain. 'Adam is the old lady who had the stroke – I mean, he's her grandmother.' She stamped her foot. 'I mean, he's her grandson.'

'Hi,' Peter said. 'Great to meet you.' He squeezed Tess's shoulders. 'Hi, honey.' He kissed her lightly.

'You wanted to ask me something?' Tess said softly.

'Yes,' he said. 'I need to talk to you, in fact. But it can wait for now.' He turned back to Adam, watching them both and frowning. 'I know you guys must have a lot to talk about. I'm sorry about your grandmother, Adam. Hope it works out for you.'

'Er – thanks,' said Adam. 'It's nice to meet you too . . .' He stared at the two of them, squinting in the strong sunshine. 'This has been a long morning. I need some coffee.'

'I'm coming,' Tess said, and she turned and followed him, blowing Peter a kiss goodbye. He watched her go, waving, and as she and Adam walked towards the café, he stayed there, watching, and when she turned once more he smiled at her, and went back towards his flat.

CHAPTER TWENTY-SIX

They sat down in silence at a café on the edge of the Campo. After the waiter had gone, Tess leaned forward and looked at Adam. 'Wow,' she said. 'Adam, what the hell –'

He met her gaze. 'Who's that?'

'Peter?' Tess was stumped. 'He's – a friend.' He stared at her.

'How did you meet him?'

'We – we sort of bumped into each other,' Tess said, suppressing a smile at the memory. 'He's a journalist. He lives here.'

'And you're seeing him? What's – so what's going on with the two of you?'

'Adam!' Tess said, astonished. 'Who cares! That's not important at the moment, is it? I mean – what's going on with *you* – that's the question, isn't it?'

She was spluttering, and he nodded, bowing his head slightly. 'I know,' he said frankly. 'I know. Tess – I owe you an explanation at the very least. I'm sorry, I couldn't tell you before –'

'Doesn't matter,' she said. She tapped the table with a teaspoon, beating out a rhythm. 'It really, really doesn't matter.'

'Well, it does,' Adam said. 'I think – it's affected everything.

Even keeping it a secret has. I sometimes think, if things had been different, you know, would Mum still be here. Even –'

He broke off, and looked miserably down at the ground. She looked at him, tearing her thoughts back to the present – and the past, the ever-present past. 'Oh, Ad,' she said eventually. 'Do you really think that? How would that have made a difference?'

'I don't know,' Adam said. 'But Tess –' He stared out, across the colourful square where the market was in full flow, the flower stall next to them thronged with people. 'I don't know. Just all that lying, what it did to Mum, to the two of us. I feel no connection to that woman. I don't think I could ever.' He jabbed a thumb back in the direction of the river, towards the hospital. 'Even though she's my own flesh and blood. The only real family I have.' He breathed in the sunny midday breeze. 'Diana's been more like family to me, for all her odd ways, these past ten years, than she ever has.'

'So – when did you find out?' Tess said tentatively, not knowing where to start, she had so many questions. 'About Leonora, about her being your – your grandmother?'

'When Mum died,' Adam said. He smiled grimly. 'Yeah. Nice present for the funeral, isn't it? Your mother's dead, you're all alone in the world, but hey, there's something she never told you, and you can't tell anyone else!' He was fiddling with a sugar cube, in a plastic sachet; he crushed it, suddenly, and the brown sugar shot across the table.

'What happened?'

'Well, you know the summer after she died,' said Adam.

'Sure,' said Tess.

'I didn't want to go back to the cottage. I was spending a lot of time out.' His eyes met hers. 'With you, mostly.'

'Yep,' she said.

'So – someone kept ringing. We didn't have caller ID back

then, but the phone would ring, quite often, and they never left a message. I'd be on my way out, or – busy.'

She remembered it well. They were embroiled in their own secrecy so well, that when the phone kept ringing they took it as evidence of their duplicity. It didn't occur to either of them, as they lay tangled up in the ancient quilted bedspread on the rickety iron frame in Adam's room, the attic with the sloping rooves, high at the top of the house. Six, seven, eight hours could go by in the day, lost summer days spent inside, sleeping, eating, having sex. People would knock at the door, wanting to check up on him: he ignored them. The phone rang: he ignored it. If they wanted to leave a message, they would. By the end of that summer, they knew each other's bodies better than their own; the mole high up on the inner thigh, the bump of skin under the breast, the scar beneath the ribs. It was their own world, created to keep the world outside at bay.

Tess closed her eyes, willing the memories away, and said, 'How did they contact you? Who was it?'

'It was Clive. Good old sensible staid Clive.'

'Clive Donaldson?'

'Yep. Turned up at the door one day, after you'd gone off, it must have been. "I've been trying to reach you, young man. I've something rather important to tell you." That's what he said – I remember it so clearly.'

'*He* told you?' Tess was appalled.

Adam's smile grew twisted. 'He called Diana. They'd agreed she should be there. She was Mum's best friend, after all. So we wait around for ten minutes, in the sitting room, making polite conversation about the football, the weather, you know. And then Diana appears, they sit me down on the sofa and tell me –' he flung his hands open – 'all this.'

She shook her head. 'My God. And your mum – she never said anything to you about it?'

'Nothing, nothing at all.' Adam tapped his menu. 'I don't blame her though. She probably thought she'd pick the right time to tell me. She didn't know she was going to drop dead, did she.'

'No, no, of course. But – who else –' Tess began, but a waitress appeared to bring them water, and the moment passed.

When the waitress had gone Tess said, 'Adam, you know, I'm so sorry.'

'Sorry for what?' he said, gazing at her in amusement. 'It's not your fault.'

It was weird, sitting here with him like this, all tension vanished. Again, she realized he was like a new person to her, the person she'd seen in the lobby of the hotel that morning, not the Adam she'd screamed at outside Claridges, cried over once again. If only it could always have been like this, she thought. If only – if only she could have been a friend to him, a proper friend all these years. If only she'd known . . .

'I know it's not my fault,' she said. 'It's just that you must have been through such a lot. And you had no one –' She grimaced, and took his hand, squeezing it lightly. 'No one to help you.'

'Hey,' he said, squeezing her hand back. 'It's a bit late for regrets, my dear. Where were you when I was twenty-four and in the depths of depression? Living it up in London, miles away.'

She looked at him. 'Do you really think that?'

The mood had altered. 'I don't not think it,' he said eventually, his voice neutral. 'There wasn't anyone else I could talk to.'

There were several things she wanted to say, but now was not the time. Later, perhaps. She bobbed her head as if acknowledging the blow. 'I'm sorry you felt that,' she said.

'Don't worry,' he said, keeping his voice level. 'Now's not the time.' She smiled. 'What's funny?' he asked.

'Nothing,' she said. 'Nothing at all.'

'So,' said Adam, after a pause. 'This guy, Peter – what's the story there?'

She stared at him, her eyes wide, searching his face. 'Oh, Adam. He's – it's not important now. Just a guy.' She bit her lip.

The waiter set their food down and withdrew, murmuring to himself.

'Looked pretty important to me,' Adam said. 'American, is he? What's he doing here?'

Er . . . he moved to Italy when he married a crazy-sounding lady who turned out to be having an affair with her oldest friend after he stalked her for a couple of months . . . Tess weighed up the plausibility of this statement, then decided against it. 'He's a journalist,' she said eventually.

'Journalist, eh?' Adam plucked a chunk off the side of his toasted sandwich. 'And –'

Tess wasn't ready for a conversation about Peter, not with anyone, certainly not with Adam, not now. 'Did you really mean that?' she asked, swallowing. 'That there wasn't anyone else you could talk to? You really think I wasn't there for you?'

Adam stared at her in surprise. 'Well, it's true, isn't it?' he said. 'I don't mean you, as such, like it's your fault, Tess. I just mean – well, here we are, we're supposed to be best friends, oldest friends, whatever it is we are. And we've done it all wrong. We've slept with each other, we've lied to each other, we've not been there for each other, we've grown apart – 'He looked at her, and took a deep breath. 'Really, what a mess. Don't you think?'

It was the nonchalant way he said it that upset her most. 'How can you sit there and just say all of that?'

'Why not?' Adam said, a curious look on his face. 'It's true, isn't it?'

'I –'

'Tess, if this whole stupid business with Leonora has taught me anything, it's that life's too short. I was sitting there in the airport this morning, waiting for a flight, any flight out to Rome, to come and see you – to see her. And I was dreading it, because of how we left things last time, that night in London. How stupid we were.'

'Oh,' she said, fiddling with the corner of her napkin. 'Yes, we were.'

'You think so too?' he said carefully. 'I'm glad. I thought so. I'm sorry – Tess, I feel like we constantly do this to each other. And it's so silly.'

'Righty-ho,' said Tess. She drank her coffee, and swallowed hard. 'Right. What are you going to do now?'

'With Leonora?' Adam stared down at the sugar granules again. 'I've thought about it a lot. I think we have to try and bring her home. There's a hospice near Thornham, they'll take her.'

'You've rung already?'

'Yes,' he said. 'Did it yesterday afternoon when I found out. Spoke to Clive – he's my solicitor now. Well, the Mortmain solicitor.' He shook his head, and a flash of anger crossed his face. 'God, the whole thing's bloody crazy. Anyway, he has all her requests noted in some file in his office. He went and checked it all over. She covered every provision.' He gave a short laugh. 'Every provision except the one where she acknowledges her daughter or her grandson, in public.'

'So you saw her? You'd go and –' Tess couldn't get her head round it.

'About every six months, yes,' he said.

'But she was –'

'I had to,' Adam said.

'For the money?' Tess said, and then instantly wished she hadn't. He stared at her.

'Do you think that's what it's about?' he said, in amazement. 'Seriously, Tess? You think I want money from her?'

'But isn't that what –'

'I haven't taken a penny off her,' Adam said, his voice cold. 'I wouldn't touch her money. How can you say that? I saw her twice a year because I'm the only family she has, I had to. But don't ever say she gave me money with my knowledge.'

Tess felt ashamed for briefly assuming he had. How little she knew him.

'The scholarship at school –' she said, slowly. 'She must have set that up to help you out.'

Adam nodded. 'Yes,' he said. 'And I never got to talk to Mum about it. She must have thought she was doing it for the best, getting her to help us out. That's why Mum moved back in the first place – she didn't have anywhere else to go, no money, and Leonora gave her that cottage. I didn't know till Mum died – she would have hated me knowing.' He spoke slowly, and swallowed. 'But God – I'd rather have failed every exam under the sun and had a day more with Mum had I known that's what the plan was.' His nostrils flared. 'Well, I did anyway, so that got fucked up too.' He ran his hands through his hair. 'Sorry. There's so much I've made my peace with. But a lot of it makes me furious.'

'Do you know what happened?' Tess asked, curious. 'Who he was? Who Leonora had an affair with?'

'No idea,' said Adam. 'That's the thing. She won't tell me. I don't think Mum knew either – but then Mum never told me who her own mother was.'

'And your dad – you don't know him, either.'

'That's different. At least I know who he *is*,' Adam said. 'I've met him, once or twice, when he's been over. I just don't *know* him. And Mum was always completely open about it: she wanted a baby, he didn't, they weren't a couple, really, they went their separate ways. This . . . this thing with Leonora, it's different. Perhaps now –' He winced, and stopped. 'When she dies, whenever that may be – then I'll find out. It's hard to imagine, I must say. The idea of Leonora Mortmain . . . well, the idea of her as a young woman's pretty hard to swallow, for starters. Let alone her as an unmarried mother.'

'Perhaps.'

'I don't know anything about it,' he said. 'Just a clue, that's all I want. I'm in that town, and I'm from that family, and I don't even know the most basic things . . .' He rubbed his temples.

'Nor does anyone else,' said Tess. 'And when people start finding out she's your grandmother . . . that's going to be strange.'

'I know.' He was silent, staring across at the square, and then he rubbed his temple with one finger again and looked at his watch. 'I'd better go in a minute.'

'Where?' she said, startled.

'Back to the hospital. I told Dr Veltroni I'd be back to see her in a couple of hours.'

Tess wrinkled her brow. 'Really?'

'Yep.' Adam crushed his paper napkin into a tiny ball. 'So, we should talk when I'm back.'

'Er –' said Tess. 'Yes.'

He drummed his fingers on the side of the chair. 'I mean, what have you decided to do about the group? When are you going back, have you had a meeting about it? What do they want to do?'

'I don't know,' said Tess.

'But you're in charge,' he said, half-smiling at her.

'We'll work something out,' Tess said crossly. 'I don't know what they want to do yet.'

'What, you still haven't talked to them?' He sounded mildly surprised.

'No,' said Tess, breathing through her nose, trying to stay calm. 'What with being at the hospital for hours, and talking to people back home, and trying to get hold of the next of kin and everything.'

'You found time to see your Italian boyfriend though,' Adam said, raising his eyebrows.

Tess turned to face him, but his expression gave nothing

284

away. 'He's American. Well, half-Italian. Oh, it doesn't matter.'

'You said he was –'

'He was with me when your – she – when Mrs Mortmain collapsed! Of course he came with me, and it's a bloody good thing he did!' Tess said and she realized she was shouting. She calmed down. 'Sorry. But he was the only one who knew what was going on, who could talk to the ambulance people, the doctors. So leave it.'

'Fine,' he said, holding up his hands. He put some money down on the table. 'I'm sorry. I didn't mean to imply anything. It's none of my business, anyway.' He stood up, and she stood up too.

'Here –' She thrust a paper map from the hotel at him. 'This'll help you find your way round.'

'Thanks,' said Adam, sticking his wallet inside his jacket. 'Bye. So – will you be OK?'

'Yes, of course,' she said, squinting into the sun to look up at him. 'See you later, then.'

'Yes,' he said. 'See you later.' The sun was blinding her, she couldn't see his expression. 'We'll need to discuss things. When you've had the meeting, and I've decided what to do, is that all right?'

'Fine,' said Tess. 'Absolutely. Take – take care.'

'Thanks.'

He stalked off, without a backwards glance. Pigeons scattered, flying into the air as he headed back the way they'd come across the square, leaving her behind, watching him go.

CHAPTER TWENTY-SEVEN

'You haven't rung the insurance company?' Andrea said, sitting on her hands and rocking forward.

'No,' said Tess. 'I thought we'd better all discuss it first.'

'Well, dear – if we're going to go home, we'd better do something about it,' said Jan. 'Sooner rather than later.'

'I know,' said Tess. She looked around, trying not to sound helpless. 'That's why I thought we should put it to the vote.'

There was a murmur of discontent from the back row (Ron and Andrea), a muffled sigh from the stalls (Carolyn Tey), and a 'harrumph' from the circle (Diana Sayers). They were in a small meeting room off the reception area of the Albergo Watkins. It was a dark, mean room, with an ancient ceiling fan that clanked on every circumference, and a vague smell of drains.

It was after one, and very hot. They were all tired, and hungry, and fractious, like a group of schoolchildren. Tess wished she knew how to calm them, how to make it better.

'I think you'd better call the insurance people, Tess, before we make any decisions,' said Jacquetta rather crossly. 'There's no point in us voting to all go back a day early first thing tomorrow if you ring them and they tell us we're not covered for it.'

'Absolutely,' said Carolyn. 'Tess, dear, I do think we ought to know what provision the school has made for this kind of eventuality.'

Tess said snappishly, 'What, the eventuality of one of you having a stroke and an unduly complicated family history? Do you know, I don't think we have an eventuality for that,' she said.

'Tess,' Diana Sayers said chasteningly. Carolyn sank back into her seat like a scolded child. Tess blushed, ashamed of herself.

A voice from the back spoke up. 'I'd like to stay on till Monday,' said Liz. 'But I don't mind if we go back tomorrow, either. I'll go with the majority.'

'Me too,' said Claire. 'Tess, do you need us to do anything?'

Tess flung them a grateful glance, even more ashamed of her childish behaviour. 'No, thanks,' she said. 'Thanks, though.' She felt they were giving her an inter-generational vote of confidence. 'Hey. Can you all just hang on here for a few minutes?' she said, looking at them all. 'I'll call Beth and the insurers, and see what results and I'll have some answers for you then. Ladies – I'm sorry about this. Give me a few minutes.'

'Ladies *and gentleman*,' Ron muttered crossly under his breath as Tess went out of the room.

'So – all those who vote to go tomorrow, put your hands up, then.'

'That's it, isn't it?'

'I think that's pretty clear,' Tess said. 'So, by a clear majority, you vote to go back tomorrow. There's an easyJet flight in the morning, the insurers are pretty sure they can put us on that. I'll have to –' She paused. What would Adam want to do? She didn't know, and then she remembered his rather caustic tones. *But you're in charge . . . What, you still haven't talked to them?* Well, he was right. Her first loyalty wasn't to him, it was to her group, and that's what they'd voted, and so they were going, and he could follow on later, when he'd sorted out whatever needed to happen with Leonora Mortmain.

'So, this is our last night,' Jan said, with a rueful little smile. 'I must say, Tess, I didn't expect it to end like this, did you, dear?'

'No –' said Tess. 'Our last night, you're right –' She suddenly thought of Peter. One more night, would she even have time to see him, what with packing the ladies up and sorting everything out?

Jan misunderstood her. 'It's been wonderful, Tess dear. Don't you start thinking it hasn't been.' She rolled her eyes. 'And you know, until Mrs Mortmain went and dropped practically dead, it was a lovely holiday, wasn't it, Carolyn!' She pinched Carolyn Tey hard on the arm.

'Um – yes,' said Carolyn, smiling weakly at Tess. 'Lovely, Tess. Lovely holiday! Excuse me,' she finished, hurrying for the door.

'Silly woman,' said Diana. She winked at Tess. 'All right, Tess? What else is there to do?'

'Nothing. You'd better pack. Please, everyone!' Tess clapped her hands. 'Carolyn! Just a moment. The flight's at nine twenty-five, that means leaving here at seven o'clock in the morning, is that clear? I'm afraid it's a very early start, but . . .'

The group edged out of the room in single file, Tess last. She looked round at the badly lit room, and turned the light off on her way out. It wasn't like Rome any more, none of it was. Real life wasn't riding around on mopeds, drinking Prosecco with Peter, lying on the floor in his arms, dancing to Ella Fitzgerald. No, no. This was real life. She sighed and went upstairs. She had to pack. Her phone rang as she climbed the stairs.

'Peter?'

'Hi, sweetie.' Peter's deep voice resonated down the phone, as if he were next to her. 'Look, can you talk? I just want to—'

'I'm going tomorrow,' she said desperately, unlocking the door to her room and closing it hurriedly. 'We're leaving, first thing.' She reached into the cupboard and got out her suitcase.

There was a silence. 'Shit,' he said eventually. 'I need to see you, then.'

'I know,' she said.

'I'll come over later. We need to talk.'

'"We need to talk"?' Tess said, trying to sound light-hearted.

'Something's happened, and I don't know what to do about it,' he said. 'And now you're leaving. Perhaps I should go for it.' It was as if he were talking to himself. 'You're really going?'

'I have to, Peter,' she said, fiddling with her necklace, looking around the room; it was a mess, everything was a mess. She breathed deeply. 'What's up? Can't you tell me?'

'I'll explain later,' he said. 'But it's not you. You're wonderful. See you soon.'

'I –' she began, but the line had gone dead.

There was no sign of Adam at tea-time, and by six o'clock Tess had had a busy day. She'd packed, spoken to the insurers again and to easyJet. She had checked with everyone that they were getting on OK, and had explained everything to the hotel, ordered three cars to take them to the airport and had booked Brian's minibus in Langford to pick them up from Gatwick at the other end and take them home. Claire and Liz were going to the bar in the main square of Trastevere one last time, and they had asked Tess along.

'Come on. One more Prosecco,' Liz had said, when she knocked on Tess's door to ask her.

Tess had smiled, caught between a laugh and a sigh. 'OK,' she'd said. 'That'd be lovely. Thanks, Liz.'

It was early evening, and the square was at its most alive. There were street performers and Senegalese guys selling silver discs which they threw up into the air with a stick, which stayed up in the sky for what seemed like minutes, suspended as if in mid-air, before coming down again. The glare of the discs as they caught the evening sun flashed on the building opposite, as the three girls sat in silence, watching children jump up and down, screaming with excitement. A priest came out of the church and hurried across the square, smiling indulgently at the children, scowling at the street-sellers. Tourists and locals ambled past – the early evening *passeggiata*, the stroll through the streets, had begun.

'This time tomorrow,' Liz said dreamily. 'Ah, it's sad to think we'll be back home.'

'I know,' said Claire. 'I think we're doing the right thing, leaving early, but it's still –'

'I know,' said Tess. 'I know. You two could have stayed, though.'

'I didn't mean that,' Claire said. 'I want to come home with everyone. We did this as a group, we should go home as a group. It's just it's been so wonderful – and now it's over.' She said impulsively, 'Oh, Tess, do tell us. What's the story with Adam and Mrs Mortmain? Is he really her long-lost grandson? Of course – if you can't say anything then don't. But I'm so curious, we all are.' She clasped her hands together. 'Is it *true*?'

Tess said, 'It's a long story. And I don't know most of it myself, yet.'

'Where's he been today, do you know?'

'No idea. I was just wondering myself.' Since they had parted abruptly at midday she had not heard from him. She told herself that was typical Adam, he hadn't changed that much after all, he was always flaky. He was probably off looking at the Pantheon or, more likely, chatting up some random Italian girl, or even Dr Veltroni, who had taken rather a shine to him – and he wouldn't even have to remember her name, since it was the same as his supposed girlfriend's, Tess thought cattily.

290

Claire nodded. 'Oh, I see. Sorry.' She saw that Tess wasn't going to give her any more information, and said, 'Well, we'll find out, I'm sure.'

'I hope so,' said Tess, trying not to sound dismissive. Liz nodded.

'Well, anyway, you're right. It has been a wonderful week,' she said. 'I wish we weren't going home.'

Tess nodded in agreement, looking at Liz in sympathy. It was true, but it was also true that what lay in wait for her at home was not so wonderful, compared to the life she'd been living this past week. Her old-lady life in Langford, replete with trips to tea shops, constant rain and bad fashion. Hell, she had spent fifteen minutes one Saturday night in April *balancing fondant fancies into a pyramid shape on a cake stand*. Let alone the fact that she had unwittingly started buying the same clothes as the population of Langford. When Jan Allingham started complimenting you on your look it was long overdue time for a makeover.

But this week with Peter had transformed her, she thought, as the warm evening sun shone on her bare arms. She wasn't ready to put on reading glasses and get a subscription to *People's Friend*. Not yet.

She was going to see him later, he was coming to the hotel. One last night . . . one more time, a few snatched hours with him. Tess could see him so clearly, as if he were in front of her, and the power of her feelings for him shocked her. He made her feel alive. She hardly knew him, but it didn't really seem to matter. And this time tomorrow she would be back home again . . . She turned impulsively to the other two.

'Do you like living in Langford?' she asked them. 'Are you ready to go back?'

'I don't live in Langford,' Claire said sheepishly. 'I live in Salisbury, do you remember? We had that conversation once, about the cathedral there, and you said—'

'Oh, yes, yes,' said Tess, though she didn't remember this at all. 'Sorry, of course. What, so – how do you get to classes?'

'I drive,' said Claire simply.

'But it must be about an hour each way?'

'Yes, but it's totally worth it,' Claire said. 'I have time to practise my language tapes in the car, and listen to audio books. It's wonderful. That's what part of me giving up my job was all about, trying something new, getting to spend more time on me.'

Liz cleared her throat. 'I'm not ready to go back, to answer your question,' she said, ignoring Claire. 'I love it here.'

'Me too,' said Tess. She hugged herself.

'I could move here,' said Liz. Her eyes followed a child running across the square; she smiled at him. 'Quite happily. It makes me think, when I left London, why did I just drive west and plump for Langford? Why was I so ready to assume I couldn't stay in London and just do something else? Like work for a pub theatre, instead of working at that vile agency? Or at a garden centre, or train as a teacher, or . . .' She shrugged her shoulders. 'I got here in April, and all my friends told me I was doing this amazing thing and now – well, I love it there but it's hard, isn't it? Moving into a new town.' She looked at Tess. 'Not for you – you know everyone there. But it's hard.'

Tess thought of the times she'd seen Liz in the deli, or walked past her on the street, and had said hi and been perfectly friendly but never pursued the acquaintance at all. There was something a bit – what was it? Dubious, perhaps, about people so obviously desperate for attention, it made her want to shy away from them. She looked at Liz, then, and chided herself. Liz wasn't desperate for attention. She was just a bit lonely. She'd been braver than Tess had, for goodness' sake.

'Are you thinking you might leave, then?' Tess asked her. 'Move to Rome, maybe?' She was half joking, but Liz nodded.

'Maybe. Not Rome, necessarily. Paris, perhaps! Or Madrid. I've always wanted to learn Spanish.'

'I'm learning Spanish,' said Claire. 'In the car, it's wonderful.' She beamed at Liz. 'It's stuff like that, I mean, you get to do when you give yourself a bit more time. I've been pressing flowers, you know. And making salsa with my own tomatoes! I couldn't have done that last year, could I? Aren't the three of us lucky!' She raised her glass, and Liz, slightly ruefully, clinked hers with her. They turned to Tess.

Tess stared at her, feeling a rising panic. 'Yes,' she said. 'Yes, lucky.' She raised her glass to clink theirs, but their faces had changed, and they both smiled girlishly.

'Oh, hello,' Liz said, a little too enthusiastically.

Tess said, 'What?'

'Tess,' came a voice behind her. 'Hi.'

She turned around. There was Adam. In the uncertain evening light he loomed over her, seemingly taller and darker than before.

'I've been looking for you,' he said. The two others started fussing over him, as if he were a celebrity.

'Adam, sit down and have a glass with us,' Claire cried. 'There's plenty left.' She swallowed. 'So. Gosh. How – how are you?'

Adam looked down at her. 'Who are you?' he said. 'I'm sorry,' he added, correcting himself, as Claire blushed awfully.

'This is Claire,' said Liz, patting Claire's hand. 'Hi, Adam.'

'I know who *you* are,' he said, shaking her hand and smiling. 'It's nice to see a friendly face. I'm sorry,' he said, turning to Claire and taking her hand in his. 'That was really rude of me.'

'No, no,' Claire hastened to assure him. 'I'm sorry about your grandmother,' she added. 'Is she—'

'She's still alive,' said Adam briefly. 'That's what I came to find Tess for. I need some information to give the hospital, and I need your group insurance number.' He patted her curtly on the shoulder. 'I'm sorry to disturb your drinks.'

There was something about the way he said *your drinks*, as

293

if they were lolling around on cushions drinking champagne and eating sweetmeats while Leonora Mortmain was calling out for their help. Tess got up.

'Do you need it now? Let's go back to the hotel and I'll find it for you.'

'I don't want to disturb—'

'No,' she said, equally curtly. 'I'm meeting Peter in a bit, so I'd better do it now. Let's go. Hope that's OK.' She turned to the girls.

'Yes!' cried Claire eagerly.

'Of course it is,' said Liz. 'See you later. Give us a call if you want to meet up.'

Tess smiled gratefully at her and put some money down on the table, fumbling slightly. Her fingers were shaking, she didn't know why. 'Thanks, you two. That was lovely.'

'No,' Liz told her, handing back the euro note. 'Keep it. Buy us a drink next time.'

Tess nodded, acknowledging her point, and she smiled. 'Right,' she said and turned back to Adam. He looked at her, unsmiling. 'Let's go then, shall we.'

CHAPTER TWENTY-EIGHT

Adam walked fast. They hurried back along the uneven streets, past the knots of tourists and restaurants, dodging the pots of geraniums that clustered at the corners of the streets. She kept her arms crossed and so did he; they said nothing, but some kind of tension was mounting by the time they got back to the hotel. Tess fumbled again for her keys, her fingers all thumbs. Adam waited, frowning, by the door.

'So – what did you decide to do, in the end?'

'We're flying back tomorrow. I texted you.'

'Right. My phone isn't working.'

She unlocked her bedroom door, and he held it open for her to go inside.

'Well, I didn't know how else to get in touch with you,' she said, going over to the chest of drawers. 'Sit down.' She gestured to the spare twin bed and he sat down, his hands between his knees, picking at a piece of skin on his finger. She saw how tired he looked.

'So – what time's your flight?'

She picked up the folder with all her information in it, and started leafing through it. 'It's early, I'm afraid. Nine twenty-five. We're leaving first thing.'

'Right,' Adam said again. 'I'll have to come back on my own.'

Tess slammed the folder down on the chest of drawers. 'Adam, come on. What the fuck do you want me to say?'

'Nothing,' he said. 'Nothing, Tess, why would you accommodate me in all this?'

'*You told me to ask them!*' she yelled at him, surprised at the intensity of her own feelings, at how tightly she was wound up. 'You bloody told me to sort it out, this morning! Don't sit there and act like that. I did what you said, Adam. I'm sorry the flight's not later, but you've got your own stuff to sort out.'

Adam said scathingly, 'The "stuff", as you so charmingly put it, is coming back next week, and they've said I should just take a normal flight back and meet her at the airport.'

'Oh,' said Tess. 'Fine.' It's not my fault, she wanted to say, bewildered. She didn't understand him, didn't know what to say to stop him being like this. 'Let me write down the details for you,' she said. 'You should get some sleep after you've sorted it out, you look exhausted.' She scribbled in silence for a few moments, the sound of her biro on the notepad loud in the hot, close room.

'I won't take up much more of your time,' Adam said evenly. 'I know you have to go off and meet the Italian Stallion, and have your *Roman Holiday* fantasy for one more night.' He paused as she turned and gave him the piece of paper. 'You don't have time for—'

'Give it a rest,' Tess said, breathing in deeply through her nose. She closed her eyes, trying to keep her cool. 'Adam, I know this has been a long, horrible day, I know this is all awful for you. But stop taking it out on me. What have I done?'

He folded the piece of paper over and over in his hand. They were facing each other, staring intently at one another in the gloom of the room.

'Nothing,' he said, after a while. 'You're right. You've done nothing wrong. I shouldn't take it out on you. You don't realize.'

296

He turned for the door, but she caught his arm. 'Adam – I'm sorry. I'm here for you. You know I am. I always will be.'

'When it's convenient for you,' he said, and there was grief in his voice, a catch in his throat. He turned away, sliding the paper into his jeans pocket. 'So just forget it, Tessa. We don't always have to do this.'

'Is this about after your mum died?' Tess said, banging her hand against the wall, so she could lean on it. She gritted her teeth. 'You don't know—'

'I do,' he said. 'I know how much I hurt you.' She stared at him. 'I do. You think I don't but I do. It's just that you disappeared. You totally disappeared, for eight, nine, ten years. When I needed you most. You were my family – and . . .' He shook his head, his smile bleak. 'No. Forget it.'

Tess laughed, her voice hollow. 'Adam! Don't you remember what happened between us? There were reasons – there was a reason I didn't want to see you, you know.'

'What – the abortion?' he said, his voice low. 'I know. I know.' She stared helplessly at him. 'But my God, everything was pretty black then. Mum – the news about the family – you know. That summer – I'm sorry, I shouldn't have done what I did to you. I never regretted it, T. Never.' He gripped her arm. 'But it happened.'

'You didn't *do it to me*,' Tess said, trying not to sound furious. She took a deep breath. 'We both did it. But I was the one who had to get rid of it. And that happened, too, you know. Even though you –' Her voice cracked. 'You didn't even ask. You never asked: And I'm still so angry with you – I'm still *so angry* –' She breathed in again, trying to stay calm, trying to catch that scent of jasmine, and she smoothed the folder in front of her with her hands. 'You're right. We should just forget it.' She took a deep breath. 'Let's not get into this, Adam. It's not a good idea. Not now.'

'Not a good idea.' Adam nodded solidly. 'Fine, Tess. Fine.'

'I just mean, now's not the time. Your grandmother—'

'Don't call her that.'

'Oh, grow up.' Tess slammed her hand down on the chest of drawers, the sweat from her hand slimy on the varnished wood. It shook, violently. 'Just grow up, Adam!'

'Me, grow up –' Adam said, his expression black. 'Me, grow up! Tess, my God, coming from you, that would almost be hilarious, if it wasn't so –' He shook his head, searching for something. He spat the words at her. '*Tragic*, that's it.'

'At least I've got a fucking *job*, and a house of my own, and a life!' she screamed at him, so angry that she feared she might lose control. Her mouth was dry, she could feel the blood pounding in her ears, around her clenched jaw. She opened her mouth, staring at him in contempt. 'You bastard! You smug stupid bastard! I'm sorting my life out, I'm moving on, I'm changing things and you – you just stay the same. Your whole life, you've been in the same place, drinking in the same pub, you've had the same job, the same friends – and you tell me I'm not grown-up?'

'My life's not a fantasy,' he said. His voice was ugly. 'I'm not trying to live my life like something out of a film, Tess. I don't fall in love with people just because they live in a romantic city and they whisper a few sweet words to me late at night after some wine.'

'Peter and me are—'

'Peter and I,' he corrected, and she could have slapped him. 'Peter's nothing, Tess, he's a phantom, he's a dream, you can't see him for what he really is! What are you doing? It's like Will all over again.'

'He's nothing like Will,' she said furiously. 'Shut up.'

'You wanted someone stable and boring and staid who'd tell you how great you were and lo and behold, there was Will, except he was so stable and boring he couldn't even get around to having sex with you,' Adam said, as if he were reciting a lesson. She stumbled back. It was like a slap in the face.

'That's not true,' she said, her voice a whisper.

'And now here you are and you're pissed off with me, and you're pissed off with Langford, so hey, presto! Wow! Here's this handsome stranger who's on the rebound and wants some no-strings sex, so I'll just convince myself I've fallen in love with him, and then it'll all be OK, and I'll be able to justify it in my mind!' Adam's eyes were blazing. 'Because you always can, Tess, even when you're most at fault, you always can. But you don't understand, he's not offering you a future. He's offering you a distraction from the past, and that's not the same thing.'

She stared at him. 'Man. I didn't realize you hated me so much,' she said brokenly.

He was silent, and his hands fell to his sides. She looked at him, almost afraid, and was astonished to see his eyes filled with tears.

'It's not that,' he said quietly. 'It's that I loved you so much.'

'What?'

He nodded in the gathering gloom of the room; she could hardly see his face. 'For years, after you left. And I needed you so much. I missed you so much. And you were my best friend.' He gave a ragged sigh. 'You're right, T. Sorry. That's the trouble, isn't it. With you and me. Always has been.'

'What?' she said again, calmer now. She pressed her hand protectively to her neck. He watched her, and touched the hand, lightly, sadly. He looked at her, his eyebrows raised, and scratched his hair which was standing up in tufts, the way it used to when he was angry, or hurt, or confused about something.

'It's nothing, now. We know how to hurt each other, more than anyone else. Don't we? And we have done, comprehensively. I don't understand why it should be like that, but it is.'

His words saddened her profoundly. 'Oh,' she said. 'Perhaps I know what you mean.'

'I couldn't hurt Francesca like that, not if I thought about it for a fortnight,' he said. 'And compared to you, she's nothing to me.'

But with the mention of Francesca it was as if a spell had been broken, and Tess stepped back a little. She touched her forehead, the back of her neck; she was perspiring in the sultry heat, still breathing rapidly. He watched her.

'I'm sorry again,' he said.

'Do you think there's a way back for us?' she said, but she knew the answer.

'I don't know,' he said. 'I don't know. I don't think we can be friends, the way we wish we could.'

'Maybe,' she said. She looked at him, seeing him again as she'd seen him that very morning – it seemed a lifetime ago, now. 'I don't think so.' She cleared her throat. 'And you – you have a lot of stuff you need to sort out,' she said without rancour.

He nodded. 'I know.'

But he didn't know, that was the trouble. It was as if they were playing in the dark, tripping over things, hurting themselves, each other, and it had to stop. Perhaps the only way was if they accepted that too much had happened for them to ever be friends. Perhaps this was goodbye, and perhaps it should have happened a while ago.

'I probably won't see you tomorrow morning, then,' Adam said. He was standing by the door.

'You won't,' she said. 'Goodbye, Adam. I hope – I hope she gets home OK.'

'You too,' he said, and he bent forward as if he were going to kiss her forehead, but then he stopped. He gave a short, sad sound, something between a laugh and a cry, and he went out, shutting the door behind him.

Tess sank slowly down onto the bed, staring at nothing, not noticing or caring that the room was now in darkness. She didn't move. She sat there for ages, trying to see where it had gone wrong. Where her friendship with Adam had become impossible. Perhaps, she thought to herself finally, perhaps the seeds were sown long, long ago, and there was nothing either of them could do about it. What those seeds were, she knew she would probably never discover.

Her time in Rome was nearly over, and in a hospital in the middle of the river lay an old woman, clinging to life, the only one who could explain what lay in wait back for them back in Langford, away from this magical city where it seemed anything could happen.

Tess got up and opened the window, gazing out into the still night, waiting for Peter to arrive, and she did not move for a long time.

CHAPTER TWENTY-NINE

When Peter finally arrived and she opened the door, the rest of the hotel was asleep. She saw his face and something about his expression worried her, a warning note ringing in the distance.

'Hi, honey,' he said, coming into the room, putting his hands on either side of her face and kissing her, a long, deep kiss. 'What a day you've had, hey?'

'It's OK,' she said, though when she looked back to this morning and Adam's appearance in the lobby of the Albergo Watkins, she was astonished to find it was the same day, and not several weeks earlier. She put her hand on his chest, looking at him.

'How are you?' she said.

'Good,' said Peter. 'But I need to talk to you.' He was always direct, he didn't dart around the subject. He took her hands and pulled her so they were sitting on the bed. 'I had the interview for the job today. The West Coast job.'

'What?' Tess's bleary mind struggled to fit the pieces together of the last week. 'The job . . .' She was rewinding in her head. 'That first night . . . you told me about it.'

'Yeah, and I just interviewed with Donald today, on the phone. He wants me to fly to New York next week.'

'Wow, that's exciting,' Tess said, trying her best to sound incredibly positive, as though that was the best news she'd ever had. 'What does that mean?'

'I don't know,' Peter said, his eyes scanning her face. 'What do you think it means?'

'Well, *I* don't know, do I?' said Tess. 'But they must like you. And why wouldn't they? You're—'

'No,' he interrupted. 'What does it mean for us? I'm thinking about us.' He leaned forward and kissed her neck gently.

'Oh.' It had been a long, long day, and Tess was tired, not least by the scene she'd just had with Adam. With horror she felt tears budding in her eyes, plopping down onto the coverlet of the bed. 'That's – that's wonderful,' she said, sniffing.

'It's wonderful that I'm going?' Peter said, looking uncertain.

'No, you idiot.' She slid her arms around his neck, kissing him. 'It's wonderful that you're thinking about us. Because –' she gave a watery gulp – 'I am too.'

'I don't know what I'd do if they offered it to me,' he said seriously. He pushed a lock of her hair away from her face. 'It's a great job, Tess – I just have to be straight with you.'

'That's why I love you,' she told him. 'Because you're straight with me. It doesn't matter. If it's the job you want . . .'

'This isn't a holiday romance, then?' he said. 'Is it?'

'We don't know what it is, darling,' she told him, kissing him again. 'But it's something. Isn't it?'

'Yes,' he said. He picked up her shawl, which was lying on the bed. 'We've got one more night together. Let's go out. Just for a while.'

So for one last time, she grabbed her bag and they left the hotel together, and for one last time she walked through the dark, uneven streets with Peter, hand in hand, kissing and laughing in the warm night air, not really saying much, just enjoying the fact that they were by each other's side. They stopped in a tiny vinoteca by the river and had bread, salami

303

and wine, and talked about silly things, their favourite films, Americanisms and Britishisms, like getting the floor numbers mixed up the first time she came to his flat (or apartment, as he insisted she call it). They climbed onto his moped and rode through the deserted moonlit city, theirs alone, across the river and back to the hotel, and the wind was cool on her face, her neck, her collar bone, as she clung onto him one last time.

When they got back, they pushed the narrow single beds together in silence. He wrapped her in his arms and drew her close, kissing the back of her neck, holding her tight to him. She didn't sleep, though she desperately wanted to. She lay all night, blinking, her mind racing, always in a circle, reaching no conclusions, while Peter's cool breath blew steadily on her spine.

Early the next morning, she said goodbye to him at the door of her hotel room. They kissed for a long time, the extended handle of Tess's suitcase banging against the plaster walls as she leaned against it, clutching on to Peter, feeling as if she would cry the moment he let her go. Tears pricked her eyes, and she held onto his shirt.

'Don't go,' he said eventually, laughing as he removed her hand from his buttons. 'Stay here.'

That was why she was sure she loved him, that idea that they could say these quite monumentally important things to each other and there was no game-playing, nothing sinister about it. That she could look into his eyes and see – what? Nothing. Nothing other than kindness and affection and a need to be loved in return, the way she did. Adam was wrong, wrong, *wrong*! Peter wasn't a passion junkie, and he wasn't on the rebound. Well, he was – but that was what was great. She knew that! She knew his faults as well as his strengths, and that only made her like him more. Because she wasn't playing a game, she was totally herself. She didn't lie to him, or conceal things from him. He wasn't a different person from the one she thought he had been.

'You know I can't,' she said, touching one of the buttons lightly with her index finger. 'I have to go.'

As if on cue, a car horn sounded outside.

'That's us,' she said.

'Come back here, then,' Peter said. 'Come back and stay with me.'

'You might not be here,' she said, laughing.

'I changed my mind. I won't go for the interview. I want to stay here.' She shook her head questioningly, and he pressed on. 'Imagine it – us in the apartment, just the two of us. We could go out to supper every night. You could speak Italian, buy a scooter, eat pasta . . . walk to everywhere you need to be, live a proper life here, buy fresh flowers in the market every day.' She was laughing; she opened her mouth to speak but he put his finger on her lips. He said, earnestly, 'You'd get a job at a school here easily, they're always short of English-language speakers. There's room for your books – you can even have your portrait of Jane Austen. Why are you going back there?'

He reached forward and kissed her gently on the forehead, and the tenderness of this small, perfect gesture touched Tess somehow, more than she could possibly have said. Her stomach turned over, and she breathed out, deeply.

'You have to go and I have to go.' She scrunched up her face, so she didn't cry.

'That's a good look,' Peter said.

'Don't,' said Tess. 'I – I'm trying not to.' She took a deep breath. 'I'm trying not to cry.'

'Aw, sweetie,' he said, and his voice was kind. He put his finger under her chin. She looked away from his eyes, at the chipboard door next to them. 'Whatever. When you're back home, just remember how it felt to be this way, to be this person. Remember. It's too easy to forget that kinda stuff.'

Why are you going back there? She could still feel it all: the warm breeze in the room, the smell of the hotel, jasmine mixed with coffee and heat, most of all heat, the kind of warm terracotta-petrol-tarmac-y heat you never found in England, certainly not London, let alone Langford. The smells of Langford were wet grass, petrol, certainly, rain, a certain 'farm-yard smell', as her mother used to put it, and something else . . . the smell of an English country town, whatever that was. Mustardy? Wet tweed? Cheap, horrible scented candles, the kind that were on sale everywhere?

Tess tore her mind back to the present. She wrapped her arms slowly around Peter's neck.

'I won't forget,' she said, and she raised herself up so she was on tiptoe. 'I won't forget. I will always remember you, darling.'

His hand slid over her hip, onto her bottom, and he pulled her towards him again, and for a few moments more she was lost in the deliciously familiar feeling of total happiness, of Prosecco and moonlight and sex. Then Peter opened the door, wheeling her bag towards the stairs, and she followed him. As she did, closing the door behind her, there was a soft click down the corridor and Tess looked up. There, in a creased shirt and jeans, his hair standing on end, was Adam. He had dark, almost black, shadows under his eyes, and he looked as though he'd got up in a hurry. There was no time to say anything – they had said too much already. She gave him a small smile.

'I'm off, then.'

'Of course,' he said.

Peter was halfway down the stairs. 'Hey, is that Adam? Bye, man. It was good to meet you.'

Adam leaned towards the staircase. 'Bye, Peter. Good to meet you too. Tess, can I have a word?'

'Sure,' she said. She patted Peter's shoulder, motioning for him to go ahead, and he took her bag downstairs. 'What's up?' she said, opening her handbag to check her passport was there. She didn't look at him, didn't want him to see how upset she was.

'She's dead,' Adam said briefly. Tess's head snapped up.

'Leonora?'

'Yes,' he said. 'The hospital just called. I'm on my way there now.'

'What happened, do they know?'

'She just – drifted away, they said.' He scratched his head and closed his eyes briefly. Tess looked down at the waiting group, at Peter talking to Diana. 'You should go,' Adam said.

'We can cancel—'

'No, no,' Adam said firmly. 'Absolutely not. It wouldn't make any sense.'

'My God.' Tess put her hand on his. Outside, the minibus hooted its horn impatiently. 'I'm sorry. Adam – I don't know what to say.'

'It's over,' Adam said, nodding, not meeting her eyes, looking past her into the distance. 'That's all. We can go home now.'

It was only later that Tess would think how very sad it was that the end of anyone's life should be greeted like this. Even Leonora Mortmain's.

April 1943

Neither of them knew it was going to happen. She would look back and marvel that she could have woken that day with no idea of what lay ahead of her. That she could start the day as a – oh, as a child! – and end it in his arms, his hands clumsily stroking her hair, their slick bodies clinging to each other, exhilarated, exhausted.

The atmosphere was tense in the Hall that early April morning; it was tense throughout the town, throughout the country. They had been at war for three and a half years now; there were men and women from the town out in the Atlantic, at danger from U-boats, fighting in Tripoli and Tunisia, in Italy and somewhere in occupied France. And what lay between France and England? Nothing, except the Channel. And so they worked, and watched, and waited.

Leonora was tense, too. A spoon had vaulted out of her hand – she had watched it spinning, almost leisurely, through the air, crashing into the wooden dresser that stood in their breakfast room and breaking a vase. It was bad luck, it wasn't her fault. Father's dogs, Bonhote and Tugendhat (named after First World War generals), had started to scrap in the hallway, barking loudly and suddenly, and she had jumped.

'You're eighteen, Rara!' her mother had said, trying not to raise her voice, her face contorted into an agony of suppressed anger. Her mother never shouted, no one did in Langford Hall. 'Why are you so clumsy? You *must* be more careful!'

'The dogs barked, Mother. I'm sorry. I didn't realize they were so close – I jumped.' She didn't add, couldn't add, that she hated dogs, always had. Their big slathering jaws, the way they didn't care, thought it was fine to simply *leap* on one, whether one liked them or was terrified of them. Once, Tugendhat had pinned her up in the corridor – he was an Alsatian mix, an ugly brute – snarling and growling, and when Leonora had screamed, Sir Charles Mortmain had hit her on the hand with the ruler three times. For raising her voice.

Her mother was harassed to a point almost past sanity. 'I do *not* care. You should be ashamed of yourself. Look at this mess. Your father will be extremely angry.' Mama was leaning forward, shouting at her daughter now, the pent-up anger of the tension and the sudden spring heat releasing itself. Her face was red and shiny. A greasy tendril of hair flapped out from behind her ear.

'I'm sorry, Mama,' Leonora said, genuinely contrite in the face of her mother's rage. 'I didn't mean to, but the dogs –'

She was going to say, 'The dogs scared me,' but she halted, not convinced this would be the answer her mother was looking for. Her parents had no sympathy for her fear of the dogs, her father in particular.

'Doesn't matter,' her mother said, stifling a sob. 'I'll need to find Eleanor, to see if we can have this mended. Oh, Rara, just – just go away!'

Leonora did, without a backwards glance. She ran to the door, pulled it open, ran out into the sunshine without saying goodbye, her heart heavy, her teenage sense of outrage already melting away into guilt, and sorrow, and a resolve to bring something back for her mother. An ice cream? Some flowers? A book? Her eye wandered as she caught her breath, diving down the warren of sidestreets that was Langford's medieval centre, and through a gap in the houses she suddenly caught a glimpse of fields, of the countryside beyond, a flash of enticing green. Spring was well under way, it was the first really warm day of the year. She shivered. She would slip quietly through the streets, out through the gap in the ancient city walls, down the stairs to the water meadows. An apple and a book, that was all she needed, she'd pick some flowers for her mother on the way back. She had a beautiful primrose-coloured hardback of Catullus's poems in her pocket; Leonora was a romantic soul, though given scant opportunity to explore this at Langford Hall. And now she was free. She jumped excitedly in the air, scratching her bare arms. Everything was all right again, the memory of Mother's face as she picked the coloured shards of china off the floor but a distant memory, with the extreme callousness of youth.

'Hello there, Atalanta. What mischief are you up to now?'

She jumped, and turned around guiltily.

'Philip! My goodness, you gave me a fright.'

'Exactly.' He smiled, and took her hand from her mouth. 'If you weren't up to something awful,' he said, mock-slapping her fingers, 'you wouldn't be looking quite so guilty. What is it, eh?'

Philip Edwards was awfully annoying this year; so pompous. One year away from Langford at Cambridge, and he thought he was God's gift to the universe. She snatched her hand back to her side, mortified at the blush she felt at the warmth of his touch. 'Nothing,' she said. 'I'm just escaping home, that's all. Ma's furious with me. I've been awful.'

'I bet you have.' There was laughter in his voice, but a note of sympathy too. She heard it. 'I was just off for a walk,' he said. 'Got some reading to do.'

'Oh, me too,' she said airily. She patted her coat pocket.

'What's in there?' he asked, leaning forwards.

She was instantly embarrassed, as if he had caught her in

a lie, or exposed a secret part of herself. 'Get off,' she said, wriggling away, but he pulled the slim volume out of her pocket and held it above her head. He grinned.

'Love poetry!'

'It's not,' she said, though she was blushing. 'All sorts.'

'I know, I know, my little Atalanta,' he said.

'Don't call me that,' she said, though actually she liked it.

He jabbed a finger. 'Look – Atalanta the swift-footed huntress, who rejected all men and wouldn't get married until whoever it was dropped the golden apples and distracted her. Second poem.'

'That's not true!' The stain on Leonora's cheeks deepened; marriage, indeed any relations with the opposite sex, had never occurred to her, raised as she was in the oppressive atmosphere of the Mortmain home. Never – until recently.

'Oh, come now,' he said, slightly wolfishly. But then, seeing her embarrassment, he softened instantly. He patted her arm and she relaxed. 'I was heading down to the water meadows. I wanted to see you, wanted to talk to you about something.' He shifted on his feet. 'Um – fancy coming with me?' He looked down at her. He was so tall these days, and she felt so little; when had he grown so much, outstripped her, turned into this tall, broad-shouldered man? Where had the eight-year-old Philip who could fit into her pink silk party dress gone? Who was this stranger, almost a man, in front of her?

She was suddenly shy, which was ridiculous. 'Of course,' she said, drawing herself up to her full height. 'I was intending to go that way, anyway.'

'Really?' He smiled. 'We are of one mind, then.'

'Absolutely,' she said, and they set off together as the morning sun crept up and over the rooves of the town, flickering through the silent streets.

She shouldn't have let him. But the truth is, she wanted to. Wanted to feel his arms around her, his body on top of her. They were close, always had been. She sometimes hugged

311

her maid, Eleanor, the person to whom she was probably closest other than Philip. But no one else in young Leonora's life hugged her, touched her, was physical with her, and so it was easy, really, to move to that stage, since he was the only one she had ever spontaneously thrown her arms around, tripped over and wrestled to the floor, kissed.

And so when they were lying side by side, on the rug he'd brought with him, in silence, listening to the wood pigeons coo dolefully in the trees at the edge of the park, feeling the blazing, lazing summer warmth steal over them, she did not move when he leaned over her, nor was she wholly surprised. Leonora Mortmain was an impeccably brought-up young woman. She would simply not have known how such things should be initiated. She only knew she was terrified for a second, and then completely happy, when he leaned up on one arm and stroked her shoulder, kissed her cheek.

His hair flopped into his face, shading his features as he hung over her.

'Are you all right?' he said, his hand stroking her leg. She could feel the warmth of his palm on her skin, through her thin cotton dress.

She wiggled a little, her hair fanning out behind her, and smiled up at him. 'Of course I am. Are you?'

'I am now, Rara.' His fingers moved more slowly, he was staring down at her. 'I missed you. It's been a long term. Christmas seems like a lifetime ago.'

At Christmas, at a party, she had kissed him, or rather let him kiss her, in a dark corner of a house filled with old men and women, the people who had been left behind. It was just the two of them in the study, as music blared out from a wind-up gramophone in the drawing room. He had pressed up against her, his hands clutching the back of her head. She had enjoyed it, even though it should have felt wrong, this boy who was now a man, her oldest friend, doing these things to her.

The next day, he had met her, walking along the lane back to the Hall, on the way back home, and he had kissed her again, pushing her gently against the old oak that had stood for centuries at the crossroads. His body was warm against hers in the cold, his tongue in her mouth alarming at first and then exciting. This time they had both wanted it, and it only stopped when they heard the uncertain roar of a motor engine coming towards them. They had broken apart, and it was only then she realized his hand was inside her dress, on her breast, and that she liked it there.

Now, here in the fields, Leonora didn't know what they were doing; she wasn't sure he knew either, only that it felt right. And that's when Philip kissed her. He undid the buttons on her delicate lawn cotton dress, gently kissing the skin each button revealed, one by one, and parting it until she was almost naked. He took off his trousers and shirt, and then he removed her starched, semi-corseted brassiere, draping it gently over the high grass; it bobbed as if held up on stilts.

'Do you remember coming here in the summer, when we were little?' He pushed her hair off her face, kissing her eyes, her cheeks, her lips. 'Just the two of us, down here?'

'Of course I do,' said Leonora shyly. Her fingers beat a light motion on the back of his neck. She stroked his skin, it was smooth, it smelt comforting, of hay and incense and – oh, of Philip, her oldest, most beloved friend, and being naked with him, which should have felt so extraordinarily strange and wrong, felt wonderful, delicious, right.

'When I was at school, when I was utterly miserable, I'd close my eyes and think of you, of us, here, in the summer, and it would all seem manageable suddenly.' He moved her arms so they were above her head, pinning her hands there, so he could run his hands over her body, over her breasts, kissing her stomach, her breast bone, her nipples – she could feel the scratchy hairs on his face, rasping against her skin. She smiled, looking down at his soft hair, his hands on her

313

body, then she looked up, to the sky above her, the trees around them, and breathed in. She was happy – a little scared, but happy. She kissed the top of his head.

'It's all right, now,' she said softly. 'You're back here. And so am I.'

'I know,' he said, his voice muffled. 'Oh – Rara.' He kissed her passionately, and she him, and he wouldn't let her move until he came up for air and they moved together, and she took him in her hand, instinctively, curious, and stroked him till he groaned. He was quiet for a moment, and she nodded up at him, and his eyes were enormous, his face serious.

When he finally pushed slowly, carefully, into her it hurt, but only for a moment, and then it felt strange and wonderful. As if he was plugging something, filling her up. They hardly made any movement in the field; he rocked his hips urgently against hers, and she welcomed him in, till he came inside her, his cry strangled, as if she was hurting him. Then silence.

And then it was as if she was snapped back to reality and they were two teenagers again, one in a half-undone dress, her knickers in the grass, the other with his trousers discarded, his pants around his knees, breathing heavily against each other, rocking again, just the two of them, as his breathing subsided and she stared up at him.

'Hello,' he said, pushing the hair off her forehead. 'My little Atalanta.' He smiled, blinkly heavily at her.

'Oh – hello,' she answered. 'Oh, Philip –'

'I've been wanting to do that for a while now,' Philip said, with an attempt at composure, and then a smile broke out over his face, the one she knew so well, and he shifted his weight from on top of her, and covered her mouth with kisses.

It was scorching hot, deadly quiet in the grass where they lay. She was silent, wondering what they had just done, amazed at how powerful it felt, knowing it was right.

'I'm going away,' Philip said after a while, his breath in her hair. 'Next week, I'm going.'

He rolled off her, and fiddled with his trousers. She lay there, not sure what to say, his sweat drying on her, cold in the heat. Wetness slithered between her legs. She felt suddenly grubby, there in the dusty grass.

'Where?'

'To the barracks, I suppose.' He cleared his throat.

She still didn't understand. 'Barracks?'

'Local barracks, over in Thornham. Mum was hoping my eyesight'd stop me from enlisting. But I went yesterday. The sergeant-major said it was fine.' She stared at him, aghast. He said, almost proudly, 'There's no way I'd stay at home like a lily-livered little snake, not like Roger Bowen, getting his daddy to get him off the hook. There's a war on and I'm eighteen now.'

'Philip – you're not going to fight,' she said, sitting up, clutching his jacket. He turned to her in surprise. 'You can't!' she said, her voice sounding weak and silly, even in her own ears. 'You –'

'I've got to, Rara,' he said, looking puzzled. 'How can I not?' He smiled at her gently, smoothing her hair off her forehead again. He caught her to him, and held her, still naked, against his chest. She could feel his heart, hammering inside him, the cooling sweat on his strong body. 'What would you think of me if I didn't go and fight? Listen to me. It's a dirty fight but we're going to beat Hitler. You'll see, I'll be home by Christmas, and we'll be married, and your father can go to hell. I wouldn't have – I wouldn't have taken you like this, if I wasn't sure.' He looked down at her fiercely. 'D'you hear me?'

His hand enfolded hers, caught between their bodies, as he cradled her.

'Don't go,' she said, realizing now the severity of what they had done, and of what he had always meant to her. She pulled away from him. 'How can you go? How can you say we're going to be together? We can't be!'

315

'Yes, we will,' he said, and it was almost as if he were laughing at her, which only made her more furious. 'Everything's changed, Rara. The world has changed. This war is changing it.'

'Not with my father,' Leonora said. 'Philip, they won't ever let us, ever . . . It's not the war, it won't change anything. Oh, my God – you shouldn't have . . .' Emotion overwhelmed her; she picked up her shoes, a sob catching in her throat. 'I hate you!' She scrambled in the grass for her underthings, pulled her dress on over her shoulders, her fingers trembling on the buttons.

'Leonora!' he said in surprise as she stood up, stumbling away from him. 'Leonora, come back!'

She ran through the heavy lush fields, the morning dew drenching her bare feet, her hair flying behind her, and when she stopped at the bridge over the stream to gather her breath, he caught up with her.

'I love you,' he said furiously as the water rushed beneath them. 'I don't care that you're a Mortmain, that I'm the vicar's son. It doesn't matter, can't you see? Everything's changing. I love you, Leonora, and it'll all be wonderful when I'm back. This war's nearly over. It's got to be for the good. We're going to lick the Germans.' His hand ran down to her stomach, almost as if he knew, and he kissed her. 'It's just you and me after this. I promise. I'm offering you a future. Not the past.' She clung to him, sobbing a little, her hair falling around her face. He smiled. 'Now kiss me again.'

She kissed him, even as she tasted the salt of her own tears in her mouth. He cupped her chin in his hand, and with his other hand pushed her thick, golden hair behind her shoulder.

'You are such a beautiful girl,' he said. 'Doesn't it feel right?'

'Yes,' said Leonora, because it did. It honestly did, no matter who her father was, who Philip was. She had never, ever felt more alive than she did at that moment. 'Yes, it does.'

'I'll see you tomorrow,' he said, as she turned to run back

to the town. She nodded, smiling at him, though it gave her pain. 'And the day after, and the day after that. You and me, Rara, just you and me. Promise me you believe me.'

'I believe you,' she said, poised for flight, but she turned and kissed him just once more, feeling deliciously wanton as she lifted her face up to his, feeling her hair fall between her shoulder blades. 'I love you,' she said, no longer timid.

'I love you too,' he whispered, as they kissed on the bridge. It felt so private, just between them. She couldn't have imagined, have foreseen, the result of that one spring day.

PART THREE

Omnia mutantur, nos et mutamur in illis.
All things change, and we change with them.

Roman proverb

CHAPTER THIRTY

When Mick Hopkins first moved to Langford in 1970, to take up a job as barman at the Feathers, the local pub was a very different animal. Mick, who was no innovator, but a keen, if impassive, observer of human nature, liked to compare it – only to himself – to a ham and cheese sandwich.

As the years went past and Mick eventually became the landlord, he noticed the change, but it wasn't until the nineties that it was obvious. In 1970, not only was the price of a pint after decimalization just eleven pence, but the customers he served were mainly men, all locals, all born and brought up within a mile radius of the pub. The food was sandwiches: ham, cheese and pickle. In the thirties, the ham would have been local, the cheese proper, creamy, sharp Somerset cheddar, the pickle made in the kitchen by the landlord's wife, but by the mid-seventies, the ham was processed and reshaped into shiny, slippery slices, the cheddar was pre-packaged and plastic, and the pickle from a jar, with a faint taste of washing-up liquid about it.

Mick just kept on serving pints, and emptying the ashtrays, bringing out plates of food, and listening to his customers as they complained about the weather, about the strikes, about the cost of living, the government ... And as the seventies turned into the eighties, and Langford tidied itself up a bit, the number of tourists increased tenfold, and Mick, who was by then the landlord, opened up the garden at the back, which had been a concreted-over space where the bins were kept. He put some benches down, a couple of potted plants, and a couple of spaces for cars, and started serving cream teas, with synthetic whipped cream in a can, as well as ham, cheese and pickle sandwiches. Janey, his young, nubile barmaid, was dispatched to Bath to buy some Laura Ashley curtains and duvet covers, fake plastic flowers in vases, and pale blue and pink towels, for the four bedrooms upstairs. The tourists loved it.

Then, in the late eighties, someone on the council suggested Langford enter the Britain in Bloom competition. Mick didn't mind: he could see it would be good for business. So the Feathers was festooned with purple anemones, coral geraniums, Busy Lizzies and the like, every available windowsill and patio square given over to bumptious boxes of colour. The car park was turfed over, made into grass, and patrons were allowed to use the town hall car park. A play area was erected, and the denizens of Langford brought their children there on summer's evenings, at the weekends, and for parties. The ham and cheese sandwiches came with a frothy lettuce garnish, and were cut into triangles. They started serving Pimm's.

When the Jane Austen Centre won a fairly substantial Lottery grant in the nineties, the town seemed to think this was confirmation of what it had always known: Langford was a cut above other places, a classy step back in time. It conveniently forgot that it had made its money from the now-defunct coal mines ten miles to its west, and from farming. It only remembered – and saw – the golden stone, the Beau Brummell connection, the high-end visitors, the Mortmains, the glamorous bits. When Jacquetta Meluish arrived from Chelsea in 1997, and opened her tasteful gift shop on the high street, Mick knew things were changing.

Within five years there were two more shops of its ilk: a delicatessen and a glamorous off-licence that specialized in Spanish wines. They were soon followed by the world-renowned Mr Dill's Cheese Emporium, and Vistas, an art gallery specializing in insipid watercolours of the surrounding countryside, which always made Mick feel a bit nauseous. He loved the countryside around Langford, it was dramatic and full of surprises, whether it was the lush, almost tropical greenery of summer, or the shocking colours of autumn, or the stark, black beauty of the hills and hedgerows in the depths of winter.

Now, the cream teas they served at the Feathers had local clotted cream from George Farm, jam made by the long-suffering Janey – now married with three grown-up children – and the cheese was proud Somerset cheddar again, the ham from local pigs. But the pickle was still out of a jar, the fish and chips were still from the freezer, and the deep-fried brie was still the most popular starter on the menu. Some things you could change and you should, some you couldn't and you shouldn't, Mick reasoned. He was getting old, now, he knew it, and some might say forty years was a long time to be serving drinks to people, but he still loved it.

This summer, though, things were different. It was odd being in Langford these past few weeks. June had passed, and it had become hotter and hotter, the roads dustier than ever, the usually sweet air of Langford – which, unlike Thornham, was high on a hill – became still and oppressive, with no wind to blow through the town. It hadn't rained for over a month by the time July was over. In cottages and houses built to keep the warmth in across town people sweltered, babies cried and didn't sleep, the inhabitants tossed and turned, praying for rain.

Mick had his rooms above the shop – that is, at the back of the courtyard of the pub, overlooking the valley, where the oldest part of the town spilled down the hill, down towards the water meadows. On summer's nights, he slept with the tiny casement window open, so he could hear the wood-pigeons cooing in the trees below, the blackbird singing loud in the dead of night.

Once, a wasps' nest camped out in the eaves by his shutter, and he had come in one afternoon, looking for his glasses, to find the room black with hundreds of swarming creatures. It wasn't a humming sound, either, it had sounded like an approaching storm. He had shut the door behind him, standing in the centre of the room, dumbstruck for what seemed like an eternity, until common sense got him out of there. Adam had been downstairs, behind the bar. 'Oh, my God, what happened?' he'd said, as Mick had stumbled into the pub again, and it wasn't until he'd looked down at his arm and seen three angry red marks, that he realized he'd been stung. He'd had to go to hospital.

That, he thought, was the ugliest invasion he'd had to deal with since he'd been here. For the most part, Langford was a lovely place to live and – after only forty years here – some people had let it be known that they regarded him as as good as local, now. Of course, that meant less and less now the place was increasingly full of tourists and DFLs (down from Londoners), but it was still nice.

On this particular morning in August Mick was up and about early, though he hadn't slept well. Even opening the windows wide late at night out onto the valley had not brought any wind in. Mick was a quiet-tempered man, but even he was feeling a touch out of sorts. His bones seemed to ache more than usual and, as he lifted the old blackboard with the day's specials out onto the high street he paused for a moment, enjoying the cool of the narrow road where the morning shadows were still long. As he always did he looked over at the house opposite, but Leda House was shuttered up, as it had been since Leonora Mortmain died. Mick shook his head as he stood up, wiping his hands on his apron, and went back inside.

It wasn't right, he told himself. The woman had been dead for nearly two months now, and no one knew what was happening. They hadn't even had the funeral yet, for God's sakes. She was still in Rome, in some freezer there, waiting for clearance to come back – because of red tape, they said. It wasn't good for anyone, especially Adam, and Mick didn't like it. He hesitated in the corridor by the courtyard as he fumbled with the keys, and unlocked the door to the bar.

Now, Mick had been no fan of Mrs Mortmain's, but he wasn't the type to take sides, either. Do as you would be done by, was his motto. So he had always smiled and greeted her politely, even if she'd ignored him, these forty years and even if, over the past decade, she'd grown more and more unreasonable, even a little crazy, he thought. He was, Mick told himself as he let himself into the warm, dusty bar, old enough to remember her when he'd first come to Langford, and he remembered things that other people – like Ron, or Clive, or Diana or even Adam – might have forgotten. But he remembered she wasn't always that bad. She'd been in her late forties, then.

Though Mick was fastidious about keeping a clean bar, and though Janey, and Janey's daughter Kirsty, now part-time and looking suspiciously like Mick, had cleaned up the night before, the old room still smelt close, yeasty, a little sweaty, in the heat. Still moving slowly, Mick went over to the leaded windows that gave out onto the street and opened them. He stared at the house for a moment again, and then nipped behind the bar.

He'd often thought to himself that Leonora must have been a fine-looking woman, in her day. She had dark, dark eyes, pale skin, cheekbones that stuck out a mile, gave her an Audrey Hepburn kind of look. She wore headscarves and a lot of black, and she had an angular, almost tomboyish way of moving.

Mick started checking the barrels, letting his mind run along. That was the trouble, he'd always known it. Thin women, they all too often turn scrawny. It happened to Audrey Hepburn, didn't it? Mick liked them with a smile on their face and some meat on their bones. He couldn't say that out loud, of course, it wasn't right to say it out loud, but in the course of his rich bedroom life at the Feathers, it was the Janeys of this world who still brought a smile to his face. And that had been the trouble with Leonora Mortmain, as the years passed and he settled into his life as her neighbour. She grew thinner, seemed to shrink before his eyes, as if something was eating her up. Before, she'd had a bit of spark. But these last few years she'd become downright scary, always twitching those curtains, always scowling, rarely venturing outside, preferring to keep her world within those four gloomy walls. It was a big, lovely house, that one. A real shame.

No visitors, either. Apart from Jean Forbes, of course, and a couple of others. Solicitors, men from London who looked after the estates. Mick didn't pass judgement, so he made no comment when he saw Adam slip across there, after his day shift was over, once every few months. He liked the boy, and he had loved his mother – everyone had. In fact, after she'd moved to Langford, Mick had enjoyed a brief affair with Philippa, one summer when Adam was a toddler. It had ended amicably on both sides, though Mick carried a small torch for Philippa thereafter – she really did look like Audrey Hepburn too, and though she was a bit too thin, she was lovely, she smiled and laughed an awful lot. He felt protective towards her son ever afterwards, especially when she died. He didn't know where she'd come from, but from a few things she'd said, he wondered. He saw how Philippa never had any new clothes, how Adam didn't have a lunch box for school, how sparse their house was, and he wondered. And when Philippa died – well, he'd often thought they looked alike, but it was clear that was where the similarities between them ended.

Even Mick would never have guessed what they were saying in Langford now. That not only was Philippa the old woman's daughter, but that she'd refused to speak to her after she came to Langford, heavily pregnant, reluctantly looking for her mother. She was given the cottage, that was it. Mick didn't understand it. Philippa – how could you not love her? She'd been the kindest, warmest woman in the world . . .

Mick shook his head, surprised to find himself thinking about all of that, of Philippa's lovely face, her wild hair, her beautiful naked body straddling his, her big generous smile as she leaned forward to kiss him . . . He leaned against the bar, breathing heavily, not knowing why today, of all days, this memory should upset him so much.

''Ullo Mick!' came a voice out at the back. Flustered, Mick jumped out of his reverie.

'Oh,' he said, turning round slowly. 'Oh. It's only you. Hello, Ron.'

Ron Thaxton came sloping into the pub, and put his elbows wearily up on the old bar. 'All right there, Mick.' He blew air out of his bottom lip onto his forehead. 'Oh, it's hot. Isn't it.'

'Certainly is, Ron.' Mick turned back to the bar. 'Only nine o'clock, though, I can't serve you yet,' he said with an attempt at humour that, even to him, sounded pretty weak.

'I don't want a beer, don't you worry,' said Ron. He sighed. 'When we were in Italy, Andrea and I both developed something of a taste for Campari, you know. Campari and sodas. In a nice square, of an evening. Quite delicious, I must say. Slice of orange, some ice. *Andrea* –' he emphasized her name again, heavily – 'she sometimes preferred hers with orange juice, and then you say "with *sugo d'arancia*". You know.'

'That's nice,' said Mick. He wiped a cloth over the wooden surface of the bar. 'Never got a taste for Campari, myself. I like a whisky with water now and again, though.'

'Whisky's nice too, yes,' said Ron. He paused, and exhaled loudly again. 'Oh, dear.'

'What's up, then, Ron?' said Mick patiently. 'You all right?'

'I dunno,' said Ron. He clambered wearily up onto a bar stool, and started fiddling with a beer mat. 'I'm not sleeping too well at the moment, that's the trouble. Don't know what it is.'

'It's the heat,' said Mick. 'Five weeks without rain, it's no good for anyone, you know.'

'You're probably right,' said Ron. 'But it's something else, too. Ever since we got back from Rome, I've been having trouble with it.'

'Well, that were eight weeks ago, too,' Mick pointed out. 'I remember, 'cause Mrs Mortmain died early June, the day after you all got back, wasn't it?' Ron nodded. 'And we're in August now, ain't we. And still no funeral.'

'I know,' said Ron. 'And I think that's what's my trouble.' He looked pertinently at Mick and lowered his voice. 'I think she's haunting me, you know. That woman. She's not in the ground, yet. She's like the undead.' He licked his lips. 'I've been getting into vampire books lately, Mick. It's all the same thing.'

'Ron Thaxton, you can't say that,' Mick told him, chuckling. 'You can't speak ill of the dead.'

Ron said sagely, 'Well, I was blooming rude to her while she were alive, so it'd be hypocritical of me to start weeping over her now she's dead, don't you think?'

'Suppose so,' said Mick. He ran the tap, pouring out a glass of water for himself and handing one to Ron, who accepted it with a nod. They sat in silence for a moment.

'I keep thinking about her,' Ron said after a while. 'You see, we had words, when we was out in Italy. She had something on me.' He paused, as if he would say more. Mick said nothing. 'Well,' Ron went on, almost defiantly. 'She was an evil old woman, I don't care what anyone says. She was stirring up trouble, she was on that trip so we couldn't have the hearing about the water meadows. She knew what we was all saying about her. It's like she didn't care!' He looked up at Mick, mystified. 'I don't think she cared if we hated her. It's strange, isn't it?'

'It is strange,' said Mick.

'And she weren't being nice to young Tess Tennant – to be honest, poor Tess didn't know if she were coming or going with that one. She'd look at her, I'd see her, like she wanted to –' He shivered. 'I don't know. Nasty woman.'

'Ron,' Mick said sternly, but Ron shook his head.

'It's just – we were there when she had the – the stroke, me and Andrea. And I feel responsible. I didn't like her, but I didn't wish harm on her, you know that.'

'Course I do,' said Mick. 'It's a strange situation, though, all the same.'

Ron looked up at him. 'What, with young Adam Smith? Strange? I should say so. Who was the father? Does anyone know that?'

'Not to my knowledge.'

'Me neither,' Ron said incoherently. 'Whoever he was, he was a brave man, that's all I can say. Wonder if Adam knows?'

'Think he's had enough secrets to keep these last few years,' Mick said.

'Suppose so.' Ron wasn't convinced. 'Still, what's he doing, hiding that little fact all these years, eh?'

'I don't blame him,' Mick said solidly. 'I'd keep it to myself, too.'

'Well, maybe,' said Ron. 'Only now it's worked out pretty well for him, hasn't it?'

'Hey, there, Mick, you in there?' A sluggish voice called in to him through the windows.

Mick put out his hand, to silence his companion. 'Yep,' Mick said loudly. 'That you, Suggs?'

'Yep,' said Suggs. 'I just wanted to check, mate. Do you want me on Friday or not? Thought I'd best make sure.'

'Not,' said Mick. 'I thought you was coming in Saturday and Sunday, that all right?'

'No problems,' said Suggs. He peered in through the window, leaning on the old settle and squinting while his eyes adjusted. 'Thought I'd best check, what with everything. Who's that? That you, Ron?'

'Yep,' said Ron. ''Ullo, Suggsy.'

'I'll come in, then,' said Suggs and, with miraculous ease, he vaulted through the open window and onto the settle, jumping down on the floor. 'You got any coffee going?'

'Too hot for coffee,' Ron said moodily.

Mick indicated with his head. 'Back in the kitchen, mate. Help yourself.'

'Thanks, Mick.' Suggs disappeared into the kitchen, whistling loudly, and Ron turned back to Mick.

'All I'm saying is,' he said, 'that Adam Smith's gone from having no money, no job, nothing –'

'Hang on a second,' Mick said lightly. 'He works here, that's a job!'

'You know what I mean,' Ron said. 'He's gone from having nothing to . . . well, the man's a millionaire now, inn'ee? Must be. All just because of a bit of luck with his parents.'

Mick stared at him. 'I wouldn't call it luck,' he said, as Suggs came back in. 'I'd call that proper bad luck, if you ask me.'

'That's better,' Suggs said, flopping happily down at the bar next to Ron. He took a gulp of coffee. 'I was up a bit late last night, drinking with Adam. Got a bit of a headache this morning, you know.' He looked up. 'What's bad luck?'

'That's who we were just talking about,' Mick said, and Ron had the grace to look slightly ashamed. 'Adam, and his news.'

Suggs nodded, and wiped his mouth. 'Well, like I said to him, if you're going to get money who cares how it comes to you, long as it's legal? I don't think he feels the same way though.' He stared ruminatively into his mug. 'Poor bugger, you know. He's got a lot to deal with.'

'Like what?' said Ron, more curiously than anything else.

'Like, tonnes of crap that's been chucked on him. Getting that body back from Italy – well, that's been a right horror story, you wouldn't believe it.' He shook his head. 'Poor sod. And the meetings with the solicitors, and the land people –'

'About the estate?' Mick said.

'All of that stuff. Then there's the water meadows, the people who bought the land, they want to start building straight away, and he's got to deal with them about it –'

'What?' Ron said. 'So – so he's really going ahead with it, then? He's going to let them build? After all that?'

Suggs looked at him. 'That's what he says, Ron.' He made a face. 'But poor bugger, like I say. He's got enough on his plate without me diving in and having words with him.' Ron opened his mouth. Suggs said firmly, 'Not right now, Ron. Still, now the body's coming back, and the will's being read and all, and the funeral's happening, he can start to sort it all out.'

'The funeral?' said Mick, as Ron simulaneously cried, 'What?'

'That's why I wanted to check if you needed an extra hand here on Friday,' said Suggs. 'I'm sorry, Mick, I thought he was going to call you. Funeral's been fixed for Friday, three o'clock at the church.'

'My goodness,' said Mick. 'So – right. So it's finally happening.'

Suggs said, 'You know what, Mick? I reckon you'll have a full house in here afterwards.'

'Yup,' Mick said, nodding grimly. 'Poor lad.'

'It'll be a busy day for you, Mick,' Ron said with relish. 'There'll be a lot of people wanting a drink after that funeral's over, I'm telling you.'

Mick looked around the deserted pub. 'Reckon you're right,'

he said. 'Well, let's be having it, then.' He was adding barrels up in his mind; his eye scanned the shelves for gin and vodka; his lips moved as he tried to remember the last time they'd got more white wine in. He clapped his hands together. 'We'll make sure there's enough beer for everyone. Let them come.'

CHAPTER THIRTY-ONE

'Christian, dost thou see them, on the holy ground?
  How the troops of Midian, prowl and prowl around?
  Christian, up and smite them, counting gain but loss;
  Smite them by the merit of the holy cross!'

'Are they all going to be like that?' Francesca whispered to Tess, after the first hymn was over. 'I feel like I'm in a Victorian novel.'

Tess wiped her forehead as she sat down. 'I think so,' she said. 'In fact, it's probably going to get worse.'

St Mary's was airless; the lilies decorating the altar and the coffin were wilting, their perfume overpowering, sickly. The congregation, dressed in sombre colours, was weary, the atmosphere oppressive.

Francesca and Tess were at the back of the packed church. They had escorted Miss Store, their neighbour, to the funeral. Miss Store was in her eighties, nearly blind, and sported an impressive moustache and beard. She had been a maid at Langford Hall from when she was a young girl until the house was sold in 1960 and, as she said to Tess, when she came round to ask if she and Francesca would take her to the funeral, 'I feel I should, my dear. After all, she was a difficult woman, but that father of hers was a monster. And I feel that

333

someone from the Hall should be there, to pay their respects.'

Tess and Francesca had said of course they'd take her. Apart from anything else, as Tess said to Miss Store, it gave them a cast-iron excuse to go to the funeral. They weren't sure, either of them, whether it was appropriate for them to go – was it a small, private funeral? Adam had said not, but Adam didn't say much else, either. They would set out early, to get a good seat, so Miss Store could see what was going on.

But, though the funeral was due to start at three, and the girls and Miss Store arrived just before half past two, they were astonished to find the church already packed, and by the time the service started, it was standing room only, with about thirty people crammed at the back, some standing on the steps of the font to get a better look. It seemed virtually everyone in Langford wanted to be able to say, *I was there*. Rumours, since the date of the funeral had been confirmed only a few days before, were running at fever pitch.

It was the bug-eyed fascination Tess found so – distasteful, almost. The fact that she could walk down the street with Francesca and – as had happened a couple of weeks ago – someone on the other side of the street could nudge their friend and hiss, 'Hey – that's her. Francesca something. That's Adam Smith's girlfriend. I wonder what she –' and then trail off, their voices disappearing into nothing under the glare of the girls' annoyed stares.

Looking around her as the first hymn ended, Tess was glad of their position in the church, now. At least here, right at the back, they were relatively free from prying eyes.

'And now,' the Reverend Joanna Forster said, the acoustics muffled by the sheer number of bodies sweltering in front of her, 'Now we will have our first reading, from St Paul's letters to the Corinthians. And this will be read by Clive Donaldson.'

The Mortmain solicitor, a thin, scholarly-looking man, strode up to the lectern and smoothed the great Bible, adorned with the Mortmain coat of arms. He looked up and at the front pew, where Adam sat with Jean Forbes, Diana Sayers, and Carolyn Tey. He cleared his throat, and then began.

'For since by man came death, by man came also the resurrection of the dead. For as in Adam all die, even so in Christ shall all be made alive. But every man in his own order: Christ the firstfruits; afterward they that are Christ's at his coming. Then cometh the end, when he shall have delivered up the kingdom to God, even the Father; when he shall have put down all rule and all authority and power. For he must reign, till he hath put all enemies under his feet.'

'For as in Adam all die?' Francesca hissed loudly to Tess. 'Is she having a laugh? What the hell does that mean?'

'No hell in church, please,' Tess said primly, as a tweedy gentleman in the row in front turned around and gave Francesca a quelling glance.

'Seriously,' her housemate said moodily. 'This is not on. This is a joke. Who picked this stuff?' She stared out, across the massed ranks of Langford inhabitants, down the aisle to where Adam sat. Tess followed her gaze, trying to extract some information from the back of Adam's head as to his emotional state. 'This place,' Francesca said. 'This place is fricking crazy.'

The truth was, neither of them knew very much about what was going on behind the scenes, and it showed. Since her return from Rome, Tess had seen Adam only a couple of times. She had texted him – *You will let me know if there's anything I can do? I mean it. Genuine offer.* – and had heard nothing back. He had been away a lot, out of the country, in meetings. As the weeks of waiting for Leonora's body to be released from the hospital in Rome passed, she thought how flimsy that offer sounded – there wasn't anything she could do, was there? She wasn't an Italian bureaucrat, or a diplomat at the British Embassy.

She had seen Adam in the pub one evening when she was meeting Liz for a drink, and had said, 'Hey – if you want Peter to do anything out there, you know he'd be happy to go and talk to someone –'

'Peter? Why?'

'Well –' Tess was flustered. Saying Peter's name, back in Langford, was a luxury. She missed him, and Rome, with an aching pain. She wanted to bridge the gap that had now sprung up between them. 'He's there. That's all. I knew he'd –'

Adam had held his hand up, politely but firmly. 'Thanks, T. That's really kind of you, but it's fine. Thank you.'

'So are you planning the funeral?' she had asked boldly. 'If you want me to help –'

'It's all written out,' he'd said. 'There are instructions. So I don't have to do anything. No one does. We just have to wait for the body to get back here. Thanks, though.' He had smiled briefly but kindly, and turned back to his conversation about the cricket with Suggs, who was behind the bar that night, leaving Tess with the distinct impression that a door had been gently but firmly shut in her face.

There are instructions. She knew now, from Diana, that there were indeed instructions, typed out, kept in the Tey & Donaldson safe along with the will. The instructions for the exact funeral service Leonora Mortmain wanted, down to the layout of the order of service. And the will to be read after she had been committed to the ground, in the family vault by the church.

Reverend Forster stood up, and looked around. 'The next reading is from Job, chapter nineteen, verse twenty-five:

'For I know that my redeemer liveth, and that he shall stand at the latter day upon the earth: and though after my skin worms destroy this body, yet in my flesh shall I see God; whom I shall see for myself, and mine eyes shall behold, and not another; though my reins be consumed within me.'

By this time, the congregation was growing restless. There were a lot of hell and brimstone Biblical warnings about death, and not nearly enough eulogies or dramatic revelations. When was Adam going to get up and give an impassioned plea for mercy on the soul of his long-lost, dead grandmother? When was he going to say, 'Drinks for all, on me! And the water meadows plan – that's gone away!'

Some people were saying that Adam was no better than his grandmother. There was something about the secrecy of it all that made people uneasy. No smoke without fire, they said. Tess had heard Ron saying to Andrea, a couple of days before in the post office, 'There's something fishy going on, you mark my words. Why hasn't he said anything about it all, eh? I don't trust him, you know. I think he'll turn out to be no better than his grandmother.'

Tess wanted to hit him. *No better than his grandmother*. What about his mother, what about Philippa? No one mentioned her in all this, it was all about the legacy, the Mortmains, the secrecy . . . No one said, He lost his mum, he never knew his dad, give him a break! And no one knew what had happened, either.

The temperature was rising inside the old building, it seemed. It wasn't even sunny outside; the sky was thick that day with dirty clouds that seemed to press down on the town and the surrounding hills. Tess looked anxiously at Miss Store, who was breathing in a rather wheezy way. 'Are you all right?' she said softly.

'Yes, dear,' Miss Store said perkily, looking up at her. 'Oh, it's a good send-off, isn't it! What's next?'

'Oh, dear,' said Tess, looking down at her order of service. She smothered a smile with her hand. 'I don't think I can take much more of this.'

'And now,' Reverend Forster said, 'before our final reading, we will sing one more hymn, "The Sun is Sinking Fast".'

The congregation sighed heavily, and stood up. Miss Store

was at the end of the pew, next to the aisle, and Tess was next to her. As Tess helped Miss Store to her feet, biting her lip, suddenly overwhelmed by the surreal absurdity of the situation, she looked up to find Adam turning round, staring at her. He gave the ghost of a smile, and turned back almost immediately, but she knew what he was thinking. She looked down at her order of service, trying not to smile, as the organ started playing the dirge-like tune.

> *'The sun is sinking fast,*
> *the daylight dies;*
> *let love awake, and pay*
> *her evening sacrifice.'*

Tess glanced at Francesca a few times during the hymn, to see if she was all right. She was more aware, today, of Francesca's outsider status than she had been. And she was slightly envious of it. Francesca seemed taller, more confident, more herself these past few weeks than she had before.

There was a curious constraint between them now; as if something had changed. A few days after Tess had come back from Italy, she had arrived home from the college to find Francesca in her usual position on the sofa. But she had been crying, Tess knew.

'Is everything . . . OK?' Tess had asked her, almost timidly, offering her a glass of wine.

'Sure!' Francesca had said brightly. 'Yep. Everything's *great*.'

Tess had been wanting to ask this since she'd come back; now seemed the perfect time. 'How have things been with you and Adam?'

'Good, good,' said Francesca, faux-enthusiastically. She reached forward for the bowl of crisps. 'Yeah, great. You know, we broke up and got back together and it was great. Until he went away and didn't say why, and I find out it's because he's got a secret family I know nothing about. Yeah, totally brilliant.'

'It's been weird for him,' Tess said loyally, but then she

338

thought of Adam's hard, cruel face as he taunted her about Peter. *He's not offering you a future. He's offering you a distraction from the past, and that's not the same thing.*

Perhaps it was true. Was it? She just didn't know, now she was back here. What had seemed so simple and straight-forward in Rome was anything but. Her heart contracted, as it did whenever she remembered Peter. When would she see him again? He was so far away. 'I'm sure he hasn't been delib-erately lying to you,' she said. 'No one knew.'

'I know,' said Francesca. 'It's just it makes me think about what I'm doing here.'

'Really? How?' said Tess.

Francesca drank some wine. 'Well. You know, in my old job?'

Tess nodded encouragingly, though she wasn't sure what the question was. 'Mmm.'

'Well, in my old life, really.' Francesca blinked. 'I was so busy, and I hated it, and it was so stressful, in a suit, barking orders, watching as millions of pounds went down the tubes – when they made me redundant, I wasn't one of those people who lost her identity, I really thought, *Hurrah*. But you know what I miss most of all about it?'

'No,' said Tess, curious.

'The order. Having a place in society,' Francesca said. 'I hated school, hated the structure. But I loved my job for the same reason. I liked knowing where I was in the ant colony. This is where I work, that's the cafeteria I eat my lunch in, here's the bar next door where I go and get twatted with all the other bankers because they're the only people I have time to hang out with.'

She sounded desolate.

Tess nodded. 'I guess . . .' she said, uneasily. 'But you can't live like that for ever.'

'No, and I couldn't have done it for much longer. But my point is, I thought I hated it, that I needed to get totally away from it, but actually I think we all need some structure.' She blinked, and threw a section of her hair behind her shoulder. 'A plan. I – I need to be doing something. We both do.'

Tess didn't know whom she meant by 'both'. Her and Francesca, or Adam and Francesca? She was about to ask, but Francesca's phone had rung; she'd picked it up. 'Yep. Yep. Sure. About twelve? Fine.'

She'd put the phone down and gone back to reading her magazine.

'That Adam?' Tess had asked curiously.

'Yep,' Francesca had said. 'He'll be round after his shift's over.'

This was how it worked, now, and this was why she never saw Adam. His relationship with Francesca these days seemed to be only about sex. And it was weird. Really weird. It reminded her of that summer they'd had together, though she would never say so to anyone else.

In bed, gazing out at the night sky through the too-small curtains that never quite drew shut, Tess would hear him arrive, let himself in, and go upstairs to Francesca's room. She could hear them, though she tried not to: she could hear the bed creaking loudly, Francesca crying out and occasionally Adam too, and she found it upsetting, she didn't know why, not for what one might think were the obvious reasons but because there was something so desperate and undercover about it.

In the mornings, he was always gone – she was usually up around seven and Adam was never there. Once, coming up for three weeks since Leonora had died, when there was no news, Tess had heard him arrive late, after midnight. It was a particularly sultry, airless night and she had got up at three in the morning to get some water. Tiptoeing silently across the uneven floorboards to the bathroom, she saw Francesca's bedroom door was wide open, with Francesca asleep, alone. He had been there for less than three hours. It wasn't just once or twice, either. It was at least four times a week, so that she got used to it, though she never saw him.

She asked Francesca once, during those weeks, 'Is Adam OK? I haven't seen him properly for ages.'

And Francesca said, 'Not really, no. But you wouldn't expect him to be, I suppose. The poor bastard.'

'What does he say? Anything at all?'

Francesca put down her magazine, and gave her a searching look. 'He doesn't say anything. He's looking for some sort of release, I guess. And that's fine by me.'

And then she'd got the email from Peter, only the night before the funeral, which only served to emphasize how far away those days in Rome were.

> *Dearest darling Tess, cara mia –*
>
> *I'm sorry I missed you. Darling, I'm going to stay here and take the job. The good news is – perhaps this is good news? Hope so – it's only for around three months and then they want me back in Rome for the new year, to finish work on a big piece about Berlusconi we've been doing. It's probably going to be a book, and they want me to pull it all together when I get back. But here, I can start straight away. Perhaps it's good for me to leave Rome for a while, get away from bad memories: but there are good ones too, and they are all to do with you.*
>
> *So, the long and the short of it is that, thanks to a crazy Italian PM, I will be coming back to Rome for Christmas. Christmas in Rome is the best place to be. Can we meet then? Will you come over then? I think what we had was worth exploring. I think of you and it is magical. Don't you agree?*
>
> *I'll call you later.*
>
> *All my love*
>
> *Peter*

*   *   *

'I am sure Leonora Mortmain would be gratified to see the church so packed,' Reverend Forster said, after the hymn was over. She paused, and patted down the green silk stole around her neck. 'As you know, she lived in Langford all her life and loved this town.'

The silence in the congregation was broken by a few, faint noises of dissent here and there, and by a couple of people clearing their throats. Reverend Forster pressed on, undaunted.

'Her family has asked me to let you all know that tea is being provided at the Feathers, after the service.'

'*Tea?*' Tess heard someone say loudly.

'I'm sure we could all do with a refreshing cup of tea in this muggy weather!' Reverend Forster said, grinning and resting her hand comfortably on her stomach. 'Thank you, all of you, for coming. We finish with a few lines from John, chapter fourteen – like all these other readings, chosen by Miss Mortmain herself.' And then she opened her Bible, and read:

'. . . *Philip saith unto him, Lord, shew us the Father, and it sufficeth us. Jesus saith unto him, Have I been so long time with you, and yet hast thou not known me, Philip? he that hath seen me hath seen the Father; and how sayest thou then, Shew us the Father?*'

'What did that mean?' Francesca asked as they were filing out. 'Who's Philip? What was that about?'

Tess had no idea, but Francesca was speaking loudly and people were turning round. 'Um –' she said. 'I think it was about how we should acknowledge God more in our lives.'

'But I'm an atheist,' said Francesca. 'I don't want to.'

'Well,' said Miss Store, leaning on her as they reached the door and stepped outside. 'Absolutely don't, then.'

'Did you enjoy that?' Francesca asked her. 'I mean, not "enjoy", exactly, but are you glad you went?'

'Ooh, ever so glad,' said Miss Store, beaming and waggling her hairy chin. 'It was a very good service, I thought. Something for everyone.'

'Hm,' said Francesca. 'Not sure about that.'

The majority of the congregation stood chatting outside the church before slowly trickling towards the high street and the Feathers. The clouds were thicker and darker than before and Tess turned to watch the little procession to the side, making its way to the open grave, where the committal was to take place. Reverend Forster walked behind the coffin, borne aloft by four very erect but small pallbearers, her head bowed, and behind her Jean Forbes, Carolyn Tey and Clive Donaldson followed sombrely, with Diana Sayers behind them and, last of all, Adam, taller than any of them, his suit especially black in the darkening gloom. Diana turned to him, put her arm around his shoulders, and squeezed him.

'Aren't you going to wait for him?' she said to Francesca, who turned away from Miss Store and looked at her.

'No,' Francesca said shortly. 'He knows where I am. He'll want me later, not now.'

'Right,' said Tess. 'Well – do you want some tea?'

'Tea? Oh, you old lady.'

'I meant the wake, at the Feathers,' said Tess. 'I won't be ordering tea, for what it's worth. I will be very much on the gin. Do join me, Miss Jackson.'

'You betcha,' said Francesca.

'Miss Store, shall we walk you home?' Tess asked politely.

'No, thank you,' said Miss Store. 'I shall be going to the Feathers for a cup of tea. Or perhaps a little gin and tonic, now you mention it. I must say,' she said, blinking at Tess and Francesca, 'I know he's had a difficult time, that poor boy, but he's lost his mind if he thinks we'll be wanting tea. Shall we adjourn?'

'With all possible haste,' Francesca said, striding grimly on

343

ahead while Tess grinned uneasily at Miss Store and gave her her arm.

'Well, isn't this nice,' said Miss Store. 'To see all the town together.'

'Quite a weird reason for them to be together,' said Tess. 'I mean, I don't wish to speak ill of the dead, Miss Store, but she wasn't exactly popular, was she?'

'No,' said Miss Store. 'In fact, she was a nasty woman. But you should have known her when she was little. Sweet thing.' She smiled. 'We were almost friends, she and I. We were the same age when I was a maid there, and we have a similar name.'

Tess tucked Miss Store's arm even tighter into her own. 'Oh, what's that?'

'My name's Eleanor,' Miss Store said. 'And hers was Leonora, you know that. We used to say we could have been twins, we were the same size, same age.'

'I didn't know that,' said Tess. 'So you knew her when she was a girl?'

'Yes,' said Miss Store. 'Used to bring her tea in the mornings. I'd lay the fire in her room, put out her clothes. We'd talk about the day ahead, she'd ask me about my day, we'd have lovely little conversations. I – yes, I liked her.' She looked up at Tess, smiling. Tess wished Francesca could hear this too, but Francesca was several strides ahead, her mind somewhere else. Tess bent down.

'So when did she become – like this?' she said curiously.

'I don't know,' Miss Store said. 'It was sometime towards the end of the war. She went away for a few months, and when she came back she was very different. And she never smiled again. Isn't it funny.' There was a pause. 'I suppose that's when she had the baby. Of course.' She shook her head. 'Funny, it never crossed my innocent mind. And we'll never know what happened. Poor dear.'

Someone patted Tess on the shoulder; they turned and

parted to let the empty hearse that had carried the coffin drive through the crowds. Tess looked thoughtfully towards the procession in the graveyard, as they turned onto the high street and walked slowly towards the pub.

CHAPTER THIRTY-TWO

Tess knew what they'd let themselves in for when she opened the door to the main bar of the Feathers, standing aside to let Miss Store go in front of her. To her question, 'Shouldn't we be going in there – where the tea is?' Miss Store had looked scornfully at the parlour at the back of the courtyard, with a sign on it which read, '*Private Function – Tea*' and said, 'Goodness gracious, no. We want to be in the bar.'

She was right, too. Everyone else in Langford had had the same idea, it seemed, for on opening the door Tess was hit with a wall of sound, the smell of sweaty bodies, beer, perfume – and heat. The heat was overpowering – the low-ceilinged rooms of the Feathers meant it was always warm but today of all days, it was almost unbearable.

Miss Store, who was small and surprisingly wiry for a woman of her years and vision, disappeared almost immediately into the crowd, worming under the armpits of her fellow citizens while Tess and Francesca hung back at the door, almost afraid to go any further.

'We could just go home . . .' Tess said. 'It's pretty –'

'Are you kidding?' Francesca said. 'No way. This is a last hurrah. In more ways than one. We're staying, *mon amie*, and we're getting trashed.'

Tapping the two old men in front of them, and with a charming smile saying, 'Excuse me, so sorry, can I just –' she slid her way to the front of the bar, Tess following in her wake.

The path to the bar was at least eight people deep. Tess saw people she hadn't seen since she got back all those months ago, like Donna Roberts, who bullied her at school, still wearing a ponytail to the side of the head – or perhaps it was just the crush that had dislodged it, Tess thought crazily, as she pushed past her. Joe Collins, the elderly owner of the fields beyond the water meadows, who'd been involved in a boundary dispute with Leonora Mortmain for decades; he was standing up straight, chatting merrily away, a gleam in his eye. With him was Guy Phelps, owner of George Farm, drinking moodily at his side and talking loudly to Mick, who was smiling politely at him while frantically filling glasses. There was Suggs's girl-friend, the surprisingly respectable Emma, who ran the mobile library between Thornham, Morely and Langford. She smiled at Tess as she squeezed past.

'All right, Tess? What a day, eh?'

Tess smiled. 'You're telling me.' She patted her on the arm and rolled her eyes, as if to say, 'I'm going this way, see you later,' then turned and bumped into someone.

'Hello, Tess, dear,' said Jacquetta Meluish, clutching a large glass of wine. She paused to remove her paisley scarf. 'Well, what a day. It seems a long time ago when it all happened, doesn't it? Ah, Roma. Oh, dear me, it's hot in here, isn't it!' She patted her forehead dramatically. 'I hate the heat. Don't mind it when it's somewhere exotic, hate it here.'

Tess nodded, having unexpected sympathy with this point. She smiled at her. 'Oh, your scarf –' Tess pointed to the floor where the offending article had slithered, as Francesca moved further towards the bar. 'Look, you've dropped it.'

'Oh, my God,' Jacquetta crooned, slightly unnecessarily. She looked down, then up again. 'Oh, well – I'll just have to get it later,' she said, draining the rest of her wine and turning back to her companion, whom Tess couldn't see. 'More wine!' she called out, like the Lady of the Camellias at a glittering Paris soirée.

'What do you want?' Francesca yelled from the bar.

'Wine,' said Tess. 'Let's get a bottle.'

'Where's Miss Store?' Francesca yelled. 'She OK?'

Tess stood up on tiptoe, and swivelled round like a ballerina. 'She's by the bar. Talking to the vicar. She's fine.' Francesca nodded, and Tess turned back, catching sight of someone. 'Liz! Hi!'

'Thank God,' said Liz with relief, turning round with some difficulty. She was wedged between Ron and someone from the Parish Council whom Tess recognized but couldn't put a name to. 'This is crazy,' she said. 'First the funeral – then this. It's biblical, that's what it is. If you know what I mean.'

'I know,' said Tess. She looked at Francesca, at the bar. 'Are you OK?' she mouthed. Francesca nodded. 'We'll stand back – can you get three glasses?'

'Sure,' Francesca bellowed back.

Tess squeezed through the massed ranks, clutching hold of Liz by the arm, feeling strangely protective of this relative newcomer in the insanity of Langford.

'I'm OK!' Liz exclaimed, as they burst forth from the throng, almost falling over, by the windows. 'Thanks, Tess, though. Phew.' She put her hand on the back of her neck. 'It's boiling in here. I think I'm about to melt.'

'The windows aren't open, for God's sake,' said Tess. 'There's no fresh air in here, it's mad.'

'It's just as hot outside,' Liz pointed out. 'It must rain soon, mustn't it? It can't go on like this, it's been weeks.'

'I know,' said Tess, as she looked up to see how Francesca was doing. It was like a Brueghel painting, she thought fancifully, the wooden interiors, the apple-cheeked villagers, the beer tankards frothing, sheafs of wheat in the corners – only the villagers were apple-cheeked with alcohol, heat and hysteria, and the sheaves of wheat were old, dusty, dried, and stuck up as decorations around upon the ceiling. She patted her forehead and stepped forward into the crowd to help Francesca, who was carrying three glasses, and a huge plastic cup filled with ice.

'How on earth –' Tess said, in admiration. 'Francesca, you are amazing.'

'Ask and ye shall receive,' Francesca said. 'Thanks,' she said to Andrea Marsh, who handed her a chilled bottle in a wine cooler.

'No probs,' said Andrea. Francesca took the glasses and poured out the wine.

'Do you want some, Andrea?' she said.

'No thanks. I'm drinking Campari and orange juice.'

'With an Amaretto chaser, eh?' Ron said from behind her, patting her flank. Andrea blushed, looking not unpleased at this rather public display of affection. Ron raised his glass to them. His cheeks were slightly flushed. 'Well, I'm glad you're here, Tess. It's a big day for Langford –'

'Please, Ron,' Andrea said, in quelling tones. 'We don't want any speaking ill of the dead.'

'Wasn't going to!' Ron said in outrage. 'I just meant –'

Francesca turned from them, taking a glass and giving it to Liz, and another to Tess. 'Well –' she said. 'Here's to –' She raised her glass. 'Not sure, really.'

'Cheers,' said Tess. 'I think we just say cheers.' She took a sip. 'I'm going to open the window,' she said, moving the ice cup and bottle of wine off the sill. 'It's boiling. No one's going to steal our stuff,' she said to Andrea, who looked alarmed. 'There's no one else left, is there? Everyone's here.'

She undid the catch, pushing both windows out wide, and breathing in. She closed her eyes at the tiny rush of fresh air from outside. Then she looked up, and across the street.

'Oh, my God,' she said quietly.

There, directly opposite, framed by the window as if by design, was the drawing room of Leda House, powder blue and cream, and through the glass, clearly visible, stood a stiff, weary-looking group, clutching very small glasses of sherry and standing in apparent silence. Jean Forbes and her husband Mike, Clive Donaldson, his bald pate glistening in the heat, Richard and Diana Sayers, Carolyn Tey and, his face a mask, Adam.

Once again Tess found herself fleetingly thinking how unlike the Adam she had known he now was, in his black suit, his hair combed, his eyes dark with grief, trapped in a situation not of his own making, and she could not help him. For one second he turned, his gaze caught by the movement from the pub opposite, and he saw her. She stared at him.

'Look –' said Ron. 'There they are.'

In the distance there was a faint, almost ominous sound.

'That can't be thunder,' Andrea said hopefully. 'Is it going to rain?'

'Oh, my goodness, look,' said someone behind Tess, and she turned around. It was Beth Kennett, her boss from the college, curiosity written all over her face. She was with Jen and Guy Phelps.

'Must be about to read the will,' Beth said. 'That'll be an interesting conversation, I bet.'

'I bet,' said Guy. 'Well, Adam's a sensible man.' He drained his pint; he was a little drunk. 'I'm sure he'll see us all right.'

'Do you think?' Francesca said suddenly from the corner. 'What do you mean?'

'Hello there,' said Guy, reddening slightly. She raised her glass to him, but didn't move. 'I just meant – it's good a chap like Adam's inheriting all that dosh. And the water meadows. No chance of that shopping centre going up now, that's for sure.'

'What makes you say that?' Francesca said. She looked bored.

'Well . . .' Guy said, slightly uneasy under her unwavering gaze. He licked his lips. 'Just mean – he's one of us, isn't he?'

'What's "one of us"?' Francesca asked, putting her glass down. Her voice was soft over the din of the pub.

'One of the village, the town. From Langford, I mean. He's a local.' Guy sounded flustered. 'He knows what we want.'

'I doubt that very much,' said Francesca. She smiled her cat-like smile. 'Being "one of us" didn't stop Leonora Mortmain, did it? She sold you all out for the money, and why?'

'Oh, you don't know what you're talking about,' said Guy. He smiled in a frank way, that curiously posh English combination of politeness and contempt.

She raised her eyebrows. 'Perhaps he wants to keep the money,' she said. She put her bag over her shoulder. 'Perhaps he feels he doesn't owe this town anything, anything at all. And I have to say I can see his point.'

'What do you know about it?' Guy said. 'It's Francesca, isn't it?' She nodded, and he gave her a lazy-lidded smile. 'How long have you lived here?'

'Oh, not long,' Francesca said. She nodded at Tess. 'Only a few months, really, but you see you're forgetting I'm in a unique position. I know him a lot better than you.'

Guy looked unconvinced. 'I know him pretty well actually. How's that?'

'I'm fucking him,' Francesca said. She grimaced. 'And, unless there's something you want to tell me about your relationship with him, I think that means I win.'

'Oh,' said Guy.

Tess watched her friend, not sure whether to intervene or not and wondering why she had picked this day of all days to roll out her biggest loose cannon. Guy was looking distinctly ruffled, she couldn't work out if he was drunk, aroused, annoyed, or all three – possibly the latter, she decided. 'Francesca –' she said.

'Right,' Guy said. 'You –'

Francesca turned to her, then. Her eyes were bright. 'T, I'm off, sweetheart. Just fancy an early night, you stay on and I'll see you later. Bye, Liz,' she said and, without so much as a by-your-leave, sat on the windowsill and swung her legs over. 'Bye,' she said, and she gently pushed the windows shut, leaving the others gaping after her and only Tess, holding her wine glass, unaccountably disturbed by what she'd just heard, though she couldn't say why. And outside, once again, she heard the rumble of distant thunder.

In ten minutes or so the 'wake' was in full swing again, the noise even louder, the heat even greater, and the takings better than they had ever been – since Mick could remember, anyway. He stood behind the bar, yelling orders to his fellow barmen, wiping his brow and looking out at the sea of people. Half the town was crowded into that one room, and for what? What were they hoping for? Some kind of shared experience, he supposed, though they were mad to think they'd get it from this, the funeral of a woman who'd done nothing for the town her whole life. Perhaps they wanted answers. Perhaps they just wanted to acknowledge what was an extraordinary situation: that the boy they'd known their whole lives was now the sole heir to that estate which, some said, ran into millions. Mick didn't know. All he was sure about was that if he was a punter he'd rather be here, in the bar, than in the deserted function room Adam and Jean had half-heartedly booked. He turned to Suggs.

'Run down to the cellar, will you, Suggsy? Thanks, mate.'

By ten thirty, the pub was still full to bursting. Tess had had a few glasses of wine by then, and she and Liz had stayed in the corner by the window, grateful for the small amount of fresh air it gave. The wind seemed to be picking up, she thought – or was she just drunk? She didn't want to open the window in case Adam saw her and thought she was pruriently looking in. She had long since stopped worrying about how sweaty she was, the tendrils of hair glued to the nape of her neck. There was no point – everyone else was much drunker than her, they wouldn't have noticed.

After a while, over the other side of the bar, she caught sight of Diana talking intently to Jan, who had been drinking white wine spritzers, she had informed Tess, in a rather sweet but ultimately futile attempt to limit the amount of alcohol she consumed. Jeremy was next to his wife, practically half-asleep. Occasionally he slapped the bar, and looked across at Jan through almost-closed eyes, and Jan would turn to him and say, as if he'd just done something hilarious, 'Oh, Jeremy, what are you *doing*!?'

Jeremy would smile and turn back. He seemed to be conducting a conversation with Ron, though Ron was doing most of the talking, and there was a group around him. Phrases like, 'I heard . . .' and 'He won't even listen to me . . .' and 'Well, I knew him when he was a little thing . . .' floated over to her, above the heads of the drinkers. Tess set down her drink, and went over to the bar.

'Hey, Diana,' she said boldly. 'How did it go, over there?'

Diana turned to Tess. 'Hello, my dear. How's that boyfriend of yours?'

'He's not my boyfriend, he's Francesca's,' Tess said, uneasily. 'You—'

I meant the Italian one,' Diana said beadily. She drank some more wine. 'I thought you were supposed to be going to Rome this weekend?' she said inconsequentially.

'Oh – yes. Yes, I was,' said Tess. 'I'm going soon instead. I hope.'

'I hope? Why, isn't he there?'

Tess said, 'He's not in Rome . . . He's had to go to the States for a bit . . . we're meeting in Rome.' She didn't want to go into it, not now.

Diana wasn't really listening. 'Be hot in Rome,' she said,

blowing cool air onto her forehead. 'Almost as bloody hot as it is here.'

'It's not till Christmas,' Tess wanted to get it straight.

'*Christmas*?' Diana bellowed. 'That's not very *satisfactory*, is it?' Tess blew her hair away from her face, trying to cool down.

'No,' she said sadly. 'It's not . . .' She felt rather drunk, all of a sudden. 'Diana,' she said. 'Is he OK?'

'Who?'

'Adam. Did it go OK? The will and everything, did they read it?'

'Yes, and yes, and yes,' said Diana, Sphinx-like. 'Pretty straightforward. Though I didn't get anything. Oh, well. Richard and I will move to Mauritius next year instead.'

Tess took another sip of her drink; it was a big mistake. The room, which before had seemed full of people she knew, chaotic, messy, exciting, was now full of strangers, the floor seemed to be shifting, the heat was unbearable.

'I'm going to go,' she said suddenly. 'I've got to go. OK?'

'Sure,' said Diana. 'You're all right, Tess?'

But Tess didn't hear her. Hot waves of panic, or was it merely drunkenness, were washing over her. She pushed through the rest of the drinkers, outside into the courtyard. Peter. *Peter*. She hadn't thought about him all day, not once, and the thought of him now flooded over her like a cool breeze.

He was enjoying working in San Francisco; if she was honest, Tess really didn't know what was going to happen after he came back. She wondered whether he would stay in the States, but she just couldn't tell, despite the fact he said he wasn't. That was the hard thing about communicating with someone who wasn't in front of you. They spoke every day, and if they didn't speak they were on Skype, which was hard to get used to, but they were both coming around to it. And they emailed and texted all the time. But nuances were lost, jokes didn't work, the inflections, little eye movements were missing, all small things that built up into big things. And the intimacy of the smell of his skin, the touch of his hands – they were all gone.

Peter had promised he'd be back in time, insisted she book her flight to get in an hour after him. She didn't know what was going to happen, but she knew one thing for certain. This time next week she'd be in Rome, out of this strange town, drinking chilled wine in a square somewhere, feeling Peter's arms around her, his lips on hers . . .

There it was again: another rumbling sound – was it in the distance? She couldn't tell. Tess walked across the courtyard, looking up at the almost night sky. The moon should have given her light; as she stepped out onto the high street it showed the streaks of dark, leaden clouds running across the sky towards the horizon. She felt sick, full of wine and no food, full of some kind of foreboding. She looked almost desperately across at Leda House, but it was in darkness. Whatever had happened was now over and the actors in that strange little drama had dispersed. Her eyes felt heavy; she felt as though she had been drugged; sweat beaded her skin, and her feet ached as she walked along the high street, a lone figure under the inky sky. Everyone was in the pub or at home, she realized. It was her, her alone, out here.

It was with some relief that she turned into Lord's Lane a couple of minutes later. She stood in the dark, fumbling mechanically for her keys, feeling drunk, still sick to her stomach. But as she did, suddenly the door flung open, and she jumped back.

'Adam,' she said, almost with relief. 'My God – hello.'

He was doing up the buttons on his suit jacket. He looked at her. 'Sorry,' he said. 'Didn't mean to scare you.'

'You didn't,' Tess said, leaning against the door frame. 'You been paying Francesca a visit?'

Her tone was more judgmental than she'd intended, and

she realized she must sound a little drunk. 'I'm just leaving,' he said in an odd voice. 'It's nearly midnight. I have to go.'

Tess looked at her watch. It was after eleven thirty; how could it be so late?

'I hope today went OK for you,' she said, putting her hand clumsily on his arm. Something wet fell onto her shoulder. 'You know. Not too . . . awful, I suppose.'

'It was fine,' he said, not meeting her gaze. 'Could have been worse.' He scratched his head. 'When are you going to Italy?'

'Next week,' she said promptly, unfazed by the question after her rehearsal with Diana. 'Can't wait.' She looked at him. 'Adam, do you want to stay, have a drink, talk about the day and – and stuff?'

He shook his head. 'Tess – no. Sorry, sweetheart. Like I said, I have to go.' He looked up. 'Wow. It's finally raining.'

She stared at him. 'You can't stay, have one drink with us, instead of disappearing off like – like a thief in the night? Where do you have to go that's so urgent this time?'

He laughed, and she blinked, feeling another drop fall on her face. 'Sorry,' he said, suddenly serious. He stepped past her, onto the cobbled street. 'I'm going away from here, T.' He bent forward and kissed her forehead. 'Just for a while. But I'll see you when I get back, OK? Have a great time in Italy, too. You deserve it.'

It was definitely rain; it was falling in droplets now, on her shoulders, in her eyes. Tess shook her head, blinking rapidly. There was still no wind. 'Where are you going?'

'Just away,' he said.

'What on earth does that mean?' she said, the alcohol and the day itself loosening her tongue so she was talking to him like the Adam she knew of old.

He brushed the rain off his forehead. 'You told me in Rome I needed to change. That I'd stayed the same for too long. Stayed here.' He raised his voice as a clap of thunder hit them,

356

and the rain battered down even harder. 'Well, I didn't agree with you then, but I think maybe you're right.'

'Adam, I was being stupid, I was—'

He interrupted her, holding up his hand. 'I'd better run, I have loads to do. You get inside. It's going to chuck it down.'

'But –'

'And look out for Francesca, will you?' he said.

'I always do,' Tess said, shaking her head. 'For God's sake, Adam, this is – it's crazy. Stay for a drink!'

But he wasn't listening 'No. Sorry.'

'Isn't there anything I can do?' Tess said desperately.

He looked into her eyes, as if he were looking for something, and then he patted his pockets. 'There is,' he said. 'There really is. Look after this for me.'

He took out of his suit jacket a battered, yellowing, slim little hardback, no bigger than her palm. Tess remembered it from Rome. He put it into her hand. 'This was with my grandmother when she died,' he said. He swallowed. She glanced down at it, then up at him.

'What is it?'

'It's a book of love poems. Catullus's love poems. God knows why she was carrying it around. She's marked bits of it.'

Tess clutched it. 'She carried it everywhere,' she said.

'Just – I want you to have it,' Adam said. 'Look after it. It must have meant something to her, if she held onto it all this time.'

'Why do you want me to have it?' she asked.

'Because . . .' He trailed off. 'Because I – I want to believe that there was some love in her, somewhere. And this might be the only actual proof of that. So you should look after it, while I'm away. It'll make me feel OK, knowing you've got it.' He didn't look at her, but he folded her fingers around the book and clutched her hand. 'Night, Tess. I'll see you – I'll see you one day.'

'I'll see you one day?' she repeated blankly but he merely

smiled and walked away, down the tiny street. She stood, watching him, and then the rain began in earnest, heavy drops that pattered down on the stones with fury. Thunder cracked overhead, and in seconds, water was running in rivulets down her neck, washing away the sweat and grime of the day, and she stood there until long after he had turned the corner, until she was completely wet through, staring into nothing. She turned, then, back to the house, where a golden line of light shone through the crack of the door, and pushed it open.

CHAPTER THIRTY-THREE

Francesca was inside, sitting on the sofa as usual. She was dressed in her Francesca summer lounging outfit, which comprised a small pair of polka-dot cotton shorts and a flimsy pale blue vest. Tess shook herself as she shut the door. Drops of rain flew off her, hitting Francesca, but she did not move.

'Hey,' said Tess, trying to sound more sober than she felt. She put the book onto the bureau. 'It's pissing it down out there, have you seen? I saw Adam outside. Have you two had a . . .' She trailed off and looked around her, in horror. 'Francesca, what the hell's going on?'

The tiny sitting room looked as if a poltergeist had been on the rampage. Books were pulled off the shelves; a vase (not a very nice one, from Francesca's peak period of buying rubbish) lay in bits on the floor; Tess's beloved cake stand next to it, cracked in half. The huge flat-screen TV had moved position, and was by the door; there was a smooth patch of rug to show where it had been before, with DVDs littered around it, crumbs and even an apple core as evidence of the girls' laziness when it came to housekeeping. Tess stared at it all, her mouth dropping open. By the entrance to the kitchen was a huge suitcase, Francesca's suitcase, with clothes hanging out of it, half folded, spilling onto the floor. A lamp, some iPod speakers and some coat hangers sat next to it, the only orderly notes in the room.

'Oh, my God,' Tess said, sitting down next to her on the sofa. 'What did you do?'

Francesca said nothing, but continued to stare at the wall opposite. Tess said gently, patting her arm, 'Francesca –'

'I'll get you a new cake stand, OK?' Francesca pulled away from her, and stood up. 'I'm packing.'

'You're packing? Where are you going?'

'I'm leaving,' Francesca said, standing in front of the door, her arms folded. 'I'm leaving first thing tomorrow.'

Tess blinked, and rubbed her eyes. She was in a daydream, she must be. 'Are you going away with Adam?' she said.

'No,' said Francesca briefly, and she went into the kitchen. 'I'm going back to London,' she called. 'Had enough here. I'll pay you rent to the end of next month, that'll be OK won't it?'

'Um –' Tess stood up, and followed Francesca into the kitchen. 'Yes, of course, but – Francesca, what's happened? What's wrong, darling?'

'Leave me alone,' Francesca said, bending over and getting some plates out of the cupboard. 'I don't want to talk about it, all right?' She glanced up at Tess, her hair falling in her face, and gave her a really strange look. 'It's not your fault.'

Tess folded her arms, watching her flatmate. 'Is it Adam?' she said tentatively. 'Have you broken up again?'

Francesca laughed, her hair flowing like silk as she did. 'Broken up? Darling, we're not together, we can't break up.'

'But –' Tess shook her head, casting off the last vestiges of her drunkenness. She had sobered up pretty quickly. 'You and he – you're –' She reached out her hand.

'Don't touch me,' Francesca said. 'Look, it's just an exercise. It follows a set pattern.' She swallowed. 'Yeah. He texts me to see if I'm free. He comes round after you've gone to bed and we fuck each other until we're exhausted, then we fall

360

asleep. We don't talk, before or after. It's just sex,' she said flatly. 'Amazing sex. That's all there is to it.' She chewed her bottom lip, almost ruminatively. 'That's – he's not sleeping, since his grandmother died, and I don't sleep well anyway, so – might as well enjoy ourselves, no strings, get some rest afterwards.'

Tess thought of the times she had heard Francesca crying out wildly in the night, and she thought that she didn't believe her. Francesca looked up at Tess again and made a sad, odd sound like a sob and Tess realized she had caught her lip in her teeth to stop herself from crying. 'Oh, Francesca,' she said, sadly. She put her hands at the base of her spine and leaned back against the kitchen surface, as if to emphasize that she wasn't going to touch her, and looked at her flatmate. 'You really like him, don't you?'

'No, I don't,' Francesca said, but it was unconvincing, and she put her hand over her mouth. 'Whatever it is,' she said, rocking backwards and forwards and frowning, as if she were trying not to crumble, 'whatever, it's just that I can't do it any more. I don't want *this* –' she waved her hand around, gesturing to the debris on the floor of the sitting room – 'any more. I've rung my friend Kate, she and Mac are away on holiday, I'm going to go and stay at her flat for a couple of weeks.' Tess knew about Kate, she was one of Francesca's best friends. She nodded, watching her.

'Francesca – are you sure?' she said boldly. 'It's just – you were pretty screwed up before you got here, and being here's done you good, hasn't it? When you think what you used to be like? You'd been made redundant, you were behaving erratically at work. You were a bit . . .' She searched desperately for the right word, but couldn't find it. 'A bit . . . mad.'

She said it awkwardly, trying to lighten the mood.

'You're hilarious,' Francesca said, walking back into the sitting room. Tess followed her.

'Why?'

'I'm mad?' Francesca cried. 'You total hypocrite, Tess. *I'm* mad! That'd be funny if it wasn't so totally patronizing. And wrong, by the way. Can't you see we're just playing at real life, here? With these –' she gestured to the broken china – 'with these cake stands and stupid sofa cushions and – arghh.' Her shoulders sank down and her arms fell heavily to her sides. 'We're grown women and we're both hiding from where we belong.' She cleared her throat. 'I'm not mad, Tess. I had a crappy job and it made me unhappy. But I know where I belong, and that's back in London, with my friends, getting another job, living the life I had before.' She stared up at her. 'Someone rang me about a job last week. Doing pro-bono work, only taking on needy cases. There's a load of competition, obviously. But I'm going for it.'

'Oh,' said Tess. 'That's – well, that's great.'

'I'm sorry I didn't tell you.'

'Hey –' Tess shook her head. 'That's not important. I just want you to—

Francesca interrupted her. 'Tess, I know where I belong, and if I stay in Langford it'll be like – like being wrapped up in cotton wool. I'll be throwing my life away, doing some half-arsed job and waiting for Adam to come round at midnight and leave three hours later. I know where I need to be, that's all. Can you say the same thing?'

Tess said, faltering, 'Of course I can –'

But she remembered something Leonora Mortmain had said to her, their first night in Rome, a line that had been playing at the back of her head all through this long day. Her beaky face, beady eyes, watching her carefully as she spoke. *A woman should live for herself, not in the shadow of others.* She had been referring to herself, as much as to anyone else.

'Really,' said Francesca, picking up armfuls of clothes from beside the sofa and dumping them into the open suitcase. 'Tell me, why haven't you seen Peter since you got back?'

'I – we haven't been able to. And the funeral was today so – You know that.'

Francesca nodded. Tess looked around her, her eyes resting on the broken cake stand briefly before she realized she didn't want to look as though she was bothered about it.

'I'll get you a new one,' Francesca said. 'I've said I will.' Tess shook her head impatiently – it didn't matter. 'Oh – oh, Tess.' Francesca sounded almost imploring. 'You've got to see what I'm talking about.'

'I don't,' Tess said, trying not to sound as upset as she felt. 'I think you're trying to make me feel bad so you can justify your own behaviour, but I don't want to have an argument with you about it, Francesca, not if this is your last night.' She laughed shortly, and shook her head. 'Why are we even – this is crazy! Your last night. Don't go!'

'I have to,' Francesca said loudly, too loudly. 'God, Tess, don't you see? Look at this, look at us!' Her face was a rictus of rage; she relaxed, and a tear ran down her cheek. 'We live in a town that's still controlled by the family that ran it two hundred years ago! You teach things that happened two thousand years ago! You think you're in love with some guy in Italy who's about to move to the other side of the world, and you seriously think the two of you are going to be together!' She winced, as if it was painful to say these things, but it didn't stop her. 'You talk to a picture of Jane Austen, because a picture on the wall is the closest you've got to having a friend here, apart from me and Adam. And you two aren't friends, whatever you've got you're not friends.' Francesca paused, panting, and then she said, 'And everyone here is over fifty, apart from us and Adam, and he's the biggest hypocrite of them all, he's in bed with all of them!' She was sobbing now. 'It's like I woke up today, and now I see it I can't stay here another day. I just can't.' She shuddered. 'I need to get my own life, I want to walk on wet pavements again, I want to be annoyed when the tube's cancelled, I want to fall in love with someone who loves me back, and I don't ever want to see a *fucking* tea towel, ever again.' She kicked the side of the sofa. 'Tonight made up my mind for me.'

'Is that why you –' Tess gestured at the mess, not knowing what else to say.

'This? This wasn't just me. It was your precious Adam too.' She smiled, almost pleased she could shock Tess like this. 'I knew I was going after that ridiculous service, that awful wake at the pub. I knew I had to go. But he – he merely hastened the process.'

'Adam – did this?' Tess didn't believe her.

'Well, both of us,' said Francesca shortly. 'He was almost mad.'

'You must have had quite a bad fight . . .' Tess was bewildered. 'How can you be like this with each other?'

'Ha.' She smiled again, a great big smile. 'You think I'm mad, babe. You have no idea.' She looked at Tess, her hand on her cheek, her face flushed, hair tumbling about her. 'You should look in the mirror sometime. Or at that man you think you know so well. You're welcome to him. To all of it. I don't know what happened with his mother, or his horrible old grandmother, but whatever it was, it's screwed him up for life.'

'It's kind of understandable,' Tess said, trying to be loyal to Adam, and the memory of lovely Philippa, whom everyone missed every day. 'I can't blame him, you know.'

'Nothing can be that bad,' Francesca said. 'I'm sick of it. I'm getting out of here, darling, it's the only way. I can't stay.'

'What time's your train, then?' said Tess, not knowing what else to say.

'It's at eleven,' said Francesca. 'I'll be home by lunch-time, and you can go to college in the afternoon, and by the evening you'll have forgotten I was ever here.'

With an air of total finality, she dropped her dressing gown, the blue Chinese dressing gown, into the suitcase, and flipped the lid shut.

Spring 1977

The younger woman walked heavily across the lawn to the striped deckchair facing away from her. She could see a pair of feet, shod in pointed black pumps and crossed elegantly beneath the chair, and she cleared her throat tentatively.

'Hello?'

No answer.

'Um – hello?' she said, slightly louder, trying not to wheeze. She wiped the sweat off her brow; she was nervous.

Silence.

'Er . . . Mother?' she said. 'Is that you?'

A low, drawling voice came from the chair, but nothing moved.

'If you take only one thing away from this meeting, please, it is that you are never to call me Mother again.'

Philippa shifted her weight from one leg to the other. It was hot, even in her cheesecloth kaftan, and she was very pregnant, and she wished she were sitting down, there, under the shade of the spreading magnolia tree at the edge of the lawn, in a deckchair like this one, sipping something cool. These days her feet seemed to have permanently swelled to twice their natural size. Everything ached: her feet, her back, her breasts, her neck; she felt sick all the time, and had head-aches that never went away, always had done, and she couldn't take anything now to stop them. She was always uncomfort-able, especially since she'd come to Langford. She had never wanted to find her mother, never felt the urge to make a neat story out of her life. Philippa was used to self-sufficiency. But now she was desperate. That was the only reason she was here.

How they found out where she was, she never knew. Since Tony left, went back to the States, Philippa had been increas-ingly alone, her already-small band of friends in Dublin dwindling by the day. She had always been a loner, preferred her own company to anything else. She was an only child, after all. From the moment she had been able to escape the kindly but suffocating ministrations of her adopted parents, she had escaped as far as she could; it was the sixties, and though she didn't know it, she was far less alone than she would have thought in this desire to flee. She didn't particu-larly care who her real parents were, nor did anyone ever ask. The baby-boomer generation was made up of so many different kinds of families, fractured by the Second World War, and in those days, there was no real guarantee of ever finding out. Besides, she wanted to live her own life now. That was in the past; she wanted a future.

The next few years were like a dream come true. She had gone to Morocco for a year, travelling around with a girlfriend from university, had driven along the Silk Route in a minivan, ending up in India, living in Varanasi for a few months and selling beers to fellow dropouts. She had crossed the States with friends in another minivan, and somehow ended up teaching English in California, she didn't know how. When Philippa crossed the Atlantic again, she knew she couldn't go back to the safe, dull Home Counties of England she had learned to despise. She went to Dublin and stayed there, gaining her PhD, becoming a lecturer, living a gently bohemian life, drinking long into the evenings, arguing about poetry, discussing politics and art, taking off for strange places at a moment's notice, having sex with whomever she pleased. Nothing that tied her down, nothing that made her feel like little Philippa Crabtree from Basingstoke, growing up in one of a row of identical houses, hair plaited like every other little girl in her street, shoes, satchel and dolls identical to everyone else's.

She vowed that would never happen to her.

And then she fell pregnant.

She told everyone it was an accident, but that was not strictly true. She was in her mid-thirties now, and inside her was a deep longing for a baby. Tony – the sweet, kind, Irish lecturer in Early English with whom she had been having an affair these past few months – was appalled at the news, but man enough to hide it when she told him. The relief on his face when she explained she wanted to bring up the baby by herself was almost comical. Philippa remembered, again, why she preferred being alone.

But that was before she lost her job – employment law in the mid-seventies not being what it was later to become. Tony had happily fled to take up a teaching post in America. Many of her other friends had either lost their jobs or been drawn back to the UK, since this was during the height of the Troubles and even Dublin was affected by the mood. Everyone was on strike, inflation had never been highter: it felt as though the world which to her had seemed so full of golden possi-bilities was going to hell in a handcart. The Crabtrees, her adoptive parents, had scented the wind of change early and migrated to Australia several years previously – presumably hoping, Philippa wryly thought, to put as much distance between themselves and their disappointing daughter as possible.

Suddenly, free-wheeling, happy-go-lucky Philippa realized

she was pregnant, broke, with rent due in three days, no savings, absolutely no plans, and almost totally alone. It was then, like a miracle, that she was contacted one day by a solicitor from a small town called Langford.

'Miss Crabtree?'

She had almost not answered the phone; it was in the hallway, too far for her to walk when she was lying prone on the grubby corduroy sofa, silently weeping and patting her stomach.

'Miss Crabtree, my name is Edward Tey. I am contacting you on behalf of a client of mine. We have been aware of your whereabouts for some time now. I wonder, could I interest you in a trip back to England? We have a proposal for you.'

And that was how Philippa found out who her mother was. Two days later, she was back in England for the first time in over a decade, walking across a typical English lawn at the height of summer, feeling like a fish out of water, wishing with all her heart she were back in Dublin. But it was too late for that now. It wasn't just her any more. She wasn't alone any more, nor would she ever be again.

So Philippa stood there awkwardly, pushing her thick hair away from her perspiring face and waiting for this woman to turn around, hoping more than anything else that she would let her sit down.

When she stood up and turned around, Philippa squinted. She was wearing a wide-brimmed straw hat, which kept most of her face in the shade, and huge sunglasses. Her large hands were folded together, and she wore a blue silk jersey tunic – obviously expensive, even Philippa could see that. She said nothing.

'Hello,' Philippa said, slowly. 'It's nice to—'

'Here are the deeds to the house,' Leonora Mortmain said, picking up an envelope of papers from the iron table beside her. A trickle of condensation ran down the jug of water next to it. Philippa watched its progress longingly. 'It has been painted, only last year for the previous tenants. There is furniture in there, again from the old tenants. You will find an envelope in this pack. It has five hundred pounds in it. That is for clothing, et cetera, for the baby, and for the two of you for the first few months, until you are able to get another teaching post. Yes?'

Philippa squinted, as if she were a bit drunk, to try and make out some of her mother's features. 'It's nice to meet you at last,' she said. 'Thank you so much for—'

'Please listen to me,' said Leonora Mortmain, and her voice was awful, horrible to hear. 'I have always monitored your movements, first through the Crabtrees, then through private means. We know you are desperate, that you have no options, and that you and that child, which will be born a bastard, are basically alone in the world. That is why I have said I will help you.' She cleared her throat, a small, precise gesture. 'Yes, you are my child, and the child of someone else too, and that is why I will help you. But we are not to be in each other's lives. I do not want to hear from you again. I do not want anyone to know, most of all that child in there, where you came from. Do not tell him. Do not tell *anyone* that you are a Mortmain. You will have to change your surname, to be totally sure no one can make the connection. These are my only conditions. Is that understood?'

The baby inside Philippa – the reason she was there, rooted to the ground in this small town, forced to settle for something when it was really the last thing she wanted – suddenly kicked. She put her hand on her stomach, feeling the smooth, taut skin of her rounded belly underneath the cotton of her dress.

'Don't call my baby a bastard,' she said softly. 'I won't take the house, thank you very much. I don't want anything from you.'

There was a silence.

'You have to take it,' Leonora Mortmain said flatly. 'You think you're quite the bohemian, don't you? Living a life of Reilly, no cares or responsibilities, but you're not quite so selfish as to turn this down, are you? I know you really have nothing.' She took her sunglasses off, folded them neatly and put them on the table. The baby kicked again, and the vice-like grip around Philippa's head, from the sun and fatigue, tightened a little more as she looked into her mother's dark eyes for the first time since she had been a new born.

'Don't you care?' she said wonderingly, blinking back sharp tears. 'Didn't you care at all about me? Did you think of me, ever, when I was growing up?'

'Not really,' said Leonora Mortmain. Her eyes were impossible to read. She stared impassively at her daughter. 'You were a mistake, you see.'

'You can't be this horrible,' Philippa said. She reached forward, and took the envelope. 'You just can't. I'm going to let you know when the baby's born, what it is, how he or she is. Don't worry –' as Leonora held up her hand to speak – 'I'll make sure no one finds out, I won't say a word. Thank you. Thank you for the house, and the money. It is kind of you, though apparently you don't want me to think so.'

She desperately wanted to pee, to sit down, to cry. She had to go.

'I have already explained,' Leonora Mortmain said. 'I don't think I need to explain any further. I have a duty to you, in as much as I cannot let you become destitute. You are clearly the sort of person who needs control in her life. Perhaps that is what I can give you.'

Philippa could feel sweat pooling between her breasts. 'Can you tell me who my father was?' she asked quietly.

The older woman put her hand up to her eyes, as if she were shading them from the sun, and when she spoke her voice was wavery. 'No. I cannot. I've said all I'm going to say to you. Take this envelope, please, and consider this entire matter closed.'

And Leonora Mortmain simply walked away, walked into the house, shutting the door behind her, leaving her daughter on the lawn in the midday sunshine, tears in her eyes. Philippa clutched the envelope. This was like a bad dream. This baby was a terrible mistake, she knew it now.

Perhaps she should give it away, get out of this town, start all over again.

Then she realized with cold, calm certainty that she stood on a precipice. That she would be in terrible danger of repeating what had happened to her. That would not happen to her baby, never, ever!

She was still crying a little as she walked through the silent house, down the corridor and out of the front door. No one said goodbye, but she felt as if there were eyes watching her the whole time. Philippa stood on the high street and looked around her, as if trying to remember where she was. It was a whole new world. There, opposite, was a pub called the Feathers. Philippa wiped her nose and walked in.

There was a man behind the bar, polishing some glasses and whistling. He looked up as she came in, giving her a curious glance, and then he smiled.

'You all right, my dear?'

'Um – not sure,' said Philippa, stroking her stomach again as the kicking intensified. 'I've just moved here, actually.'

She didn't know why she said this.

'If you don't mind me saying,' said the man behind the bar, 'you look as if you could do with a nice sit-down and a cup of tea.'

'That would be lovely,' said Philippa. 'But I need the loo first.'

'Well, let me point you in the right direction and I'll get you your tea.' He leaned across the bar. 'Welcome to the

Feathers. I'm Mick. Nice to have a new face in Langford. You're very welcome, my dear.' And he grinned, kindly.

Philippa shook his hand and gave him a watery smile and, as she took in her new surroundings, blinking back tears, for the first time in a long while felt that she might not be entirely alone.

CHAPTER THIRTY-FOUR

'I know some people have been put off by what happened back in the summer,' said Beth Kennett, her fingers drumming the admissions lists in front of her. 'But what can I do? *We* didn't kill her.'

'I don't know,' said Andrea Marsh, stacking a group of papers smartly together; the paper made a loud, sharp sound on the old wooden desk. She glanced up at her boss. 'But numbers are down, and there has to be a reason. And I'm telling you, if we don't sort it out soon –' she tapped a folder in her in-tray significantly – 'you'll be in real trouble.'

Beth sighed. 'I know I will.' She scratched her head and breathed in heavily. 'Oh, dear. You'd think it'd make a difference, having this connection with the Mortmains, but no. Bookings are down nearly thirty per cent on last year. It's the live-in people doing the music lessons and the cookery courses and all that, they're the ones who bring in the revenue. And they're down –'

'Nearly forty per cent,' Andrea said briskly. 'I'm afraid, Miss Kennett, when times are hard people don't want to learn about some emperor and some civilization that happened two thousand years ago. What's the point?' she finished, as if she was the last person in the world to have recently enjoyed a free Roman civilization course that was a perk of the job, and even less likely to have spent early June wandering round Rome hand in hand with someone gazing at statues.

'There is a point, Andrea. Of course there's a point.' Beth gazed out of the leaded window, down the driveway, at the setting sky. It was a beautiful autumn evening, with a real chill in the air. Halloween was the following day, and the leaves in the park were at their most beautiful: terracotta red, citrus yellow, orange and green. Autumn had arrived gradually, the long summer's nights had lasted well into September. They had sat outside to eat their sandwiches on the long grass until only a couple of weeks ago and it had seemed, after the long, hot summer, as if winter would never come. Tonight, she felt suddenly, it was just around the corner, and it was going to be long. She shivered.

'Goose walk over your grave?' Andrea said, standing up. 'I'd better be off, you know. I'm meeting the committee at the Feathers in a bit. Don't want to be late.'

She zipped up her salmon-pink quilted jacket, and pulled her grey-streaked dark hair out of the collar. Beth watched her.

'You've a committee meeting? I thought it was all over with the water meadows, now Leonora's er – gone.'

'*Au contraire*,' Andrea said grimly. 'We don't know where that Adam Smith is – Adam *Mortmain*, I suppose I should call him,' she said, heavy disdain in her voice. 'And as far as anyone knows, they're still going ahead with the plan. They're scheduled to start draining the land and building the foundations in January.'

'But I thought –' Beth looked surprised. 'Wouldn't he have pulled out of the whole thing?'

'He's getting two million off them,' Andrea said, shrugging her shoulders. 'That's the problem.'

Beth said thoughtfully, 'That's such a shame. I always liked him so much.'

'"Like" has nothing to do with it,' Andrea said. 'I used to

like him too, we all did. Thought he'd had a rotten time of it, what with his mum, even before that when he was little, no dad, such a wiry, clever little thing he was. Always laughing, used to run around town like a puppy, he would.' She gathered up some files and hugged them to her body. 'Don't mean he's a decent person.'

'So – where is he?' Beth said, ignoring this. 'Can you tell him what's going on?'

'Could if anyone knew where he was,' Andrea said. 'He's vanished, and that Francesca vanished the same day. Most peculiar.'

'The two of them?'

'That's right, and there's Tess Tennant left all on her own in that house. I wonder what she makes of it all. If she knows where Adam is.' She cleared her throat and wound her scarf around her neck. 'She'll be lonely now, you mark my words. I always thought she took that Francesca in too quickly. I never trusted her, you know? Little bit sly, I thought.'

'Francesca helped you with the committee, didn't she? She nearly got them to delay, till Mrs Mortmain steam-rollered it through.' said Beth staunchly. 'And Tess is a sensible girl.'

Andrea was in an unsentimental mood. She raised her eyebrows. 'You think? I like her, don't get me wrong, but she's a bit . . . well, I wouldn't have said anything before that trip to Rome, but she's a bit flighty.'

Beth cleared her throat. 'She handled the whole thing very well, I thought.'

'Did you? Well, that's good,' Andrea said, in a voice that showed she didn't mean it. 'If you ask me, it's a good thing Adam whatever-we're-calling-him showed up when he did. We'd all still be there if it wasn't for him lighting a fire under her to sort it all out. Going off with that Italian man – and we haven't seen hide nor hair of *him* since, have we?'

'I think she did very well,' Beth said firmly. 'You lot are a tricky bunch to control, especially when you've known her since she was born. It was very hard for her. See you tomorrow. Goodnight, Andrea.'

'Anyway, goodnight,' Andrea finished casually, as if Beth had not spoken. She paused in the doorway of the study. 'See you tomorrow.'

Left alone in the darkening room, Beth gazed into space, thinking about nothing in particular, listening to the ticking of the grandfather clock that stood by the door. There was a faint whirring sound in the distance, and she realized she'd been hearing it all day. She had the beginnings of a headache, she thought, rubbing her temples. She glanced over at the clock and began to shut down her laptop. Her eye wandered as she waited, idly wondering what the noise was. She stared at the Victorian portrait of Ivo Mortmain, which hung up over the fireplace. It was almost lifesize, the rugged-looking Ivo dressed in a ceremonial suit of armour, his expression remote and rather grand. Beth flipped the lid of the laptop down and stood up, clutching it in her arms. She looked up at the portrait again, and nearly cried out with recognition.

'Of course,' she said to herself, smiling at the Mortmain forebear. 'You're the spitting image of him. How can none of us have noticed before?' She opened the office door. 'Where are you?' she said quietly. 'I wonder where you are?'

'Where who is?' a voice behind her came.

Beth actually jumped into the air with shock, practically dropping her laptop. She gave a little scream and then turned around. 'Tess!' she cried with relief, for the corridor was dark, and Langford Hall had always been a bit Gothic, even in broad daylight with the lights on.

'Sorry,' said Tess, laughing, partly with shock, partly with anything else. 'I left my glasses here – came back to pick them up. I'm sorry! Did I give you a fright?'

'Something like that,' Beth said.

'Have you got everything?' Tess asked, looking behind her. 'Who were you just talking to?'

'Oh . . . no one,' Beth admitted. She looked at Tess's face; she thought she was rather pale. 'Did you get the glasses? Shall we go?'

'Great,' said Tess. 'How nice, running into you like this.'

'Absolutely,' said Beth as they reached the great vestibule of the hall, a circular room in black and white with two vast staircases leading up each side. The residential students slept in a separate wing, and so the building was deserted. Beth fished around in her pocket for the keys; there was a house-keeper on the premises, but in the separate wing. At night, the old part of the house was locked up.

'Funny to think she grew up here,' Tess said, hugging herself as Beth unlocked the door.

'Who?'

'Leonora Mortmain,' Tess said. 'That she was a little girl, who grew up here. Weird, isn't it. She probably played in the gardens – I can't picture it, myself.'

'She was never the kind of person you could imagine as a child,' Beth said. They stared around them, at the empty hall. She pushed the front door open and the evening sunset hit their eyes. The whirring noise she'd heard before grew louder. Beth blinked. 'Yes, it's strange to think she lived here. Over-looking the water meadows, too – you'd think they'd have meant something to her.'

Tess said quietly, 'I know.'

'What's that noise, do you know?' said Beth. Tess looked surprised.

'What noise?'

Beth shushed her, and they walked down the drive in silence, under the gathering dusk.

'Don't know,' said Tess eventually. 'How weird.'

'How's the course going, then?' Beth asked, after a pause. 'Roman Civilization – you've taught it twice now, I think?'

'Nearly,' Tess said, smiling. She pulled a navy blue beret over her hair. 'It's cold, isn't it? Tomorrow's Friday, so it's

Catullus, then I'll have done it twice. It's been good. It's a bit quiet –' She trailed off.

'How many in this class?'

'Ten,' Tess said. Beth sighed, and Tess shrugged her shoulders. 'I don't know, though. Perhaps it's just not as popular as it was. I don't think it's the school, Beth. All the cookery classes seem to be quite full, and that really random stuff I never understand why anyone would want to do a course in, like shrubs and potting, or Victorian architecture – well, they're full to bursting.'

'You get to play with things, that's the difference,' Beth said, smiling.

'You know what I mean, though?' Tess said anxiously.

'Sort of. All the numbers are down across the board, trust me. Perhaps it's just –' She trailed off. 'Oh.'

'Perhaps it's just me? Or perhaps it's just no one wants to do Classics any more?' Tess said lightly. 'Or perhaps it's a combination of the two.'

'I didn't mean that,' Beth said uncomfortably. 'I'm very glad we hired you.' Tess put her hand on Beth's arm.

'Hey, it's OK,' she said. She gave a mock grimace, but her heart-shaped face was pale in the gloom.

'Have you found a new flatmate?' Beth said, changing the subject.

'No, not yet,' Tess said, her voice uneasy. 'I need to though – Francesca paid nearly two months' rent but even so it's already run out. I haven't –' She trailed off. 'Yep, I definitely need to. Seems like a long time ago.'

'What does?'

'Her leaving, I mean. The summer –' Tess stopped, and fiddled with the buckle of her boot. 'It all seems a long time ago.' They were under one of the spreading beech trees and Beth could not see her expression in the darkness. 'All of it.'

'Are you missing that Italian chap?' Beth said, kindly. 'What was his name?'

That Italian chap. 'Peter,' Tess said. 'He's – only half Italian. Yes, I am, rather.'

Beth peered at her. 'Wasn't it just a summer thing? Holiday romance?'

'Er –' Tess didn't know what to say. 'No, it was –' Was she right? Probably she was . . . it hadn't occurred to her while she was there that it was a holiday romance, born out of a time and place. Here in the damp English autumn chill, she wasn't so sure.

Beth bit her lip. 'Sorry, am I being really tactless? I am, aren't I.'

'No, no,' Tess hastened to assure her. 'I've been thinking all along it's something with a future, and perhaps I have to accept it's not.' She didn't quite believe she was saying it, though.

Beth stared at her, clearly at a loss. 'Oh, I see.' Tess wondered if Beth was thinking she was over-doing it a bit, and an awkward silence fell, only broken when Beth said,

'Good grief, what's that?'

A car was screeching up the driveway, the headlights flashing. Someone jumped out.

'Who on earth is that?' Beth said. 'Andrea? Andrea, is that you?'

Out of a battered white Golf flew Andrea Marsh, waving her arms at the two girls. 'Look!' she cried, running towards the wall at the edge of the house that divided the formal garden from the side of the valley. 'Look! It's started! It's bloody started!'

'What has?' Tess cried, following her.

Andrea's eyes were wild, she pulled her hand rapidly over her shoulder, as if swatting a fly. 'Come!' she called out. 'Look!'

They followed her to the low wall, and looked out. It was getting dark and, down at the bottom of the valley, it was darker still. But they could still make out a swarm of vehicles on the grass amongst the yellow and orange trees.

'What are they?' breathed Beth, over Tess's shoulder.

'Diggers,' said Andrea grimly. 'Look.'

The whirring sound that had been bothering Beth all day now revealed itself to be the churning of a tractor, cutting up the earth on one side of the thin footbridge. Beth shook her head grimly. 'My God, that's what it was.'

'You heard it?' Tess said. She was deathly pale.

'Yep, all day.' Beth nodded. 'Did you know –'

'No,' said Tess, staring down at the water meadows. 'No idea. I haven't heard from him . . . since he left.'

'The little tinker,' Andrea said, her voice dripping with venom. 'That bloody little bastard. It's dishonest, that's what it is. Greedy.'

'There must be a reason for it,' Tess said quietly.

'Name me one,' said Andrea flatly, looking over into the valley again. High up in the trees at the edge of the estate, the rooks called, bleakly. Andrea jangled her car keys in her hand. 'I have to get back,' she said. 'I've got to tell Ron . . . And the others.' She turned to Tess. 'You give me one reason why he'd do this.'

'I can't,' said Tess, and Beth looked at her face, miserable in the gathering gloom. 'Oh, dear. It's awful.' Beth patted her on the arm.

'Come on,' she said. 'Let's go home.'

CHAPTER THIRTY-FIVE

One of the effects of Francesca's departure and Adam's disappearance was that Tess wasn't sleeping. She wasn't tired out. As autumn arrived, hers became a sedentary life, and she was glad of the shortening of days, the excuse to stay in; it was embarrassing, this excess of sunlight, it showed up her paltry existence even more. It showed her that her life back in Langford was . . . reduced. Small. In the late long summer's evenings, she would sit, full of melancholy, on the sofa, watching TV, leaning on the large A4-sized hardback *Guide to Langford* to eat her supper, as light poured in through the windows, as birds sang in the hedgerows and the sound of people laughing and having fun echoed around her, down the small lane, in the nooks and crannies of the town.

With autumn came an endless mist that descended on the town and wouldn't shift, and rain and wind, and log fires and darkness and, finally, an excuse to stay in. She made endless hearty meals, casseroles rich with sage and chestnuts, roasted chickens dripping with garlic and thyme, thick onion and potato soups. She couldn't stop eating, like an animal preparing for hibernation. She listened to the radio, she read voraciously, she prepared for class, arranged her books and other possessions, to cover the absence of her flatmate, or her loneliness, or the fact that she missed her flatmate, or her oldest friend, or her summer romance . . . the trouble is, she didn't know whom she missed the most.

Time and again, she got out Leonora Mortmain's slim book of poetry, turning the volume over and over in her hands, wondering why the old lady had kept it with her all these years. She read the poems, or tried to re-read them; it was years since she'd actually read in Latin that which she didn't have to teach on a course, and it was much more taxing than she remembered. Some of the poems were underlined; some had markings by them. Asterisks, mostly. And then at night, she tried to sleep, but she couldn't.

It should have worried her. It bothered her vaguely, that a whole weekend could go by, and she could stay inside for nearly all of it, holed up on the sofa, chatting to Meena, her parents and Stephanie on the phone, only venturing out to get the paper and to buy more milk. She avoided her fellow townspeople unless she had to have contact with them. They were starting up the Save the Water Meadows Campaign again, with renewed vigour; she ought to go along to a meeting. The bridge had been torn down, the land was fenced off already – it was all underway, and still she couldn't quite believe it would happen.

The rain fell, the leaves turned to mulch, the skies clouded over, and autumn came, shrouding the town in fog, and Tess carried on cooking, eating, sitting – and then going up to bed, and turning things over in her mind again, blinking at the ceiling, trying not to be scared by the noises outside, the screams from a creature in the claws of another, the cats fighting, the birds caught by the foxes. She was mentally, but not physically, exhausted.

At the start of the new term at college, Tess was assigned new classes – the same week-long or term-long courses on a variety of subjects – and she was also, to her pleasure, teaching the Latin A level class, which took place over one year and was six hours a week. They were an interesting bunch, more committed than her previous students, women who'd been at home with children and wanted to go back to their studies, people who'd retired and wanted to accomplish something, a retired company director who loved sword-and-sandal epics and had always promised himself he'd learn Latin when he retired, even a priest who needed Latin before he took up a post in London and, most bizarrely of all, a librettist who was writing an opera about a gladiator in ancient Rome.

It gave Tess something of a start, she knew, to realize that this was the autumn term of a course that would last till the following summer – and that she was the one teaching it. They wanted her to sign a new contract. The lease on the cottage would be up in January, too, she had to renew it. She supposed she was staying in Langford. That was her life now. The summer was long over. She should be looking to the future, not sleepwalking through her life. She needed several things to happen. She needed to find a flatmate now. She needed to put all the events of the summer behind her, and concentrate on her life here – and her life with Peter, starting again at Christmas, and how she could possibly reconcile the two. And then things started happening.

One of the first things that happened was in her new Latin A level class, teaching the poet Catullus. They were studying his second and third poems, about his adored mistress Lesbia and her beloved sparrow.

'What are those three lines on the end of the second one?' someone asked. 'They haven't got anything to do with it.'

It was Friday, and it was a long day. Tess was tired; she hadn't slept the previous night. She looked down, reading the words out.

'Tam gratum est . . .'

> *Tam gratum est mihi quam ferunt puellae*
> *pernici aureolum fuisse malum*
> *quod zonam soluit diu ligatam*

Tess stared down at the paper. '*Tam gratum est mihi quam* – but I'm grateful that . . .' She looked at them again, remembering now the layout in the book of poetry Adam had given her. She could see the page. Throughout, Leonora had doodled, drawn lines, but this poem, or just these three lines, were furiously underlined, with stars around them.

'That's really weird.'

'What is?' asked Sandy from Esher, who was in the front row.

'This poem,' Tess said without thinking. 'It's in a book I've got. Someone underlined it. Many times. It obviously meant something to them.'

'Whose book was it?'

'A lady. She died. It's a bit of a mystery.'

'Wow!' Sandy said, holding her pen ready. The class looked expectantly at Tess, – this was exciting! Much more so than Catullus and his girlfriend Lesbia, which was a weird name to give a girlfriend anyway.

'Is it like a treasure hunt?' asked Lynda, Sandy's best friend.

'No, listen to her, it's a mystery! Like – oh, do you like Cadfael?' Sandy said. 'Because they had a manuscript that some monk had been murdered over, with poisoned illuminated parchment, and—'

Tess held up her hand. 'Er, not so much like that, I think. More –' she lowered her voice – 'more like an insight into their state of mind.'

'Oh,' said Lynda. 'That's not very interesting, is it?' She rolled her pencils and pens, which were lying perfectly straight together on the wooden desk, over the knotted surface with her immaculate pearlescent nails.

Tess sighed. 'Perhaps it's not,' she said.

Suddenly a voice at the back spoke up. 'Isn't it about marriage?' said Tom, the librettist. Tess looked with delight at her favourite pupil, as Tom, still waggling his hand to be noticed, went on. 'I always thought it was about Atalanta, wasn't she an Amazon?'

384

'Yes, it's about Atalanta, but she wasn't an Amazon,' said Tess, though she was impressed. 'She could have been, though. She had many suitors, and she was extremely beautiful, but she just didn't want to get married. She didn't see the point of men.'

'Oh,' said Tom, quashed.

'Ha,' said Sandy, who was recently divorced. 'I can see her point.'

Jemima, the competitive mother who had recently moved to town, looked slightly embarrassed for Sandy.

'Atalanta was a great hunter,' said Tess, settling on the edge of the desk. 'I always liked the sound of her, I must say. She helped catch a boar that had been terrorizing the local countryside.' She crossed her arms and looked down at all of them. 'She roamed around, doing what she wanted. Not constrained by anyone. And then, she decided to get married.'

'Why?' said Sandy, disappointed.

'Don't know why,' said Tess. 'Because she wanted to, not because she was told to. I think that's the point. Anyway, to find the best suitor, she decided to race against them all, to see who was the fastest. She was very fast.' She looked down at the book. '*Puellae pernici* – it means fleet-footed, swift girl. She raced them all and one of them – Hippomenes was his name, I think – he dropped three golden apples, one by one, and Atalanta stopped to pick them up and so he beat her, and she married him.'

'So – women are easily distracted by golden baubles,' said Lynda, disappointed. 'Even a woman who's renounced men and gone off and become a hunter in the forest will still run after some twinkling gold. Pathetic.'

'I can testify to that,' said Gerald, the ex-managing director (whether retired or fired, Tess couldn't tell), who was extremely rubicund and jolly, but who referred to his wife as 'the little lady', making Tess want to punch him. 'Hah! Hah!'

'I don't think that's the moral of the story,' Tess said slowly.

'I think the point is, she had rejected marriage too strongly, for the wrong reasons. Run away from it. And the golden apples were the symbol, the distraction – after all, if Usain Bolt was running round a stadium and someone chucked some golden apples in his way, he'd be distracted, wouldn't he?'

'Well, he wears golden shoes anyway,' said Sherry from Thornham. 'So probably not. He wouldn't notice them.'

'Look,' said Tess hurriedly, 'the point is, the speaker is glad – in this case Catullus, talking about his girlfriend, I suppose, although it's a tiny fragment so we're not really sure – that the golden apples loosened her girdle. I.e., took her virginity. Because it had been too long.'

'What's the translation then?' said Jemima the competitive mother. She was an ex-marketing director who had just moved to Langford with her husband and two children, and was extremely literal. 'What does it mean?'

'Um – well, it's . . .' Tess paused. It was cryptic, in the extreme. Jemima tapped her pencil impatiently. Tess wrinkled her nose, was silent for a minute. 'OK,' she said eventually. 'Here's a rough stab, I suppose it would be something like, *"But it's pleasing to me, as they say, that the swift-footed girl had the golden apple, and it now loosened her girdle, which had been tightly tied for too long."*

'The girdle as in her virginity. Picking up the apple meant she would lose her virginity, that's signified by the girdle. She was going to be a wife and mother. A proper woman, they would say. And the speaker of the poem is pleased about this.'

There was a silence as some people digested this, and others merely looked bored. And then Sandy, watching her with interest, said, 'So, dear. Does it explain something to you, then?'

'Yes,' said Tess, smiling up at her. 'I think it does.'

CHAPTER THIRTY-SIX

Tess ran home from class that day, barely even stopping to say goodbye to Beth and the other teachers. She flung open the door and threw her bags on the floor. There was a note on the floor too. She picked it up.

Tess! Hi! I'll be round at about six, hope that's OK! I can't wait!

Tess read it swiftly, distracted. She went over to the bureau which stood by the window, her shaking fingers pulling papers and books out of the shelf, and she translated the poem again, looking the words up in her old battered leather-bound Latin dictionary, which she had had since she was a teenager. Perhaps the words meant nothing but she knew, suddenly, that they did. They meant something to Leonora, no one else.

Finally, things were starting to change. She had a new flat-mate moving in that evening, and she was fairly sure she wouldn't stand for Francesca-like levels of untidiness. Tess got up to make herself some tea, and looked down at the open bureau where, in one corner, her computer sat unopened. She ought to see if Peter had emailed her, but somehow she couldn't face it. The previous night, she had woken in a cold sweat, clutching the duvet with her fingers aching from the tension, from a dream where she had gone back to Rome for Christmas. But as she walked through the Piazza Farnese, to

Peter's flat, people were walking past her, saying hello and she stared at them in panic as they streamed past. She couldn't remember what he looked like; couldn't at all. She had no photos of him; his face, when they talked on Skype, was bleached out by the camera, indistinct, his voice high-pitched and full of static. That wasn't the Peter who had ridden with her on his moped, drunk Prosecco with her, kissed her in front of the Trevi Fountain, no – no. She just had to find him again, both in Rome at Christmas and in her head, fall back in love with him again. But it seemed so far away! Like a dream, as strange as the dream she'd had the previous night.

Funny, Tess thought, as she headed into the kitchen. She had fallen in love with him so easily the first time – surely it should be enough, the second time, too?

She looked around the kitchen, at the curling notice stuck on the pinboard about the Harvest Festival; the postcard from Francesca, a cut-out photo of the London Eye; another post-card, from her parents on their holiday in October and the notice of the rubbish collection dates over Christmas and the New Year. There was a letter, too, from the letting agency, reminding her politely that they were still waiting to hear if she would be renewing the lease on the cottage for another six months. Tess had opened it but put it back in its envelope and it stared up at her, the light catching the sheen of the cellophane so it seemed to wink at her. Would she be here for another six months? Or should she just be impulsive, and go to Rome?

What would Rome in January be like? Rainy, grey – just like here, but Rome. Rome, with Peter. Wine, food, Italy, scooters, classical ruins, speaking Italian, her new flat-heeled patent-leather boots, walking everywhere in the greatest city in the world . . .

It was raining outside and it was already dark. Tess stared out into nothing, her mind racing over everything. The poem today, Atalanta and how she refused to get married. How she was tricked into loosening her girdle – how must she have felt? The book of poems . . . she stared down, they were still in her hand.

Once again, Tess felt that strange connection to Leonora Mortmain that she had felt before and which she couldn't explain. She was pretty sure the old woman had devised the gloomiest, most hellfire and brimstone service there was, so that absolutely no one enjoyed themselves. And all that stuff about *for as in Adam all die* – it was vindictive and spiteful. No wonder her only living family member had cleared out of the country for – how long was it now? Nearly three months. The order of service from the funeral was tucked inside the book of poetry. Tess flicked idly through it, her eye falling on the penultimate page of the service, the final reading.

Philip saith unto him, Lord, shew us the Father, and it sufficeth us. Jesus saith unto him, Have I been so long a time with you, and yet hast thou not known me, Philip?

What Philip had to do with it, she had no idea. Who was Philip, anyway?

The front door opened, and a head peeked around it. 'Hello,' it called. 'It's open, are you decent?'

Had she been sitting there thinking for that long? Tess jumped up guiltily. 'Hi, Liz!' she said. 'Welcome to your new home! I'm so sorry about the mess.'

'No worries,' Liz said, untangling her scarf. 'It's raining out there. Horrible evening. I meant to come over earlier, but Jen insisted on doing a stock check *again*. So annoying.' She rubbed her hands and looked around her. 'I've got all my stuff in the car, shall I unload it and then park it round the back?'

'Absolutely,' said Tess. 'I'll give you a hand. Kettle's just boiled – do you want a cup of tea first?'

'Only if you've made a pot,' said Liz simply, and Tess loved the idea that she would have steaming pots of tea waiting around for people, rather than the depressing single soggy teabag in the sink that tea usually meant in this house. She had to remind herself to be nice. That Liz was lovely, not the girl whose Dealbreaker with Adam was that she cried during sex. At the thought of Adam telling her this, in horrified ghoulish tones, Tess smiled with a half-sigh, and rubbed her shoulder.

'I'll wait if not,' Liz was saying. 'This is lovely! Tess, thank you so much for letting me move in. Jen's was nice, but living above the shop . . .' Her face clouded over. 'Well, it's not ideal. You know. So – to have a proper home!'

'Ah,' said Tess, feeling guilty. 'Bless you.' She patted her arm. 'Let's get your bags inside.'

Liz had packed neatly, economically and sensibly. Even her boxes had easy-to-carry handles on them, and she had marked everything. 'Books'. 'Bathroom'. 'Kitchen utensils (small)'. 'Toiletries'. In less than ten minutes they were back inside with the boxes correctly placed in each section of the small house, and the kettle was on again.

Liz came into the kitchen, her long thin face red and slightly wet from the rain. 'Hey, I got some of those Swedish ginger thins you like, by the way, as a moving-in present! They came in this afternoon.' She put them down on the counter as Tess poured the water into the teapot. Liz watched her.

'This is bloody great,' she said. 'When I think about a year ago, how miserable I was.'

'Really?'

'Oh, yeah,' Liz said, matter-of-factly. 'Working in that awful agency. Squeezing onto a smelly bus every day, sweaty all the time, in winter and in summer.' She breathed in. 'It's funny, there have been some good times and some not-so-good times since I moved to Langford. But I've never doubted it was the right decision.' She smiled at her. 'You must know what I mean. After all, you grew up here.'

'Here you go,' said Tess, handing her a cup of tea.

'Thanks,' said Liz. 'Ooh, this is nice. This is just what I need.'

'Good-o,' said Tess. 'Have a ginger thin.'

Liz took one, smiling. 'You know, Tess, I can't thank you enough. You've no idea what a difference it makes.'

'What?' Tess said, taking a biscuit for herself.

'Having a proper place to live. It's just lovely. I've only been here half an hour, and it's lovely.' She smiled, and took another sip of her tea. 'Aren't you having any?'

Tess leaned against the counter. 'I might in a bit.'

'What are you looking at?' Liz asked, noticing the order of service on the surface.

'Oh, just something from class today,' Tess said, handing her the biscuits again. 'Reminded me of the funeral. These are absolutely lovely. Thanks.'

Liz bent over the order of service. 'Gosh, what a gloomy business that was,' she said, nodding. She looked down at the open page. '"Hast – hast thou not known me, Philip" – and what was that about? Some kind of message from beyond the grave?'

'What?' Tess said. She put down the teapot.

'Well, I mean, because wasn't Adam's mother called Philippa?' Liz blushed slightly, as she always did when talking about Adam, as if she were embarrassed to have this know-ledge. 'What –?' She stared at her flatmate, who was gripping her wrist. 'Ow.'

'Yes,' said Tess. 'Yes! She was. I'm so stupid, Liz.'

'Who's Philip?'

'I don't know.' Tess opened the fridge. 'I don't know, perhaps we'll never know, but she wanted someone to find out, that's the point, Liz. I'm having a glass of wine, I'm afraid. Will you join me?'

'Oh, I'll join you,' said Liz happily. 'Only one though, I've got yoga tomorrow. Wow,' she said, taking a wine glass. 'First night in the house, and it's like Rome all over again. Wine, women and song – all on a Tuesday evening. Who knows what'll happen next!'

CHAPTER THIRTY-SEVEN

'But you said you'd book your flight right away,' Peter said. 'I don't get it. They'll be kinda expensive if you wait, Tess. Don't you want to come?'

'It's not that –' Tess cradled the phone under her ear, and took another bite of the ginger thins. At the moment Tess was going through a box every couple of days. She swallowed hastily, the biscuit scratching her throat. 'Arrh.' She coughed.

'You OK?'

'I'm fine,' Tess said. 'Sorry.' She rubbed her eyes; she was tired. She felt tired, and fat, and lonely; these conversations with Peter, which had once been such a source of joy to her, now sat uneasily with her. The time difference was severe, which made it hard to find a time to talk. And there was so much to ask him, she felt she could never really know where he was. Just as he didn't know where she was.

'I'm sorry. It's just I feel like you're slipping away from me, sometimes,' he said, after a pause.

'Don't say that,' Tess told him. 'It's just – I feel like a fraud. I don't feel like I'm –'

She glanced up at the picture of Jane Austen, which hung in silent splendour by the door, and caught sight of herself in the mirror, which made her stop in her tracks, biscuit dangling from her fingers, halfway to her mouth. Dress it up however you like, it was the plain truth that Peter would not love her were he to see her now. Her hair needed washing, and was kept in place with a kirby grip and a scruffy ponytail. She was wearing an old, scraggy pair of jeans and an outsized and unloveable but very warm navy cardigan that she had found in the cupboard underneath the stairs when she moved in. Her pale face was free of any make-up, her eyes had dark circles underneath them. Her nails were bitten and uneven.

She wanted to explain, to tell him she wasn't the girl he had known over the summer. She couldn't remember that girl, the one who danced through cobbled piazzas in the moonlight and lay on sunny floorboards while someone kissed her hair, stroked her breasts, her soft, sunkissed skin. Who on earth was that girl, and where had she gone? She stared at her reflection, horror creeping across her face.

'You're still the same to me,' Peter said, a note of impatience detectable in his tone, even through the echo on the line all the way from California. 'Still the same beautiful girl . . .' He trailed off. 'I kinda really miss you,' he said.

Tess could feel herself melting. 'Really?' she said, pleasure creeping into her voice.

'Yes, of course,' he said.

'You're in San Francisco!' she said. 'You're having a whale of a time. I don't believe you.'

'That's not true,' he said, laughing. 'I call you in the morning, I work all goddamn day, I walk back to the apartment, and I email you.'

'So you're not enjoying it at all?' she said sceptically. 'You didn't like the day in the vineyard last week? Or the weekend in Big Sur? How strange, because I don't believe you.'

'Well . . .' She could hear a smile in his voice. 'I just wish you were here with me, that's all.'

She sighed. 'Oh, Peter, Peter. You honestly wouldn't say that if you could see me now.'

'I honestly would,' Peter said. They were silent for a moment. 'So you'll book the ticket?'

'I'll book the ticket – or you know, you could always come here.'

As she said it she knew it wouldn't happen – Peter striding down the high street in his chinos and expensive sunglasses, his handsome face biscuit-tanned, to be confronted by Mrs Store, or Mick Hopkins, or someone. He would think it all a joke – he thought where she lived was a joke.

'To the British toy town? Where Winnie the Pooh lives? Sure, after Christmas maybe,' he said, trying to sound enthusiastic, and she didn't push it, but a sinking feeling washed over her.

'Where's Liz?' He changed the subject.

'She's away on a hen weekend,' said Tess.

'A what?' She could hear him whispering under his breath. 'Just a beer. Thanks a lot.'

'A bachelorette party,' Tess said, summoning up her *Sex and the City* lexicography. 'They're in a cottage in the countryside.'

'Doesn't she live in a cottage in the countryside?'

'Well, yeah,' Tess said. 'If I was her I'd be pissed off about it.'

'How's it going?'

Liz had moved in nearly a month ago now, and so far it was going extremely well. She was incredibly good-natured, kept herself to herself, didn't want to be best friends and do everything together and – Tess hated to say it, but was forced to privately admit it – was more the kind of girl with whom you'd expect to share a cottage like this. She was what Diana would call a Good Sort. She was quite hearty. She owned wellington boots, she listened to Radio 4, she sang loudly in the shower, she volunteered at the local primary school, she belonged to Amnesty International and spent a lot of time trying to open up a chapter in Langford. She never lounged on the sofa. She didn't drink wine out of the bottle, or order foie gras through the post, or have incredibly loud sex. She only appeared outside her bedroom in pyjamas and a towelling robe, and would have reared back in horror had Tess loaned or given her anything as frivolous as a Chinese silk dressing gown.

And no, she never messed up the kitchen making mojitos, and she never forced Tess to do karaoke, or made her laugh so much that wine came out of her nose, but it was fine. It was different, that was all.

'It's going really well,' Tess said truthfully. 'But I've got no one to go out with.'

'I don't believe that,' he said. 'What does a nice girl like you do on a Friday night in the English countryside?'

Tess glanced at the sofa, at the near-empty biscuit packet, the TV listings guide, the new copy of the John Lewis catalogue that had arrived that morning and which she had been looking forward to flicking through. 'Oh,' she said. 'Nothing much.'

'No drinks for you at an ole luvverly British pub?' said Pete lightly. His English accent was awful.

'Afraid not,' said Tess, wondering what he would make of the Feathers, and quailing at the thought.

'No programmes about the Queen?' There was rustling in the background, she could tell he was distracted.

'No,' said Tess. 'No drinks at a British pub. No programmes about the Queen, or chimney sweeps wearing fingerless gloves and talking like Guy Ritchie. No women wearing bonnets and saying, "Good day, sir," and no people openly weeping in the street about Princess Diana, either.'

'None at all?' said Peter.

'None at all.'

'That sounds awful.'

'It's OK,' said Tess. 'I'll manage.'

'What about Adam?'

Tess was reaching for another biscuit. 'What?'

'Adam – you heard from him yet?'

'No,' Tess said. 'Not a word.'

'Man, that's weird.'

'It is,' said Tess. 'I hope he's OK. I hope he's sorting himself out.'

She didn't really know what she meant when she said that. She didn't know where he was, what he was going through, how he was. She just knew that the person who had wrecked her flat and driven Francesca nearly to the brink, and then out of town, was not the Adam she remembered. She screwed up her eyes, trying to remember another Adam, the one she thought she knew, who'd helped her find the cottage, who'd matched her and a bunch of Swedes drink for drink in a strange pub in London, who'd dipped her in front of Will and Ticky and called her 'sweetums'. It had been nearly three months now since he'd taken off, and she honestly didn't know when she'd see him again. Perhaps he would never come back.

When she had said goodbye a few minutes later, Tess put the phone down and, gritting her teeth, turned and stared into the mirror, gazing unflinchingly at what she saw.

She realized, suddenly and with blinding clarity, that with Peter and her it was Rome at Christmas or nothing. She tried to imagine leaving here, and it was much easier than she'd thought; in the mirror, her reflection winced.

'Right,' she said, glancing up at Jane Austen. It was only eight thirty, it was Friday, and she really couldn't face another weekend of mouldering away in her cottage again. She wrapped a pink woollen scarf around her neck and tying her coat at the waist she picked up her bag, sliding a couple of sheets of paper into it, and shut the door behind her, stepping out onto the street.

It was late November, and the bitter smell of bonfires and the faint trace of fireworks still hung in the damp air. The watery mist that had descended on the town in October was still there, muffling everything; Tess's shoes echoed on the cobbled ground as she turned onto the deserted high street, walking swiftly, feeling the bite of the cold as she went. She turned into the courtyard of the Feathers, and pushed the door to the pub open, taking a deep breath as she did so.

'Hi there, Mick,' she said casually, as though it was usual for her to go for a drink by herself. She pulled up a stool at the bar, just as she'd done all those months ago, the night she first met Francesca, when spring was in the air and she'd just got back.

'Evening, Tess,' said a deep voice.

'Oh, sorry, Suggs,' Tess said, wrong-footed. She blushed. 'Sorry.'

'No worries. What can I get you?' Suggs rubbed his hands together.

'Um – pint of Butcombe's,' said Tess, and she got out her book. 'Thanks a lot.'

She opened her book – she was rereading *I, Claudius* – and took a sip of her drink, pretending it was normal she was here, that there was nothing unusual about it. She peeked a look around her, and saw that, apart from a table of people having a birthday dinner, it was quiet tonight. A couple of men drinking by themselves at a table, a couple having food in a booth by the window, and a youngish man up at the bar along from her, reading the paper.

'How've you been?' said Suggs, putting her pint in front of her. 'How's Liz getting along?'

'She's great,' said Tess. 'She's away this weekend, though. So I'm all on my own.'

'Oh, really,' said Suggs, leering suggestively over the bar. 'Come up and see me sometime, Tessa.'

'Right,' said Tess. 'Definitely.'

'I totally would, you know,' Suggs said, giggling. 'Just so you know.'

'How is Emma, by the way?' Tess asked pertly, smiling.

From the other side of the bar, nubile young Kirsty the barmaid looked sharply at Tess. Suggs said awkwardly, 'Er, she's fine, fine.' He rubbed the back of his neck. 'Ah, fine.' He lowered his voice. 'Actually, we split up.'

'Oh, I'm sorry.'

'Don't be,' he said, sneaking a look at Kirsty. 'There were Reasons, you know.'

'Right,' said Tess, nodding.

'And she found mould in my socks. A whole pile of them, by the door. I've been letting the washing get a bit out of control, since Adam went away.'

'Stop!' Tess cried. 'Jeez, that's horrible.'

'I know,' said Suggs. 'No wonder he left me.'

'You heard from him lately?' Tess asked, taking a sip of her drink.

'No,' said Suggs. 'Not really. He rang me a couple of weeks ago, but that was it.'

'He rang you? Where was he?'

'Well, he didn't say,' Suggs said, lowering his voice. 'I presume he's still in Morocco, have you heard anything else?'

Morocco? Tess didn't want to say, *I didn't know he was in Morocco, actually.* 'No, I haven't heard anything,' she said. 'How long was he planning to spend there, do you know?'

'Walking the Atlas mountains, how long does that take?' Suggs held up his index finger. 'Just a minute, my love.' He turned to serve someone the other side of the bar, and Tess glanced, unseeing, down at her book.

'Hello, Tess,' said a voice behind her. She looked round to see Diana Sayers leaning on the bar next to her.

'What a nice surprise,' Tess said, pleased. She patted Diana on the arm. 'I haven't seen you for a long long time.'

Diana smiled briefly back at her. 'That's quite true. How've you been?'

Tess shook her head. 'I'm fine, thanks,' she said. 'Are you eating?'

Diana jerked her thumb behind her. 'Richard and I came out for a meal,' she said, and Tess realized they were the couple seated by the window. She looked over at Diana's husband Richard, who was rarely seen out and about. 'He's just back from a trip, so we thought we'd treat ourselves.'

It was odd, seeing Diana: she represented the early summer and that heady yet awful week in Rome so clearly for Tess, and since Mrs Mortmain had died and the new term had begun, Tess hadn't seen her. She had thought of her several times, of her gruff kindness, her calm demeanour during the storm, the way she had supported Adam, the son of her best friend. Tess looked over to the window again. 'It's strange,' she said frankly. 'Last time I saw you, I was where you were – I opened the window, at the wake –' Diana was looking blank, so she said hurriedly, as though it was embarrassing, 'After the funeral, Leonora Mortmain's funeral. I saw you all, in the sitting room of Leda House, drinking sherry.'

'My God,' Diana said, catching Suggs's eye. 'Has it been that long. That was a grim gathering, I can tell you.' She brushed something imaginary off her sleek grey fringe.

'I can imagine,' Tess said, watching her.

'Have you heard from Adam? Is he still in Morocco?'

'Well, I don't know –' Tess began, and was glad when Suggs appeared.

'Yes, my dear,' he said.

'Two more glasses of the Pinot Grigio, please. Small this time.' Diana turned to Tess. 'There's something in that wine. Don't know what it is, but it's quite *strong*. Do you want anything, Tess, dear?'

'I'm fine, thanks.'

'You meeting someone?'

'No,' said Tess. 'Just popped in for a drink.'

'How nice,' said Diana.

'Well,' said Tess. 'Seemed like the sensible thing to do.

I can't stay in another night eating so many biscuits my stomach swells up like a drum.'

'Anyway,' said Diana, wisely ignoring this conversational offering, 'I don't know where he is or what he's doing. I'm sure he's fine, I'd just like to know. You know?' Her brow wrinkled, and she pushed her lip out. 'Silly boy. He never did know what was best for him.' She patted Tess on the arm. 'He should have snapped you up all those years ago when he had the chance, instead of messing you around and driving you off to London.' Tess's eyes widened. 'Right, I have had too much to drink. I should mind my own bloody business.'

'I don't think he'd agree with you about that,' Tess said, smiling and shaking her head. 'And for what it's worth, I don't, either. We never thought that, it's that everyone else here did in this ridiculous town.'

'Rubbish,' said Diana, as Suggs appeared with the wine. Then, 'Do you really think that?'

'I can see why he needed to get away from here,' Tess said. She thought of the lease, the letter on the fridge which she still hadn't answered. Diana put the two glasses back on the bar.

'Need a hand, dear?' called a quiet voice from the back, and Diana batted the request away fiercely with her hand.

'Do be quiet, Richard,' she called in his direction. 'What do you mean?' she said to Tess. 'It's not ridiculous here.'

'I'm not saying –' Tess said, scared by her expression. Diana's eyes were cold. 'I'm not saying it's ridiculous for you. I'm just saying . . . sometimes – it's like a theme park. Oh, a toy town.' She thought of Peter, of their conversation earlier. 'You know. The tea towels, the tourists, the – all that stuff.'

'Well, shame on you, Tessa,' Diana said, and Tess leaned back, so frosty was her tone. 'There may be a gift shop, and there may be tourists, but it's still a proper town. A place where people live.'

'I know that,' said Tess. 'But sometimes – I can't stand it. Everyone in everyone else's business. Getting things wrong most of the time, too.' She was thinking of Adam and Philippa, and how no one had known anything.

'I know,' said Diana, her grey eyes sad, as if she understood. 'But this is a community. We support each other. They'd support you, if you let them. There are people here whose grandfathers' names are on the war memorial, young people who can't afford to buy a house here because of the second-home owners, people who remember the water meadows before all of this happened. So remember that,' she said. 'Everyone comes from somewhere, and lots of people come from here and are proud of it. It's not a theme park to them.' She took a deep breath. 'Real life isn't about sparkly fantasies and new things, you know. Real life is hard work, but it's what you have in the long term, and occasionally you treat yourself to a cake from the deli and a nice Cath Kidston tea towel and that's how you find the balance.'

Tess stared at her, not knowing what to say. She looked around the pub; Suggs was chatting to the man sitting by himself at the bar, and she saw it was Guy Phelps. Had they heard? Did they agree if they had? She closed her eyes, almost in pain, and Diana shrugged her shoulders. 'Gosh,' she said. 'I didn't mean to say all of that, Tess. I'm sorry.'

'It's fine,' Tess said. She felt as if a heavy mist was clearing. She shook her head. 'Honestly.'

'Too much wine. That's what it is. It's none of my business to say it to you, dear. I meant to say it to Adam, before he left. For the last ten years, probably.' Diana smiled bitterly. 'I've taken it out on you instead, haven't I?'

'It's fine, though,' Tess said, a bit shakily. 'You're probably right.'

'It's not fine,' Diana said. 'It's true, though,' she added, in her blunt way. 'I am being unforgivably rude, I'm afraid, and I like you. Always have since you were eight and you asked

402

the Mayor at the village fete why he was so fat.' Tess laughed, astonished. 'I'm glad you're staying here.'

Tess thought of Peter; then she thought of the book of poems on the bureau at home and the contract for work she still hadn't signed, and the mist, the smoky smell of approaching winter out in the dark streets tonight. She sipped her drink and squeezed Diana's hand. 'You're right.'

Peter would be in a bar somewhere, in San Francisco: she'd never been, so she couldn't imagine it, the way she could if he were in Rome. If he were in Rome he'd be in the Piazza Navona with a beer, his dark, beautiful eyes resting on the waitress, flickering across the long, beautiful piazza, the sound of laughter and water from the fountains in the background, his elegant brown fingers playing with a sachet of sugar . . . She could picture him in Rome, they seemed to go together. She couldn't picture him in San Francisco. In a bar too, perhaps, playing pool, slapping some buddies on the back? No, Peter didn't like pool – or did he? She didn't know. So much she didn't know . . . Tess stared at Diana, colour returning to her face.

'You're right,' she said again.

'Damned right I am,' said Diana, picking up her glasses of wine again. 'See you later, m'dear.'

Tess drained her drink and walked to the noticeboard, her eye caught by something. On the worn, dry cork, next to an advert for yoga classes in the community centre and another for Carolyn Tey's flower-arranging course, was a pink flyer for Knick-Knacks, Jacquetta Meluish's shop. Tess gazed at it.

PRETTY THINGS & FRIPPERIES & GIFT IDEAS
OR JUST TREAT YOURSELF

Then she turned, clutching her book and her bag, and walked out into the night. It would be nice to say the mist outside had cleared too, but it hadn't. Still, she walked home, smiling. She tidied up a bit, she folded the funeral service sheet into her book of Catullus's poems, stacking it next to the Bible and a few other books. She would work it out, she knew it. And then she went to bed where she slept soundly, for the first time in a long while.

CHAPTER THIRTY-EIGHT

'Come on, Sandy,' Tess said, a pleading note in her voice. 'You don't need to do that here, you can do it when we get to the villa, it's really not that far away . . .'

'I'm just going to tie the laces properly *now*,' Sandy said. 'Because I know it's all very well preserved, but the grass and everything will be terribly muddy, and I don't want to get these shoes wet, Tess, dear.' She tugged at her spotless hiking boots. From inside the minibus, Brian the driver sighed loudly.

Tess stamped her feet, hugging herself in the bitter cold air. 'You can do it on the minibus,' she said firmly. She patted Sandy on the arm, propelling her gently up the steps, and nodded apologetically at Brian. 'Right, everyone. Ready?'

'I've been ready for forty minutes,' said Brian grimly. 'Where to?'

'Langford Regis,' said Tess sternly. 'You know that.'

'Just checking,' Brian said, and eased the minivan into gear. 'Just making sure.'

'Can you turn the heating on?' said Sherry, as the creaking old vehicle juddered out of the gates of Langford College and down the high street. In the back row, like the cool kids from school, Gerald the company director, resplendent in tweed, and Tom the usually mute librettist, nodded.

'Bloody freezing,' said Gerald briefly. 'Gosh.'

'I have *absolutely* no idea why you would have picked this day to go on a trip like this,' Tom said, patting the cream cashmere scarf at his neck.

'Because we get it to ourselves and we can have a private tour,' said Tess. 'I told you to wrap up warm, Tom. There are spare jumpers up here,' she said, pointing to the overhead shelves. 'You'll just have to put one on if you get too cold.'

They were right, though: it was a bitterly cold day in early December, when it hurt to breathe, and the air caught at the back of the nostrils and throat. Frost gripped the yew trees in the churchyard as they drove past; along the road the hanging baskets outside the Feathers were a forlorn sight, black and covered in ice. Tess patted her bag as if reassuring herself that she had everything: notes, water, mobile phone and, of course, a First Aid kit. She didn't want to get a reputation for being the killer of old ladies. She stared out of the window. It was a lovely day for a drive, cold though it was; the air was clear and the sky was ice-blue sharp.

'We will be back in time for tea, won't we, dear,' said Sherry.

Jemima looked alarmed. 'I have to pick Gideon up at three,' she said. 'And Maisie has a flute lesson at three thirty. I'm afraid I really have to be back by two thirty,' she said, her voice rising slightly hysterically, as only the English middle-class woman can make it. 'Tess?'

'We'll be back well before then,' Tess said patiently, for the third time. 'Don't worry.'

'I want to get back early too. 'Cause the Christmas lights are being switched on in Thornham tonight and I don't want to miss it,' Sherry told Jemima.

'Well, the children are *so* excited about ours.' Jemima smiled dampeningly, and went back to reading her book.

'Who's switching them on?' Gerald demanded from the back. 'We had Dale Winton in Chislehurst last year. Funny chap. Very funny.'

'Actually, we've got Frank Roberts this year,' Sherry told him proudly.

'Who's that?' asked Tom.

'Frank Roberts, the rugby player?' Sherry said. 'Played for Bath for years. Runs a cab company now.'

'I've never heard of him,' Jemima said coldly, looking up from her book.

'I have,' said Gerald. 'Prop, am I right?'

'You're right,' said Sherry. 'Lives locally, ever such a nice man. So yes, we've got him. Who's doing Langford?'

'Look,' Tess said, tapping the window as the bus slowed down for the traffic lights at the pedestrian crossing. 'As if by magic.'

She pointed out of the window at a figure taping a poster to a wooden telegraph pole. It was Jan Allingham, chatting gaily to some unseen figure while she wrestled with curls of sellotape attached to her fingers. She turned at the sound of the bus and, catching sight of Tess in the window, waved wildly, sticking the sellotape together.

'Are you coming tomorrow?' she called, her voice faint through the glass. 'Look!'

In the doorway of the health-food shop Tess saw her companion, Diana Sayers, leaning against the shut door, watching her and chatting back. She saw Tess in the window of the bus, squinted to recognize her, and then smiled back. She mouthed something. Tess couldn't make out what she was saying, but she waved back at her, smiling.

'So yours is tomorrow, then?' said Sherry with relief. 'That's good. Avoid a clash. Who is it?'

'Martin Riviere,' Tess said, pointing at the crumpled poster in Jan's hand. 'Again.' Jemima looked crushed.

Martin Riviere (real name: Martin Trowton) was a fairly ancient quiz show presenter, a local boy made good who had retired to a big house in the valley below Langford ten years ago, since which time – as the only celebrity in the near vicinity – he had been prevailed upon to open the church fete in Langford twice, in Thornham once, the summer fete at Langford Primary twice, made a cameo appearance at the Organ Fund Fundraising Spectacular as the Angel Gabriel, and switched on the lights in Langford now three times.

'Oh, not again,' said Sherry, with all the bitchiness of the local rival. 'How *boring.*'

Along the high street, signs that Christmas was coming were everywhere. The lights were hung across the street, ready for tomorrow's ceremony. The window of Knick-Knacks was filled with brown parcels tied with beautiful red velvet ribbons; Jen's Deli had a tasteful plethora of panettone and Vacherin cheeses; but the rest of the town had no such scruples and silver-fringed signs saying '*Merry Christmas!*' and large plastic cartoons of Santa, small pearlescent-coloured Christmas trees and pink, green, red and purple baubles and strings of fake glass beads hung in every other shop window, and every house in town. Even Tess and Liz had been involved in their own Christmas tree decorative tussle – Tess being very much of the 'more is more' mind-set when it came to tinsel and orna-ments, and Liz, who was of the same persuasion as her boss Jen, rearing her hands up in horror every time she saw a bit of tinsel. Still, they had found agreement and their tree stood proudly in the window, the bureau having been moved out of the way so it could take pride of place in their sitting room, along with every other house in town. Almost every house.

As the minibus moved off again, Tess glanced towards Leda House, where the window boxes, like the rest of the facade, were empty, blank and a little dirty. She gazed at the shut-tered window.

Lynda clutched Sandy's hand. 'It's freezing in here,' she said, shivering.

'I know, but it's not a long drive,' Tess told her patiently. 'We'll be there in twenty minutes or so. And it really is a wonderful place, if you haven't been there before. The best-preserved mosaics in – oh, my God.' Her jaw dropped. 'Brian – stop! Stop the bus!'

The front door to Leda House was open – it was never open. She could see just inside, into the hallway; the ceiling lampshade swung in the breeze.

'Can you stop, please, Brian?' Tess called, her voice louder than she'd intended.

'What?' Brian called.

'Just pull over, quickly,' Tess said. 'I just need to see something –'

Brian screeched to a halt, as the members of the Langford College A level course all tipped over to the left, and Gerald and Tom clutched each other, to stop themselves falling to the floor.

'Don't be long,' Brian said. Tess shot him a look as the door swung open and she climbed down the steps. She hopped across the road and, uncertainty striking her only then, paused at the front gate and looked inside.

No one had been seen in Leda House since the funeral. Jean Forbes had received a nice pension and she and her husband had immediately shut the house up and left for a lengthy – and well-deserved – cruise. The windows were shuttered; the furniture covered in dust sheets. Peering into the darkened hall, Tess called out, 'Hello?'

The rumbling sound of the minibus's engine behind her was distracting. She advanced, little by little, so that she was standing on the threshold.

'Adam?' she called into the gloom. As her eyes adjusted to the light, she could make out a beautiful, threadbare wine-red carpet, and on the walls row upon row of prints, on exact lines, engravings of classical ruins, of statues, pillars, temples, all in black and white. The long hallway had four white doors, two on each side; they were firmly shut, and the only remaining light came from another door, out to the big garden, with its immaculate lawn that she had glimpsed only once, when as a child she had climbed on Adam's shoulders to peer over the thick stone wall. Tess slowly stepped further forward. She was standing on the carpet now, in the house.

Suddenly she heard footsteps, a kind of scuffling, shuffling noise, somewhere in the house. She jumped, and breathed out, in a gasp.

'Adam?' she said, more loudly, and moved to the staircase at the back of the hallway, looking up. She ran up the steps, peering onto the landing, around to the first floor, but all the doors there were shut, and there was no answer, no sign of anyone. And the noise had come from downstairs, she was sure . . . Shaken, Tess came down the stairs again, retreating swiftly towards the front door. She peered back out onto the street, but Diana and Jan had disappeared. Perhaps the door had just blown open; there was no one there. Her fingers itched to open the sitting-room door, and she wrapped her hand round the smooth black doorknob. But she couldn't open it, something inside her stopped her. There was no one there, and this was ridiculous. She shut the heavy front door carefully behind her and turned back to the van, where the members of her class were watching her expectantly, their faces pressed against the windows.

'Sorry,' she called, crossing the road again and hopping on board once more. 'Sorry, stupid of me. Must be a gardener or something. Thought someone was back in there.'

'Or a ghost,' Jemima said, clutching her hand to her throat. 'Jacquetta – you know Jacquetta Meluish? She's my neighbour. She said her friend Carolyn said there were *ghosts* there . . .'

She looked around momentously at the others.

'Ooh,' Sherry whispered.

Brian nodded, unimpressed, and jerked his head, motioning for Tess to sit down, which she did. She shivered as the bus drove off again, glancing back once at the house, still shuttered up, as though its eyes were closed.

* * *

410

'It was really weird,' Tess said, that evening, hovering over her flatmate. 'I got the feeling someone was there. I really thought there was. But it was nothing.'

'Perhaps it was a *ghost*.' Liz turned around from the hob, and licked one of her fingers. 'Perhaps it was Leonora's ghost. How spooky.'

'That's what Jemima said,' said Tess uncertainly. 'But I highly doubt it. I'm sure it wasn't that at all. It was just – weird.'

'Well,' said Liz reasonably. 'He has to come back some time, doesn't he? Adam, I mean.' She paused, and then shook her head and said, 'Anyway, let's get these apples started. We can put them in the fridge, for tomorrow. Why don't you be in charge of dipping?'

'Sure,' said Tess, feeling like a five-year-old, but comforted by Liz's soothing voice.

'Here, have a lolly stick,' said Liz. 'Be careful before you dip them in, though. The sugar's really hot.'

'OK,' said Tess meekly. She glanced at Liz quickly. Francesca had never made toffee apples. She, Tess, had never got back from a long day at work to find Francesca putting the finishing touches to a stew 'to have later'. Nor had she ever found Francesca ironing her sheets, 'because I was doing mine and I thought I might as well do yours at the same time.' Francesca had bought some very expensive lavender linen spray in a cut-glass bottle which was never used. That was as close as she'd got to ironing, in the five months they'd lived together.

Tess paused, holding her apple over the golden, bubbling sugar. She wondered where Francesca was now. She had to call her again, it had been weeks since they'd spoken. Of course, she didn't *desperately* miss her, it was just . . .

'Tess!' Liz cried sharply, but it was too late. Tess dropped her apple. It fell into the molten sugar with a resounding *plop*. The girls both leapt back, but not far enough to avoid a few small drops of boiling sugar hitting Liz's bare forearm. She howled.

'Shit!' she said, composure gone. 'That really hurts.'

'God, I'm so sorry!' Tess cried. 'Oh, my God! Are you hurt?'

'No, I'll be fine,' said Liz. She patted her arm. 'Just stings. Just stings! Er,' she said, looking round at Tess. 'Why don't you go into the sitting room and relax? I'll just finish off here and then we can start supper. Sound OK?'

'Sure,' said Tess gravely, smothering a smile. 'Will do. Let me know if you need any help.'

She went into the sitting room and sat on the sofa, looking at the tree with its twinkling white lights, the little stucco angel on the top that Liz had found at the church Christmas bazaar the previous week. Christmas was almost three weeks away, and she wasn't feeling Christmassy at all, yet.

She thought back to the previous year and the flat in Balham, and how she and Meena had bought their tree from the dodgy man in the corner shop who also sold them illegal fireworks. They had gone after the pub, dragged it down the street, narrowly avoiding dog shit, and when it was back in the crowded, cold sitting room, they had lovingly festooned it with red, green and gold tinsel, some plastic lamps left over from Diwali, some gold bangles Tess had bought in Accessorize and a feather fascinator that Meena had worn to a wedding the previous summer perched on top of the tree. They had sat in silence, their arms round each other, drinking wine, and then Tess had gone to bed and cried all night: for all it was two months since she'd split up with Will, it was only that night she really realized it was over. She was leaving London, and she was moving away.

Tess shifted on the sofa, tucking her feet under her and gazing at the tree again. It was coming up for a year, now, since she'd moved back. What did she miss about London? Meena, definitely. The flat, with the bed with the loose spring that dug into her back, and the dog next door that howled in the night? No. Fair View, the optimistically named school where she'd taught? No. And yet – though it was unwelcome, Tess's mind flashed back to earlier that day, as the Langford

412

college A level course poked around the ruins of the villa. Gerald, looking at his watch, had said, 'Can't believe this place got a Lottery grant. Bloody ridiculous.'

'These are the best mosaics we have from Roman Britain,' Tess had pointed out to him, stamping her feet in the cold, working off some of her aggression.

'Yup, but I don't believe in preservation like this,' said Gerald casually. 'If this Roman johnny's place wasn't meant to survive, it wasn't meant to survive. Much better to spend the money on widening the road here. Bloody ridiculous an A-road only has one lane on the busiest stretch.'

'I agree with you about that, Gerald,' said Lynda. 'It should never have taken us an hour to get here. It's ridiculous. Now we'll be late getting back, too. I don't know what they're thinking.'

What who are thinking? Tess wanted desperately to ask, but she didn't want to get into it and so, regretfully, said nothing, but once again the thought occurred to her: she loved teaching Classics, loved helping these people learn new things, but God, there was no satisfaction in it, compared to how it used to be. When you could interest a bored fourteen-year-old in how the Romans conquered every people around them, from Turkey to the most savage British tribes, or how the Greeks invented the Olympics, or how the general in the first Iraq war used the battle strategies written down by the ancient historian Xenophon because, distressingly, history always repeats itself, then – *then* you felt you were teaching people something. When you were listening to an idiot like Gerald Mottram talk about how there should be more roads built and you were actually having to pay attention to what he said . . . well, that was a silly job.

'Penny for them?' Liz called from the kitchen. Tess sighed.

'Nothing interesting. Do you want a glass of wine?'

'Oh, I won't, thanks,' said Liz. 'Want to keep myself fresh, you know.'

Tess carried on staring into space. 'What's the date tomorrow?' she said, suddenly.

'Er . . .' Liz licked some sugar off her fingers. 'The seventh of December.'

Tess sat up. 'That's tomorrow?'

'Yep,' said Liz. 'Christmas nearly here. Why, what's special about the seventh?'

'Nothing,' Tess said. 'It's someone's birthday. That's all.'

CHAPTER THIRTY-NINE

It was a bright, clear afternoon. There was a haze on the fields, a shimmering quality that was deceptively like summer; the grass was golden, and the dark green-black of the yew trees in the churchyard framed the view down across the valley.

St Mary's was an old church, the oldest building in the town. It sat behind the high street, looking out over the countryside, its small but perfectly proportioned stone walls mellowed over the centuries into a golden-grey hue. On this crisp, cold day, there was no one around, save Tess. She closed the gate behind her and walked briskly up the path; the faint scent of eucalyptus in her nose as she passed the porch which was festooned with boughs of pine for Christmas.

She turned into the churchyard which stretched out behind the building, looking out over the hills, and picked her way through the graves as the rooks called loudly in the trees. The same family names, Taylors, Frobishers, Edwards, repeated over and over again, the lichen-covered stones listing slightly, as if they were slumbering in the frosty, ice-blue grass. The view was beautiful. Here would be a pretty good place, she thought, to spend eternity.

At the edge of the graveyard she stopped, holding in her

hands a little poinsettia plant she'd bought from the flower shop. She had found the grave she was looking for.

Philippa Smith
Beloved mother of Adam
7th December 1943–9th April 1995

Someone had recently cut the grass and a wreath already lay there; Tess looked at it, not giving it much thought, and gently put her plant down on the smooth turf. It was so quiet. She could hear a rook calling, the sound of a car on the road down towards the water meadows, and that was it. The sunlight filtered through the bare trees where the birds had built nests, casting a hazy light over the graves. She took a deep breath.

'Happy birthday, Philippa,' she said.

She looked again more closely at the wreath, realizing it was brand new. Philippa had been much loved; it wasn't that strange, but this wreath was beautiful; lush, glossy ivy leaves and white lilies, shot through with red beads of holly berries and a card resting on top, in handwriting she didn't recognize.

Always my beloved mum. I miss you every day. Adam xx

Tess stared at the card, suddenly hot even in the chill, but then she realized he must have paid someone to leave the wreath there. It wasn't Adam's handwriting, it was a stranger's, and she should just calm down. She closed her eyes and thought of Philippa. Funny to think she would be sixty-five today – she was older than Tess's mother, and yet she had always seemed younger, younger than most of her parents' generation. Perhaps it was her attitude. Where had it come from? Tess breathed in, thinking of how well she still remembered Philippa – her bouncing, curly hair, her ready, wide smile, her penchant for terracotta-coloured clothing, straw bags, wide skirts with deep pockets into which she was continually thrusting her hands enthusiastically, her terrible obsession with tagines, joss sticks, and mangoes. She loved

416

mangoes – she was always serving them up when they went round for tea, and Tess and Stephanie hated them. She gave a little chuckle. Perhaps she should eat a mango, as a birthday tribute to her and to her son.

'Tess?' said a voice right behind her. Tess screamed and jumped half out of her skin, clutching onto the gravestone for support. She turned around.

'Adam?' she said. A silhouetted figure, black against the bright sunlight, was standing behind her holding something. She screwed up her eyes. 'Oh, my God,' she said. 'Adam! It's really you, isn't it? Oh my bloody God.'

'Not very pious language for a churchyard, Tess,' the figure said, walking towards her. 'You're by my mother's grave. Do you mind not swearing like a navvy and using her headstone as an armrest?'

It was Adam. He was wearing a long grey coat; he seemed to be taller. His face was weatherbeaten and tanned, laughter lines etched in white at the corners of his eyes. She stood up straight, laughing, and ran towards him.

'Oh, my God!' she cried again, hugging him hard. 'You're back!'

He hugged her too, squeezing her tight. 'It's good to see you, T,' he said, and the sound of his voice was overwhelming. She realized how much she'd missed him. 'It's bloody good to see you.'

She drew back, smiling wide. 'Adam Smith.'

'You remembered too,' he said, looking at her, and then at his mother's grave. 'Bless you. You remembered.'

'Of course I did,' she replied, hugging him tight once again. 'Welcome back.'

He was the same old Adam, yet he was different. More grown-up. Distant, perhaps. He was carrying some rosehip stems and holly, wrapped carefully with twine, and a battered flask of coffee.

'They were the only things growing in the garden at Leda House,' he said, after he'd laid them gingerly down on the grave and they had stood in silence, lost in their own thoughts, for another moment. 'And she loved roses.' They retreated to the low wall at the edge of the churchyard, and Adam poured out a cup of coffee, handing it to Tess, and taking a swig out of the flask himself. They both fell silent once more.

Eventually, Tess said, 'So. Where have you been?'

He smiled. 'I was in Morocco.'

'That much I gathered,' Tess said.

'Sorry I wasn't in touch,' Adam said frankly. 'I didn't really know where I was going. I just knew I needed to . . . get away. It wasn't till I was far away I realized how bad it had got. How – bad I felt.'

'Really?' she said.

He nodded. 'The whole thing. Leonora having her stroke. Having to face up to it all so suddenly. Us rowing. I'm sorry.' Adam spoke softly, staring down at the ground, holding the flask between his legs. 'Then – her dying. And all of that. Waiting for the damn body to come home.' He breathed in as if it hurt, and closed his eyes, drawing himself up a little. 'All at the same time. Man. The funeral – that funeral.' His eyes lifted, to the Mortmain tombs by the side of the church, and the recently dug grave. 'And – do you remember how hot it was? Those nights. I couldn't sleep. I couldn't damn well sleep. No matter what I did, no matter how much I tried to tire myself out.'

There was a silence.

'Have you heard from her?' he said quietly.

'Francesca? We've spoken a couple of times. I had an email last week. She's OK.'

'Have you seen her? Is she –'

'She's OK,' said Tess.

He nodded, as though he understood. 'I have to talk to her.' Tess also nodded briefly. 'I treated her so badly. That last night, before I left. We totally lost it with each other. Took everything out on each other.' He closed his eyes again for a moment.

'What happened?' Tess said softly.

He looked warily at her. 'It was all very dramatic, but when I look back on it it was stupid. She hit me.'

'Did she?' Tess didn't entirely blame her. 'Hard?'

'Pretty hard.' He shook his head. 'She gave me a few home truths. Then I threw your cake stand on the floor,' he said. 'I was furious. Sorry, darling. I know how much you loved it.'

'Don't worry,' Tess said, the flicker of a smile crossing her lips. 'She gave me a few home truths too. She was –'

'– right,' they both said, in unison.

'You treated her badly,' Tess said. It was a statement.

'Yes,' he said. 'But not because I didn't like her. And I've treated a lot of people badly.' He took another swig of the coffee. 'God, this is maudlin. Enough. T, tell me how you've been. What's happened with Peter?'

She stared at him in astonishment. 'Adam, we're in a grave-yard, it's your mother's birthday, you've just got back from nearly four months away, we're allowed to be maudlin. What on earth are you talking about?'

Adam stared back at her, and then gave a shout of laughter. 'You're right.'

'Course I am,' she said. 'I don't even know where you've been. Tell me.'

'I went to Morocco.'

'Yes, you told me that already,' she said. 'More, please.'

'OK, OK.' He held up his hands, and shuffled along the wall away from her a little, turning so he was facing her. He said, 'Well, I didn't really do anything much. I flew to Spain, got a boat over to North Africa, and then I travelled from town to village, hitch-hiking, you know. I stayed in the Atlas Mountains. In all sorts of different places.' He stopped, and drew breath. 'I didn't know where I was going. It was – great.

Sometimes I'd spend a night with a family in a tiny house, sometimes in some lovely mansion with a courtyard and a fountain. Once I slept in a tent, out on the edge of the desert.'

'Wow,' said Tess, looking ruminatively out over the view. 'That must have been amazing.'

'You'd love it, I kept thinking that,' he said. 'And you know, I kept thinking how much Mum would have loved it, too. She loved the food. Remember those tagines?'

'That's weird, I was thinking about all the things she liked when you arrived,' Tess said. 'How much she loved tagines. Mangoes, and all of that. I wonder who –'

I wonder who she got that from, she was going to say.

The mood had changed. Adam gave her a sideways glance, and then stared ahead again. 'Now it's back to reality, I suppose,' he said. He drained the rest of the coffee, and then fastened the lid on the flask. He cleared his throat. 'So – how have you been? What's been going on here?'

'Well, guess,' said Tess, trying to keep her voice light. 'Not much, really. They're turning on the Christmas lights tonight.'

'Oh,' he said flatly.

'I've got a new flatmate.'

'Who?' He turned to her.

'Liz.'

'Liz? Oh – oh, Liz.' A flash of something, a bit of shame, a pretence of looking cool, crossed his face, and then he smiled, shaking his head. 'Right. She's nice.'

'Yep,' said Tess, not really wanting to say more. 'She's very nice.'

'Bit different from Francesca, I bet.'

'That's oh so true. Very – organized.'

'Hm.' His eyes twinkled. 'Do you remember when Francesca ordered a case of champagne for my birthday, and shook the bottle up as she was opening it because she wanted to know what it was like to be a Formula One winner? God, it went everywhere.' He grinned at the memory.

420

'No, I don't,' said Tess, primly.

'Oh,' he said, trying not to smile. 'Well, you were probably out. Hanging out at the cake shop or chatting to Jan and Diana about sensible socks and where to buy them.'

Tess gasped in outrage. 'I wasn't as bad as all that. Was I?'

'Well, for a bit,' he said. 'Till you went to Rome.'

She nodded, a bit too eagerly. 'Right.'

'You probably needed a bit of downtime, after leaving London.'

'What does that mean?' Tess didn't like the turn the conversation was taking.

'You know, growing your eyebrows all bushy. Wearing those thick cardigans,' said Adam blithely. Tess shook her head in disbelief.

'You really know how to lay on the charm, don't you?'

'It's you,' he said, pushing her gently, his tone contrite. 'I'm only joking. You know – you know I don't mean it.'

She put her arm round him, and patted his back.

'How're you feeling about – about everything?' she asked.

'About the Mortmain situation?' he said, accentuating the words. 'I don't know, T. There's still loads to sort out, I haven't really got my head round a lot of it.'

She squeezed his shoulder. 'What do you have to do first?'

'See people, say hello.'

'Adam –' she said. 'You should know, you're not the most popular person round here at the moment.'

'Right,' he said, flinching a bit. 'Because of what's happening with the water meadows.' He glanced up at the spire of the church, as if to look behind him would be too much. 'I have to decide what to do.'

'They've already started, you know that,' she said. Perhaps he didn't know. Perhaps they'd gone ahead without him. 'People in the town are—'

Adam's jaw was rigid. 'People in the town,' he said, throwing her arm off his shoulder. 'All my life it's been people in the town who've dictated this and that. Who cares what they think?'

'They live here, Adam,' Tess said gently. 'They love it here. It's going to change everything.'

He put his hands on his hips, and stared ahead. 'Well, they knew it was happening. And where were they when Mum got here and no one would look her in the eye, because she was unmarried and pregnant and living alone? Where were they when she died? When—'

'That's not fair.' Tess spoke softly, and rose to stand next to him. She said, 'Remember how Diana helped you clear out the house? How Mick let you stay with him, all those nights when you were too drunk to go back to the cottage? Mum and Dad, they lent you money for the funeral.' Her throat was thick. 'And Ron, oh, I know he's a busybody and a silly old man, but he gave you that bag of clothes, in case you needed stuff. They wanted to help you. You just didn't want them to help you back.'

'Now you're the one who's not being fair,' he said, but in a mild voice. His hands dropped to his sides: 'Oh, T, I don't want to get into all of this again. That's why I went away – I just can't face it . . .' He bowed his head, as if his voice would crack. 'It's this damn inheritance. It's all this.' He jabbed his thumb at the Mortmain tombs. 'I didn't ask for it. I never got to talk to Mum about it, I don't even know how she felt about it. It's like – it's like there's a huge part of her I didn't know, and I loved her so much and she kept it from me.'

'She had her reasons,' said Tess. 'Your mum was a wise woman. She was wonderful. If she didn't tell you, there's a reason. She knew what Leonora was like . . .' She trailed off, tactfully.

'She knew her own mother was a cow, you mean,' Adam said sombrely. 'I keep thinking . . . who was my grandfather? Who was Mum's father? Because he must have been a wonderful man, to offset her.'

422

'Perhaps she changed,' Tess said. 'You don't know.'

'I don't know,' Adam acknowledged. 'But she made it very hard to like her. And she wouldn't tell me anything. I can never like her for that, you know.'

'That's an awful thing to say.'

His eyes were cold. 'Perhaps it is, but when both your parents are dead and you haven't seen your dad's family for decades, and the only family you've got is this – this woman who looks at you with –' his face contorted, and he spoke in a rush – 'with *hate*, Tess, like she thinks you're the lowest of the low because she hated your mother, because having her was so shameful to her she couldn't ever tell anyone she had a family, a daughter and a grandson . . . and you can't do anything to change her mind . . . it's, yeah, it's pretty unnerving.'

'She wasn't very lovable,' said Tess.

'She wasn't, I'm afraid.' Adam nodded. 'All these years I've been, I've been keeping this secret, because I had to, and trying to . . .' He shook his head. 'Trying to meet her halfway. But she gave me nothing. Responded to nothing. Acted like she didn't care. I'd have tea with her twice a year, and she'd berate me for an hour and a half about how I'd let her and the Mortmains down, how I should have gone to university, why didn't I have a job? What was I doing with my life? And then I'd leave, and that'd be it. And I couldn't tell anyone.'

'You couldn't have told me?' Tess said.

'She was desperate for me not to tell anyone. Said they could know when she was dead and that was it.' The corners of Adam's mouth turned up, swiftly, sadly. 'I wanted to talk to you about it. But you know perfectly well, T, we weren't close after that all happened. I treated you abominably badly. I couldn't burden you with anything else. I don't think you'd have listened anyway.'

Tess didn't know what to say. After all these years of getting over him, of losing the friendship that meant so much to her

423

and then finding it was repairable, gradually, of wondering what on earth he was thinking and why he was the way he was, and he had given up all his secrets to her in five minutes. She tugged his arm.

'Look, Adam. I know it's going to be hard, coming back, but you've done the right thing. And you know something? I'm here for you, brother.'

He smiled. 'Thanks.'

'I mean it. You need a friend.' She nodded. 'I'm sorry I wasn't one before. But I'm your friend now. It's going to be OK, all of this. You'll sort it out. It's a fresh start, remember? Not going back to the past.'

Adam nodded. 'You're right,' he said, his voice lightening. 'Now the will's nearly sorted out, and I've cleared my head, I can sort of see the horizon again. I just need to leave the past behind.'

'That's a good thing,' she said fervently.

'Perhaps we both do,' he said. He held out his hand, and she shook it, then he put his arm round her, and pulled her towards him. 'Buy you a drink?' he said. 'If you think I dare show my face in the pub.'

'I'll be with you,' she said. 'Remember, that's a promise.'

'OK,' he said. 'Thanks, T.'

'Just don't sleep with my housemate again, OK?'

'That's also a promise.'

They walked through the graveyard, his arm still around her shoulders. Tess's feet were freezing, she noticed now, a clammy coldness that was almost painful. She stamped her boots on the ground.

'It's beautiful here, I have to say,' Adam said. 'All that time in this totally different landscape, and I'd think of being back here.' He looked behind him, down into the valley. 'All these people who were here before us. They had the same view.'

They turned towards the church, to avoid the Mortmain tombs. 'Do you think you'll change your name?' Tess said.

'No,' said Adam. 'Too weird to do it now. And – it comes with all this stuff. Stuff I don't want.'

They were in front of the church now, in the shadow of the building. Tess stamped her feet again and stopped, in front of a row of graves, fiddling for her gloves in her coat pocket. She stared at the grave in front of her.

'Adam . . .' she said. 'Philip, Adam.'

'What?' Adam was tying his scarf a little tighter. She pointed.

'Philip Edwards. Adam . . .'

And she read:

> In Loving Memory of
> Philip Edwards
> 1924–1943
> ଚ
> He died for his country that we might live in freedom
> Beloved son of Thomas Edwards, vicar of this Parish, and
> Mary Edwards
> ଚ
> Brother of Primula Edwards
> ଚ
> Have I been so long a time with you, and yet hast thou not
> known me, Philip?

They both stared at the stone. There was silence for a full minute.

'Philip Edwards,' said Adam. 'My God.' He bowed his head, collecting himself. 'You know, that was one of the readings Leonora asked for, at her funeral.'

'I remember.' Tess had now read the order of service about twenty times. Thoughts were jostling for space in her brain. 'That's him. She – she called out his name. When she –'

'What?' Adam said.

'Just before she had the stroke.' Tess remembered it now,

as clearly as if she were back there. She could hear the traffic, smell the fumes, see the rage and hate, the expression – was it despair? – in the old woman's eyes. *Where's Philip? Where is he?* 'It must be him. It has to be.'

Adam slowly shook his head. 'My God.' He looked back at the grave. 'So it was you, old chap,' he said. He stared, unblinking. 'He was only nineteen.'

'You can find out –' Tess began. 'Make sure. Perhaps there are relatives—'

He stopped her. He was smiling. 'I am sure. That's the weird thing.' He tensed his shoulders and then let them drop. 'Right,' he said, as he breathed out at the same time. 'God, what a welcome back.'

'He's with his daughter,' Tess said. 'In the same graveyard. I wonder if he ever knew?' She bit her lip; tears filled her eyes, and she turned away, so he wouldn't see how upset she was.

'We'll never know,' Adam took her hand. 'Let's go and get that drink, T. I think we deserve it.' They walked to the church gate. 'Happy birthday, Mum,' he said softly as they turned onto the high street, towards the Feathers. 'I miss you.'

October 1943

She was sent to her room after she had told her mother, like a little girl. A little girl with a six months' pregnant belly.

'Go to your room, Leonora.'

'Mother—'

'Go to your room.' Leonora had never seen her mother so – was it angry? No. Terrified, she thought. Fear was written on everyone's faces these days as a matter of course, though people tried to hide it, pretend everything was all right; but Leonora saw it magnified on her mother's face that sunny autumn day, when she finally plucked up the courage to tell her.

'I'm – I'm sorry,' Leonora whispered. She was clutching the fine lawn cotton of her dress in her hands; it was creased and puckered, her hands were clammy. It was cold in her mother's sitting room; the fires were never lit now, much of the house was shut up. They were getting ready to turn it into a girls' boarding school, and much to her father's displeasure the family was packing up to move into the town, to Leda House, her mother's family home.

Alexandra Mortmain looked out of the window, down towards the black iron gates of the entrance to the hall. She swallowed, and Leonora felt sick, sicker than the nausea that had gripped her for months now and that never seemed to go away. Her mother was scared, too. That made it worse.

'Mother, I haven't told you everything – who –' She paused. She simply didn't know how to frame the words. *It's Philip, Philip Edwards*, she wanted to say. *I love him, I've always loved him! We're going to get married, Mother, he comes back on leave in a month, I'll tell him then!* Somewhere in Leonora's mind was the tiny kernel of an idea that perhaps, just perhaps, it could all be satisfactorily resolved. Couldn't it? It said in the marriage service, 'with my body I thee worship', didn't it? For he had, oh, he had, and what had happened was because he honoured her and she him. And she loved him, yes she did . . . But Leonora knew, if she was absolutely frank with herself, that it was not to be. The look of horror, disgust, fear, written so large on her mother's face was evidence enough.

For months now, Leonora had kept the growing secret to herself; she was sure Eleanor, her maid, must have had some idea. For she was sick every morning, she felt sick all day, in fact. She felt as if something were dragging her down, pulling her inside out. She didn't know what it was and, because menstruation was something shameful, to be discussed only in the most urgent of circumstances, she put her lack of monthly bleeding down to one of the many symptoms that seemed to be assailing her. She was dying; she was being punished for what she had done with Philip, for loving him.

It wasn't until she felt her baby kick, and carry on kicking, five months into her pregnancy, that Leonora realized what was happening to her. And what could she do? There was nothing she could do, nothing at all. She couldn't tell anyone. She might have told Eleanor, but she wasn't there, she had been put to work at Home Farm. She had no friends, now school was over, and young Miss Mortmain had not been encouraged by her parents to befriend any of the girls at her school. She couldn't tell Philip – how could she put this in a letter? One day, one of her father's dogs, whom she feared almost as much as her father, jumped up and nearly pushed her to the ground. The dogs were kept permanently hungry, the better to run after anything that trespassed on the grounds. Tugendhat's black expressionless eyes, his snarling teeth glistening with saliva, terrified her.

When she knew there was no other option, it somehow gave her a strength of purpose. She knocked on her mother's door one afternoon, holding her head up high, waiting for the slightly querulous, petulant 'Yes?' in answer, entered the room, and told her.

Leonora sat in her room, ten minutes later, swinging her legs off the edge of the old bed which creaked as she rocked gently back and forth. The baby moved inside her; she rubbed her stomach tenderly, as she could only do when she was by herself. She gazed out of the window, trying to find order in the rhythmical ache of the bed; the curtains around the bed swayed slightly, giving off a haze of dust that swam in the golden light flooding through the glass. There was nothing she could do; she had to tell them.

She thought of the last time she had seen Philip, at a tea dance her parents had given for the town after the church fete. It will not stop us, this war, everyone said; we will carry on having church fetes, tea dances, living our lives. They had smiled across the room all evening, talked briefly in front of others, sharing secret looks, knowing they would see each other at some point. Then, as Leonora returned from the kitchen where she had been supervising the lemonade, Philip had emerged silently from the shadows, and pulled her towards the back corridor which led out to the kitchen garden, where the boots, the coats, the servants' things were kept. They kissed, they did not say a word, and she gasped, shocked by her own pleasure in him again, amazed at this – this which was was happening to her – as he ran his hands up her bare legs, unbuttoned her dress, kissed her skin, held her breast in his hand, boldly moved her hands to the front of his trousers, so that she could feel what she did to him. He would have gone further –

'No,' she said, smothering a laugh. 'Not here, Philip – how can you!'

'But I'm going away,' he said, kissing her neck. 'I want you so much, Rara.'

'I know,' she said, soothing, mothering him, stroking the back of his neck where his painfully short cropped hair met the top of his spine. 'Soon, I promise.'

'Very soon,' he said, kissing her again. 'My Atalanta.'

She laughed softly again, and put her head on his chest; he touched her hair gently, and sighed. From the grand sitting room came the strains of a song, played on the wind-up gramophone.

'What is it?' she said. 'What are they playing?'

'I heard it in London,' he said. 'They play it all the time, in the officer's mess.' They swayed slowly together, just the two of them, silhouetted against the light pouring through the door from the setting sun and he sang to her, so softly, as the song played faintly, the notes echoing on the polished floor.

I remember you,
You're the one who made my dreams come true,
A few kisses ago . . .

He held her hand, put his finger in the centre of her palm so she felt the pressure of it, fleetingly, as they separated, and walked back towards the drawing room again.

And that was the last time they had spoken. That was all she had. That, and the strangely sunny certainty that he loved her and he would come back for her – for that she never doubted.

So as Leonora waited in her room, and the minutes turned into an hour, maybe more, she thought of that last meeting, relived it over and over, her hands resting on her bump, the rocking motion of the bed and the memories of Philip soothing her, lulling her into a sort of calm.

The sharp rap at the door, when it eventually came, made her jump. 'Miss Mortmain. Your father wants to see you. In his study. Says immediately.'

It was dark now. Leonora climbed gingerly off the bed, put on her sandals, and opened the door.

She came down the stairs gently in the dark, the gloom of the unlit hall making the slippered wood treacherous. A strip of light slid out from under the door to her father's study. She raised her hand to the dark oak, and saw it was shaking. She knocked.

'Come.'

For months now, Leonora's father had been writing a new book, his first since *Roman Society* which had been published nearly eight years ago. It was about the army, about battle stratagems and campaign fighting, and it had a peculiar resonance now, of course. Leonora had often wanted to ask her father about his work, but she never could pluck up the courage. He terrified her.

Sir Charles Mortmain stood by the window behind his chair, with his back to her as she entered. Piles of books surrounded him, and a pipe rested on the green leather surface of the desk, the edges of which were tooled in gold. The door creaked loudly behind her as she gently shut it. The loud ticking of the grandfather clock was the only sound in the room.

'Father –' Leonora began. She stood by the door, all composure gone. She didn't know whether to advance further.

'You will not call me so.' Sir Charles did not move; she strained to see his face in the reflection of the glass. 'You will leave here tonight. A motor car is on its way now. I have spoken to—'

'Father, if I could—'

'Stop!' Her father's hand was held up, and his voice was loud, clear and sharp. 'I. Have. Spoken. To.' He paused. 'To Miss Wheeler, who is your mother's old nurse. You will go to her tonight.'

'Father—'

'DO NOT CALL ME THAT NAME AGAIN.'

At the rage, the venom in her father's voice, Leonora stepped back, involuntarily, bumping into the door.

'You are not my daughter,' her father said. 'We simply –' he paused, as if choosing his words – 'yes, we simply do not have a daughter any more. You will have this bastard, God damn it to hell, and you will return to Langford, and we will never refer to it again.' And then he turned round, and she saw his face, and fear washed over her anew. 'But be clear on this matter. Be very clear. You are not my daughter, nor shall you ever be.'

The baby kicked inside her. Leonora leaned against the door; the varnish was cool; her head was swimming.

'Do you have anything else to say?'

She shook her head, miserably.

Sir Charles stepped out in front of the desk. 'Do you accept what I have said?'

Leonora bowed her head. A tear dropped onto the floor; her hair hung in front of her face. Her father walked towards her.

'So that we are clear, I shall say it for the final time. You are no longer my daughter,' he said, and then he hit her. His open palm smacked hard onto her cheek; the force of it sent her head flying to one side, and the bones in her neck clicked loudly. She cried out, briefly, clutching her cheek, tasting blood. Her other hand covered her mouth, to muffle her sobs, and Leonora stared up at him, her eyes wild.

He did not look shocked, or upset, or even discomposed by what he had done. His eyes were utterly cold. He looked at her with faint disgust, as if she were a beggar on the street obstructing his path, and then he stepped behind the desk and sat down, cracking his knuckles as he did.

'You may go and pack now,' he said, and he picked up his pen again. He waved it at her, dismissing her, and Leonora turned and opened the door, feeling the blood pool in her mouth and wondering if she was going to be sick. She did not look back, but closed the door behind her and ran towards the great staircase. She put her hand on the bannister, and looked up to see her mother framed in the doorway of the drawing room, watching her with a peculiar expression, her hair escaping from its bun. Alexandra Mortmain nodded, and simply turned away from her only child.

'The motor car will arrive in an hour,' she said, as she retreated into the drawing room, and the door shut behind her, leaving her young daughter standing in the darkness. From outside, she could hear her father's dogs barking cruelly, their jaws snapping viciously, a violent and fearful sound. She shivered, tears running down her cheeks, and climbed slowly upstairs.

Leonora's baby, a little girl, was born in a nursing home fifty miles from Langford, in deadliest secret. She came in early December, a month early. The day before, Leonora had received a letter from Primmie, Philip's sister, telling her he had died in Greece in November 1943, one of thousands of men to die out in the Aegean as the British tried to recapture the Dodecanese Islands from the Italians.

Sweet, unsuspecting Primmie had written:

I knew you and he were particularly close. He was always extremely fond of you – I hope I may be so forward as to remind you of this? – and I know he cherished your friendship. I thought that, although this news is of the worst kind, you would wish to hear from me, while you are away completing your nursing training. He would have wanted you to hear before others, I am sure.

The baby came early. Leonora knew it was because of the shock of hearing about Philip. They both nearly died; Leonora lost a lot of blood. She never knew how much, she was never told, never asked. She cradled the letter numbly in her hand when she woke, two days later, to the mewling sound of her tiny daughter in the wooden cot by her bed. She called her Philippa, and when she gave her to be adopted by a family twenty miles away, that was the only thing she asked, that they keep her name.

Leonora went home a month later. Years afterwards, when she briefly allowed herself to think of that black, awful time again, she would wonder how she got through it. The answer was that she honestly didn't care any more if she lived or died. She discovered that it was possible to live, to put one foot in front of the other and walk, to smile and say hello, to wash one's face in the morning, brush one's hair in the evening and everything else in between, and yet be totally dead inside. For whom was she living, anyway? Who cared about her? Philip was gone, her baby was gone, taken away from her, and she had been told flatly that she would never see her again. Who else mattered?

Her family never mentioned it again. Unless forced to, her father never spoke to her after that. She was rarely allowed out of the house. So many of the young men of her generation, one of whom she would have been expected to have married, died. And so Leonora inherited the ruined estate when her mother finally died, and moved out of the Hall as soon as she could. She stayed on in the house in Langford, sitting at the window, watching the world go by, ruminating inwardly on what might have been. She had waited for years for her parents to die, so that she might do as she pleased.

But by the time it happened, it was too late for Leonora, too late to save her. Perhaps it was a wind that blew through the town one day, like the old saying, and changed her for ever. Perhaps she was more her father's daughter than she realized. But something inside her had been poisoned, and the poison stayed within her, until not even her beloved Philip would have recognized her. She forced her own daughter to hate her, and her grandson too. It was a tragedy, and perhaps saddest of all is that, with time, the wind that changed Leonora made her forget the girl she had once been, the love she had once felt, the man she had once remembered and the baby she had held for two short weeks, crying over her tiny writhing form as if her heart was breaking – which, in fact, it was.

CHAPTER FORTY

Dear Tess,

An early Christmas card for you from San Francisco. It is beautiful here, raining a lot, but when it's not it's crisp and sunny. There's a great bar round the corner where we hang out after work, which shows the game, I am quite converted to the 49ers these days. I've been hiking a lot and hanging out with the guys from work, it's all really cool. I think you'd like it here, too!

Thank you for the postcard of Langford, I can see where you get your quaint charm. It's very British, isn't it? Like something from a film set. Funny.

Thinking of you always, only a few weeks to go now till Christmas. I can't wait.

Peter

x

The whole town would out to see the lights being switched on, though it was a bitterly cold night. Tess walked along the lane towards Leda House, where she was to pick Adam up on the way. The streets were strangely deserted, and she hugged herself, shivering in the sharp, cutting cold. It was a clear night and a nearly full moon was out, while hundreds of stars studded the sky. It hurt to breathe in, though, and frost was already gathering on the car windows and the hedgerows.

She sang to herself:

> '*O little town of Bethlehem,*
> *How still we see thee lie,*
> *Above thy deep and dreamless sleep*
> *The silent stars go by . . .*'

She slapped her palms against her arms, to warm herself up. Ahead of her walked a couple, each holding the hand of a child. Their progress was naturally slower than hers and she caught up with them. Only when it was too late to turn back did she realize with a sinking feeling that it was Jemima, her student, with her husband and two children.

'Hello!' Jemima called, as Tess unsuccessfully tried to walk briskly past her. 'Tess, it's me!'

'Oh, hi there, Jemima.'

Jemima was beaming almost graciously. 'Look! This is Gideon, and this is Maisie!' She pushed the two small figures at either side of her forwards. They stood there, shyly, Maisie's stubby plaits swinging from side to side as she furiously sucked her thumb.

'Hi,' said Tess awkwardly. She looked at Jemima's husband. 'You must be Jon,' she said, congratulating herself heartily on remembering his name.

Jon smiled and shook her hand. 'Nice to meet you,' he said. 'You're Jemima's teacher, right? Sounds great, your course.'

'I don't know about that,' said Tess. 'Thanks.'

'I'm very envious of your trip to Langford Regis,' Jon said. 'I'm an architect, I'm really keen to go there sometime.'

'Shall we carry on walking?' said Jemima urgently. 'Jon, I really don't want to miss getting a good position, it'll be so incredibly disappointing for the children if we do.'

'Oh,' said Jon. 'Right.' They all carried on walking; they were nearly at Leda House.

'What are you working on at the moment?' said Tess.

'Actually,' said Jon, 'It's nothing very flash, but I'm pretty excited about it. It's a new community centre in Morely. It's solar powered. They want it to be as green as possible.'

'Jon! Tess doesn't want to hear you droning on about your work,' Jemima said, and Jon shrugged, sliding Tess a smile. 'Tess, I was meaning to ask you, are there any programmes here you think the children would like?'

'Er –' Tess looked blank. 'Like what?'

'Well, just activities, organizations, that sort of thing. It's *so* frustrating when you hear everyone else's children have gone to the water park, and the water park was only open for two bloody weeks back in April!' She laughed, almost frantically.

'I don't know,' said Tess politely. 'I'll keep my eyes open.'

'Would you, please? I do so want the children to get the most out of living in the country. Maisie! Don't suck your thumb!'

They were at Leda House now, and ahead of them, where the high street gently curved to the right, one could just glimpse a few flashing lights. Jemima said, as she grabbed Gideon by the arm and practically shoved him back onto the pavement, 'Just things like – I heard there were music appreciation lessons at the church hall once a week, and no one told me anything about them.'

'This is going to be hilarious, I have a feeling,' Jon said. 'If my poor dad could see me now, he'd laugh.'

'Why?' said Tess.

'I grew up in Brixton, right? My dad was from Jamaica, my mum's from Clapham, when Clapham wasn't a nice place to be from, you know.' He nodded ruefully as the front door to the house opened. Adam was standing on the threshold, smiling at her. 'Catch me, the architect living in the English village with the daughter who's not even four yet and she's learning the flute.'

'This is Jon,' said Tess, as Adam held out his hand.

'I know what you mean,' said Adam. 'We had a cat when I was little that had vet bills so big my mum always said she and her family could have lived for a month off what it cost to keep him alive for a couple of weeks.'

'Oh, hi!' Jemima said, coming forward, holding a wriggling Gideon under one arm. 'I'm Jemima.' She shook her hair, and actually slightly pouted a little. 'So this is who you were looking for yesterday, Tess!'

'What?' said Adam.

'Nothing,' said Tess, embarrassed. 'I thought I saw – the door was open, I came in and had a look. Nothing,' she added again, wishing Jemima to hell.

'We'll leave you to it,' Jon said, nodding. Jemima looked at him crossly.

'We can walk together. It's lovely to have a Mortmain back in the house again,' she said, in a tone like one of the BBC commentators during the Remembrance Day parade. 'And when did you get back?'

'Yesterday,' said Adam, with a note in his voice that Tess knew meant, Don't go any further. 'So, you're an architect, Jon?'

'Yes, I am,' said Jon. 'Mainly working on green stuff. I'm just finishing off a town hall in Morely, it's been great.' He looked at Adam. 'You're the guy with the water meadows, is that right?'

'Yep,' said Adam.

'Ah,' said Jon. ''Cause I love it down there, man. It's really nice. Right,' he said, taking his wife's hand. 'See you later, guys. Nice to meet you both.'

He held up his other hand and they moved off.

'He's nice,' said Adam.

'His wife's awful,' said Tess grumpily. 'I have to teach her.

One of those super-competitive women who thinks every-thing's a race. I can't stand her.'

'Good teaching attitude there,' said Adam. 'Nice to know you're completely impartial.'

'You'd be bloody partial if you had to teach her too,' said Tess. 'Have you got everything?' She looked behind her, at the dark house.

'Yep,' said Adam. 'I've got everything, which is to say I've got nothing, really.' He sighed. 'I should bring my stuff over here, I just don't want to.'

'So you're going to live here, then? Sell your mum's place?'

'I think I have to,' said Adam, as they set off down the street at a slow walk. He pushed his hand over his forehead, through his short hair. 'But – man, I don't want to. God, it's cold, isn't it?'

Someone came out of the Feathers opposite. 'Hello, Tess,' she called. 'Are you –' It was Andrea Marsh. She stopped and looked at her, and then saw who she was with. 'Oh. Hello, Adam. I heard you were back. Good trip?'

'Yes, thanks, Andrea,' Adam said politely. 'How are you?'

'Good, thanks,' said Andrea. She sniffed. 'Lot of people interested to know you're back, Adam.'

'Oh, right,' said Adam, still polite. He nodded and smiled at her. 'See you in a bit? We're just heading down to the lights.'

'Right you are,' said Andrea. 'Just waiting for – someone.' She sniffed again, disapprovingly. Tess and Adam waved, and carried on walking.

'Blimey,' said Adam under his breath. 'I really am *persona non grata*, aren't I?'

Tess didn't know what to say. 'Um – well, you know,' she began. 'You know, a lot of people thought, when they found out about you – I guess the bridge being demolished was a bad sign. They thought it was all going to be cancelled.' She felt awkward, being the person to say this, but he had to hear it. Adam looked quizzical. 'The bridge? Oh.'

'Go down there tomorrow,' she said. 'Have a look.'

Adam frowned. 'I –'

'Don't you love it down there?' Tess said curiously. 'I still do.'

He stared at her. 'I never thought about it.'

'Well, you should.'

'I will,' he said, meeting her eyes. 'I promise I will.' He patted his pockets. 'Right. Have I got the keys to the house? It's confusing, having these two places.'

Tess wrinkled her brow. 'It is. Could you – could you ever sell this place?'

'I can, but it's difficult. It's Grade One listed, and the terms of the will mean I'm not allowed to for five years.' He sighed. 'She wanted me to stay on here.'

The sound of people in the street grew louder as they drew closer to the lights.

'I've been thinking about Philip Edwards,' Tess said. 'You should talk to Joanna, see if there are any church records you could look at, find out a bit more about his family, all that.'

'Definitely,' he said. 'Especially since his family is practically the only family I've got. Do you know what my only beef with my mum is?' he said suddenly.

'Er, no?' said Tess.

'I just wish I knew something about my dad. He was a lecturer like her, they had an affair, he was Irish – at least I think he was Irish, he could have been from Greece or Japan or Toxteth for all I know.'

'I think you'd know if he was from Japan,' Tess pointed out. 'And I think it's understandable, what she did, even if she might have wished it was otherwise. When you think how she'd grown up.'

'Maybe.'

'She wasn't close to her parents, was she?' said Tess. 'I mean, her adoptive parents.'

'No, luck of the draw, I think,' said Adam. 'I feel sorry for them, I think she was foisted on them, poor thing. It was after the war, they couldn't have kids of their own, I don't think they had any choice. They moved to Australia when she was twenty, I don't think she saw them much after that. I never met them, anyway.' He looked up at the starry sky. 'God, it's so ridiculous, isn't it. My only family – what? – some random great-aunt's relatives and I don't know the first thing about her or where she lives or anything.'

'Primula Edwards,' said Tess thoughtfully. 'Awesome name. Straight out of Miss Marple.'

'It's cool, isn't it,' Adam said. He grinned at her.

'I love that name,' Tess said.

'Go on, change it,' he said seriously. 'I can really see you as a Primula. Grow your eyebrows again and find that old cardigan. Then you can move in with someone called Lettice and breed cats together.'

'Oh, you can just bog off,' Tess said snappishly. 'Liz is coming along later, by the way,' she added meanly. 'If anyone's going to be my Lettice, it's her.'

'I'm sure,' said Adam solemnly. 'By the way – I keep forgetting to ask.' He scratched the back of his head. 'What are you doing for Christmas?'

Tess said, 'Well, Mum and Dad are going on a cruise, so—'

'I've been thinking,' said Adam. 'Do you want to come round for Christmas? I was going to do a thing. Get Suggs, Mick, Diana and Richard, a few other people over, cook up a storm –' He trailed off, watching her expression of dismay. 'Don't look so horrified, T.'

'It's not that,' Tess said. 'It's just – oh, that's a real shame. I'm going to – um, I'm supposed to be going to Rome for Christmas.'

'Rome?' he echoed blankly. 'Why?'

The door next to Jen's Deli banged loudly as someone came out, shutting it behind him. It was a young man, who glared when he saw Adam and carried on down the street.

'Er – well,' Tess said, feeling this ought to be obvious. 'To see Peter. Because Mum and Dad are away, that's why.'

'You're – wow.' Adam nodded, a bit too enthusiastically. 'You're still with Peter?'

'Well, I'm clearly not *with* him,' Tess said, gesturing around her. 'But – yeah.'

'Well, that's great!' Adam stopped in the street. 'When was the last time you saw him?'

'I see him all the time,' Tess explained. 'On Skype.'

'On Skype,' Adam echoed. 'Right. But actually, in the flesh, instead of the two of you being like those weirdos who get together because their avatars meet on Second Life. Actually in the *flesh*, when was the last time you saw him?'

Adam was so annoying sometimes. 'Well, when we were in Rome.'

'So – you haven't seen him since June.'

'Yes, but—'

'Right,' Adam said, barely controlling a smirk. 'Wow. That's a real trajectory you've got going on there, Tess.'

'Shut up, Adam!' she said touchily. 'We have tried, it's just things got in the way. Things like – well, your grandmother's funeral.'

'That was in August,' Adam pointed out. 'And?'

'Well, he's been away,' Tess said. 'Working in California.'

'You couldn't fly to see him?'

'Not to California, no. He's coming back for Christmas, I told you.'

'So you Skype.'

'Yep,' Tess said airily. 'It's brilliant. We chat *all* the time.'

'But you haven't actually *seen* him since June.'

Tess ignored this. 'Anyway, I'm going over for Christmas. Five days. And it's going to be great. Rome at Christmas, how wonderful will it be?' She tugged Adam's arm. 'Hot chocolate sitting in squares, all muffled up! Walking along the river! Going to see the Pope on Christmas Day, *urbi et orbi* and all of that.'

443

Adam looked as if he would say something, but didn't. 'That's great, T.'

She looked gratefully up at him. 'Thanks, bruv.' She slid her arm through his and he squeezed it.

'Come on,' he said. 'Time to face the music. And the lights.'

They walked towards the crowd, arm in arm, and as Tess grew accustomed to the noise and the sudden darkness – the street lights had all been switched off along that stretch of the road, in preparation for the Christmas lights being switched on – she looked around her, with a growing sense of amazement. She knew people, it was weird. She knew lots of people, that was weirder.

'Hi, Tess,' someone called out, and Tess turned to see it was Jen from the deli, holding a tray with little things with cocktail sticks attached. 'How are you?'

'Good, thanks,' said Tess.

'Ah,' said Jen, recognizing the man at her side. 'Adam.'

She offered Tess what turned out to be a fig and prosciutto snack, and then turned on her heel before Adam could take anything.

'I think you'd better leave me,' Adam said with resignation. 'Sooner or later someone's going to try and punch me, and I don't want you at risk from a stray fist in the eye.'

'Hello, Tess,' said a male voice in the darkness. 'How've you been? Enjoying these delicious snacks?'

'Guy?' said Tess uncertainly. 'Is that you?'

'Yes, it is,' Guy Phelps said. 'I've just been telling someone all about your delicious flatmate and her amazing skills.'

'Oh,' said Tess. 'Actually, Francesca's moved out, Guy, I thought you—'

'No, silly!' said someone brightly, next to her. Tess lurched forward in surprise, and grabbed Adam's arm tightly.

'Liz!' she yelped. 'Oh, my God, sorry, I thought you meant—'

'No,' said Liz, who really did have the sweetest nature imaginable. 'I'm sure Francesca has many amazing skills, far more than me!' Her face shone in the candlelight from a nearby window. 'Here are the toffee apples, Tess. Have one! George says they're very nice, so I must trust him! Hello, Adam! How very nice to see you!'

'They look delicious,' said Adam gravely. He smiled. 'How are you, Liz?'

'Oh, I'm very well indeed, thanks very much, Adam!' Liz said gaily. 'Take one.'

'They are extremely nice,' Guy Phelps said stiffly. 'Anyway, I see Ron over there. Excuse me, please.'

He nodded at Tess, ignoring Adam, and pushed through the crowd towards the edge of the kerb. Tess watched him, and saw Ron Thaxton and Andrea standing side by side, chatting to Diana and Jan. In front of them, Jemima was talking to another mother, both of them holding children, their heads nodding animatedly. As Tess looked, Diana caught sight of her, and saw the person next to her. She excused herself and came over.

'Adam, my dear,' she said, hugging him briefly. 'How lovely to see you.'

Adam bent down and kissed her on the cheek. 'It's lovely to see you. I called you earlier.'

'I know, Richard said.' Diana patted him on the arm. 'It's good to have you back. Are you staying at the big house?'

'Yes.'

She nodded. 'Fine. There's things we need to discuss. I'll come and see you tomorrow.' She looked as if she would say more, but suddenly she said rather loudly, 'Ah, here's Jan. Right. How nice.'

'Adam Mortmain, is it, you're calling yourself now?' Jan said, coming up to Adam. 'Hello, Tess, dear,' she added. Behind her, Ron and Andrea stood silently, like the massed ranks of foot soldiers at the beginning of *Gladiator*. 'So, Adam. What's happening with the development, eh?'

'Oh, dear,' said Diana, running her hand through her hair in a manner almost identical to Adam's.

445

'Hello, Jan,' Adam said in a hearty voice, which really didn't suit him. Beside him, Tess tensed. She wished, just for one evening, his first evening back, they could leave him alone. 'Nice to see you, how've you been?'

'Fine.' Jan waved her hands, distracted. 'Listen. What's going on? You promised you weren't like your bloody grandmother, so why have you let the developers start on the water meadows?'

Adam put his hand lightly on her arm. 'Jan, I'm sorry, but I only got back this morning. I've got to catch up with them. It was my understanding they weren't starting the work till January.' He bowed his head. 'I need to find out what's going on. I'll do it first thing tomorrow. You understand.'

'Er, yes,' said Jan, as Tess looked at her friend admiringly. 'That – of course that makes sense.'

'You're becoming more and more like a Tory MP,' said Tess, as Jan, much mollified, moved away, followed by Diana who smiled briefly at them. Adam looked at her in horror.

'Don't say that!'

'That's what you're going to need to be, round here,' she said frankly. They were in the middle of the road, buffeted by people walking past, gathering in front of the small podium a few metres away. Tess spoke quickly. 'You do realize that, don't you? Like it or not, the Mortmains were the big family for years and years, you know they were, and there are people who'll still look on you as the young lord. Especially now you've got the –' She stopped. 'Anyway. Let's go, shall we?'

'Money,' Adam supplied grimly. 'Especially now I've got the money.' He shook his head. 'It's pathetic.'

'It's not just about the money,' she said, trying to sound reasonable. 'People here have long memories. The Mortmains were the big grand family in town. Look at someone like Miss Store, she was your grandmother's maid for years. Now they know about you, it's going to take a long time for them to see you as someone else.'

446

He stared at her. 'When did you become such a local expert?'

When you and Francesca both went away and left me, she wanted to say, but she didn't. She smiled at him. 'Come on. I see an ancient celebrity and a fat local councillor on a rickety makeshift stage. If that's not a recipe for fun I don't know what is. Let's go.'

Suddenly, there was a loud crackle, and half the assembled crowd jumped. 'Lay-dees AND jennelmen,' came a smooth voice incredibly loudly over the speaker system, 'PURleease welcome TO the stage . . . THE one and onleee –'

Tess nudged Adam. 'He's introducing himself!'

Sure enough, the small wizened figure of Martin Riviere was bent slightly with his back to the audience, speaking into a microphone.

'You KNOW HIM from those CLASSIC TV shows *Fall Out* and the LEGENDAREE *Blind Man's Bluff* . . . Misterrrrrrrrrrrrrrr . . . Martin . . . RIVIERE!!!!'

It was the kind of introduction that couldn't fail to leave you clapping, even if – as was the case with some of the crowd, especially those under twenty – you had no idea who was being introduced. As he finished, Martin Riviere dropped the microphone, spun round, and smiled brightly for the audience, clapping them back and twinkling like a cut-price Norman Wisdom. He gestured for the microphone to the large councillor who stood next to him and he, after scrabbling in a bewildered way on the ground, handed it back to the smaller man, who said, in a more normal voice, 'Good evening, ladies and gentlemen, boys and girls! And Happy Christmas to you all!'

'Happy Christmas!' the crowd chorused back, the voices of the children loudest. Someone started crying.

'Oh, dear, I've lost a vote already,' said Martin Riviere. 'Who's crying?' A mother at the edge of the crowd smiled ruefully and pointed at the screaming little girl on her hip as she bounced her up and down.

'Come up here,' said Martin Riviere to the mother. She shook her head. 'Go on,' he said. 'I won't bite. I've got a present for your little girl.'

'Dodgy tactic,' said Adam and Tess bit her lip, trying not to laugh.

But the mother was persuaded, and she moved towards the front of the crowd. 'What's your name?' Martin Riviere said to her.

'Della,' said the young woman. 'And this is Katie.'

'Hello, Katie,' Martin Riviere said, crouching down next to the little girl, who had stopped screaming and was staring intently at the old man, her face still flushed. Her pink, fur-lined parka jacket had its hood up, and she looked like a very cross small pink Eskimo. 'Here. Have this donkey.'

'This is really random,' Adam whispered to Tess.

'Go with it,' said Tess. 'That's what I'm doing.'

Martin Riviere handed Katie a small toy donkey. It had tinsel round its neck.

'*Little Donkey, Little Donkey,*' he sang, standing up, making a heaving sound as he did.

'Sing along, everyone!'

'*Bethlehem, Bethlehem . . .*'

Tess wanted to laugh again, but she found herself moved. She disliked the heavy-duty Christianity that people like Leonora Mortmain had loved to employ. But here, on this cold, clear night, as a group of people she lived with all sang, their voices soft in the winter air, she could imagine the donkey walking towards Bethlehem in the late-afternoon heat, guided by Joseph, carrying the pregnant Mary, all of them tired and weary and looking for shelter. She looked up at Katie who was standing on the stage, holding Martin Riviere's hand and singing shyly along.

'Right,' said Martin Riviere, as the song ended. 'Now I'd like to ask someone for some help, switching the lights on. Who's that down there? What's your name?'

'Maisie!' someone yelled loudly. Tess wondered if, like Martin Riviere, Jemima could actually imitate her own daughter's voice, the better to get her up on the stage.

'You're a pretty little thing, aren't you, Maisie?' said Martin Riviere, smoothing down his silver silk tie. 'Do you want to come up on stage and help me with something?'

'Stop it,' hissed Tess, as Adam stuffed his fist in his mouth.

Maisie came up on the stage and, after a whispered consultation, her brother Gideon accompanied her too.

'We press the button now,' said Martin Riviere, and Maisie, Gideon and Katie all put their hands on a big red button he held out, and the crowd drew its breath. 'Happy Christmas, everyone,' he cried, and signalled behind him to the man in charge of the lights, who was, in fact, Suggs. Suggs flipped down a switch, and there, down the high street, illuminated snowflakes, stars, Christmas trees and baubles flickered into life.

There was a loud 'Aaaahh'. Tess joined in, and Adam looked down at her and smiled.

'Sorry,' she said. 'I can't help it. It's so lovely.'

'Don't apologize,' he replied, looking up at the lights, around at the crowd, then back at her. He nodded. 'You're right. It is. It really is.'

CHAPTER FORTY-ONE

There was nothing Tess liked more than singing carols loudly while pottering around the house making seasonal things like mulled wine or mince pies or wreaths for front doors, but in the days after Adam came back, Liz went on a Christmas domesticity drive that even Tess herself found somewhat overwhelming. She made her own crackers (with crêpe paper and loo rolls), she tied mistletoe and holly everywhere, so that casually putting one's hand on a stray surface became a hazardous activity, and she had a CD called *King's College Carols* constantly on a loop. Tess started to think that if she heard 'I Saw Three Ships' one more time blood would ooze from her ears.

'I've made a carolling corner!' Liz cried when Tess came back from work the following Monday. 'Look!'

She pointed in the direction of the far corner, which was what Tess and Francesca used to refer to as the Dead End, because it was simply the bit of the house where furniture and things went to die. They had kept the recycling box in this corner, and the empty box from the flat-screen TV.

Now, under Liz's gentle care, there stood a small slightly wobbly round table, which Liz had recovered from outside a house on Lord's Lane where it was about to be thrown out.

She had rescued it and brought it back to Easter Cottage and now, at Christmas time, it was fulfilling its purpose, finally, as a table with –

'What the hell is that?' said Tess, putting her bag down on the chair by the bureau. 'Is that a cardboard house?'

'Yes!' said Liz, patting the cardboard box which she had cunningly transformed into a house by dint of bending the top flaps together to form a roof. 'A Knupfer House!' She took on a dramatic expression and spoke like someone narrating a Disney movie. 'It's an *old* Austrian *tradition*, dating back *centuries*. We're going to cover it with icing sugar and then stick cinnamon biscuits over it, *just like* Hansel and Gretel!'

'Is that the box Francesca's face cream came in?' Tess said, staring at it. Francesca had been addicted to ordering all her many Dermalogica skin products and Bumble and Bumble hair products on a website which kindly gave you one item free, but only after you'd spent fifty pounds on a very small phial of moisturizing fluid that promised to make your skin glow brighter than Tutankhamun's tomb. Thus the house was still full of narrow, high cardboard boxes, suitable for storing and delivering body lotions, cleansers and soothing boosters and now, apparently, also making gingerbread houses.

'It's not mine,' Liz said merrily. 'Ah, it's going to be so exciting. We'll put the icing on, gather round and sing carols. Just like they do in old Austria.'

'Right,' said Tess tentatively, not wanting to rain on Liz's parade. She remembered, with a flash, the day she'd arrived back from school particularly blue about Will, and the strap on her shoe had broken, meaning she had lost her balance and stepped into a puddle. She had opened the door to the cottage to be greeted with the sound of Francesca and Adam upstairs having sex so loudly that Tess had at first thought one or other of them was being murdered.

'Ah,' she now murmured to herself, not without nostalgia.

'It'll be fun,' Liz said, a small frown puckering her brow as she saw Tess's expression. 'I've asked a couple of people to drop round.'

'Oh?' Tess said, examining the Knupfer House and not really listening. 'Who?'

'Well, I think Beth's coming over, for starters. Sorry, Tess, I should have checked.'

She sounded guilty, so Tess smiled at her, feeling bad. Why wasn't she always as enthusiastic about everything as Liz? Yes! 'Great! It'll be fun. Brilliant. Shall we ask Miss Store round? Give her a bit of mulled wine and some minced pies? Oh, I'm properly in the Christmas holiday spirit now, Liz!' She squeezed her housemate hard, and Liz looked at her in consternation, alarmed by this sudden change in mood.

'Great!' said Liz, drawing back a little. 'I'll just finish mulling the wine. Why don't you go and ask Miss Store if she's free?'

Ask Miss Store if she's free, Tess grumbled to herself, as she stood on the doorstep of the tiny cottage next door and rang the doorbell. She's hardly going to be busy, is she? Good grief –

The door was opened by Miss Store, whose sweet face broke into a hearty smile when she saw who it was. 'Tess, dear! Look who's here!'

Tess looked over her shoulder to see Adam sitting in one of the low chintzy armchairs that gave Miss Store so much trouble now her knees were bad. He stood up. 'Hello, love, how are you?' he said. 'Just chatting to Miss Store about my grandmother. She knew her from when they were both girls, you know.'

'Course!' said Tess, pleased. 'That's great. That's – really great!'

'What can I do for you?' Miss Store said. 'Come in. Sit down.'

Tess – somewhat regretfully – declined. She explained her mission, and invited them both to drop round after they'd finished chatting, then retreated back next door. She wanted to check her emails, before Carolling Corner – as that was what they were evidently calling this evening – began.

She'd emailed Francesca a few days ago, and not heard anything back. As Liz hummed 'I Saw Three Ships' melliflu-ously in the kitchen, Tess ground her teeth, waiting for her computer to crank itself into life. Amongst the emails giving her tips on how to get Free TV Downloads and the latest releases showing at the Streatham Odeon (she had booked tickets online once, eighteen months ago, and was now receiving emails from them on a bi-weekly basis, despite her best efforts to cancel them), was one from Francesca:

Hi from London, young Tess –

I am writing this sitting in Kate's flat. Still haven't found a place yet and the people renting my flat aren't due to move out till February. So annoying. So I'm sleeping on a succession of floors or in spare rooms. It's kind of liberating. Hey, you don't need a flatmate, do you? Hahahahaha.

I got that job. It's weird. I'm working as a lawyer again. For an ethical firm. My main client's an inner-city farm. Someone's trying to build a bit of the Olympic Village over it, it's all really dodgy. They loved my experience helping out on the water meadows campaign. Isn't that weird, me working for a farm? Like I'm a country girl all over again. Me!

Tess, just want to say this once and then not again – I'm sorry about flouncing off that night, all the things I said. It's nothing to do with you. I couldn't take it any more. The whole thing with Adam those last few weeks, it was poisonous. I was mental, that night, I feel really guilty. I guess I liked him more than I ever told him. And I'm not right for him. I behave badly when I'm with him. Like a princess. I look back on some of the stuff . . . Argh. Well, he's not right for me, either. I can see that now. I hope we both can.

& I think my time in Langford had come to an end too, don't you? Never expected it to last as long as it did. It was a blast and I'll always remember it. Can I come and stay, some time soon? What are you doing for New Year's?

Come up to London, even if it's just for the day. Love you, miss you lots, and thanks for everything again,

F

PS Have you seen my citrine earrings? They were probably under my bed. Quite valuable but don't worry if they've been hoovered etc. And my silk sleepmask? I think I used it to tie the wardrobe doors together.

XXXX

There was a knock on the door. Tess jumped up to answer it, her eyes still glued to the screen.

'Oh, hello,' she said in surprise, as she opened the door to find Guy Phelps standing on the threshold, somewhat anxiously clutching a bottle of wine.

'Er – um. Hello,' said Guy. 'Is – Liz around?'

He looked past Tess as if she were a housemaid.

'Guy!' Liz appeared from the kitchen, drying her hands on a tea towel. 'How super that you've come!' She smiled at him, her eyes shining.

'Oh, huh!' Guy stepped into the cottage, looking pleased. 'Delighted to be asked, lonely fellow like me all on my own up at the farm! Not often I get an invitation to venture out on the town.' He handed Tess the bottle of wine, without looking at her. 'Er. There you go.'

'Thank ye, zurrr,' Tess said under her breath, in her best yokel accent. He turned away, and she did a quick curtsey, then muttered under her breath.

'So!' Guy said, rubbing his hands together and advancing

454

towards Liz. 'What's this evening in aid of?' He was determined to enjoy himself; this was clearly a big night out for him.

'Oh, just an excuse for some mulled wine and to sing some carols,' said Liz happily. 'Get us into the Christmas spirit.'

'Excellent. *Excellent*.' Guy looked around the room, as if trying to spot the other partygoers. 'Hey! I see mistletoe!' He waggled his eyebrows. Tess cleared her throat and he looked at her, as if seeing her for the first time. 'Oh. Hello, there, Tess. How are you?'

'Oh, I'm super duper, thanks very much, Guy,' Tess said chirpily. 'Thanks for coming.'

'No problems!' Guy said, bouncing on the balls of his feet. 'As I said. Christmas party! Delighted.'

'Yes,' said Tess, retreating into the kitchen. 'Thanks for coming to our party *that I had no idea we were actually having*,' she hissed to Liz. 'What's he doing here?'

'He's nice,' said Liz staunchly, ladling out some mulled wine. Tess stared at her. 'And I want to get in the Christmas mood.' She handed Tess a glass.

'Thanks.' Tess took a sip, diverted. 'Ooh. That's delicious.'

'It's for Guy. There's – oh, that's the doorbell! I wonder who that'll be?'

'I wonder, too,' said Tess. 'Blimey.'

She stomped towards the door, practically flinging the glass of mulled wine at Guy.

'Oh,' she said. 'Hello, Beth.'

Beth Kennett stamped her feet on the ground, wiping them on the iron grate. 'It's freezing out there. Thanks. This is nice!' She stepped inside.

'Beth!' Liz called. 'Thanks for coming! Welcome to Carolling Corner!'

'Oh, well,' said Beth uncertainly. 'Er. Thanks for inviting me to – er, be in your carolling corner.' She looked at Tess. 'You too, Tess.'

'I had nothing to do with it,' said Tess.

'Mince pies are on their way,' Liz called from the kitchen. 'Beth, let me get you a glass.'

'Hello, Beth,' said Guy, clearly overwhelmed by the already dazzling display of female companionship on show this evening. 'How exciting. Jolly nice to see you again.'

Beth pulled her top down self-consciously over the waist-band of her jeans. 'Er, thanks,' she said.

'Drinks are on their way!' Liz called from the kitchen.

'Marvellous!' Guy called back. 'Anything we can do to help?'

'Nothing, but you can help yourself to the mince pies!' Liz put a beautifully stacked pyramid of hot, golden, crusted home-made mince pies on the breakfast bar. 'They'll get cold in a minute!'

Tess thought of her synthetic fondant fancies, piled up on the now-dead cake stand, and she had a sudden flashback to the evening she and Francesca had made margaritas. Francesca had been out to Thornham on the bus – she loved the bus, strangely – and had bought the right glasses, some salt, margarita mix, a brown bag crammed full with limes, and some tortilla chips, which turned out to be all they ate that night. They had invented a narrative dance routine to 'Copacabana' and 'What Becomes of the Broken Hearted', and set up a production line to make the margaritas to music, like the famous Morecambe and Wise sketch in the kitchen. It was hilarious – less hilarious when Francesca, merrily chopping the limes in half with a motion akin to the guillotine, nearly removed her own finger, instead embedding the knife in the chopping board with such force it took both of them to remove it. She withdrew, standing halfway up the stairs in the dark-ness while Beth and Guy made polite conversation, and swiftly texted Francesca, suddenly desperately anxious not to let another minute go by without telling her how great she was.

Got your e, ta so much. Just thinking of margarita night. Miss you! Course you can stay any time. Speak soon. Lots of love. T x

456

The bell rang while she was texting. 'I'll get it,' Tess called out, with no real enthusiasm. She flung the door open. Suggs stood on the threshold with his arm round Kirsty, his fellow barperson at the Feathers. 'Hi all,' he said. 'We bought some beer, too.'

Kirsty, who looked a bit as though she might be a daughter of Bob Geldolf – lots of eyeliner, mute but pissed off expression – nodded, with a half-snarl.

'Hello, you two! That's brilliant, thank you so much!' Liz said, rushing towards them. She kissed Suggs on the cheek and went for Kirsty, who veered back in horror.

'Oi.' Tess put her phone back down on the table. 'When did you know about this?' she demanded of Suggs. Kirsty watched her curiously, chewing some gum and standing with one hand on her hip

'Oh, this morning,' he said airily. 'It's quite last minute.'

'You're telling me!' Tess said, going into the kitchen.

'Who else have you asked?' she said casually to Liz. 'Just so I know with whom I'll be carolling in a corner in a short while. Want to get my harmonies right and all that.'

'Oh, I'm sorry I didn't properly mention it to you,' Liz said desperately. 'I'm really sorry. It was a bit last minute, and then I kept seeing people all day, and it turns out everyone's free – it's just a few carols and singing and mince pies, you don't *really* mind, do you?'

'Course not!' said Tess, seeing the anxiety on her face. 'Absolutely not! Great idea! Just – who else is coming?'

'Well, Jen's coming along later, and Joanna, and—'

'Joanna the vicar Joanna?'

The doorbell rang again. 'I'll get it!' Guy cried, near-hysterical. 'In charge out here, don't worry!'

'Great!' Tess shouted back. 'Thanks!' She turned back to Liz.

'Yes,' Liz said innocently. 'Joanna the vicar Joanna. Why?'

'Nothing, no reason at all,' said Tess. She thought of the

climax of the dance routine to 'Copacabana', which involved Francesca as Lola – of course – sitting on a chair, legs daintily crossed, whilst Tess – as Tony, the passionate barman lover of Lola – emerged from the curve in the stairs and flew across the room to defend her honour from Rico. They had found a fan from somewhere, and Francesca batted it seductively, whilst Tess clutched the front of her cardigan as if it were a proud matador's jacket and then sank to the ground, shot by the imaginary Rico. (They called up Adam, but he was working at the pub and couldn't be persuaded to leave and come and join them.) Who, really, could say that was a more worthwhile evening? Of course not.

There was another knock on the door. 'I'll get it,' Tess said, determined to be nice. She threaded her way through the crowd in the tiny sitting room. It had expanded, she was sure.

'Hi! Hi there, hi,' she said, pushing past people. Was that Claire? And Ryan, from the greengrocer's? And Alice Gilkes, from the Packhorse and Talbot in Thornham? What was this flash mob of a Christmas drinks party? When had they all arrived?

She opened the door. There, clutching *Carols for Choirs 4* and a box of biscuits, stood Joanna and, next to her, holding a bag of amaretto biscuits and a bottle of wine, was Jen.

'Hi!!' Jen said brightly.

'Look, you've each brought your area of speciality,' said Tess, trying to sound bouncy and hugely pleased to see them. They looked back at her blankly. 'Joanna's brought some carols, Jen's brought some exciting deli-style food! Hey, come on in!'

'Right,' said Joanna pleasantly. 'Oh, what a nice crowd. Hello –'

'Room for us?' came a voice behind the two new guests, and they jumped and turned around.

'Adam. Miss Store. Course,' said Tess, with relief. 'Come in. The event has expanded somewhat since I issued my

458

invitation,' she said, thinking she sounded like Lady Bracknell. Adam stared at her. 'I'm afraid it's a bit crowded.'

'Well, I like a bit of a do,' said Miss Store, with pleasure. 'How nice!' She advanced enthusiastically into the room.

'Have you had a nice chat?' Tess asked Adam.

'Er – yes,' he said. 'Heard all about life at the Hall. I'll tell you later. Sounds pretty grim to me.'

Jen and Joanna stared at Adam. He smiled politely back at them.

'Good evening, you two.'

'Evening,' they said. Tess smiled at him.

He held his hand open, like a maître d'. 'After you,' he said. They scuttled in, to be greeted with cries of pleasure from Liz, leaving Adam standing in the doorway.

'What the hell is this?' Adam muttered in Tess's ear.

'Don't say hell, there's a vicar here.'

'What's going on?'

'No idea,' said Tess quietly. 'Can I ask you something?'

'Yes,' said Adam, looking around, as the assembled guests surveyed him with displeasure. He caught sight of Suggs, and raised a hand. Suggs smiled back.

'It's an etiquette question.'

'Go ahead. You know I'm an expert on this kind of thing.'

'How long do I have to stay at a party at my own house before I can leave?'

Adam looked at his watch. 'Ten minutes.'

'You think? How do I . . .' Tess felt awful. 'How do I get out of here?'

Adam thought seriously for a moment. 'No worries. Just tell Liz you'd arranged to go for a drink with me. I do need to talk to you, actually.'

Tess thought then how straightforward boys were. No messing about, no tying oneself into knots with a hugely complicated story. 'Oh. Perfect,' she said, as Joanna produced a portable keyboard from her satchel.

'Hurrah!' cried Liz, clapping her hands. 'Guys! Guys! The music's here!'

'Brill,' said Guy Phelps appreciatively. 'Bloody great party, Liz.'

'Yay!' said Tess, clapping loudly, the better to later cover her tracks. She downed a glass of mulled wine that was resting on the table. Adam gave her a disapproving look.

'It's my house,' she said grumpily. 'Ten minutes, yes?'

'Yes,' he said. Someone plucked at his shoulder. 'Hey – hi, Liz. Good to see you again! Yes, great party.'

Tess watched him, watched the room filled with people laughing and chattering, watched as Liz poured drinks and Guy appreciatively watched her, watched as Miss Store opened her eyes wide with pleasure at something Joanna the vicar said to her, watched as Suggs surreptitiously squeezed Kirsty's bottom, jolting her into expression; and she felt strangely removed from it all, as though it was happening to other people. Perhaps it was the little suitcase, poking out from the cupboard beneath the stairs, which she would shortly be packing for Italy. Perhaps it was nothing more than that, because she didn't want to miss Christmas here. But she should have felt happy and didn't, and she didn't know why.

CHAPTER FORTY-TWO

An hour later, Tess and Adam stood at the bar of the Feathers, breathing out as if they'd both just completed a gruelling marathon.

'Well, young lady, young gentleman,' said Mick, ambling over. He shook Adam's hand. 'Good to see you again, son. I wasn't in when you were here the other night, was I? How've you been?'

'I'm pretty good,' said Adam, clasping Mick's hand between both of his. 'It's great to see you, Mick.'

'Now, will you be wanting me to put you on the rota for next week's shifts?' Mick asked, his eyes twinkling. 'I've still not replaced you with anyone permanent, you know. When you coming back?'

'I might need to talk to you about that,' Adam said. He smiled back, embarrassed.

'A'right,' said Mick. 'What can I get you, in the meantime?'

'Pint of Butcombe's, please,' said Adam. 'Tess?'

'Same for me, please,' said Tess. 'Maybe a tequila chaser.'

'Serious?' Mick said.

'Almost,' said Tess. 'No.'

'So, I hear there's a bit of a do going on at your place tonight,' Mick said, sliding the pint over to Tess.

'You knew,' Tess said moodily, taking a sip of her drink. 'That's nice. First I heard of it was when half the town started arriving on my doorstep.'

'Oh,' said Mick.

'Come on,' Adam said, gesturing to a table. 'Come over here and stop whinging.'

She followed him over, smiling, and they sat down. 'Do you want some food?' she said.

'Maybe, what do you think?'

'Not sure. There'll be loads at home, I'm sure. And I might be a nice housemate and go back in an hour or so, you know. Finish off the rest of the evening. I don't want Liz thinking I wasn't having a good time or that I'm pissed off she's trying to re-enact *Songs of Praise* in my living room.'

'But you are pissed off with her for trying to re-enact *Songs of Praise* in your living room,' Adam pointed out.

'Yes, but I don't want her *thinking* that, do I?' Tess was shocked at his naivity.

Adam shook his head. 'Female friendships,' he said. 'Never understood them, never will.'

'Liz isn't my friend, she's my housemate,' Tess said, 'and it's much more important you have a good relationship with your housemate, frankly. Friends – well – if they're meant to stick around, they'll stick around.' She clinked her glass against his.

'Ah,' said Adam. 'I see, I see. Charming.'

A companionable silence fell, during which they both drained their drinks. Adam scratched his neck and looked around the pub, as if taking it all in for the first time. The ceiling was covered in hanging decorations made of red and gold foil, and the casement windows were sprayed with fake snow.

'We sat here that first night with Francesca,' said Tess, speaking aloud without meaning to. She cleared her throat. 'Do you remember? Londontown,' she added meditatively.

He looked at her in surprise, but she was staring into her pint.

'What are you thinking about?' Adam asked, after a pause. Tess looked up.

'Oh, just that night in London,' she said. She took a deep breath. 'I think enough water's under the bridge that we can talk about it, now, don't you?'

The rest of the pub was virtually empty; they could only hear the clink of glasses being cleared away in the silence that followed, and the faint hum of a car going past outside on the street.

'Totally,' Adam said, nodding. 'I'm really glad you said that. I've been feeling like—'

'I missed you so much when you were away, bruv,' Tess said abruptly. 'You know, I just can't be bothered to have all these resentment things saved up against you. That's the trouble with knowing someone so long.'

He put his hand on her knee. 'I know.'

She swivelled in her seat, turning her face to his and looking up at him. 'I never said this to you, but when you arrived in the hotel in Rome –' She shook her head and stared back down at her drink. 'Nah, forget it.'

'No,' he said, intrigued. 'What?'

Tess blushed, and then she nodded and said, 'OK. Well . . . I wasn't expecting to see you.'

'Obviously,' said Adam.

'And you walked in and – I saw you like other people see you.'

'What do you mean?'

Tess gazed up at the shelf above the bar, where a row of regulars' silver tankards hung. They were covered in tinsel. 'You know when you see someone without expecting to. And you see them – without preconceptions.'

He nodded. 'I do know.' He smiled. 'That's really strange. I had the same thing, with you.'

'Really?'

'Yep,' he said. 'You just appeared, at the top of the stairs, and I didn't recognize you. You looked – so different. I remember it very clearly. Just staring at you. All these things going through my head. Isn't it funny.'

'Why?' said Tess. 'What did I look like?'

'Well, it's kind of hard to explain,' he said awkwardly. 'How did I look?'

'You looked like a man,' Tess said, biting her lip. He gave a shout of laughter.

'A man? I looked like a man. Well, that's good.'

'I mean –' she said, nudging him – 'I always see you with all these old archaeological layers, you know. How we were when we were both five, thirteen . . . eighteen.' She looked at him. 'I saw you as a grown-up man. I know, it's silly. But I don't think I had before.'

'Well,' Adam said, and his voice was suddenly serious. 'That's how I saw you, T, that is strange.'

'As a man? Thanks.'

'No.' He shrugged his shoulders; he was awkward all of a sudden. 'You looked – like a siren. Like this beautiful woman. You had this white shirt on. You were pushing your hair out of your face, you looked so – serious. Grown-up. Beautiful.' He smiled at her incredulous face. 'Honestly! I suppose that's what –' He stopped.

'What?'

'That's what falling in love does to you.'

'Me?' Tess said.

'Er – yes,' Adam replied. 'That's to say – I mean – you, you and Peter.'

'Yes – of course,' she said. 'Yes, I suppose so.'

'When are you going to Rome?' he asked.

'In ten days' time. The twenty-third,' Tess said. 'I can't wait.'

'I bet,' he said, looking pleased. 'Ah. Lucky thing. And lucky him. He's a fortunate man, I hope he knows that.'

'Thanks,' she said, putting her hand on his and smiling into his eyes. 'Thanks a lot, Adam. I have no idea if he knows it or not. Frankly, I'll be amazed if he recognizes me. It's been six months . . .' She shook her head. 'I don't know. Am I crazy?'

'You'd be crazy if you didn't go,' said Adam. 'You'd never know. And I've seen you with him.' He finished his pint. 'It makes sense, I'm telling you.'

Tess shrugged her shoulders. 'Thanks, Adam.' She shivered. 'I am excited.'

'You should be.' He stood up. 'Another pint?'

'Yes, please,' said Tess. 'Great.'

'So,' she said, when he returned a couple of minutes later. 'Do you know how long you're staying in Leda House, then?'

'For the next few months. That's why I want Christmas there.' He chewed the inside of his mouth, thoughtfully. 'By the way, I'm going up to London next week. Do you want to come with me?'

'Are you joking?' Tess asked, scanning his face.

'I'm not, I promise. I have to go, something to do with the estate,' he said vaguely.

'What?' said Tess.

He didn't answer. 'And – well, I thought I'd treat you to a pre-Christmas present. To say thanks.' He scratched the back of his neck, awkwardly. 'And everything.'

'For what?' Tess laughed. 'I've been a terrible friend to you this past year.'

'No,' he said seriously. 'You haven't. You've been the best friend I could have hoped for. And you've shown me up, too.'

'How do you mean?'

He looked uncomfortable. 'I've treated people badly. I treated you badly.' She shook her head. 'Yes,' he said gently. 'I did. And there are loads of others. Girls, mostly.'

'Everyone sleeps around,' Tess said unconvincingly. She coughed.

'I've come to see it wasn't right, though,' Adam said. 'You know. Trying to get over my mother dying, and trying to cope with having to carry this secret around with me. I think I did Mum a disservice.'

'No, you didn't,' Tess said, a break in her voice. 'That's ridiculous.'

'Is it?' Adam smiled, but it didn't reach his eyes. 'I just can't help thinking, if she could see me now, she wouldn't be proud of what I'd done. How I've spent the last thirteen or so years.'

Tess didn't say anything. She hadn't been there for him for so much of it, she'd been so angry with him, what could she say to that?

Adam said quietly, 'The way I drove Francesca away. The way I treated her over the summer. Man!' He looked up to the ceiling. 'It makes me feel really crap, when I think about it.'

'Adam!' Tess hit him gently on the arm. 'Stop it. She knew what she was getting into. And she was ready to go back to London. She needed to leave.'

It was true. But he was right, and he knew it, and so did she.

'I spoke to her earlier,' Adam said. 'I'm going to see her in London, I think.'

'Really?' said Tess. 'That's – wow.'

'Yep,' said Adam. 'I called her just before I went to see Miss Store.'

'Wow,' said Tess. 'Good. Good for you.' She wasn't sure it was a good thing for Francesca, but she knew enough now to let them just get on with it. 'Do you think –?'

'Do I think what?'

'Do you still fancy her?' Tess said, after a moment's hesitation.

'What is this?' Adam asked. '1989? Are we in a time warp? Do you like Bros or do you prefer Wet Wet Wet? Are you still going out with Daniel Mathias?'

'Oh, be quiet.'

'*Fancy* her.' Adam made a 'pshaw'-ing sound. 'Honestly.'

'So – yes,' Tess said.

'That's not why I'm going to London,' he said.

'I believe you,' Tess said, laughing, and she was glad, gladder than she could say that it was OK, that everything was OK. She raised her glass to him. 'Thousands wouldn't.'

'Good,' he said. 'Let's change the subject.'

'Fine,' said Tess, emboldened. 'What are you going to do now?'

'Now now?' Adam blinked, looking bemused.

'I mean when Christmas is over. What are you going to do with the rest of your life?'

'That's partly why I'm going to London next week. Got to see a man about a dog. Timing's a bit weird, five days before Christmas, but I think it's going to be good.'

'Great,' said Tess, only half concentrating. 'So – Francesca, eh?'

'You're really not going to ask me what I'm doing, then,' he said. 'That's nice.'

'Of course,' Tess said, chastised. 'Sorry. What's going on?'

'OK,' he said. 'Well, it's not a big deal, really. But I've put the cottage on the market and I've cancelled the deal with the water meadows – they're threatening to sue me, so's the council.' She gasped. 'I know. It's no big deal, but Francesca's got a friend, a lawyer who specializes in this stuff, who can help me.'

'You're really not going ahead with it?'

'No,' Adam said simply. 'You know, I could try to convince myself that it might be OK. But it's not. They should be left alone.'

She shrugged her shoulders, her eyes full of warmth. 'That's great. Oh, you are doing the right thing, you know it.'

He looked embarrassed. 'And –' He cleared his throat, carrying on as if he were reciting a shopping list. 'Um, I'm going to turn Leda House into a community centre, arts centre, have plays and concerts there and stuff. And there'll be a fund, to help finance – um, to help finance local people who want to buy their first place but can't because of horrible down-from-Londoners like you.' He held up his hands. 'That last bit was a joke.'

Tess stared at him, her mouth open. 'Are you serious?' she said eventually.

Adam nodded. 'I am serious.'

'Oh, my goodness.' Tess pursed her lips together, to stop herself from grinning widely, laughing hysterically, jumping up and bursting into tears and throwing her arms around him. 'I'm having to control myself.'

'So I'm going on an arts administration course,' said Adam, ploughing on. 'I need to know how to set up a charity, and to administer a fund like this one. We'll need people to help . . . I'm going to talk to Beth, see if I can rent some rooms off her at the Hall, for offices. Kind of like the symmetry there,' he said, and then stopped, his brow wrinkled. 'Tess – you do think this is a good idea, don't you? Say something.'

Tess shut her eyes briefly and then opened them and reached for his hand. She was incredibly moved by him. 'It's a brilliant idea,' she said simply. 'Your mum'd be proud of you, you know.'

He nodded. 'Thanks, T. I don't know about that, but I hope she'd be pleased with this.'

'And your new grandfather too, I bet. Who knows, maybe you've got loads of grandfatherly relations who'll come out of the woodwork now. They'd be proud of you too, I know they would.'

Adam clasped her hand back and nodded.

'And I'm proud of you,' Tess said softly. 'I'm really proud of you –' She wanted to say 'bruv', in the old way, but looking at this calm, measured, mature Adam she couldn't – she realized she knew him still, but something about him had

468

changed, grown up, gone for ever. He wasn't her bruv any more. 'I'm really proud of you, Ad,' she said simply. 'Cheers.'

'Cheers,' he said, smiling, and they drank. 'This is the life, isn't it.' He sighed, looking round the pub. 'This is all I ever wanted. And after next week . . . everything'll be even better.' He nudged her. 'So glad you're going to come down to London-town with me, T. Francesca'll be chuffed, too.'

'Yep,' said Tess, hesitating a little, and then taking the plunge. 'Of course I'm coming. It sounds brilliant, all of it.'

'It is. And you're off to Italy straight after that,' he said, nodding encouragingly. 'Christmas is nearly here. Everything's working out the way it should!'

Tess hesitated again. 'Yes, that's it. Everything's working out the way it should.'

He touched his glass to hers. 'I'll drink to that.'

CHAPTER FORTY-THREE

One of the great things about moving away is that you get a sense of distance. The people with whom you feel no kinship but a nagging sense of responsibility: gradually they can just be weeded out. The old college friend with whom you shared everything from hair dye to tampons and with whom you have absolutely nothing in common now: in London, preserving the edifice of the friendship would be more noticeable than it is when you are a penniless teacher living one hundred miles outside London with no car, no interesting contacts and no stories of the high life. And yet, as Tess read her old friend Fiona's Christmas card, she started thinking about how they had been, thirteen years ago, two stumpy, shy students together in the big city, and how scary it had been, how they had formed a friendship – based on the shock of the new – and what Fiona was like now. What were they both like, now?

Happy Christmas, Tess! Hope yokel land is all it's cracked up to be and you are still enjoying your new life. We were just at a hotel near you, I think it's owned by the Soho House people? Really lovely. When are you coming down to London? We're

off to Thailand for Christmas and New Year but come any time
after that. Tom's work is going well and we just got a new car!
Happy New Year!
Love Fiona.

The new best friend from your first teaching job, where
you went to the pub after work and got hopelessly, helplessly
drunk on cheap white wine, crying with mirth and sadness
over shared twenties experiences: she left teaching five years
ago to work in HR, and though you have dutifully met up
for drinks once every six months, each time it gets harder and
harder. Because basically your friendship was based on sharing
the same office. And that was it.

Dear Tess,
Merry Christmas!
Wishing you all the best for 2009 . . . Must put a new date
for drinkies in when you're next up in London!!!
Pippa
xx

And, of course, the ex-boyfriend, with whom you shared
over two years and several friends, some fantastic holidays
and a crucial period of each other's lives: if Tess had stayed
in London, would she have been forced into some semblance
of friendship with Will and Ticky?

Dear Tess,
Merry Christmas and a Happy New Year.
I hope this finds you well and your life in Langford still
enjoyable. Hope too that things are still going well with Adam;
he seems like a nice chap. Ticky and I are engaged. I thought
you ought to know. I really hope you will join in our pleasure
at this news. That sounds rather presumptuous, but I have been
thinking of you lately, and thinking that, while I was unsuited
to you, I was lucky to have you in my life for that time.

I often feel that you and I may not have said the things to each other that we might have and I wanted you to know this, at least.

~~With best wishes~~
(sorry!)
With love from
Will
x
(and Ticky)

This last arrived the day Tess went to London with Adam again, a couple of days before she was due to go to Rome. She read it, wincing slightly, sitting on the sofa as weak winter sunshine shone into the sitting room of Easter Cottage. She tried to imagine what she could write back that would set the record straight.

Thanks so much for your charming Christmas card. Actually, Adam is not my boyfriend. We lied to you so that I would not look like a sad loser, but I now realize this was a bit pathetic. I am in fact off to Rome for Christmas, to stay with a gorgeous American called Peter, and I hope that we will pass the holiday period having lots of sex. He is not really my boyfriend, either, we merely shared an amazing week together, silly though it sounds, and when I think of him I think of a truly magical time when I became myself again – after dating you for two years had worn my soul bare, a bit like paint stripper. Anyway! Best wishes to you and your family for a cool Yule –

There was a sharp knock at the door. 'Tess?' came a voice from outside. 'I'm late, sorry.'

'Hi,' she said, scrambling to stand up. 'Just coming.'

She opened the door, smiling at Adam; though it was two weeks now since he'd been back, the sight of him was still a sheer pleasure to her. He kissed her on the cheek, and glanced over her shoulder.

'What on earth is that?'

Tess turned around. 'Oh, dear. It's my packing.'

Adam surveyed the huge mess on the floor, a pile of tangled trouser legs, tights, and knickers. 'Right,' he said politely. 'When's your flight?'

'Day after tomorrow, at eleven,' she said. 'I'll be there for late lunch, hopefully.'

'Wow.' Adam rubbed his hands together. 'Tess, this is exciting, isn't it?' He put his arm around her. 'You must be really looking forward to it.'

'Yes,' said Tess. She kicked a stray pair of tights disconsolately towards the corner of the room and slung her bag over her shoulder. 'Come on, let's go.'

'So how do you feel about seeing him again?' Adam said, shoving his hands in his pockets. 'Have you two guys made any more plans?'

Tess stared up at him as she picked up her keys. 'Who on earth are you? Oprah Winfrey?'

Adam looked at her. 'What do you mean?'

'All these questions,' Tess said crossly, opening the door. 'I don't know the answers. I haven't seen him for months, you know. And he's been away too. I have no idea what it's going to be like.'

After a pause, Adam nodded. 'Right,' he said. 'Sorry, of course. I'm just rather cheerful today.'

'Why?'

He looked at her. 'Well – you know. Going to London, seeing – everything. And – ah, finding out about the course and everything. Still,' he went on hurriedly. 'I can see why you'd be a bit nervous, I bet. Like, you're looking forward to seeing Peter again, but you're wondering what it'll be like.' He whistled.

'Absolutely,' Tess said, nodding. She felt relieved that he had said it out loud; she felt disloyal admitting anything negative about her trip, about Peter, about anything to do with it. Still, she watched him, wondering if he was thinking the same thing as they left for London, to see Francesca once again. 'Yes, that's exactly it . . .' She shut the door and locked it and they walked down the street together. She chewed a nail, thoughtfully. He looked at her.

'Well, it's nice to know,' he said, 'that it wasn't just a fairy-tale romance.'

'Yes, I –' Tess began, but she stopped. 'What do you mean?' she said fiercely.

Adam gestured, his hands still in his pockets. 'Well, like you said, it was this magical time et cetera, et cetera, and you worried it wouldn't come to anything. You said that,' he said mildly.

'Oh, right,' answered Tess doubtfully. 'Well, yes – that's the way it is, yep.'

They were at the end of her road, and they turned left, towards the town hall and the station. Tess looked back towards the high street, at the Christmas tree lights, shining dully in the cloudy day, at the thick yew trees that fringed the edge of the churchyard, at Langford in the middle of the morning. She didn't want to go to London. She felt cross, crotchety, as if some unnamed irritation were upon her, like a rash settling on her skin. Adam was already walking ahead.

'We'll be late,' he called. 'Hurry up, T, we don't want to miss the train.'

Mist was in the air; Tess shivered and pulled her collar around her, as she ran to catch up with him. They were going to London again.

Tess had forgotten things about Francesca. She had forgotten how clear her skin was, and how she smelt of something – jasmine? It was delicious, anyway. And how curiously impassive she was, how you had to know her well before you knew what she thought about something. Remembering the last time she'd seen her, that awful day in August after Leonora

Mortmain's funeral, Tess realized that was the only time she'd ever seen her lose her composure, really. She didn't cry to get attention. Inside, she might be a melting pot of insecurities, but outside, she was cool as a cucumber.

She met them off the train at Waterloo. There were carol singers from a local church underneath the famous clock, singing lustily to a crackling backing tape. Francesca stood beside them, looking vaguely irritated by their presence. A new bag, a beautiful blue Anya Hindmarch patent thing, hung from her arm. She was in dark blue jeans, patent black boots and a thick black cloak-like wool coat with a hood. She looked, more than ever, like a famous person, someone from a film, and Tess thought of Liz, humming cheerfully away in the kitchen that morning, making pancakes and wiping her hands on the apron while she chatted happily to Tess about the day ahead. Funny to think how different they were.

'Hello, old girl,' Francesca said, casting one last look of vehement dislike at the choir as she walked towards them. She kissed Tess on the cheek. 'All right, Adam, my man. It's great to see you both.'

She did not kiss Adam, but she squeezed him on the arm, and grinned her catlike grin briefly at both of them. 'Fancy some lunch?' she said. 'I'm bloody starving.'

'It's only twelve,' said Adam, smiling at her. 'Have you had breakfast?'

'Breakfast, and a snack,' Francesca said. 'I tell you, since I went back to work my appetite's out of control. Langford wasn't great for my metabolism. I get hungry just walking up the stairs.'

'I don't know why you're surprised,' Tess said. 'You did virtually nothing for five months.'

Francesca's eyes widened for a second, and then she laughed. 'Oh, piss off. Who bought the margarita mix, eh? And the karaoke machine?'

'And the flat-screen TV,' said Tess. 'And all those huge boxes of shampoo and face cleanser I used to pick up for you at the post office while you were – er – asleep.'

'Oh, yeah,' said Francesca. 'I left them all behind, sorry. I meant to clear them away. There must be loads. They could be recycled,' she said generously.

Tess looked at Adam. 'Don't worry,' she told Francesca. 'They have been.'

They walked across the Hungerford Bridge to Embankment, still talking. Tess looked down at the swirling, choppy water, the huge vista of London all around her, and thought of Rome, how small it was by comparison. It was not yet twelve thirty, so they went to Gordon's wine bar and were able to get a table. It was five days before Christmas – the centre of town was busy but with shoppers and tourists, not with workers, and a curious air of misrule hung in the air.

Gordon's was strangely empty, perhaps because they were early. Its dark wood interior was cosy and wintry, crammed with bottles of wine and posters. They sat at a small circular table, and Tess grabbed the stool, so that Francesca and Adam could take the wooden settle. She smiled at them both as they edged in and sat down.

They made a good-looking couple, there was no doubt of that. They were both tall, and of similar colouring: he with his light brown hair that had once been white-blond; she with her beautiful caramel-coloured mane slithering over her slim shoulders.

'Let's get some drinks,' Adam said, putting his hand on the table, exactly as Francesca did the same thing. Their hands were both narrow, with long, fine fingers; they turned to look at each other, and Tess found herself thinking it was almost comical, how perfect they were together.

'Sure,' said Francesca, and she took her coat off, picking her hair up in a ponytail with one hand and dropping it, like a silk curtain, so it fell over her back again. 'I'll give you a hand.'

They smiled at each other as they got up, having only just sat down. 'You be all right, Tess?' Adam said, putting his hand gently on her shoulder.

'Sure, sure,' said Tess, pulling out her phone. 'I need to phone Peter, confirm a few details about my trip.' She stopped, realizing she sounded insane. 'I'll be fine!' she called, though in fact they were already at the bar, chatting. Tess watched them, turning her mobile around in her hand. She could see they were both nervous; Francesca looked shy, she looked down at her purse several times and then, after the barman had taken their order, Adam patted her arm, and she looked back up at him, and smiled properly. Her eyes were shining, her cheeks were slightly flushed, her lips parted.

She's still in love with him. It was obvious. It was obvious to the barman, who looked bored as he waited for Adam to hand over the money. Why wasn't it obvious to them? Tess asked herself. And she didn't know the answer, much less what to do about it. She looked down at her phone.

Landed! Back in my apartment. Only two days to go till we are reunited. I have almost forgotten what you look like. P xx

I have forgotten what you look like, too, Tess thought to herself. She watched Francesca's animated face at the bar, and felt sick. She didn't know why.

After a relaxed but fairly brief lunch at which only generalities were discussed, such as Francesca's new job, Tess's new class-mates, Christmas plans and the weather, and nothing was said of the last time they had all met, what had transpired between them, and for Adam, and what might be happening now, they paid the bill and put their coats on. As they were leaving Adam put his hand on the door and said, 'Oh, by the way – Francesca and I need to do something. See the man about the dog I mentioned in the pub the other day. You remember?'

He nodded, significantly, at Tess.

Tess didn't remember, but she didn't want to look any more out of the loop than she already felt. She said, 'Yup, where are we going?'

'The thing is, it's just the two of us,' Adam said. 'I'm afraid. Sorry, T.'

'Oh –! Right!' Tess tried to cover her embarrassment by looking really pleased that this was happening. 'This is great! I need to do some shopping, anyway. I'll take advantage of – er – So where are you going, exactly?'

She didn't want to know the answer, but she felt she had to ask the question, and even though it was obvious that they wanted to be alone, she did feel a bit cross with them both.

'We're only going to just off Albemarle Street,' Francesca said, with a precision that surprised Tess. 'Why don't we meet you in an hour or so? It won't take long, honestly.' She smiled at her.

'Great,' said Tess. 'I'll go to the Burlington Arcade. I need to, anyway!' She wished she could keep the exclamation marks out of her voice. 'Still got lots to buy, I haven't even got Peter a present yet!'

'What are you getting him?' Francesca asked, as Adam pushed the door open.

'Oh . . .' Tess blinked, emerging into the light from the gloom of the wine bar. 'Probably some . . . I don't really know.'

'What a great girlfriend you are,' Adam said, pushing her gently out of the way as a cyclist, speeding through Embankment Gardens, burst through their little group. Tess glared at him, annoyed at being pushed around. She felt cross and awkward, a little hot from the heat of the bar and the wine they had drunk.

'I'll meet you in Burlington Arcade at four o'clock,' she said. 'Good luck with whatever it is you're doing,' and she rolled her eyes and walked, briskly, up towards Northumberland Avenue, trying not to show how she really felt.

*   *   *

The walk in the cold crisp air did her good. She walked down Pall Mall, up through St James's Square, admiring the fine tall buildings, the tasteful Christmas decorations, the old gentlemen's shops selling proper tobacco and proper Panama hats, the gentlemen's clubs with old men in waistcoats emerging from late long lunches. She thought about London, how she missed it, how she still loved it, but she realized as she came out onto Piccadilly that it no longer felt like home. And she also realized, as she walked along, calming down in the cool air, that she had done what she always did; aligned herself with a city because she had to. She had embraced London when she was eighteen, getting over Adam, having had the abortion, starting afresh.

She had embraced it because she had to reject Langford, leave behind that part of her childhood which had hurt her so much. She had loved the cool classical lines of UCL; the white stucco columns, the order in it all, the stateliness of London's squares, the white paint and black railings of the British Museum. No more higgledy-piggledy cottages climbing over each other, no more twisting sidestreets, lanes tangled with brambles, hedgerows a riot of colour . . . It seemed to Tess, eighteen, bruised, alone, that London was the perfect classical city. And up until last year, even her long, straight street in Balham had had an order she found attractive.

Her phone rang: she snatched it out of her pocket, where without realizing it, she had been clutching it tightly in her hand. *Peter mob*.

She didn't answer.

She looked through the railings of St James's church where a carol concert was in full swing; they were singing 'God Rest Ye Merry Gentlemen' in a minor key; it had a powerful, melancholy sound. Sirens wailed, far in the background, looping over and around each other. The phone stopped ringing. Someone was cooking chestnuts; the slightly burnt smell was acrid in her nostrils and she wrinkled her nose. Someone else jostled her, murmuring apologies as they hastened along the street. It wasn't a momentous moment but then, as she stared down at the phone, and then up into the sky, Tess knew, with a sadness in her heart, but also a certainty that could not be overruled, that she would not be going to Rome.

She called him back. The phone rang, and he answered immediately. She ducked into the alcove of a doorway, away from the noise on the street.

'Hey, baby,' Peter said. She knew his voice so well, now. But she couldn't picture his face. 'I just called.'

'Hi,' she said. She turned and stood, watching the cars rush by. The sirens started up again in the background. 'I know. Listen, Peter . . . I need to tell you something.'

CHAPTER FORTY-FOUR

'You can't just finish with me over the phone,' Peter said, his voice full of exasperation. 'It doesn't work like that, Tess –'

'I'm sorry, Peter.' She was almost pleading with him, because she wanted him to see that she was right, she didn't want to hurt him. 'I really am. I thought I was in love with you –'

'Hey. Hey – me too,' he said curtly. 'I don't just go around falling in love with anyone, you know. I was ready to –' He paused. 'I really thought you loved me, Tess.'

'I did too,' she said sadly. She knew it sounded weak. But Tess also knew that she was right. Like London, Rome was a distraction for her. She had fallen in love with the holiday, with the romance, with the city – with Peter a bit too, of course. But it wasn't him she'd actually fallen in love with, and that was the problem. To go and spend Christmas with him, knowing that was a lie – no. Tess had done that before, had sat passively by and let someone else make the decisions, and she had got hurt. This way, she knew, was the best way of minimizing his feelings, as well as hers. She would rather hurt him now, than hurt him much more later on. She peered out onto the street, wondering when Francesca and Adam would turn up from their assignation.

'Where are you?' Peter said. 'You sound like you're under-water.'

'I'm in Piccadilly,' she said. 'Just near the Burlington Arcade.'

'Oh, I say, how very jolly,' Peter said, in his best British accent. '"I'm Burlington Bertie, I rise at ten thirty,"' he sang. '"And saunter along like a toff."'

'How on earth –' Tess began.

'I was in a barbershop quartet at college,' he said. 'Oh, yeah. You should hear my "Mr Sandman".'

'Really?' Tess laughed, off her guard. 'Well, I never. I some-times feel like I don't know you at all.'

There was a silence, and she realized what she had said. 'Guess you're right there,' Peter said. 'Answer me something, Tess.'

'Sorry,' she said, shaking her head; she caught sight of herself in the shop window, hair bouncing from side to side as the human traffic moved along behind her.

He spoke again. 'Do you think you'd have fallen for me if it hadn't been in Rome? If I'd just been an ordinary guy who walked into the pub in your English country village one evening?'

'That's the trouble, Peter,' Tess said sadly. 'You wouldn't have walked into the pub. You wouldn't even come over to visit the pub.' He started to speak, and she said, 'I'm sorry, I'm not having a go at you, truly I'm not. I just mean – it was a place, it was a time. Don't you think? You left too.'

'Yes,' he said. 'I do think that. I've been thinking it myself, you know. Being away, it made me realize. I love it here, but only when there's something exciting about being here. I came here for Chiara. I came back here for you. But do I want to live here, now I'm back?' He laughed. 'I'm probably just jet-lagged.'

'Could you go back to the States if you wanted? Would they let you?'

'The newspaper? Yeah, I think so.' He cleared his throat.

'I kind of think they want me to. I think I want to, as well.'

So they had both decided Rome wasn't for them.

'And what about Chiara?' she asked bravely. 'I wonder if –'

'No,' Peter said firmly. 'That's over.'

'Really?'

'Tess,' Peter said, after a pause. 'It's easy for you to say "Really?" like that. But you can't stay with someone . . . when you're in love with someone else.' He gave an interrogative sound. 'Isn't that true?'

'Oh, you mean Chiara's Leon,' Tess said.

'No,' he said. 'I mean you. Think about it, honey. Call me at Nicoletta's' – this was a neighbour of his, an amazing cook – 'on Christmas Day?' he said, and his voice was warm. 'I want to know you're still feeling guilty. *Ciao*, beautiful.'

And the line went dead.

She went into the Burlington Arcade then, humming the song 'Burlington Bertie', her hand on her solar plexus, rubbing her stomach gently as though she had tummy ache. She bought some Ladurée macaroons for Stephanie, beautiful jewel-like colours, shells smooth as a duck's egg, nestling in crisp tissue paper and held in a gold and pistachio-coloured bag. She went to Penhaligon's and bought perfume for Liz, bath oil for her sister, old-fashioned soap on a rope for Mike, her brother-in-law. As she was coming out of the shop, her eye fell on the window of an old jeweller's, where antique brooches, rings and necklaces sat in plush little velvet boxes. It was a miracle she noticed it, really, tucked away at the back as it was: a brooch of three flowers wound together with gold strands, each flower a different colour, one amber yellow, one moonstone blue, one amethyst purple, with tiny green glass leaves. The work was beautiful, delicate. At the bottom, a small square of card was marked in tiny writing: 'Primula Brooch, c. 1920. Label on reverse. £45.'

Tess opened the door and went in, a smile on her face.

As she was finishing the payment, handing the card machine back to the elderly male shopkeeper, she felt a tap on her shoulder and she jumped. It was a tiny shop, and the owner looked cross, alarmed, as if she might sweep away all the little boxes, the diamond engagement rings, the strings of pearls, by too much movement.

'Hey, T,' came a voice behind her. 'Sorry we kept you.'

She turned round. 'Hey,' she said, kissing him on the cheek. 'Are you OK?'

He smiled. 'More than OK, thanks. More than.'

Tess looked out of the window onto the arcade; Francesca was standing outside, watching them through the glass. She raised her hand in greeting; her face was obscured by the reflection. 'So –?' Tess said curiously, trying to sound upbeat. 'What happened?'

'Tell you later, tell you later,' Adam said, gesturing with his head. 'Ah, but it's good to see you, sweetheart.'

They said goodbye to the elderly shopkeeper and Adam opened the shop door; just as he did, she turned, wanting to give him the present now, here. She held her hand out to him. 'Ad – this is your Christmas present. It's a bit early. And it's not really for you – you'll want to give it away. I just saw it and . . .'

'Not for me, and I'll want to give it away? Nice,' Adam murmured. She laughed, but watched his face curiously as he pressed the catch and opened the velveteen box. He stared at the brooch, gleaming up at him, and then picked it up, turning it over questioningly, as she nodded encouragingly at him. '"Primula Brooch",' he read out loud. 'Oh – T.' He picked up the brooch. 'That's –'

'It's for you to give to your great-aunt. When you find her. Because I know you will find her,' she said, squeezing his arm. 'I know you will.'

Adam stared at her. 'Tess. You don't know how much that means to me.' He nodded.

'S'OK,' Tess said gruffly. He put his finger under her chin, and made her look at him.

'What have I done to deserve you?' he said.

'Nothing,' she whispered, thinking suddenly of Peter. Her heart was full of pain, full of love too, and she wondered just why she felt this way. She turned to see Francesca still watching them, and smiled at her.

'That's nice,' said the shopkeeper, nodding his head, waggling his moustache. 'But there are people waiting outside to come in, so if you don't mind –'

'Course,' said Adam. He held the door open again, and Tess walked out. 'That is the most fantastic present, T. I have got you something. But not here. Oh, man. I don't know –' He shook his head.

'That's what friends are for, like I keep saying,' said Tess.

Francesca said nothing as they came over to her. 'Look what T got me,' Adam announced. 'It's –'

'Adam,' Francesca said, and Tess noticed then that her face was very pale, her eyes full of unshed tears. 'Can I have – can I speak to you?' She looked over at Tess. 'Alone?'

'Of course,' Tess said, answering for him. 'I'll just – I'll wait here.'

'Is that OK?' Adam said to her in a low voice.

'Don't worry, go,' she said. 'In fact –' She looked at her watch, trying to be completely blasé about this. Adam and Francesca – they were always going to be drama queens together. 'Why don't I just see you on the train? We're right by Piccadilly Circus, you can just hop on the Bakerloo. I'll go on ahead, but just in case you miss it –'

'It won't take that long,' Adam said. He gripped her arm above the elbow for a second. 'Honestly.'

Francesca stood behind him, winding a section of her hair around her finger. 'Bye, love,' she said.

Tess waved mutely at her. She watched them walk away, and stood for a moment looking down the arcade, at the twinkling lights, the silky ribbons and decorations. Then she turned, and walked back down to the street. At St James's opposite, the carol concert was still going on. Loud, harsh chords in a minor key floated across to her; a glowing light shone through the windows. The streets were four, five people deep, all in black or dark coats, clutching shopping bags. No one was talking to each other. Everyone was alone, hurrying onto the next thing. She knew Adam wouldn't catch their train. She realized she would have to go into the huge Waterstone's to get a book; she had nothing to read. She should have known this was going to happen. Tess walked, feeling tired, but with a curious freedom. She was buffeted from person to person as the music sounded louder and, high above them, the clock chimed six in the black night air.

CHAPTER FORTY-FIVE

Having at first roundly decried the Knupfer House, Tess had to admit she was becoming more and more enamoured of it. It was a good decoration. It was always there: when you got back from London after a delayed train, starving and a little sad, the deliciously sweet and cinnamon biscuits gleaming toffee-brown in the dark. It was there when you crept downstairs the following day to find the house empty, and yourself rather miserable. And it was there if you fancied a wee mid-morning snack on Christmas Eve, as you wrapped your presents. Tess had sent her parents' presents off with them on their cruise but now she was spending Christmas with her sister and Mike, and she still had a few other key people's presents to wrap, too.

She was still feeling rather blue. Her Christmassy mood had totally evaporated with Liz's departure that morning for her parents' house in Nantwich.

Liz had been making Nigella's Christmas muffins for breakfast and, as Tess came downstairs, blearily rubbing her eyes, she had excitedly thrust into her hands two wrapped presents and a tray of bulbs: 'For our garden, to brighten it up in spring, you know.'

Tess had stared back at her. 'Oh, God. Liz, I've only got

you a card. Oh! And –' She had shuffled round to the dresser, and pulled open a drawer. 'Only this.' She took out the Penhaligon's perfume which she'd bought in the Burlington Arcade. 'Happy Christmas, flatmate.'

Liz had kissed her back. 'No, happy Christmas to you, Tess.' Her eyes shone with unshed tears. 'This is wonderful,' she said, eyeing the bag Tess handed her. 'It's all wonderful. Thank you so much.'

'For what?' Tess sat down at the table; her limbs were aching.

'For *everything*.' Liz pushed a pot of coffee towards her. 'For teaching me so well. For letting me move in here. And for being a great friend.'

At that, Tess's head snapped up, and she laughed. 'I've been a terrible friend!'

'No, you haven't,' Liz said firmly. 'I think you've had a lot on your plate this year, and you've been great.'

But I'm rude about you behind your back and I leave your parties early and I loathed showing you all round Rome, and I'm a bad person, Tess wanted to say. As if she were reading her thoughts, Liz handed her a mug.

'You've had to do so much this last year, what with moving back down and starting a new job, and taking us all off to Rome. Not to mention,' she said quietly, 'everything with Adam.'

'But that was him,' Tess pointed out. 'Nothing to do with me.'

'Sometimes it's harder to watch and be powerless than to be in the eye of the storm,' Liz said firmly. 'At least you know where you are when you're in the eye of the storm.' Tess stared at her, a frown creasing her forehead. 'Being on the sidelines, watching someone and not being able to help them, if you truly love them – that's hard.'

She opened the oven door; a moist, sweetly spicy scent wafted towards Tess. She breathed in deeply. 'I suppose that's partly true,' she said. 'But it's still been much easier being me than – oh, any number of people.'

'And another thing,' Liz said, plonking the muffins down on top of the stove so that the metal clattered loudly on the hobs. 'I think it's hard, being our age. How old are you?'

'Well, I'm thirty-one,' Tess said. 'Old enough to know better.'

'That's my point,' Liz said thoughtfully. 'That's a year younger than me. And you have this job of responsibility, where you have to be a grown-up and tell people what to do. I think that's hard. It makes it hard to be normal. I have no idea what I'm doing with my life. I don't feel grown-up, it's pathetic. How am I going to meet someone or bring up children when I don't know what a spark plug is, or a hedge fund, or –'

'Can you change a lightbulb?'

'Yes,' said Liz. 'Of course.'

'And do you know what your bank account number is?'

'Well, of course I do.'

'Well then,' said Tess. 'I think you're better off not knowing what a hedge fund is, to be frank, and I have no idea what a spark plug does. Something in the car. Don't worry about it.' She stared hopefully at the plate of muffins. 'That's what I've learned over the past year. You make mistakes, you learn from them, and you try and move on.' She poured her flat-mate a cup of coffee. 'And while you can cook like this I wouldn't worry. I will always want to live with you.' She clanged her mug against Liz's. 'Happy Christmas, my dear. Thank you.'

'Oh, dear Tess,' said Liz, growing misty-eyed again. 'Thank *you*.' She put a great chunk of muffin in her mouth; it was too large, and it crumbled, small chunks falling onto her plate. Tess laughed.

'Owhse agam.' Liz said something indistinct.

'What?' Tess said. Liz tried to swallow, but got a fit of the giggles.

'Owhse agam!' she said again.

'Masticate,' Tess said, enunciating clearly. 'I can't understand a word of what you're saying, Elizabeth. Goodness, what are you, an animal? Chew it slowly.'

Liz had tears of mirth streaming down her face. She swallowed, and cleared her throat, swallowed again and gulped some coffee. 'I said, how's Adam?' she croaked eventually. 'You never said. How was the shopping?'

'Oh!' Tess banged the table with the palm of her hand. 'It was great. It was greatness. Great.'

'Good!' said Liz, eyeing her slightly oddly. 'That's great. Did you see Francesca?'

'We did. It was great to see her,' said Tess. She bit her lip, and nodded to herself, shaking herself out of the feeling of gloom she had felt on the train returning home alone. 'It was just wonderful. She's exactly the same. Brilliant. I love her.'

'Uh-uh, uh-uh,' said Liz, rather too quickly. 'Wow, that's just fantastic.' She paused fatally. 'Yes, I always really *really* liked Francesca. Seemed such a jolly, fun girl.'

Tess looked at her, her heart flowing over with affection for her housemate. She paused before speaking carefully.

'Oh, she is fantastic, and it was great to catch up with her and know we'll stay in touch.' She casually broke off a bit of muffin. 'But it was super nice to get home again, know what I mean?'

'Yep,' said Liz, also casually. 'Yep, really sure know what you mean.' There was a thump on the sitting-room floor. 'Christmas cards!' she cried ecstatically, and rushed to collect them. 'We've got – one, two . . . four, five! Look, there's one from Francesca!' she called, coming back into the kitchen. 'Ah, wonderful!'

'Oh, I'll read it later,' said Tess. 'Do you want me to check the water in your car before you go?'

'Actually, that would be great,' Liz said, shamefacedly. 'Show me how. Have *un autre* muffin.'

'*Merci.*'

Later that morning, after Liz had driven off, Tess sat, surrounded by wrapping paper, carefully cutting strips of sellotape to stick on the edge of the table, having already got herself stuck to the wrapping paper or the present a couple of times. She'd been to Jacquetta's shop and bought, at vast expense, some appropriate trimmings for her presents. It had taken her hours to do her parents' gifts a few weeks ago, and she was dreading round two. She was playing the *Messiah* to get her in the right festive mood, but couldn't find the first CD. So not for her was there a happy soloist telling of shepherds abiding in the fields, and the people walking in darkness seeing a great light, to say nothing of a happy chorus singing 'For Unto Us A Son is Born'. No, it was all 'He Was Despised and Rejected' and Jesus being crucified, not baby Jesus being born in a friendly yuletide manger with ox and ass and . . . Tess sighed, wrestling with Miss Store's bottle of sherry and box of chocolate Olivers, as the two bits of sellotape she had carefully removed from the table got stuck together.

Francesca's card was on the side. Tess looked fondly at the sloping black italic handwriting. Fine, that she and Adam were back together again, and it really was good, because she loved her, and it meant that she, Tess, would see more of her. She felt awful for doubting it, just because of what had happened before. They had changed, and they both knew what they were doing; he was different, bless him. He deserved happiness: that was all she asked for him. She bit the card and tore open the envelope with one finger.

Darling Tess,

    Forgive my behaviour yesterday! I had to write and tell you that the fact is, Adam and I are –

There was a loud banging on the door. Tess put her hand on the floor and pushed herself up, inadvertently sticking two other pieces of tape to a large sheet of tissue paper, which flapped around in her hand, tearing as she tried to pull it off.

'Hello?' came a voice. 'Tess? Are you all right?'

'Adam?' she said, relief in her voice. She pulled the door open, as the tissue paper wrapped around her hand. 'Sorry,' she explained, letting him in. 'I have no aptitude for this whatsoever. My old-lady home-maker days are far behind me. I don't know what's happened.' She looked up at him. 'Hey. You look very serious. Are you OK?'

Adam's face was dark; he had circles under his eyes and he was obviously tired. He was holding a card and a thick envelope of papers. He looked back at her.

'Well. I wanted to show you something,' he said. He held up the card.

'Oh?' said Tess, waggling her fingers. 'Dammit! This bloody paper!'

'Why didn't you tell me you weren't going to Italy?' Adam said.

Tess had forgotten. 'Oh,' she said, wrestling with the shreds of tissue paper, and tearing the last piece of tape from her fingers. 'Sorry. Yeah. I knew you wouldn't be surprised. I'm going to Stephanie's instead. I was going to come round this lunchtime and tell you. And to drop off –' She tapped his calf with her foot. 'Don't look behind me. Your present's there, I haven't wrapped it, and at this rate I never will.'

Adam didn't say anything. He just stared at her again, his chest rising and falling. 'You should have told me, T.'

Tess met his gaze in surprise. 'Oh, Adam. I'm sorry. Peter . . .' She shrugged her shoulders. 'It was never going to work. We both had to see it.' She swallowed. 'Not that he wasn't lovely. But . . . you know.' She reached behind her to the sofa, and handed him a photo. 'He emailed me this photo yesterday. He said it's my Christmas card and I have to print it out. Look what he wrote below it.' She read aloud from the back. Adam watched her, saying nothing.

> Thank you for some wonderful memories, and for helping me in a difficult time. I will always remember you con molto affetto, and with a little regret. Happy Christmas, beautiful Tess. How about you come back to Rome, before I go?'

She patted her breastbone, pleased, and tapped the front of the photo. 'Look, it's me, leaning on his moped by the Spanish Steps. Isn't it *Roman Holiday*-ish? Isn't that totally sweet of him?'

'I can see it's you,' Adam said through gritted teeth. 'I'm not stupid, though you appear to think I am. And you are, if you don't mind me saying so.' He threw the photo back onto the sofa, along with the card he had brought, and had been holding. The envelope fluttered onto the cushions. 'Why didn't you tell me?'

Tess looked at him again, astonished, as she saw he really was angry. 'I didn't think you'd be interested in me bleating on about it again, Ad. I was going to tell you today, for goodness' sake. You're not my keeper.'

'I'm not your –' He started to say something, then stopped. 'Don't you think I might have wanted to know? That it might concern me, just a bit?'

'Why?' asked Tess crossly.

'Oh, my God, Tessa Tennant.'

'Look,' she said, trying to be reasonable, though she did think he had very likely lost his mind, 'Are you OK, Adam? Why are you so upset? Have you and Francesca had a row?'

He looked blank. 'Me and Francesca? Why would we have had a row?'

'Well, quite right,' said Tess. 'Things are much better between you now, I bet, second time round.' She turned for the kitchen, batting a stray bough of holly that had come unstuck from the counter-top out of the way. 'Or even third time round, which I suppose it really is, if you're being precise.' She was gabbling. 'But honestly, Ad, I *am* glad you're back together, you know. Do you want some coffee? Or maybe even a midday glass of something? Some of Miss Store's sloe gin?'

Adam put his hand on her wrist, so that she turned sharply back. 'What are you talking about?' He was nearly shouting. 'Why have you gone *completely mad*?'

'Adam, get off!' she started slapping his hand off her arm. 'What's *wrong*?'

He released it immediately and stood only inches from her, his eyes blazing, his hair standing on end. 'I'm not back with Francesca. What are you talking about?'

She stared at him. 'What? Yes, you are.'

Adam clenched his fists and groaned in exasperation. 'Why *on earth* would you think that?'

'Because . . .' Tess raised her hands in the air. 'Well. The feelings, for starters.'

'The feelings?'

'And – the fact that you kept saying you had to go to London and it was all mysterious.'

Adam groaned. 'It was mysterious because – I had to finalize the deal, cancelling the bloody development!'

'In Albemarle Street?'

'That's where the Mortmain solicitors are,' he said, breathing heavily and staring at her. 'There were things to sort out. And I wanted to give you – this!'

He thrust the thick brown envelope he had been holding into her hand. 'This is your Christmas present. Weird present to give someone, some paper, but I think you'll get it.'

She pulled open the envelope, a quizzical look on her face. '*This day in seventeen eighty-six do I, George Mortmain*' she read. 'What is this?'

'It's the deeds,' Adam said. 'The deeds to the water meadows. They're yours.'

Tess dropped the papers on the ground. 'They're – what now?'

'They're yours.' He was smiling. 'It's cancelled. The whole thing's cancelled. It's official. And I'm signing them over to you.' He bent down to pick up the sheaf of papers, and as he crouched on the ground he smiled up at her. 'It's not a big deal, and you can't actually do anything with them, I'm afraid. They've been designated something special. You have to be on a committee.'

Tess stood in front of him, her mouth open, literally speechless.

'You can thank me whenever, you know,' Adam said, watching her.

'Adam –' She put her hand on his as he stood up. 'That's – you're really doing this?'

'Yes,' said Adam. He raised himself up, breathed out. 'We'll have to pay compensation to the developers. But I don't mind. It's the right thing to do. I should have done it ages ago.'

She touched the papers, gingerly, with her forefinger. 'Adam, this is incredible.' He handed the papers back to her, and she hugged them, looking up at him. 'I thought you went with Francesca to –'

'I took her with me to help with the transfer, and the cancellation of the sale. She was wonderful.'

'But – you stayed behind!' Tess said, shaking her head. 'She cried and you stayed behind to shag her and I had to get the bloody train back!' She smiled at him, trying to look absolutely fine about it. 'I didn't mind, honestly, even when someone was sick next to me after we left Winchester. It was lovely.'

Adam slammed his hand to his forehead. 'Tess – oh, my God. She asked me to stay because she wanted to tell me something, and she was right!' He threw the papers on the table, and gripped her hands again. 'She asked me to stay behind because she wanted to tell me I was an idiot!'

'You are an idiot,' Tess said frankly. 'I mean, this is

495

wonderful, you're wonderful. But I'm sorry, in general you are a bit of an idiot.'

Adam was breathing hard again, but he held Tess's hands in his, and looked into her eyes. 'Tess, I'm not back with Francesca, never have been. She asked me to stay behind because she wanted to clear the air between us. We needed to. And then she told me . . .' He paused, and took a deep breath. 'I'm going to have to spell it out, I can see. She told me I was an idiot, and that it was obvious to everyone that I was in love with you, and you were in love with me, and that I had to do something about it.'

Static silence fell, suddenly, looming loud in the cold, sunny room. Tess tightened her grip on his hands, and looked at him in bewilderment.

'And she was right,' he said. He bent his head, and kissed her, softly, on the lips. 'About part of it, anyway. I am an idiot. I'm in love with you, I always have been. I realized when I was away how much you meant to me, how I never wanted to live without you again.' He winced, as if he were in pain. 'How my life isn't complete if you're not there . . . But I'd already hurt you so much, and there was so much water under the bridge.' He gave a small smile. 'And you were mad about that stupid Gregory Peck substitute of yours. I just told myself it'd be enough to see you from time to time, be your friend again, hang out together again. Because it's new, it's all different now, between us. But if it's possible I love you more now, more than ever.'

She broke away from his grasp. Her heart was thumping in her chest; it was almost painful, surely he could hear how loud it was?

'Adam –' she said quietly. 'Don't – don't do it unless you're sure. Please – don't say it unless you're sure.'

'I am sure,' he said, coming towards her and stroking her hair. 'The question is, darling Tessa, are you?'

Tess put her hands on his chest. 'I don't know,' she said.

'This is – it's all a bit . . . sudden.' She swallowed. 'And there's so much history, Adam, I don't know if we can ever . . .'

Adam nodded fervently. 'I know, I know. Sweetheart, I know. But –' He shrugged his shoulders. 'All this has taught me several things.'

She held his hands, his lovely, strong big hands, that she knew so well, and watched him. 'What's it taught you?' she said, desperately wanting him to convince her.

'Well,' he said, kissing her neck. 'One, it's taught me to seize the day, even if it's terrifying. I don't want to end up like Mum. Rejected by people who should have loved her, and it just ruined things for her. Her life. And Leonora.' He nodded. 'You know, talking to Miss Store, and seeing Philip Edwards's grave, I don't think she was always that way. Her father was a terrible man, and she was unlucky. Very unlucky. I think she was probably a sweet girl once, before life went wrong. And she had no one to love her, to look after her, to set her on the right path.'

He squeezed Tess's fingers tight. 'I've got you, and you've got me, and we'll always be there for each other, we always have been, and we always will. And that's my final reason.'

'What?' she said, smiling into his eyes, trying not to laugh out loud with sheer happiness.

'It's just right,' he said. 'Isn't it? Don't you know it? Doesn't it just make sense?'

She nodded. 'It is right.' She gave a ragged sigh. 'It does make sense.' She gazed at him. 'You've been different to me, this past year. I think I fell in love with you all over again.'

'I had to go away to come back,' he said. 'I've thought about it a lot. It's really cheesy but it's true. And I've always loved you. It's just we got it all wrong before. Now it's right.' He nodded solemnly. 'Tess, darling, I promise I'll spend the rest of my life trying to deserve you.'

'You don't have to.'

'I do. I do. Because – it is right, isn't it? It just is. It's timing.'

Tess gave a small, almost sad laugh. Adam drew her hand up to his lips and slowly kissed her palm. 'I love you, Tess.'

Tess took a deep breath. She saw the boy she'd known all her life, the young man whom she'd loved, and now the grown man who was still the same, yet totally different.

'Yes,' she said. 'I love you too.'

They were silent for a long time. She could hear him breathing, feel her heart beating, and his, too. After a minute she stepped back, and looked at him, tears in her eyes.

'Oh,' he said, stroking her cheek. The card he had been holding, it seemed ages ago now, was lying on the sofa and he picked it up. 'This is what else I brought to show you. Before I got distracted.'

He handed her the card, which had a robin on it.

'Read it out loud,' he said, rubbing her back. 'It's amazing.'

'*Dearest Adam,* She read: *It was so lovely to receive your letter and to hear from you. We have never known if you existed or not, as information from Langford has been somewhat hard to come by, and it is <u>wonderful</u> now to know you are alive!*'

She stopped. 'Who's this?'

'Wait. Read to the end,' Adam said, stroking the back of her neck, and she carried on reading out loud, while he looked over her shoulder, kissing her hair.

'*Yes, I am your great-aunt –*' Tess read, with a tremble in her voice. 'Oh, Adam.' She squeezed his hand, leaned back into his embrace.

'Go on!'

'*– which is a very grand-sounding title, and I am extremely proud to be so. I loved my brother, I was very proud of him, and oh, you would have been too. He was the best brother in the world and I miss him every day . . . Every day.*

We live outside Bath, really not too far from you, and I have two children and six grandchildren, and they are all your

498

relatives – rather distant ones, but nonetheless we are related to you and shall be extremely displeased if you do not accept this invitation, which is to spend Boxing Day with us, and as many days in the future as you should care to! My telephone number is below. With very much love from me, and all of us, dear dear Adam,

Primula Jordan (née Edwards!)

P.S. I cannot wait to tell you all about your grandfather. You would have loved him.

A little time later, Adam emerged from Easter Cottage, still holding Tess's hand.

'So I'll see you in a bit.'

'Yes,' she said. 'I need to finish wrapping the presents . . . I've got a whole red and gold theme worked out, it's taking bloody ages. Liz lent me some of that ribbon you curl on the back of some scissors. And I had some holly trimmings. But it's *extremely* time-consuming.' She sighed. 'I've come to realize I'm no good at this stuff, you know. *That's* what this year has taught me.'

'Exactly,' said Adam. 'I thought your themed wrapping and ribbon curling days were behind you, Tess.' He breathed in deeply and touched her lips with his finger. 'I'm sure there's a happy medium, sweetheart. Ditch the ribbon and the holly trimmings and have a glass of wine instead.'

'You're probably right,' Tess said happily. 'Dammit, yes, you are.'

He kissed her again, against the wooden frame of the front door, and she could feel how warm he was, how strong and gentle his hands were in her hair, how unsurprising it was that here they were, on Christmas Eve, having finally realized something incredibly important.

I love you, she wanted to say to him. *It's so simple, now I can see it. I want to tell you all these things that I love about you. I feel so happy when I'm with you. Like nothing bad can happen, as if the world is saveable, as if I have a secret, a serene core at the centre of me, and it makes me want to hug people, run up a flagpole in the centre of the town, shout thank you from the hills. I want everyone else to be as happy as me now I've found you again. Because I love you.*

She sighed, and he tightened his grip on her, his lips hard on hers, until she suddenly pulled away.

'Hello, Miss Store!' Tess called out, as her neighbour shuffled past them, a bulging green string shopping bag in her hand. 'Um – we were just –'

Adam stood back, rubbing his neck awkwardly and gazing at the girl whose hand he still held, who was standing in the doorway smiling happily at Miss Store.

'Don't mind me, my dears!' Miss Store nodded and went on her way, almost ignoring them both. But she chuckled quietly to herself as she opened her own front door, and they started kissing again. She closed her door behind her and put her shopping bags down carefully, looking around her cheery, tiny cottage, and her eyes grew misty, remembering lots of things.

However, a moment later Miss Store smiled to herself again. After all, everyone knew young Tessa Tennant and Adam Smith were meant for each other. They always had been! The only mystery in Langford was why it had taken them so long to realize it.

ACKNOWLEDGEMENTS

Everyone at HarperCollins, thank you so much for everything: lovely Wendy Neale, Clive Kintoff and all the sales ladies (thanks for lunch); genius in human form Lee Motley, Lucy Upton and Sarah Radford, and to the holy editorial trinity of the great Victoria Hughes-Williams, the wonderful and inspiring Claire Bord, and as ever to my fantastic editor, for what would I do without you Lynne Drew?

A massive thank you to the one and only JLo, Jonathan Lloyd, and everyone at Curtis Brown, in particular Alice Lutyens and Camilla Goslett.

And thank you to my old colleagues on the Euston Road for putting up with me, especially Jane Morpeth, Kerr MacRae and Clare Foss. I miss you all.

For advice about Rome, advice in general, helping me to drink wine in Rome or just being great, thanks to Chris Handley, Thomas Wilson, Pamela Casey, Ariona Aubrey, Tamara Oppenheimer, James Lo, Nicole Vanderbilt, Maria Rodriguez and Vicky Watkins.

Lastly to my dad Phil, who loves Italy, especially Italian wine, footballers, and Italians themselves, but not as much as they, along with everyone else, love him. Alas, Cal and I did not inherit your Roman nose, but we both still couldn't be prouder to be your daughters. This book is for you Dad.